Caroline's Bikini

Kirsty Gunn is an internationally awarded writer who published her first novel with Faber in 1994 and since then eight works of fiction, including short stories, as well as a collection of fragments and meditations, and essays. She is Professor of Writing Practice and Study at the University of Dundee and lives in London and Scotland with her husband and two daughters.

# Caroline's Bikini

An Arrangement of a Novel
with an Introduction
and Some Further Material

*by*

**KIRSTY GUNN**

FABER & FABER

First published in 2018
by Faber & Faber Limited
Bloomsbury House
74–77 Great Russell Street
London WC1B 3DA
This export edition first published in 2018

Typeset by Faber & Faber Limited
Printed in the UK by CPI Group (UK) Ltd, Croydon, CR0 4YY

'Taken from no.90 in the *Canzoniere*; see 'Some Further Material',
'Reprise', also for a selection of verse, all reprinted with kind
permission of Professor Anthony Mortimer and Penguin Books.

The author is grateful, as always, for the support and
understanding of the publishing team at Faber & Faber, including
her editor Lee Brackstone, Eleanor Crow and Ella Griffiths and
Kate Ward, who saw the complicated pages of *Caroline's Bikini*
through to publication, as well as her agent Clare Conville.
Eleanor Rees and Peter McAdie were meticulous as copyeditor
and proofreader respectively. Her family, as ever, were patient.

A CIP record for this book
is available from the British Library

ISBN 978-0-571-33933-4

MIX
Paper from
responsible sources
FSC
www.fsc.org     FSC® C020471

10 9 8 7 6 5 4 3 2 1

For Pamela

# Table of Contents

Introduction 1

**Ready** one 5
two
three
four
five
six

**Steady** one 81
two
three
four
five
six

**Go!** one 175
two
three
four
five
six

**Finishing Lines** 241

Some Further Material 267
Acknowledgements 335

# Introduction

There's a quality of clear blue water contained in summer heat. It's there in that phrase, 'at last they came to the sea', which I can imagine writing in some short story or other. Or in 'she could smell the coolness of the swimming pool from where she stood at the edge of the grass' . . . which could be a line from this novel. It's a quality of refreshment, of relief. The idea of water, after the force of the sun, as salvation, restoration. Equilibrium regained, the story can go on.

In other sentences, too, there's the same feeling, in 'the river was a bright blue line run through a dry landscape', say, or 'the lake lay waiting for them, at the end of a long hot drive'. Or it's even part of 'the plastic hosepipe flicked beads of water against the grass' – which almost certainly could have come out of another short story I've written, as well as that lovely lake. Refreshment again, you see? Relief. But more than anything, more than those other ideas, I might think now about that earlier phrase: 'She could smell the coolness of the swimming pool from where she stood at the edge of the grass.' Adding: 'Though it wasn't close, the pool, in her mind she seemed to inhabit it already in the long seconds before she walked into it and let its blue silks and depths cover her, let her be gone.'

Yes, I can see that. Imagine writing it. Along with details of that pool at the end of a garden, surrounded by a large area of pale grey slate. There's a tree to one side in thick full leaf, like a painted tree; no wind stirs the branches in this flat, arched, midsummer heat.

So runs my introduction to what follows here, a body of water set in the midst of things. And in these pages, amongst the houses and gardens of West London laid out in sections and chapters, you will find it, in time, a particular pool, large and deep and well maintained. It's there near a certain house which you'll come to quite soon, which features, in many ways, at the heart of this story, and much later, should you choose to go there too, by the time you've come to the end of the 'novel' as I do see it – despite some discussion about that definition of fiction that features in various meetings that take place throughout *Caroline's Bikini* – you'll find some additional sections that you may also want to visit as part of your reading. In those appended pages, you'll discover background information about the people in this book – and if you want to read more about them, which could be fun, well, there they are. There are also some notes in that part of the book about love stories and where they've come from and why this 'novel' which is about to follow – in one inevitable page after another – comes from a tradition that many regard as the largest kind of love story of all.

But let me not run away with myself.

For now, let's get back to the idea of a house, a large garden and cool chlorinated water that's somewhere near. It might be in a park, in a school, in a recreation area at the edge of a sports ground, or, in this story, set in a specific part of London where the streets are wide and the gardens expansive, just down the road. But either way, somewhere, in summer, there's always a swimming pool. And here, for now, in someone's garden, it's happening, that pool . . .

It's started. It's starting now:

Ready.

Steady.

Go!

# Ready . . .

# one

'Alright,' I said. 'I'll try . . .' 'But I've never done this sort of thing before,' is what I would have said next, I'm sure, as it still seems a strange kind of thing to do, be involved in this kind of writing, the sort of project that was being suggested to me by Evan now.

'I really need you to write this story down for me, Nin,' he was saying, in no uncertain terms, if I think about it fully. 'Really, I do . . .' – and yes, it did feel like a new kind of idea for me, this, a different sort of way to spend my time. It did. It felt new.

Because though, it's true, I have published various pieces before – short stories, bits in books and essays and so on – I've never taken on someone else's narrative, had that kind of a role. 'Amanuensis' they would have called it in the old days, and I've always loved that image of Milton with his daughters; the scene by the bed: the poet and those steady scribes of his, waiting for them to come in after a night of composition with his chunks of iambic pentameter at the ready and them being there to write it all down.*

---

\* As mentioned in the 'Introduction', there are some ideas for further reading at the back of this book, in the section marked 'Some Further Material'. This includes various bits of quite interesting information about the context of *Caroline's Bikini*, how it might, if you like, fit – though that sounds like a pun! – the shape of other literary pursuits. When you've finished reading the actual story you might want to look at the section on 'Narrative Construction', for example, which details the set-up of the 'project', as the narrator refers to it here. See how you feel when you've got to the end.

'Ghostwriter', some people might say now. 'Biographer', maybe. Though neither of those terms are quite right, they're not, for the kind of thing Evan Gordonston was asking me to do.

I've known Evan a long time. I've known all the Gordonstons actually, practically forever, well, for most of my life. My mother was great friends with Helen Gordonston, and I went to school with Felicity, Evan's younger sister; his older sister, Elisabeth, went out briefly with my brother when they were in sixth form.

So . . . 'forever', yes, seems a pretty realistic description, in terms of giving the feeling of how long I've known Evan.* There was a massive time lapse, of course, between back then and now, when this story happens, because they all went off to live in America, the Gordonstons, when Tom, Evan's handsome father, got transferred there for his job. Not that any of this is particularly relevant, but to provide some kind of context here is what I'm doing, I suppose. That Evan was not unknown to me, I mean, as one might think a person might be unknown to a 'ghostwriter', say, who was going to create a narrative from that person's life, until they started work on the writing and got to find things out so that the person felt like a familiar . . . I already *knew* Evan.

So yes, 'amanuensis' could be a good word. I was closer to the subject than is usual in these things. Like one of

*And here I am again, you see, referring to those notes at the back – but really, there's no need to read the section, 'Personal History', until later. All the 'Further Material' speaks back to the story anyhow, as you'll see in time. So from now on I'll simply just refer to the sections by their titles on the pages here.

Milton's daughters, kind of, though the words Evan wanted me to write down, all about his unrequited love for the woman who would 'change my life forever', is how he first put it to me, from the moment he moved in as a lodger to her house in Richmond, were hardly the stuff of *Paradise Lost*.

Despite our close friendship, though, Evan himself was someone I'd lost touch with over the years. I had, I had lost touch, even though the family were still counted as friends by my own, with Christmas cards and calls and all of that. My mother, for example, had a summer with Helen on Cape Cod one year; my brother, when he was a postgraduate student in San Francisco, looked up Elisabeth; my father continued to send difficult crossword puzzles and books about highly evolved and researched kinds of modern history to Tom because that's what they had always talked about – 'I am fond of Tom,' my father would say, 'even though Helen and Margaret are the real friends' – so we kept abreast of the Gordonstons. We did. Yet, the fact is that I personally hadn't seen Evan through all that time he'd been away, or talked with him, or even emailed, not really, until he decided to come back to London to live, many, many years later. And, yes. He was like a different person, then, in a way, because I hadn't seen him since he was a boy,* and the one time I'd been to America he'd been on a posting in Japan and his mother told me then that he loved it there, in the States, and

* More of that 'Personal History' later – for there is lots of information in the notes about the writer's family and neighbours, friends, her childhood spent with Evan's family, etc.

might not come back – so there was some correspondence that ensued from that remark, from that period in Evan's life, between me and Felicity and what Felicity said about it . . . Even so, now, here we both were, the two of us grown up and old, and yes, of course, so different, in a way, but actually also completely the same. Because of the way our two families had always been, I suppose. All the keeping 'abreast'.

So there he was, back in London the first time, before he came back, proper, I mean – this when he was still at the point of deciding whether he was going to make that very move, 'back home', as he put it to me in his new rather American way of saying things,* though his voice in general sounded to me just the same when we were having that first gin and tonic, a drink we were going to find would serve as a sort of leitmotif set against the events and decisions that would unfold over the following months – and it was as though he'd never been gone. At that stage, he was only in town for a day or two; he was 'putting out feelers', was how he described it; the business of working out whether he could do the sort of things for some banking headhunting outfit he was working for that they wanted him to do. Though I shan't even get started there – and can't make any kind of that sort of background detail a part of all this.

For as I said to Evan when he first put the idea of this project to me: 'Don't expect me to have ONE IOTA', I

*And in that same section you'll find remarks about Evan's patterns of speech following time spent in America, along with other notes of personal interest relating to the London society of *Caroline's Bikini*.

said, in capitals just like that, 'of interest,' I said, a kind of pun, given his line of work, 'or put any time WHATSO-EVER', in capitals again, 'into the writing of a backstory.' Because establishing some kind of working life history/economic/financial context, or whatever . . . is NOT what I am going to do. 'There's not the faintest knowledge that I possess, Evan,' is what I would have told him, 'about banks and finance and the people who are employed at these kinds of places, that I can put to work here' – this, despite the fact, as I said, that our family have known the Gordonstons for years and Tom *was* a banker, for goodness' sake, so it should have been no surprise that his son would follow him into that line of work and how our two families got on, in a way, is anyone's guess – though we did, there you are, we just did, our two families, the bankers and the writers, we were close, we still are, just 'abreast', so I suppose there might be some kind of understanding in this strange account about how that other life runs along invisibly under this one, of the world and its worldly ways, after all.

I write – a bit more information may be needed here, writing is in the family – book reviews. Fiction, non-fiction, the literary end of things I suppose you could say. My father and mother are both academics, historians, and they write, and my brother, who went out with Elisabeth Gordonston and is also an historian, writes big commercial books about Soviet Russia. Along with the reviews, I myself try to write short stories, and sometimes they sell. There was a collection came out several years ago; there was another. And I get something published in a magazine here and there, or something goes on to the radio, maybe, but I keep writing the reviews in the meantime. There's also some other work I have, with a sculpture workshop in East London – I go over there, what? About once every couple of weeks, and write catalogue copy and promotional stuff, and I work on the front desk – and there's some copywriting, too, for a small ad agency, that my friend Marjorie who's very successful at that sort of thing organised for me ages ago because goodness knows I need the money, though I am not very expert at it because you have to write the kind of copy, Marjorie tells me, 'that sells' and mine goes off a bit, it tends to, on a whim. Anyhow, I am diverting, because, yes, Evan was right. I could work on this project he was suggesting to me in quite definitive terms. I could. For I imagine novels, I imagine them all the time, planning these stories that no one would be interested in, as I do realise, and my publishers say the same, so having a subject in this case that was not limited to my own imaginative outline, but was someone else's story . . . Well, maybe Evan was not so very 'out of the ball park', as he might, in his American way, say, suggesting it to me after all.

'Listen,' I'd said to him, a couple of weeks earlier, and in a way I might think of the story, proper, beginning here. 'I have an idea.'

We'd met at the pub at the end of my road, which is right by the tube, because Evan was in a bit of a rush on that first trip back to London when he was 'putting out feelers', as he described it, and had just come over for one night and was running around interviewing with various companies, I think, or organising how it would work for him at the London branch of his New York office.

'When you move back to London,' I said to him then, at my local, 'it will take time. Time to get to know people again, to find your feet. To settle in. London takes time, to do all that when you've been away; it's not the same city that you left. But,' I added, 'you'll be fine. And here's what I suggest you do: A friend of a friend of mine has a big and rather stunning, so I understand, house, in Richmond. I don't know her – the friend, I mean, Rosie's friend – but Rosie told me she has lodgers and that it's quite a fun scene there. That's a quote, by the way: that it's a "fun scene",' I said. 'I'm quoting Rosie talking about her friend; it's how the friend and Rosie both describe things there. I think it means there are lots of parties,' I continued, 'but I also think it means that it's a relaxed place to live. There are children, three boys, but they are well behaved and re-laxed, too, if you know what I mean. There's none of that crazy homework-scheduling-tiger-mother stuff going on and the friend is relaxed and glamorous and loves meeting people. Rosie knows all this,' I said, 'because she is moving out of London and was thinking for a while that she might be a lodger there herself – have a room and then be able to afford to rent in the country and have a studio nearby . . .' I was talking this way, rambling, as though Evan knew Rosie, which he didn't, though he may well have known people she knew.* 'She said,' I continued, '"This friend of mine has lodgers and it's a 'fun scene'." Because I know,

* As before, see that 'Personal History' section – with particular regard to the network of friends under the heading 'Personal Social History'.

yes I know . . .' I continued, 'one always thinks that being a lodger . . .'

'Yeah,' Evan interrupted. 'Exactly.'

Because of course everyone does know that when one thinks of being a lodger one can't imagine anything close to being involved in a 'fun scene'. In fact, the opposite is the case, that lodging is not a 'fun scene' at all but a rather more lonely, cut-off kind of human condition. A scene of being somewhat removed from the society one inhabits, actually, crouched and perching at the edge of other people's lives, inhabiting a corner of their home but not fully living there with them; as though one may have a job and even friends but that when one returns at night to those 'lodgings' one is, in fact, remote from that rich network of connections.

'Yeah.'

So the lodger comes in to a family that is not his own family, quietly taking himself upstairs while below in the kitchen happy times rage on without him; he goes upstairs quietly; to his room, to his single bed.

No wonder, then, that Evan said that 'yeah'. No wonder, I thought.

What we didn't know though, Evan and I, what we weren't close to knowing when we first discussed his possible living arrangements that night in The Cork and Bottle, over what would become our 'signature drink', a gin and tonic of various brands and strengths and volume, was that it would lead, one day, to me writing these words, Evan on the phone, constantly, it seemed, to ask how I was getting on, now that he'd tasked me with and I'd accepted the job of writing it all down, the story of what was to happen with him in Richmond. Because who would have known? Who could have? That my saying those words, casually, actually, about lodging, would eventuate in a love affair, a large, large love that, in a way, looking at literature past, is represented by one of the most expansive and intricate forms of the romance genre* and expresses more than any other type of writing a commitment to that love by way of a review of a life in all its important and absorbing but meaningless details. We didn't come close, as I was talking Evan into an arrangement that he would eventually make, having met with Rosie first, the three of us, to discuss it in full, and Rosie making the requisite phone calls to get the process started, to knowing that this talk of lodging was to be the beginning of something, a narration, a process towards a story that would happen in such a strange, invisible kind of way that many people might think nothing much was even happening at all.

'Alright,' I'd said, remember? After having had that first conversation with Evan about an idea that came from my old friend Rosie that in turn became the beginning of the next conversation and the next that all led, from hearing about their house in Richmond, to the Beresfords, to Caroline Beresford . . . It's where this story first began.

---

* 'Narrative Construction' will give you more to think about later, including the section marked 'Literary Background and Context', but no need to get into all the intricacies of this now.

## two

There are notes Evan supplied me with, when he told me that at first he'd been planning to write, himself, about the whole thing – coming back to London, going to live in Richmond, realising that something in his life was starting, something important, something that felt 'big' as he put it – this, before he thought it would be better if I could be involved and so on, be the one who would 'get the story down' as he later described my role to me, when he had relinquished the idea of being the actual writer in favour of focusing on his actions as participant in the whole affair.

The first set of papers were delivered to me by bicycle messenger the day after he'd confessed that he was not only in love with Caroline Beresford, but so in love that he could no longer think about anything else, couldn't eat properly, wasn't sleeping regularly. In other words, as he'd remarked upon, himself, he was showing all the symptoms of someone who is really almost beside himself with romantic feeling, is almost out of control with it, who has been struck, as the ancients would have it,* by fate as though by a dart from Cupid's bow. Petrarch comes to mind in all this, his love for Laura, and Dante was similar, there was Beatrice in his case, both of them forerunners

---

* There's that concept of being felled by love's arrow, and so on – and there is much of that kind of information at the back of this book, as well as metaphors and practices of a formal romantic tradition under the heading 'Courtly Love'.

for a cultural phenomenon that ran rife through the early world, right through the Renaissance and beyond, right up to a toothpaste commercial in the early eighties having a similar kind of conceit: one bright white smile from a pretty girl and the boy on the bicycle is hurled off it, flat on his face.* So, yes, was Evan also hurled. He had told me, and it was like a confession, a few weeks before.

It had been a wintry morning, a Monday, and I remember thinking how odd it was that Evan had called so early to suggest we meet for coffee at a place he said was really nice, out in Richmond, on the outskirts there. I remember asking if it couldn't be somewhere a little more central, that it would be easier for me to get to, that it would be quicker to get back home afterwards, too – I had a book review for one of the big papers I needed to finish and it was important; I didn't want to mess them around by filing it late.† And I also remember thinking how strange it was – a Monday morning and that Evan wasn't at work.

'But please,' he said. 'It's important, the Richmond part. Please come out here to the area where I now live and lodge. It's an important part of what I have to tell you, Nin. Richmond, you know. It has a role.'

Nin this, Nin that. I've always been Nin to Evan though everyone else calls me Emily, as I was christened but don't necessarily prefer. That's Evan Gordonston for you, right there: sticking to a childhood name because that's what he'd first called me when we met and I was four.

---

* See also the notes on Petrarch and Dante in 'Literary Background and Context'.
† Book reviewing is one aspect of an author's life. There's more in 'Personal History' about this: freelance writing, perilous and interesting.

'It has a role,' I said to him then, 'because that's where you now live, sorry, "lodge". It has a role because it's Richmond. It's not important, Evan, for any other reason but for the fact that it's where Caroline Beresford lives. Yes, I'll come out there,' I said. 'I'll need to take the District Line, or perhaps there's a bus. But don't think for one moment I don't know precisely why you're asking me. You want to give me backdrop. You want to set it in context, all the stuff you've been telling me about this woman who lives there. I haven't told Rosie, by the way, like you asked me to and I won't tell her. The whole thing is kind of out of control,' I said. 'But yes, alright. Though I feel like I know everything there is to know about the set-up there already, I'll come to Richmond anyhow, your cafe on the outskirts.'

It's true, I did feel like that because, before the big confession, bit by bit, Evan *had* told me, it seemed, everything, about him and 'where' he was 'at', as he put it, with Caroline Beresford. When we were children it was always like that, too. I remember from back then how he could never keep anything to himself but had to let me know straight away: his eighth birthday party when his mother said he could take seven friends to Thorpe Park as a surprise and we wouldn't know until we got there, only of course I did\*; the time he rescued a kitten from a skip and was going to

---

\* 'Personal History' contains a sample of the sorts of outings and activities the narrator and protagonist used to be involved in together when they were children, practical and creative activities encouraged by their mothers, who were both good friends and influential in the upbringing of each other's children.

keep it in his wardrobe until he could find a good home and no one was to know, only I did, and told him he would need to tell his parents about the kitten right then and there if it was to stay; there were various gifts and outings I wasn't ever supposed to know about, but did; the list goes on. Now he was an adult and back in London again he'd been keeping me in these same old loops: 'I'm taking colleagues to Nobu for a dinner party next Thursday and the chef there is going to cook the whole thing right at the table and I want you to come as my partner, Nin, but you're not to say a word because none of them have the slightest idea . . .' And then announcing it to everyone at the outset, etc., etc. . . . That kind of thing. Before he fell in love with Caroline, this is, before he'd met her. 'I have bought your birthday present ten months in advance' was another example, this just two days after he'd arrived back in London and the first time he and I had seen each other after a gap of . . . goodness knows how many years but there it was, he had reverted to his childhood habit of impulsive gift buying for Christmas or birthdays, but always telling me well beforehand what it was. So, 'I have bought a certain kind of shoe for you, Nin, that I think you'll enjoy,' he'd told me, 'in a strange and interesting colour. I am letting you know now because I am guessing how pleased you'll be with them when your birthday comes along.' So, too, then, of course I knew everything about him falling in love with Caroline Beresford. I knew everything about that.

Is it the sort of thing that can often happen to a lodger, I wonder? To a lonely person, coming and going, with a life on the periphery, somehow, with a job that is not so compelling as to make that person want to commit to a flat or house of their own; or otherwise so demanding and isolating that one never has the opportunity to go looking for a home, there's always too much work to do, and so who is stuck on the lodger-ladder; always outside looking in? I do wonder. For Evan was vulnerable to both sets of circumstances those first few weeks when he was back in London after living in the States for so long. He had me, but I was about all he had. The other friends from all those years ago had pretty much faded away, married, had families and moved to the country, or even further, to Scotland or to Wales, prompted by a feeling that London had become too impossibly expensive nowadays, turned over to the super-rich and no longer that much fun, or for similar reasons they had simply changed, moved into different lives.* And even I had my responsibilities, on that front, in order to meet the financial pressure of living in the Capital, the need to constantly keep up with the work for the gallery and the ad campaigns, along with the occasional writing of the short stories and so on, coming up with ideas for novels and having unproductive meetings with my publishers – so though I was always at the end of the phone, an email or a text, Evan must have still felt how he didn't have a whole load of people to spend time with – and on top of that, other friends my friends knew, though also friends of mine, might not be so easy to get to know. There was Rosie now, for example, away in the country-

* More 'Personal History' for later, perhaps, especially the section entitled 'Old London'?

side, and unlikely to come into town; and another friend, Christopher, had become involved with local politics and a creepy right-wing organisation that had strong opinions about tree felling and street cleaning, important issues both but I felt uncomfortable about the way his politics seemed to be bending around them and knew they would distance him from Evan. There was my other friend, Marjorie, but she was a bit like me, always writing – though in her case it was copy for a pet food giant that kept her chained to impossible deadlines that she couldn't afford to break because they paid the mortgage on her extremely pretty one-bedroom flat in Chelsea – so I barely saw her at all, let alone would manage to plan a get-together with her and me and Evan and other people. It was always dogs and cats and the spillover work that also came my way when there was a rush on, and it seemed there was always a rush.

So yes, Evan was alone a good deal of the time. He could meet friends through work, no doubt – though are friends from work true friends? Especially in that kind of work Evan was involved with? That cut-throat world of finance and manipulation, could there be real associates there who might become intimates? I am not so sure. And yes, he would have met people in his general day-to-day dealings in the way all of us do so meet – the shopkeeper at the end of the road, the dry-cleaner, and in my case the postman, with whom I have a great deal of contact due to my job* – but in general he was a man

---

* In 'Personal History' we learn more about the kinds of people one may meet regularly when one lives alone and as a freelance writer.

quietly coming into a family home in Richmond at the end of his working day, hearing the cheer going on in the kitchen, that happy chaos of family life, as I may write it, which sounds like a cliche but actually isn't, and going straight upstairs, silent as a silent brown mouse, lonely and afraid, up to his lonely room at the top of the house where he lodged alone.

Because, I write it, he was afraid. Afraid of the feelings of his own large heart. From the first moment he'd met Caroline, from the moment he'd heard her voice, even, on the phone when he'd called the number Rosie had given me to pass on to him, a charge had been set, a switch turned. She'd said, 'Oh, hi! You're Evan! Yes, I've been expecting you . . .' – and something caught, he told me, his breath, the beat of his heart. He'd faltered, 'I . . .' – but she'd simply, smoothly said, in that voice of hers, 'Come on by to the house when it suits you. After work sometime? I am always in. I never go anywhere' – which was actually just a great big charming lie because women like Caroline are never 'always in' but are out all the time, they can't help it. People like Caroline Beresford are the kind of person everyone wants to see.

That changed, of course. As I found out. As the weeks went by, and the story grew. As the first days of Evan moving to Richmond became many, many days and then weeks and a season changed, and another, Caroline would find herself staying around the house more and more; evenings, daytime, parts of the weekend . . . Stories change, they move on. It's what makes them stories.

'I keep seeing Caroline around the house and it's hard

not to think about her,' Evan told me, when it was clear by his appearance that he was deep, deep in love.* 'She says, "Hi, do you feel like a coffee? Come into the kitchen" – and that's that. I have to go in there and be with her. I must try and drink the coffee. Act normal around her. Oh, Nin. I must try.'

So there, the combination then, of Evan's vulnerability, fresh back to London after years away, and the lovely ease, the grace, of Caroline . . . was how things started for him, I know. And, in his way of things, he started telling me about her straight away, bit by bit, but it all came out over gin and tonics at various pubs and bars, in so many respects the story formed entire over the underpinning of that particular kind of cocktail, with Tanqueray or Gordon's or Bombay Sapphire or Sipsmith's or any number of the branded and unbranded gins and their accompanying designer tonics that now load the shelves and mirrored bars of West London and beyond, indicating from the first time he told me about her the depth of his love; each one after another, the glasses lining up, and many of them doubles, with crisps, or set against a bowl of nuts.

He'd gone along to meet Caroline, as she'd suggested on the phone, after he'd rung the number Rosie had texted me to give him. 'He'll have a great time there,' she'd said to me, after I'd told her he had called. It was to be a 'fun scene' after all, remember, that she'd described?

---

* People often do look different when they have fallen in love, for better or for worse. In Evan's case his appearance followed the trajectory of an early Renaissance lover; from the moment he was struck by the appearance of his beloved he started to lose his looks. See, later: 'Courtly Love'.

Rosie knew Richmond well, she'd grown up there – and no, it wasn't Chelsea or Notting Hill or Knightsbridge, where Evan could have so easily landed, courtesy of that fancy firm of his, but it was lovely Richmond nevertheless with an elegant house there of much coming and going, of parties and drinks and get-togethers and suppers. And already, as I have mentioned, something in Evan had been . . . prepared. By the sound of Caroline. By her intake of breath. By her voice. The tone of her voice. He chose a Thursday evening, to go there, to take the District Line to Richmond. It was in the early winter; he'd been back in London for a week. There was no snow but it was bitterly cold.

At that point, his suitcases not yet unpacked, if you like, he was living at the Connaught, if you believe it – I repeat: this is what these finance companies are like. He was larking about in a junior suite there, on the first floor of the hotel facing towards the front, with a little sitting area, and a dining table and four chairs. Evan would order in Chinese food, for those first few days of his 'homecoming' as I put it, and we ate spicy prawns with noodles, looking out over Carlos Place and drinking Chinese beer, me feeling so damn glamorous, myself, all because of his weird job and the way these companies 'put' their employees 'up'. Anyway, it must have been no more than a week of that, when he left his rooms there to get first a taxi, then, because of traffic, the District Line, out to Richmond, to that 'fun scene', and one of the children had answered the door, the youngest boy, Freddie, 'who is twelve', Evan told me, but Caroline came right up behind him and extended her hand. 'Hi, I'm Caroline,' she'd said. And – BANG.*

She was wearing – in my mind she wears it still – a white T-shirt and one of those skirts you pull around yourself and tie up and they look amazing. She was tall, Caroline is tall, and she was just wearing that, the skirt and the T-shirt and with bare feet and long tanned legs, though it was January. She didn't even have a cardigan on.

'Come in,' she said to Evan and he stepped into the hall.

The scent, the scent of that house, of Caroline herself, was like oranges, he said later. The whole house full of that kind of deliciousness. Oranges. Orange trees. Orange blossom. Summer in winter, fruitfulness in the dark and cold. Evan walked in the front door of the house in Richmond and, well, I'm writing it down now, it was there in his own writing, in some of the early notes, his 'life changed'.

'OK,' I said to him, this after the first set of notes had been sent, when my involvement in the project had already arisen as an issue between us. 'So just suppose I say, yes, that I'll get the whole thing down in an overall draft,

---

* Note the use of those capital letters – BANG – and the use of space following the appearance of the word, the fact that further text does not follow on from it but that the word sits out alone. This is worth a footnote, alright. Again, that word, its presentation, its dramatic appearance following the dash . . . All denote a marked and singular event on the page. See, if interested and later, the note for 'Courtly Love' for further information regarding that BANG, as well as other relevant material, notes on Petrarch and Dante, all of it. The 'all' of the story seeming to occur – the BANG, the recognition of emotion, the sense of pain – at the same time, in that second of the sighting, like an arrow as they used to write it, Cupid's dart, in that first smarting glance, the look of love. These details most important. So, BANG. Yes. It is a good word for what's happened here.

all of it, how it started, even the oranges. How her holding out her hand to you to say "hi" was the beginning of some kind of . . . big thing, I suppose, is how we might describe it. Let's just suppose . . .'

'Yes,' Evan said, and I want to write 'eagerly' – though I hate the laziness of adverbs, but adverbial was how he was being, rather, the night he actually proposed I write the story for him, the story of his love, all his little gestures so attentive and desperate and wild. Like in the way he'd said, 'Nin, Nin, Nin, you've GOT to do this for me. Please. I've never asked you for anything like this before—' when he'd first brought it up, the idea of a kind of literary project we might work on together.

'"Anything like this?"' I said to him, quoting him back at himself. 'You've not asked me to do anything for you in the past, altogether. We've not seen each other for decades, Evan. So "Nin", yourself,' I said. 'You don't need to be so dramatic and rhetorical about it. We haven't seen each other for, approximately, all of our adult life, so I need to get a handle on this, a grip. It sounds interesting but . . . I don't know, Evan. If I'm up to it, I mean. Writing it down, getting it down right, having you in there, getting Caroline in . . .'

'Oh, you will. You will. You'll make it all come together,' he replied. 'Just say you will, Nin. Please. Say.'

'Say this, say that,' I murmured, in the manner of a sage or a wise old man. The pub was cold. It was always cold in The Cork and Bottle and I was starting to think perhaps we should go somewhere else.

But for now, 'Let's have another gin and tonic,' I said.

# three

The notes Evan passed me, three weeks after that meeting, that were to be 'background reading and research' were, I have to say, inadequate. I'm going to insert some of them here, as I told him I would, as part of this book – which I wasn't expecting to do, as I'd thought with the big corporate job, and so on, his position with the Beresfords, he would want to be invisible, kind of – though I do remember that he'd had the notion, too, at the beginning of the affair, that he was going to write 'the whole damn thing' himself, so actually perhaps he didn't want to be so invisible after all. Even so, with me 'attached' to the project, as they say in the film business, and lending distance in that way, I would have thought I might, by changing some names here and there, be inclined towards protecting him to some degree. Isn't that what always happens in novels? That one protects the fact by using fiction? At one point, for sure, I did consider switching location – moving the whole *locus amoenus* as it were, to South London, say, or to Australia or Texas or the North Island of New Zealand, somewhere where they get a bit more sun – especially for the whole part towards the end that involves a swimming pool, watersports, a bikini, etc.

But no, Evan said, 'I want to be in it, Nin – the entire story, with my full name and all my feelings on show', and, as I say, I thought, well alright, 'background reading and research' after all, and so here are some of the notes now, that he made, though to my mind there's not enough story in them and too much of Evan, and to that extent I know for a novel they won't really do:

'About six weeks ago,' Evan wrote, 'I moved back to London, to an area some people might describe as suburban. I use that term "suburban" quite definitely – because London doesn't think of itself as a metropolis with suburbs – though we may read articles in magazines about the various areas being village-y or whatever; still, no one talks much about Richmond, say, as a suburb, in the way that people talk about "out in the 'burbs" in New York. It's just a term we don't use. In other places where I've lived – New York, Tokyo, for a bit, Chicago – you get suburbs in these places i.e.: –'

At this point, when I read that 'i.e.' I thought, O-ho, we're in trouble here, Evan! No one is going to want to read a narrative of yours in this kind of condition. You don't see an 'i.e.' in an ad, or in a short story, you just don't, or in any of the kind of writing for that matter about which I think of myself as having some kind of knowledge, and you certainly wouldn't see it in a love story, or romance, which is what you want to create here, Evan, is it not? Still, I let him continue for now.

'That notion of the big city', he carried on, in his terrible scrawl, 'holding itself to itself and the rest of the outside clinging on for dear life to the periphery of it, to the concept of "big city", getting "into town" to go to dinner or a show . . . is not a London notion. No. London suburbs have not been thought of in those terms. Yet I have found there ARE places here like that, after all, that are indeed suburban in appearance and nature, in . . . lifestyle. For it is "lifestyle" I am getting at here, and when my dearest and oldest friend, Emily Stuart, told me about her friend Rosie having a friend who had a big house out in Richmond, and that this friend of a friend took in lodgers, because there was loads of space, when the friend of a friend, as it were, told my friend that she had a room available, in that house, and that it was, as she put it, a "fun scene" living there . . . I thought it seemed like a sensible thing to consider it, that the arrangement might take care of things while I was getting settled, moving back to London after so many years away.

'Actually,' he continued, 'it was quite a strange thing to do. The company would have put me up somewhere much more central until I got sorted out, I could have gone anywhere. But something in me went "ping!" when the lodger idea was suggested. My own belief is that it was the intervention of fate.'

I loved the 'ping'. I said to Evan, 'I loved that "ping!" of yours, in your notes. I loved the way you let yourself go a bit, with it, but' – this all in The Cork and Bottle, some two weeks or so after I'd started working on his story – 'I have to tell you . . .' And I looked at him quite severely then, 'I do have to tell you, Evan, that we're going to go steady on the "fate" and "myth" side of things. It's too much. It's too rich. It will put people off.'

For yes, we were back in my local. It seemed, despite my various pretty much unexpressed ideas about alternative venues, we couldn't manage other kinds of meetings.

We'd reverted, Evan and I had, we had, straight away, as mentioned before, to old methods of behaviour, our old ways and habits. Not that we went to pubs back then, of course, when we were children, only that we'd always had a tendency to repeat activities, play the same sorts of games, over and over, and so on, have certain places we'd meet up at, plans we'd make that we'd stick to, day after day the same. Weeks of going over to his house, say, and Helen leaving out a certain sort of tea. Or after school every day for about a year visiting the V & A to look at the Renaissance rooms, then drawing the grand contents up in detail in special notebooks that we had. Or else my mother said we could use her garden room as a studio, and we had six months of growing tomatoes there and then painting murals of them on the walls.* We liked the familiar in that way. And it wasn't for want of trying, now, either, to be different. There had been that early morning meeting in a cafe, when the project first began, out on the outskirts of Richmond, when Evan had wanted me to go there for 'context'.† Not that Evan ever suggested going there again, but he often talked about a lunch, that I could go into Mayfair and meet him near where he worked and we could go to some fancy place there and talk and make notes about what we were calling by then 'our project', not novel, not then, and have three courses and the company would pay. He was always saying we could do that. But

* Those 'Personal History' notes come in again here; the details about the shared childhood in Twickenham, etc.; children's activities.
† The section entitled 'Alternative Narratives' may be of interest at some stage, though no need to worry about it now.

I always seemed to have some writing deadline or whatever – the gallery needed me for a catalogue, there was a pet food campaign Marjorie had passed on to me – and anyway, I had nothing pretty to wear. That night in the Cork I was just wearing my usual old jeans and a flannel shirt and that was fine, but you go into the West End and everyone looks amazing. They' ve got the hair, the tailored outfits. The bags. And yes, I own a dress, or two, a skirt, but I never seem to wear any of that kind of clothing, just the shirts and the jeans, so what was the point, really, of changing what was familiar?

'Let's just meet over here,' I said to Evan instead, meaning this part of town, just to be local, and he always came. I could make him supper at home, for that matter, I thought, though may not have said, back in the beginning,* because really, with all we had to discuss there was no need for another kind of fancy lunch, or we could go out for supper somewhere nearby – all these alternative plans Evan and I often had. But in the end we just found our routine and kept to it. There was that leitmotif of the gin I've mentioned. Those crisps or nuts. No need to do any of those other things, then, when we had our habits that we were used to. So instead of doing anything out of the ordinary, I would just meet Evan off the tube after work, the one down at the end of my road, and there he was, that second of his familiar, familiar presence, taking

* Again, this is to do with an 'Alternative Narrative', as indicated at the back of this book; here referring to an earlier part of the story, before Evan had even met Caroline, and the author had various ideas about how her protagonist's time might have been spent.

shape out of the crowd that rose up the steps before me, his lovely breaking smile, 'Hey!' like he'd never expected to see me only there I was. And, 'Let's go to the pub,' he would say, as in the spirit of 'Why would we do anything else?' and though there was no glamour there, at The Cork and Bottle at the corner, nor at The Elm Tree or The Walker's Friend, our subsequent destinations through the dark winter months, yet it was what we did, where we went, who we were.

'But I like that the whole thing felt fated,' said Evan. 'And it was, Nin. Why, if it wasn't, didn't I just get the company to sort me out with a flat or whatever? Why, if it wasn't fated, did I even think – despite the "fun scene" – that I wanted to live with another family, be a lodger?'

'You were just confused,' I said.

I was looking at him, thinking about all this as he was speaking. 'You were still jet-lagged,' I said, for something to say, because his appearance, as I could see, was a bit worn and a bit pale.

'Long-term jet lag then,' he interrupted. He fished out the lemon from the bottom of his glass and chewed on a corner like it was a little sandwich. 'Listen,' he said, after he'd eaten that tiny portion and swallowed it. 'We'll have to get the fate aspect into the story.' He paused. 'Predestination. Yes, fate. Like it or not. What I call the Big Bang factor, Nin. It was a big thing. I walked in that door in Richmond and everything changed . . .'*

* 'In 'Courtly Love' a section headed 'Unrequited Love as a Creative Act' might be of interest.

I picked the lemon out of my own glass and tore it in half. I was still thinking about his clothes. He was in a smart suit, a tie, all the rest of it, but he looked faded, somehow, drawn.

'People might read it that you were just lonely,' I said. 'That the house in Richmond, way out there on the District Line, seemed warm and welcoming and you were only recently back from—'

'But how could I be lonely?' Evan said, and he took my hand that was holding the rest of my own torn lemon. 'When I have you who I've loved for so long?' he said.

I guess I had to give him his due at that point. Sometimes writing does that, puts the words in and you can't 'write' past them. So with that 'ping!' I had loved in his notes. I couldn't deny it. I couldn't erase it in any way and now it was just there. So then I had also to allow for the fate element, the 'myth' as Evan was now dangerously starting to describe what had started as 'project'.* So, 'OK,' I said, that day, and I, too, ate the lemon; from that day onwards, whenever it was available I always would. And so here follows accordingly some more of his notes, those ideas he thought we could build into something that might have pretensions to being some kind of fable or 'myth'. Because all I could manage at that moment, after he'd spoken, was that 'OK'. It was all I could do to say it, after he'd said what he'd just said, to eat that lemon through.

'I've always been outgoing but in a retiring sort of way,'

* 'Narrative Construction' – particularly that note regarding the various descriptions and massive variations in Evan's mind as to the nature of the work under review – might be of interest here.

Evan wrote. 'I've had friends, girlfriends . . . It's just that I tend towards feelings of boredom, and can't keep the momentum of the relationship in train. I hear a kind of humming in my head is the problem, with most people; it reminds me of my father. I remember how he used to hum around the house when my mother had friends in, how he would hum and never settle. Only when his best friend from next door was over, Alastair Stuart, the historian, would you see him perk up – they used to do crosswords together or have discussions about history and historical philosophy, related literature, and whatever Alastair was writing – only generally around people, there was that humming of his. And we always knew, we kids, there was someone coming around to the house unless it was Alastair, because of it, him starting suddenly to hum, in a quiet, involved, deliberate sort of way. Anyhow, for me, meeting Caroline Beresford there was none of that business. There was no humming whatsoever.'

Caroline. 'Sweet Caroline' I started singing quietly to myself, privately, though this nothing like humming, of course, oh nothing like. It was a song with all the words. 'Sweet Caroline', in my head because by now, at home, even when I wasn't with him or reading his notes, I was getting so used to hearing Evan talking about having met someone whose name was Caroline, Caroline – the name in that terrific Neil Diamond song that everyone still loves. I would sing the whole thing quietly, start to finish, just to myself, back in those early days, even the 'Hands . . . Touching hands . . .' crescendo part that everyone gets so worked up about.

At this point, in the story, I confessed to Evan, having read his first set of notes for the first time, I had had to get up and actually put *The Best of Neil Diamond* on the CD player, that particular track. I turned it way up and sang along and danced.

'It was great,' I said to Evan. 'It's such a great song.'

'Let's go out dancing together, sometime, ourselves,' he said. 'What a wonderful idea. And that chorus – it's perfect for us! We'll find a place that has a jukebox or some kind of ancient DJ who can play it for us and we could dance along and sing . . .'

'It might be the kind of track that a young party host would have on his playlist,' I said, letting the idea develop in a lovely way, that Evan would break from our already so established routine and go dancing. 'You know, the kind of host that he might play the song in some kind of ironic, post-modern fashion . . .'

We both of us looked around us in the pub, both of us the same second. Thinking the same thing: Is there a jukebox here somewhere? But of course there wasn't.

The pub we were in that night, The Elm Tree, wasn't that kind of pub. I'd found it after realising that the Cork was too cold. It was more of a village kind of place, like we were all pretending to be in Oxfordshire somewhere because it faced on to a Green that's only about a five-minute walk away from my flat but still it's like another part of London altogether, the Green a bit like a village green, you might say, and there were dogs allowed inside and people who had been walking them, in gumboots and with Barbours on. It was further away from the tube than the Cork, the Elm, and maybe that short walk was part of it. The facing on to the Green. For it was quiet and sweet and old-fashioned inside and marked a new development in our proceedings, a slight change of mood.

'No jukebox,' Evan and I both said in unison. And then we laughed.

That seemed like a while ago, I thought subsequently, all those nights going through Evan's notes, Neil Diamond notwithstanding. Those early conversations. Early, early thoughts. By now we'd left even The Elm Tree behind us and the writing, Evan's writing, was taking us on. So 'Caroline', I read, in the spirit of that onward-moving narrative. Here we go again:

'I used to even think "My Caroline",' Evan wrote, 'though she wasn't "my" anything.' His handwriting really was appalling. 'She'd said "hi" to me, she'd put out her hand. Yet that, as far as I am concerned, was enough. That was that. She said then that since I was back in London, I ought to come and stay for just as long as I needed while I found my feet again. She said, "Can I get you anything, coffee, tea? Before I show you around the house?" And I said yes, and we drank coffee together, standing looking out through the big plate-glass "ranchers", they would call them in the States, these big sliding doors, that led out to the enormous Richmond garden.'

Evan's descriptions were clear, they were good. That part of his writing was sound, I liked it.

'The house was indeed enormous,' he finished, in this first section of his notes, 'just as Rosie and Nin had said it would be. Everything about it was on a large scale. The kitchen, Caroline's kitchen where she made the coffee and where we stood, looking out at a lawn that was the size of a bowling green, with big trees and flowerbeds and so on . . .

"'It's ridiculous, isn't it?" said Caroline. "But we are in the suburbs here so it's not as crazy as it seems."

"'I think it's lovely," I said to Caroline then. I wanted to say to her: "I think you are lovely."'

'But you didn't,' I said.

'Oh, no,' Evan replied. 'I could never do that.'

# four

The Beresfords, Rosie said, had begun with a very happy marriage. They'd had the ceremony, a really big, fancy affair – more of a house party, she described it, than a wedding – in Thailand, back in the days when everyone had holidays that were proper holidays and could also go away for big parties and occasions and not be on their phones all the time and answering emails or having to rush back to London after taking no more than a week's break for some deadline, or meeting. They were married at a time when people, by comparison, Rosie said, could take it easy.

Caroline had been a PR director then, for a company representing, mainly, thoroughbred racing stables and stud farms in Ireland; though she herself was not Irish but had been brought up – 'deep in the home counties' was how she herself put it to Evan when he asked – with ponies, and had been on horseback since the age of three, so there was 'nothing she didn't know about horseflesh', was the way Evan described her to me, when he was first wanting to describe Caroline to me on one of those early meetings when we were still going regularly to The Cork and Bottle, that first pub just round the corner from where I live. Yes, it was there, and he was ordering our third gin and tonics at the bar when I learned all of this 'key background stuff', as Evan put it, about Caroline Beresford's upbringing, background, her family, and current situation with David, her handsome lawyer husband who had been on track to make a fortune in the City but had become derailed somewhere along the line, and now all he wanted to do was read ancient Greek literature and start translation classes in the Classics department at the University of London where he'd enrolled as a part-time student and, for that reason, had rented a small flat just off Russell Square. 'He's told Caroline on a number of occasions that as far as he's concerned, they can dissolve their marriage now and he could start over,' Evan reported. 'He could happily go back to university full time and work towards a PhD, he's said, more than once – but then he and Caroline sit down and talk about the kids and the house and the horse Caroline keeps in Berkshire . . . And he loves horses, too, apparently . . . And then they decide not to dissolve things but to stick to the marriage after all, in the meantime, and see how it goes. But yeah,' Evan said, looking into his drink, and stirring the ice cubes with his finger as though he were the husband of Caroline himself, with worries on his mind about their marriage and whether he and his wife had anything in common, not handsome David, with his glasses pushed down at the end of his nose and his long legs stretched out in front of him, some ancient text on his lap and a tequila to hand. 'Things used to be great between them,' Evan said, 'but that was a while ago, you can tell. Caroline has a sadness around her, a sense of loss.'

The PR company she'd worked for represented various stables of polo ponies – it was how she and David met, through horses; his family farmed and there was a grandmother who'd always favoured David who was a great one for the races – as well as top-of-the-range brands like Rolex and Patek Philippe and Theo Fennell jewellery . . . Evan had explained all this to me, and I knew what he was getting at. These kinds of sports attract a whole lot of interest from advertisers and sponsors – I'm familiar with how that works through my own advertising activities – and Caroline was the one in charge of all of that, liaising between the various people involved. Plus she didn't just bring it together, the networking, by organising particular events – getting in the right kind of movie stars who would parade this bloodline or that, promote some particular race or the other – she was also brilliant at the writing side of things, too, the copy for the ads, the letters inviting kings and queens and princesses and Russian thugs and gangsters and goodness knows who else, London is full of these people nowadays, to the fancy polo parties and point-to-points. She could write a beautiful letter, Caroline. I saw one or two. Evan showed me. In fact I told Marjorie about the quality of the sentences I'd seen of Caroline's and even Marjorie, with her sure knowledge of what she terms 'good, solid selling correspondence', was impressed. 'Caroline sounds interesting,' Marjorie had said.

Anyhow, horses, horses, horses. Polo, polo, polo. And yes, it was at one such event that she'd met David Beresford – Rosie said, who'd known his younger brother, Robert, who'd gone out with a friend of hers from St Martins – so that was the connection there. Rosie said Robert had always been 'a complete sweetie', and that it was her friend, Amanda, who was also modelling at the time and involved in '*Vogue*-world', as Rosie put it, who had caused the trouble in *that* relationship . . . In other words, what I am saying here is that it's not that it was the Beresfords who had an unsteady gene as far as relationships were concerned. The father, Jonathan Beresford, and his wife Diana had been very happily married and 'still are', Rosie said, 'a lovely couple, kind and solicitous and smart' . . . And David Beresford was the same, she continued, I'd put all of this down in my additional notes: courteous, gentle, clever. 'And *very* good-looking' as Evan said – always a nice thing to hear: a man complimenting another man in that department – 'Charming in the proper sense of the word', he said, the 'real deal' and with a career that everyone said would go stellar. 'Well, not that stellar,' said Rosie to me much later, when I was adding to notes Evan had given me, 'because after all, they live out on the District Line, at the end of the day, the Beresfords, not Notting Hill.'

I could write about all of these details, including that slightly off remark of Rosie's that I've just recorded, and the ins and outs of the Beresford brothers and their handsome and personal ways* – Rosie had also had a crush on Robert and had been very much the shoulder to cry on after it all went haywire between him and Amanda –

---

* Those Beresford brothers! It's hard to put into words the effect of just saying that phrase aloud, as one that reaches all the way back to prep school days, when mothers and teachers might refer to them thus and hear the resonance of nomenclature then, a resonance that continues to the present day. 'Do you know the Beresford brothers' or 'Oh, they're the Beresford brothers, of course,' etc. Some sibling groups just achieve that kind of consequence in a sentence I guess. 'Personal History' might also be interesting in this context.

because, as well as Rosie and Evan talking to me directly about such matters, Evan had also by then given me his first set of annotated notes about himself and Caroline and had asked me to conduct with him – first in The Cork and Bottle when we started going there, and subsequently in The Elm Tree and The Walker's Friend, another pub in the heart of West London that was pretending to be in the country in terms of style and clientele – lengthy Q & A sessions from which I would learn 'key facts' about Caroline Beresford and 'our relationship' as he was, from even quite early on in the proceedings, somewhat alarmingly, describing his interactions as lodger to her landlady of the house in Richmond.

These Q & A sessions, he said, and he was clear about this, would be the basis from which I would construct 'a meticulous record', was his description at first, then, 'love story', to become a possible future novel entire, based upon history and fact,* which would comprise a lively and involving narrative based upon two people who had met by chance and were now, in the manner of protagonists in some early Renaissance or medieval text, deeply in love.

We may as well have been sipping on cider, these places we were frequenting so head-in-the-country in mood and atmosphere. We may as well have had a brace of black Labradors waiting for us and been wearing those Barbours I've mentioned, hung up on a hook in a wet room some-

---

* There's much discussion throughout *Caroline's Bikini* as to the nature of the literary 'project' the author and her protagonist have undertaken. Essay? Life writing? Novel? See 'Narrative Construction' and 'Literary Background and Context' for further details.

where in the West Country or the Highlands – but no, we were drinking Tanqueray and tonic in West Kensington, minutes from oligarchs and multi-million-pound show homes that were barely lived in, owned by Chinese industrialists and mobsters, no doubt; we were there, in that particular part of town. Those other 'streets of luxury', as my friend Christopher calls them, in the judgemental but also slightly avaricious vaguely right-wing sort of way of his that I find a bit sketchy, may as well have been in another world, though, as far as the establishment in which we were now settled, saying 'Cheers' and splitting a bag of nuts, was concerned. Around us, after all, were only the kinds of people who would walk their dogs in a muddy park in early winter, with not a sheikh or Russian businessman in sight but only hearty wind- and rain-swept types calling out to each other, 'What a day!' from across the steamy fug of a pub lunch and real ale.

'No kitten heels present', I made, as an early note, in one of my diaries, establishing context for the writing project I'd undertaken, with a degree of enthusiasm, by now, after all, it has to be said. No 'taster menu' or 'thrice-combed cashmere' here, I'd written. Only real ale and jolly remarking, 'What a day!' and so on. Only a mood and tone that was, depending upon the destination, pure 'Elm' as Evan and I came to call it, and in the same way, later, 'the Walker's' and then simply 'Friend'.

It was indeed uncharacteristic of Rosie to make a comment like that – 'because after all, they live out on the District Line, the Beresfords, not Notting Hill' – because she was an artist, and so should be totally unconcerned,

you might say, with money and postcodes and society . . .
But there. She did say it, about poor David Beresford's
career, 'Well, not *that* stellar,' and it stuck, somehow. I remembered it and now that I've written it down twice it
seems well embedded in this narrative; I've included it, no
denying that, so something is going on there, something.
It's as though the fact of David, the handsome fact of him
and his decision about his career, not to pursue it in the
way he might have because of 'other diversions', as Evan
described them, thoughts of a classics degree and so on
resulting in his spending time with other kinds of people,
other men and women who were not Caroline, his being
concerned with other interests, priorities, as though all
these details about the life he'd chosen may well contribute to the story I am writing here. Have input, I mean. Sig-
nificance. And there's the matter, too, of certain empathies
around the man – that I wrote 'poor David Beresford' just
there, instinctively you might say,* as though to describe
something that was straitened about him, handsome and
confident as he was, a sort of financial straitening of the
Beresfords overall, perhaps, what I am getting at here, a
feeling of there being, in their marriage and their life together, not quite enough. And this despite the big house
in Richmond, and the neighbours with, as it turned out,
swimming pools and health club memberships and so on,
all the kind of 'LA behaviour' as Evan put it, that went on
out there in that part of London with its off-road parking

---

* See 'Alternative Narratives' for further remarks regarding those involved in
the story who are not Caroline or Evan.

and what have you, the easy accommodation for lodging; despite the huge garden of the Beresfords, practically the size of a small private square, according to Rosie, and despite the number of bedrooms and en suites and so on in that house, a whole top floor with its own kitchen, for goodness' sake, given over to Evan himself, despite it all . . . there was, nevertheless, a wanting, a lack. It was as if, expressed in all the grand sweep of real estate that was Richmond, with its acreages and historical benefits, its beauties and seasonal pleasures of parks and open spaces, there was something missing in all this loveliness, withheld from them and denied. As though, all through Caroline's life, in its fullness, there had been left in her by now, not acceptance of her lot, her life, but only the desperate desire for one portion more. As though something, as I see it, a vital thing, was still so necessary, so needed, that it would articulate always the rest that had been given as insufficient by that same small immeasurable margin that could not be expressed in words or in her heart.

To go back to that phrase of Evan's about Caroline, that she had about her 'a sense of loss' . . .

And the fact that the Beresfords took in lodgers in the first place – needed to, I mean . . .

Suggests that: gap. A part that was lacking, a piece missing in the whole, let me describe it as, a space, gap, the right word entirely. And that there was an aspect of her behaviour, yes, I can see it, in Caroline's bravery about it, the circumstances that were the result of a legal career not gone 'stellar' but stopped short, rather, in a translation of the *Iliad* or of Hesiod's *Works and Days*,* in other people, scholars, professors, fellow students; the fact that she'd created a 'fun scene' nevertheless around this absence, shortfall, disguising it in order to make being way out there on the District Line a wonderful thing, so working with imagination and verve around 'that gap' – as I now found myself thinking about it – that space of missing finances and of love . . . Oh, Caroline, I found myself writing, in the vocative, a tense Evan was so fond of employing in his notes. To have, instead of a full portion, the need, the requirement instead to take in a stranger or sometimes a number of them into your home and have them living there with you, in your house, alongside your children and your husband, and with your husband away a good deal of the time, either on work assignments or because he is blocking out days and nights in the British Museum, to be in discussions with some Classics don from Cambridge or whoever . . . That you might have an unknown person living with you in the midst of your own intense domestic world . . . To have all of this . . . Want. Need. Gap. And yet be cheerful about it. To make the whole thing into a 'fun scene' . . . Well, that was the kind of person Caroline Beresford was. Barefoot in a T-shirt and groovy wrap-around skirt, thin as a rail while barely doing a stroke of exercise, one weekly Pilates class notwithstanding, because of all the running around after everybody and having the house

* David Beresford's interest in classical scholarship might merit a whole novel in itself; as it is there are some details about his personal life in the section of 'Further Material' headed 'Personal History' – as well as in notes regarding inheritance, financial contingencies, etc.

look nice with little in the way of daily household help – 'not really', reported Rosie – or big cleaning agency to be on call . . . That was Caroline. Coming to the door in the middle of winter, but still the feeling of her being tanned and carefree and summery – that scent of oranges – just pulling her hair up into a messy pony tail as she walked down the hall in front of Evan towards the kitchen, twisting up a hairstyle with one hand as she called back towards him, 'So nice to have someone my own age here,' and laughing. 'The last lot of lodgers were all international students and tiny and very foreign and exhausting. We couldn't, you know,' and at this she stopped, turned and gave Evan one of her radiant, straight-off-the-back-of-a-thoroughbred-and-jumping-down-on-to-a-wide-green-lawn, smiles, 'chat.'

That's how I see Caroline, for sure. As Evan first saw her. Tall. Tanned, even though it's the middle of winter. That sense of horsemanship hovering there somewhere in the background though we're firmly in West London and nowhere near those easy miles of republican green, the lovely and endless-seeming green-blue paddocks of 'the free State' as a compelling Irishwoman I met recently through Christopher called her place of birth. Oh, Caroline. Caroline. With that beachy dirty-blonde hair falling down her back in a gloriously sunshiny spill before she tied it up so deftly with one hand, walking down the hall in front of Evan, calling out over her shoulder in the midst of other lines of conversation about lodgers, 'Coffee? Shall we have a cup of coffee together, you and I? Before I show you around the house, I mean?' – and Evan's heart going

– Bang. Right then. Or 'Ping!' as he put it, so charmingly, in his notes.

'Yes, her receding form,' Evan said, in The Walker's Friend. He was a bit drunk. This was a much later conversation but it may as well have been one of the first, the first even, when he'd just handed over a batch of his notes and was feeling tense about it. The notes, the giving over of them, continued to make him tense though by now I'd had several sets from him, first in the Cork, then the Elm and now, as we were hunkered down in the Friend. 'Let's just go to the Friend again,' Evan had said, when he'd called me, after three or four days had passed since he'd handed over the last batch of material, in which he'd written in detail about first meeting Caroline and was recording in a metatextual, self-referential kind of way what it was like to record that moment and what it all might mean. 'Yes, her receding form,' and so on, in detailed phrases and paragraphs. 'Going to the Friend suits my mood, Nin,' he'd said, as though to be nonchalant about the import of what he'd been giving me, the latest tranche of papers. As though it wasn't a big deal. 'The Friend makes sense for us both, you know it,' he'd said.

I'd had opinions since the outset, truth to tell, about the effect the giving over of any of his notes would have, ever since our first conversation about the process of our writing some kind of story or report together, when he'd shown me his initial pieces of writing, the beginning of what he thought was going to be his own first-person account of his love for Caroline in a great pile of papers stuffed into manilla envelopes that he'd set before me on the table between us at The Cork and Bottle, round the corner from the tube. Like then, he told me this evening, having warned me beforehand on the mobile that he felt nervous about passing over more information and was planning to 'drink hard' with me to get over it, that he was apprehensive about describing his feelings in 'ink', as he put it, notwithstanding the fact that a great deal of his scrawl was in a dodgy red biro that kept running out, with pencil additions underscored and the pencil itself in need of a good sharpen. Still as far as Evan was concerned it was all 'down there', his thoughts, and 'on the page for all time', and 'in black and white'. He flung back the last of his Bombay Sapphire without bothering to top up with tonic as if to prove it.

'Have you eaten?' I'd responded, on the mobile when he'd called. I had been working on an ad campaign for dog food since seven that morning and had, myself, consumed nothing more than coffee and a packet of Fruitellas all day.

'We could have supper?' I'd put to him. Knowing how tense the giving of the last set of notes had made him, recognising how pale and drawn he'd become. 'Instead of just going to the pub, I mean,' I said. 'I could make us supper, some rice and beans if you—'

But, 'Let's just go to the Friend, Nin,' Evan cut me off. 'It's tradition. We don't need to eat, you and I. And I feel a bit nervous, you know. Having passed more of my writing your way . . .' As he was, I could see, rain lashing at the window of that same pub, jammed in as we were with a crowd of people with rosy faces and in sensible shoes, pushing towards me another envelope and slurring his words, 'Here you are, then . . .' in that gesture tipping over the little tonic bottle he could have used earlier but had chosen to ignore.

As we both watched, it seeped out the remains of its contents on the table, then over my lap. There'd been more of it left in that bottle than I would have thought.

# five

Returning to the contents of Evan's notes, a later set than those already presented with the section that had created a degree of tension, as described, resulting, eventually, in a spillage, the procurement of a wet cloth and all that a tidy-up entails, I might include here just the first page of what he gave me that night in the Friend, high, and both of us somewhat the worse for wear having not eaten properly so that the gin and tonics, Sipsmith Silver, if you please, quite fancy, had hit harder than usual and taken a real hold.

As I say, this is not from the section I included earlier that was a kind of an outline, Evan writing out an idea for the project of a traditional romance, a love story, of sorts, some kind of a novel. No – these subsequent papers were further notes he'd made to himself. His first impressions of Caroline, his response to her 'receding form' . . . He said I could reproduce passages of this writing in full if I needed to, and I think I do. Need to. For they show, as I see it, a great deal of the Evan I was dealing with here. They show how he's present, in his words. Deep in. As I'd told him that night in the Friend, across the country-atmosphere gloom of the place, with the rain streaming down the windows and the fake-log gas fire turned down low, across our little wooden table now spilt with tonic, 'I know the idea of handing these pages over makes you tense but I think we need your feelings about Caroline to be contained', and at this point I looked at him intently, 'within this document, Evan,' I said. 'And in your own words.'

What I meant, of course, though I didn't want to come straight out with it, was that the presentation of this story shouldn't always be mine. Enough, in fact, by now, of my version of things, I was thinking. It was a crucial point in the proceedings. Something about the aforementioned night, the tumble of the tonic, had made me realise that it wasn't enough for me to write about Caroline – the twist of her hair and so on, that scent of oranges – it must be Evan, too, who was speaking. That man. He must be here in the account in his own words. There must be a sense of his feeling, the expression, painful as it might be for me to witness, of his thoughts about love and hope in his own syntax and prose. For though it might make me feel strange and sad and alone, sometimes, to have access to the parts of his mind he normally kept so private and apart, a reader would need this information, I could see. Evan must have his words in this story too.

And therefore, as we have had examples before, so we have some more of his notes included here. It is where we were, where we needed to be. The former text followed by:

'Everything about Caroline Beresford seems perfect to me,' he writes. 'She has the combination of everything that's lovely,' he goes on, 'the right amount. A lot of the women I have known in my life – those in America, I suppose I am talking about, those girls I knew when I was growing up, the girls I went out with – they were "all this", or "all that". All pretty. Or all brainy. Or all tall, with no delicacy. Or all dainty, but with no strength. They were blonde, and then they were all blonde, all blonde and perky and smiling. Or they were dark, and all dark, with their own dark sophisticated thing going on. Caroline Beresford, on the other hand, is not "all" anything. She is a range, and in that range is my all.'

When I'd first read that, for example, going back to what I said before, I'd had to put the page down. It was quite full on. It was rather like the earlier metatextual stuff without the metatextual element I'd been able to insert to soften it.* This was just 'all' – to use a word of Evan's – feeling. And really – I had to keep asking myself, as I had since the beginning, since Evan had first told me about meeting Caroline – 'Do I really believe "all"? All this? "My all"?' Did I? That Evan could fall in love so deeply, so readily, so . . . availably . . . with someone he barely knew? And that it could have happened so fast, so dramatically? Did I believe that as well? That he could be 'acting out', as I might describe it, in the fashion of a Dante or a Petrarch or any of those individuals who feature in stories of courtly love – acting out a range of feelings and writing about them so as to make them real?

Still, I read on. We were deep enough in, after all, Evan and I. I was deep in.

'A range of qualities contained within her and all those qualities available at once.' Evan's notes do need to be

---

* In many ways, this sounds pretty fancy – and notes later in the book covering 'Literary Context' may help here. The remark simply relates to some sense of an overarching 'project', as the narrator sees it, that sits behind the day-to-day story of what was going on in Richmond and adds to it, to her mind: bringing in Petrarch and all that stuff making the whole enterprise more fun.

included here, important, remember, because these are sentences and phrases that are his own. This was him writing. This was only Evan. 'She has', I read, 'that easy going-outside-in-the-open-air feeling about her while also being indoorsy and intense and wanting to have big talks about society and life and art. The kind of person who wants to think about things, Heidegger's theory of *Dasein*, say, we talked about that one time, or prayer. Her hair is beautiful but also a mess. She doesn't look made up and yet she wears some sort of pink colour on her lips that makes her seem like she's someone who puts lipstick on – but then it comes off on her coffee cup, I saw the mark. This is what she said to me, her exact words, when I met her that first day, after she'd opened the door to greet me, over the course of the time we had coffee together, for the first time, and she was showing me the house. Well, maybe not exact words, but close. I know it's pretty close because that morning was when I started keeping these notes, and I do think this is what she said, pretty much:

'It's sort of suburban where we are, Evan – but there's loads of space' – is what Evan's notes show Caroline saying. 'You can have a floor to yourself, your own bathroom. It can be a kind of studio apartment for you up there, there's a kitchen area and so on, all that kind of thing, but you can also use the house as a whole, as a kind of a base, I guess is what you'll be doing, before you move on' – never guessing that Evan wasn't ever going to want to 'move on' – 'while you're getting used to being back here, I mean, in London, it can be a home for you. You can just be, you know, at home here.'

'At home', I read, Evan now continuing in his own voice, 'is an idea Caroline, of course, knows about.' His handwriting really was awful. I remembered that from when we were little, too, it had come back to me while I was reading the first set of notes and materials. He used to write me letters all the time, when we were children, enclosing them in his own hand-made envelopes and posting them through the door, and they were always in a mad inky scrawl, those dear little letters from Evan to me. Even with all this time passed that handwriting of his didn't look much better, but, you see, I was used to it. I wasn't going to mind. 'Love from your friend Evan Gordonston' they would be signed off, those letters from long ago, at the end. And three kisses: xxx.

Now we had instead: 'Being at home, feeling at home . . .' in Evan's current handwriting that seemed just the same. 'Making oneself at home . . .' I read. 'These are all ideas Caroline suggested to me from the outset, she's put her mind to that sort of understanding,' Evan wrote. 'Not that it would have occurred to her like that,' he continued. 'She's not fancily self-conscious. And yet here I am, brought up by a father who left his country, his home, for business, for finance, and a generation later, doing the same thing, leaving one place for another . . . So you might say I am the one who could be self-conscious. About home. About belonging, and where I might be. And if I have no knowledge of home,' he continued in this rich, self-conscious vein of his own that I was not used to, 'might it be that I could find it now, with this particular woman and in Richmond on the District Line? Oh Caroline, then?

Might I discover the knowledge of home in Richmond now with you?'

'Listen,' I'd had to say to Evan, having read the beginning of those first notes that had been filed in various manilla envelopes and pushed across the table towards me in the Elm and had been followed by even more florid material that had been gathered together and extended towards me in the Friend, 'it's quite poetic, what you've written, but not in a good way. To that extent, you were right, Evan,' I said, 'to be tense in the handing over of these pages. I can understand how all this may make you feel. But still . . .'

This was a few days later. We were back at The Elm Tree. That Tree, our meeting place in previous weeks, that we'd given up for the larger tables and option of Sipsmith and Portobello gins, along with the more usual Tanqueray, Gordon's and Bombay, at the Friend.* It was as though, thinking about it now, we needed to mark a change in time by our return to an older habit. For it was like that, being back in the Elm where it was darker, larger, more cavernous than it had been in the Friend. As though, in the selection of a venue with its choice of gins and tonics, the range of which had become more obvious to me in our visits to the latter, we needed a sort of process of going back to the familiar in order to go forwards, somehow, if this narrative was to continue. All very well, I thought, the 'in my own words, Nin' part of all this, Evan's idea of

* There are notes on 'Gin' and 'Pubs' in the section entitled *Caroline's Bikini – Alternative Narratives* – for those who are interested.

developing the narrative by deepening it, if you like, in his own words – but the same narrative couldn't be mired by that either. If this book was ever, ever, going to get finished some day, move on . . . If I was ever going to be able to 'get on with it, for goodness' sake' is the brisk expression I remember I used, then we needed to reach beyond the poetry, if I can call it that, of Evan's feelings, into some kind of action, drama. The return to a more straightforward range of gins seemed to define this mood – a useful metonymy for something I've found works with writing ads, actually, and my own short stories, even – that resolution can come, sometimes, when one has cast back into past time. So in the same way I felt I could be more firm with Evan in the Elm. So I felt it was my role there to have him 'move on'.

For sure, the last batch of notes had been 'poetry', I think, was how they were intended, but in a bad poetry, diary-esque-thinking kind of mode that was running through the thing entire and needed to be nipped in the bud.

'How can poetry be bad?' Evan said. 'Love poetry, I mean? If it's created in a heightened state, Nin? If to the writer it is real?'

'Well, that line there, for starters,' I replied, pointing it out to him under the low cast of pub lighting: '"Oh Caroline, then? Might I discover the knowledge of home with you?—"'

'What about it?'

'It sounds like a Gilbert O'Sullivan song,' I said. 'Inferior folk. One man and a guitar, that sort of thing, Evan. A poor man's Bob Dylan,' I was getting into my stride,

'poetry that's nothing like Bob Dylan but only something "indie", something avant-garde, that's not come off,
something—'

Evan laughed, 'Hah!' He took my hand. 'Oh, you,' he
said. 'You know I've never been a writer!' He squeezed
my hand in a merry way, three little grips. I could feel
the mood was lightening. 'You're the writer in the family,
Nin,' he said. 'Only you.'

He laughed again.

'Don't worry one bit about what I've written. I've never
been good at all that,' he continued, giving my hand another little squeeze for emphasis.

'I see,' I said. The mood had lightened for sure.

'Another?' he said, indicating our empty glasses.

'Why not?' was my reply.

Because things hadn't been easy since he'd first started handing over the notes, with the tension mounting, as
I've written, that spill. But now . . . Well, here we were.
The two of us. In so many ways just as we'd always been,
and now there was this. This lighter, merrier mood, it was
quite clear, and pleasant, too. I felt like we were nine again
and Evan was getting me to write down the rules of one
of our games. It was just like that. Evan suddenly deeply
familiar again. There was one story, I remember, a sort of
*Famous Five* he'd got me to make up when I was about
eight or nine after we'd built a fort out of discarded tree
branches that my father had assembled for a bonfire and
we were attempting to enact the story as it were, by my
inventing it and writing it down as we went along. And
there was another thing, a long poem, it was coming back

to me, there in the Elm, a sort of ballad based on a summer holiday the Gordonstons and our family took together in Cornwall, once, that was full of pirates, with Evan and me in the starring roles, with our own verses. We often had holidays with the Gordonstons, school holidays and summer holidays, before they moved away. That 'Oh, you' took me back to those projects, and to those years: my brother Felix and the way he first fell for Elisabeth on a boat ride in the Helford Estuary when he was thirteen, the time my mother and Helen organised all of us children, as well as Helen's sister's family, to accompany them on a pottery-making workshop in the Hebrides and Evan's oldest cousin showing off like mad with multicoloured glazes because she'd done ceramics in fifth form. All of it, all of it coming back to me in a lovely way since that 'Oh you' of Evan's. The bags packed. The picnics eaten. The Gordonstons and the Stuarts in two cars and we would stop on lay-bys for a thermos of something on the way. The 'Oh you' took me back alright. I felt winded by the memory of it. Lightened. And happy? Oh yes, that. I could go on and on and on.

But Evan had other things to say as well.

'It doesn't matter that what I've written is rubbish.' He'd picked up now. 'It's only my feelings that count. My feelings for Caroline, Nin. My response to her, after I met her that first time. That's all I'm trying to get at here . . .' He'd come back from the bar with two more of those fancier kinds of gin in hand and it seemed it was back to business as usual. He put the two glasses down on the table. 'Just so that you can make something of them,' he said, and sat down himself. He looked so handsome sometimes, despite his somewhat unkempt dress. 'These are just notes, remember, to help you work. Cheers,' he said, and had a sip. 'I never said you should use them, Nin, word for word. That was your idea. I feel quite relaxed about all that, actually. At one point, you know, I started making things up, even, in all this, that I'd met Caroline earlier somehow. Perhaps at Oxford, or somewhere like that, that I might be the writer of that kind of very English novel, only she was too pretty and she dropped out so I lost touch. Or that I got a message from her,' he continued, and I could see the story had taken a hold. He took another sip of his drink; it was true, he had a particular kind of Scottish handsomeness about him, that was also a bit untidy. 'A handwritten note, it was,' he said, 'saying, "You remember David, well, he and I have decided that we're going to get married . . ." I kept thinking —'

'Stop.' I cut him off. I came to, actually, because I'd been in a sort of dream. 'There's no point in making up a parallel novel, Evan,' I said, realising all at once that he was suddenly moving dangerously close to that sort of territory. 'We have our dance card full enough already with you telling me things every week, every few days, wanting to write it all down . . . We've that, plus already using some of these notes you've made . . . We've got quite enough on to be dealing with . . .'

'You're lovely,' Evan said then, and I had to look away for a second. Sometimes that happened. 'Helping me in the way you are,' he continued. 'No one else would do it,' he said. 'No one else would get it, even, what I'm trying to do here, create a record of my experiences and write a love story from it . . . is what we're doing, Nin. You and I. But you do, you get it.' He tapped my hand. 'You do.'

'Mmmm,' I said. I slugged off the rest of my Sipsmith's Silver like an old pirate straight out of the kind of story that I'd written for Evan once-upon-a-time when we had nothing but time and our families together and games to play. I'd started chapter one, 'Ready', I'd called it, but it wasn't looking too strong. 'All I can do is keep on reproducing the notes,' is what I said to him by way of response. 'The notes, the conversations we have . . . All I can do is keep writing.'

Which is exactly what I did. Kept writing. While the other kind of text Evan was working on did also progress – his own ideas, that independent or 'indie' work of his. There continued alongside my own writing his suggestions. Our meetings. The piles of material he kept passing on, in pencil, or that biro he liked, sometimes in a really fancy old-fashioned ink pen, for me to incorporate . . . How the pages did continue. They piled up, scribbled and scrawled, crossed out and rewritten . . . Sometimes I longed for Evan just to pick up his laptop and get the gist of it down in a printed format himself; it would have released me from the onerousness of the task of reading his prose so directly, made me less connected, somehow, to its dreadful qualities and passions. That I wouldn't have to peer at it, try to figure it, rewrite it, even . . . Though it hardly bore thinking about, still it would have been nice, I did reflect, if Evan had just printed out the lot and we'd committed it for inclusion as appendices or some kind of additional reading, perhaps, or in extra notes I could see we were going to need, whatever. For the days were moving on. Christopher was already leaving me messages on the answerphone asking me, in his rather Tory way, to account for my time on an economic basis: 'Marjorie says you're late with the pet insurance copy, Nin,' had been the last one. 'And I am concerned for your budgeting overall. I can do spreadsheets, you know that. Call me.' There was a feeling afoot with my friends in general that I was being careless with the practical side of things. There was more to consider in life than just some 'project' or other, they all said. There was the matter of 'realities', apparently, with my mortgage, other various financial 'responsibilities' that were slipping, all because of the amount of time I was spending, and I could see what they meant, frivolously, you might say, in straight transcription. Sometimes I did wonder if I should just get on the phone back to Christopher straight away and sign up for one of his rallies or other by way of diversion – an anti-tree-felling project he needed leafleting help with, he'd told me in another message. Work on pavement litter. Anything. Something. Any diversion, activity or practical idea that might be followed through by galvanising me into action, work for payment or 'economic certainty' as Marjorie liked to term it. Anything, really. I did wonder. That I wouldn't need to actually have to be always writing this kind of thing down instead:

'You know how we used to talk, Nin? When we were hanging out, about what it would be like to grow up and have kids? Well, seeing Caroline with her children makes me think about all that all over again.'

At this point all I could do was reproduce in full with no editing whatsoever. Though goodness knows I had seen that there were parts of the notes, pages included, that addressed me directly like that as though it were just like the old days, living-next-door-to-each-other days and he had written me a letter, still it also wasn't like that kind of communication, from him to me, the kind of message with questions in it and I was supposed to answer back. This really wasn't like one of those kinds of letters from him. This 'She's an amazing mother' kind of statement that had nothing to do with me at all. 'She did tell me,' Evan wrote on, 'in great confidence, of course, that after she'd had her first boy she was diagnosed with some sort of depression. The next two births only made it worse so as a result she was put on medication – she showed me the bottles. "Fucking weird, huh?" she said. "That I'm high on Valium half the time? Only not high, Evan, don't worry, because Valium is not like that, and this isn't Valium either . . ."' Nothing like a letter.

'Yeah, Caroline,' he'd said, he finished. 'I'm telling you all this, Nin,' he wrote, 'as though I could help her carry the load. Oh Caroline, Caroline . . .'

'More indie folk music stuff going on there,' was all I said to myself in response. But nothing like Bob Dylan.

'Oh Caroline, Caroline . . .'

Because all of this, how it was acting upon the rest of the story, what it was doing to the overall shape and style . . .

It was too much.

All the 'How can I ever be at home with you?'

It was too strange, it really was.

I decided then that I could only include it, this kind of thing, by way of small insertions, bit by bit. Because it really was –

Too strange.

It was. For me, getting all this. Strange. It made me feel strange. Despite Evan going 'Hah' and laughing. Despite him taking my hand. He'd always been a very ordinary sort of boy, when we were young. Not . . . poetic. Trying to be. He'd been just sort of . . . physical. Ordinary. The whole family on the tall side and able-bodied, if that makes sense. Full of energy, vigour, all of the Gordonstons; the sort of family who went away on walking holidays in the Alps or camping in the Highlands and doing everything with fires. Hand-knitted jerseys, despite Tom's work in the City, that was the Gordonstons. Knapsacks. And we loved going away on holidays with them, too, sometimes. Driving up to Scotland, or down to Cornwall to cottages that Helen and my mother booked that were by the sea. It was hard for me now to reconcile the man who'd come back from years abroad, in America and then Tokyo and so on, with the boy who used to come over to my house every day wearing his Cubs jersey with the badges stapled on because Helen was never going to find the time to hand-stitch them. Hard to match up that boy with this serious man who had love and poetry on his mind sitting in front of me in The Gin Whistle having an afternoon 'nip' as Evan's granny who used to live with them and looked after the two of us sometimes would have said.

Time was passing. I could feel it, winter moving inexorably on to its conclusion and entering into a new season.

We'd decided to move further out of my neighbourhood, to get away from the memory of that tonic spill, to find a fresh environment; The Gin Whistle was somewhere new.

'The only way I can describe it', I said to Evan, when we were sitting there at a long chrome and glass bar punctuated at the edges with a smashed-gin-bottles-and-their-labels feature and really feeling ourselves to be in an altogether different sort of place, 'is that you have "fallen in love at first sight".' We were going through the details of that first meeting of Caroline for the umpteenth time and I'd told him what I'd decided as far as the use of his own notes was concerned. 'I have to use that corny expression, Evan,' I said. 'I will even write it down, because it is true. It's a problem, in a way, because it's such a cliche but that's how it happened for you, it really is. You're like Dante and Petrarch and the rest of them, only your poetry isn't up to the task. I'm sorry to put it like that, but it's true. Yes, it may be very much a case of "Upon the breeze she spread her golden hair/that in a thousand gentle knots was turned,/and the sweet light beyond all measure burned/in eyes where now that radiance is rare"* as far as your feelings towards Caroline are concerned, and you very much wanting to have, in her walking down the hall and putting her hair into a pony tail and so on, something like "From thought to thought . . . Love leads me on . . . "† Alright, Evan. I get that.

* Taken from no. 90 in the *Canzoniere*; see 'Some Further Material', 'Reprise', also for a selection of verse, all reprinted with kind permission of Professor Anthony Mortimer and Penguin Books.
† From no. 129 in the *Canzoniere*.

'Because it is straight out of the late medieval tradition, your situation, of being struck by love, brought low, un-done . . . But the quality of work that comes from all that, in our case . . . Well . . . It's challenging, that's all,' I tried to finish. 'Making art from life, you know . . .' My voice trailed away.

Because, bottom line? That's the only thing that was certain at this point. That the story we had was based on what I might call the bang factor. BANG. Or the 'ping'. The 'sweet light beyond all measure' and 'her words had then/a sound that simple human voices lack . . .' It did have all that medieval and early Renaissance aspect to it only without us being the Renaissance artists ourselves that the 'project' – there I was, using that noun again – needed. There was the problem exactly. For as far as the actual story was concerned, the plot, the narrative . . . All that. We may have had the BANG, the 'ping', but we'd got no further than where we'd started: Caroline, there at the front door. Careless. Tanned. Tall, with that beachy dirty-blonde hair down her back as she walks away from Evan down the hall. That's where we were, caught in a perpetual present tense of Evan falling in love with her as she was calling out over her shoulder, 'Shall we have a cup of coffee together? You and I? Before I show you around the house, I mean?' Then, following naturally, easily, as though part of the same lovely unspooling of Petrarchan feeling: Two mugs. Two people. Fixed in place, a mug and a man, and a beautiful female reflection of the one to the masculine other across the breakfast bar, a heart also there fixed, and heart's thoughts, words . . . Two mugs of coffee effortlessly produced and a romance fiction, too, in the grand established tradition of courtly love and the early songs of the troubadours played out through the poetry sequences and epics of the early Renaissance and beyond, while Caroline chatted on about the neighbourhood and how long they'd been living there – twisting up her hair again from where it had fallen, back into that pony tail I have already described, but all of it in place, all of it. The mugs of hot drinks between them and the breakfast bar making it all the easier, too, for her to lean in towards Evan and say, 'I'd love you to live here with us. I really would. I don't even know if you like the house yet, but that's what I would love.' Is all, that's all. 'For you to just stay here, with us . . .' taking a sip of her coffee then, replacing the mug in front of her with its lipstick mark. 'Wouldn't you?' saying, quite quietly. 'Just stay?'

# six

By now, despite the folk song elements, the stops and starts, the bad handwriting, and so on, I was starting to get a feel for Evan's story, of how it contained those certain elements that spoke back to grand and epic lovelorn states of mind, how, despite the lack of 'plot', one might say, and actual chapters with activities crammed within them that might move a story along, nevertheless there was, I had to admit, some texture here that was gathering around our outline, even if it was just the beginning, and feeling, and an attitude of romance and optimism that were permeating my pages.

For they were 'my pages'. Evan had recognised this and said as much, formally, in the Friend following the ghastly tonic spill. Despite his stab at fictionalising this project of his, adding that idea about him and Caroline meeting when they were students, in the style of a certain sort of English novel, and despite the somewhat sketchy nature of his own 'life writing', as some may call it now, that was possessed of a rather alternatively styled 'indie' poetry element, the somewhat second-rate folk song tendency as already noted, the pages that were accumulating on my desk were run from my computer, my printer. Evan had said that he was keen that I be the writer for his story, he'd said that from the beginning. And he was saying it still.

And for my part, in terms of a feeling of emotional con-
nectedness to the project, now that Evan had been lodging
with the Beresfords for the best part of the winter, had
learned of some sadness there, in the family, had been party to Caroline's confession that she was dependent, 'in a
lovely way' as she put it, on mood-enhancing medication
– 'stabilising, Nin, not mood-enhancing as you call it,'
said Evan, when this had all first come up in the Friend
– now that Evan was 'deep in' as he felt he was, to life
in Richmond, the dinner parties and get-togethers that
went on there, the 'fun scene' that he overheard from his
rooms under the eaves . . . Well, I was building a picture,
as novelists like to say, that made me feel committed. I was
investing in ideas of character, setting; I was writing my
way into that kind of understanding. For example, though
Evan would not be a guest at any of the parties hosted at
the end of the District Line – not for want of being invited, he hastened to tell me, but for 'other reasons' that
I think had to do with his own feelings of privacy and
propriety – he was, as he put it, in a pun-ish way, 'party
to them' even so, and that kind of thing gave me a great
deal to think about as well. So I would write about how
he would come down early in the morning on a weekend
when David and the boys were still asleep to find Caroline
at the kitchen bar busy planning a 'fun scene' – for that
was the time of the week she liked to make her lists of
menus and ingredients, organise guests and seating plans
for the large dining-room table in Richmond, order wine
– and they would have, the two of them, over one coffee
after another, that time together, Caroline and Evan, they

would have conversations then. 'It's when we do most of our talking,' Evan said, about Thomas Aquinas or a special kind of mushroom for a risotto or a film Caroline had just seen . . . 'Any damn thing,' said Evan, expansively. 'It's when we really talk.'

And yes, building a picture is what I was doing alright. Rosie would call and ask, from her studio in Gloucestershire, 'How is Evan getting on at the Beresfords'?' and I felt able to answer in full, actually, because there were all these details Evan was telling me and I was able to colour those outlines in, somewhat – not unlike the way Rosie herself put together the beautiful paintings of people's gardens and dogs that she completed by commission from friends of friends in Gloucestershire, an outline here, some depth of colour there, from her converted greenhouse for which she paid 'a fraction', she said, 'a fraction' of what a similar kind of space would have cost in London had she decided to stay. 'That brother of David Beresford, hmmm,' Rosie might murmur, in between my talking to her about Evan's circumstances. 'Robert, remember I told you about him, Nin? I wonder where he is now . . .' she would finish.

More picture building there, I guess, to think about the Beresfords entire, their backstory so to speak. But for now I had my hands full with Evan and Caroline, those two, and my concerns on that front regarding the 'relationship' as Evan liked to call it, though goodness knows why. Because though, it's true, there may have been all these conversations then that were 'really' talking, as he put it, none of them came near to Evan actually expressing his feelings for Caroline to her, or eventuated in him leaning towards her, say, or reaching to take her hand. So I had to make something, myself, of those moments, or add to them, extend the small amount of information Evan had given me into something that might be more significant. Caroline might simply pour his coffee and sometimes their hands touched, as she poured, or he took a mug from her and his skin brushed hers . . . And from this minuscule gesture I could generate a charge, enact in those seconds the components of a great love story in the context of a grand literary tradition if I was lucky, according to Evan, in the large sunlit kitchen of the Beresfords' house at the end of the District Line.

So this layering continued. Of story, plot. I was 'getting a picture' as I described it to Evan, without him needing at this point to supply more notes. I was 'layering, layering' through all our meetings in the pub – sometimes as many as three times a week, and Evan had long discovered The Gin Whistle by then, that somewhat smarter establishment than the country-style places we'd been going to previously, with their Labrador ambience and raincoats; The Gin Whistle was on the edge of Chelsea and had the long matte chrome bar already mentioned, with the special broken glass feature – it had that kind of detail. In there, at a banquette located in the corner of such a slick establishment amply provided with all kinds of very, very fancy gin, I was doing as Evan had asked me, he was speaking, and I was taking it all down. 'Amanuensis', exactly, remember? That lovely word.

And detail, detail. More and more of it, small things that added up and did the job of creating incident without having to make a great dramatic fuss of it. There was the issue of the medication, for example, the quiet drama of that, and the moment Caroline told Evan about it, the 'mood-enhancing' aspect of whatever it was she'd been prescribed – but nothing so dramatic that it required a special section in the book. I was prepared to let that medication, for the minute, 'go hang'* and just sit there, a quiet pulse in the text, highlighting a moment I might pick up later and use.

And I already had plenty of Evan's notes to give background and support the prose I was at work on – a continuation of all those papers Evan had given me the night he said he was planning to 'drink hard'. I'd taken them home with me and filed them carefully, brought them out in sections to use. Altogether it seemed there was no shortage of material. Even so, Evan continued to pass me notes from his life, and, on our third meeting at The Gin Whistle, after many rounds of the kind of gin you didn't ask the price of, handed me yet another manilla envelope. I took it home and pulled it out one evening when he was working late and we'd had to cancel our plans.

In general, at first, the pages seemed like all the others, lists of clothes, places to visit, ideas for the book. Then in the midst, something different, it seemed. Another kind of writing started to occur. 'I'll need a place to stay while I get myself figured out,' Evan wrote, in a set of papers that read more like a journal or diary, or an essay, than the

* 'Personal History' describes more of Evan's American idioms and suggests ways the author's advertising work may have also influenced her own writing.

other pages. 'The fact of the matter is', he wrote, 'that I wasn't planning to move from London ever again. Something had gone on in California, when I went out there, after Tokyo, that made me feel I needed to get myself settled, be in one place, become of fixed abode. It was something to do with someone I'd been involved with in California – don't get me wrong, something about me, not her. It was to do, this woman told me, with the way I couldn't be "real" with her, was her word.' I stopped reading for a second – this new tone to the writing, it was . . . I couldn't describe it – then continued. Real? I thought. Real? 'A word that she used with her very lovely and characteristic insight and sensitivity,' Evan continued. 'But that's what she had said: "You can't be real with me, Evan, can you? You don't, I think, know what it means?"'

I felt strange. I put down the pages. Someone had said a very similar thing to me once, long ago. It had been a relationship fraught from the start with misunderstandings and endless recriminations followed by forgivenesses. He had been a writer too, this person, and for a while it had seemed like we could make a go of things, but in the end his feelings about me were uncannily close to this bit of Evan's journal.

'"You don't know what it means"', Evan had written, reporting on what this unnamed Californian woman had said, '"not to have to put on some show, to somehow mask yourself. To be so damn . . . capable. It's false. In the end, Evan, you don't ring true." I've remembered these words,' Evan wrote – and my own heart was beating as I read to the end of the page – 'I wrote them down after we broke up. So they would remind me, I suppose, of what kind of an individual I am, really, despite all the seeming so . . . "capable", as she'd said. It occurred to me then that in actual fact, I didn't want to ever, I think, ever let anyone come that close.'

I had to stop reading at that point. I got up from the desk where I'd been drinking tea and eating an oatcake while going through the pages. I went to the window and looked out at my street. The whole effect of having this kind of material inserted amongst the rest . . . Having it here in my hands as background, Evan's thoughts from long ago brought together this way . . . It had made me feel . . . peculiar. At once, I wanted to get back to where we'd been, in The Elm Tree or The Walker's Friend or The Cork and Bottle, one of our safe, friendly, local pubs with their country atmosphere and in easy walking distance from my own flat. I wanted the familiarity . . . of Evan. And now, instead, there was all this new chrome-bar-Gin-Whistle-style information – as though straight off one of the labels, decorated as they were with haiku poetry or excerpts from short stories, of any of those expensively fancy Chelsea gins that one could purchase there – Dark Town, Fallen Branch were two brands I'd noted – that had come at me by way of another innocent-looking brown envelope, with a different kind of person altogether, it seemed, inhabiting the pages. And why, I thought, had we to go to a different kind of pub anyway, in a different part of town – the others no longer deemed suitable? What was that all about? Even with Evan assuring me, 'No,' it was nothing as silly as him being snobbish about some postcode or 'named spirit' or 'designer distillery' or whatever and that it was just that he wanted to try somewhere new.

When I thought about it, standing there by the window, then wandering around my flat, going back to the window, looking back inside, pacing, turning, I thought: Something had been wrong right there and then, back in that first meeting in The Gin Whistle actually. Something changed; the mood, always jaunty in the past, talking of Caroline, talking of Richmond and the atmosphere there, was now turned down a notch, the gins and tonics in that swanky place so fancy you couldn't remember the ornate names of them, so thin-measured were they and so redolent of a whole range of organic matter. That night Evan had passed me the notes he had been wearing a dark blue, a navy, jersey and beaten-up old jeans that looked like he'd had them forever. His face was creased with tiredness and his grey eyes looked sad. 'I don't know what I'm doing, Nin,' he'd said to me. 'Help me, can you?'

I ran a bath and gave the whole subject of Evan my full attention. It was a different person I'd seen on our third visit to the Whistle, that fancy place; there was no doubt about it. In the light of my reading of him, I could establish that for sure. Though he'd been very much himself when I'd called earlier and though I'd thought then I could almost manage this latest departure of his into something more like an essay or journal writing, with an essay's prolix manner, to convey various thoughts from the past, now I realised I had a strong feeling about it, his sentences and words: I wanted to throw away all of the notes. Somehow, all at once, thinking about me and Evan and how I could always guess what he was thinking, was going to say, how that had been something in our friendship, part of our very . . . relationship – that loaded word, though loaded, in this case, with nothing – since the absolute beginning, when we were children together was . . .

Well, I couldn't 'go there' as they say in the States.

Evan.

Evan.

Evan.

I just couldn't.

I poured Chanel No. 5 bath gel into the running water and thought instead about his blue jersey, those jeans, how I had a jersey that colour myself and jeans that were as old. Sometimes, I thought, I felt Evan and I could have been twins. 'I know you understand,' he'd said to me that night, tired, because of course I did, I did understand what it was to love someone and they had no idea that you did and then you had to make up some long-winded story about it.

All that: 'All you that hear in scattered rhymes the sound/of sighs on which I used to feed my heart', as Petrarch begins his own 'long-winded story' . . . Oh, I knew all about that. I understood alright. I got into the bath, lay down and closed my eyes.

The next day, I called him – it was a Thursday – and we arranged to meet.

'I'd say let's go out for supper but I'm just not hungry,' Evan said. More and more, it was occurring to me, and I nearly said something along those lines, that Evan's behaviour and mien was seeming to match, increasingly, that of the famous Florentine poet of the fourteenth century about whom we'd had so much discussion. More and more it was a case of: 'the sound/of sighs'. Not being able to eat, or sleep. 'Vain hopes . . . vain sorrows', and so on. Just roaming around thinking of a woman he loved and thinking, too, of the words that would turn the love into something 'real'.

'But it might do us good, to have a bowl of soup at least,' I said. 'Gin and tonics are great but—'

'Let's just meet at the Whistle again,' he said. 'Like last time. It was perfectly good. I enjoyed it.'

'Alright,' I replied, moody. 'I suppose it will do.'

As it was, however, we went to another place altogether, Grapes of Wrath, three doors up. The old Whistle was too crowded – that smashed-glass feature at the bar drew an arty crowd – and this time I was the one who was tired. Christopher had been on the phone reminding me about my mortgage again; he said we were living in 'dangerous days' and any minute could find ourselves evicted for non-payment of any day-to-day bill as was happening to 'perfectly respectable people all over the UK', he'd said this morning, with every day passing some poor soul being turned out of his or her home and an oligarch moving in, buying up the whole neighbourhood at the same time, just like that. As a result, somewhat stricken with anxiety by his words – Christopher had always been a compelling public speaker – I'd worked all that day and very hard on a campaign for dog food, the same campaign as before, but now the company wanted to market a top-of-the-range menu for 'pampered pets'. I'd been going at it with no holds barred – so why would I want to be bothered standing at a crowded chrome bar, matte or not, was my thinking. The campaign involved foil tins of pet food that had been created to look like ready meals from Marks and Spencer but in miniature. I'd been sent them at home, in order to render them authentically in long copy and sub-heads, along with a list of ingredients, and how best to serve them: warm, with a little sachet of the crunchy biscuits that were also supplied, as a side dish. The whole thing was ornate and weird and exhausting to write about. I'd had to keep remembering to eliminate the second person from my copy, as in 'You are going to love' – you are – 'these tasty mouth-watering dishes . . .' etc. I was really tired. Around four, with Marjorie texting me, in her advertising company sort of way: 'Copy due end of play tomorrow', I changed out of my old red top and put on a grey, long-sleeved button-down shirt. I found my baseball boots where I'd pushed them behind the linen basket and grabbed a jacket from the hook on the front door. The minute I stepped outside into the air I registered that it was warmer than it had been. Could it be spring?

It took about half an hour to walk to meet Evan. The noise from the crowds at The Gin Whistle reached me as I approached. There were people standing drinking outside but it was easy to see him standing apart, off to one side, and, I saw at once, in the same dreadful jeans.

'This is too busy for us,' I said. 'Come on . . .' I led the way up the road to Grapes of Wrath, not an old pub, but not, thank goodness, new. We could make ourselves at home here, I thought. It would surely have a proper, old-fashioned and substantial gin. I started to say something about the weather, how warm it was, but Evan interrupted, before we'd even sat down he put his hand on my arm in an urgent sort of way, and scrunched up his eyes as though in pain.

'I've been wanting to ask you,' he said, his face in a grimace. He looked about seven years old. 'Did you read those latest notes of mine and what do you think? Is there a project in all this or not? Lately, I've been starting to feel this whole thing is a waste, of you, of me, of our time.'

'Steady,' I said. My breathing felt tight, like it was suddenly hard to take in air. 'Less of the "you" and "me",' I said, in a strange tone of voice I barely recognised. 'Let's rewind, shall we?' I said to Evan. 'Let's get back to Caroline.'

# Steady . . .

# one

The seasons were changing. Right back at the beginning, when it was still the middle of winter, I'd had to tell Evan that I didn't think anyone was going to be much interested in this book of his. 'Evan,' I'd had to say then. 'A story about your love for a woman you barely know, who you saw, standing in a doorway in Richmond and "ping", to use your own lovely word – that was it, love at first sight – well . . .' My voice trailed off. There's that phrase: at a loss for words. I was 'at a loss'. But it was still dark then, morning and night. The days were short.

Now it was getting warmer. And it had been a long time since I'd expressed that view; for we now had a substantial project in hand. A whole section had been completed since Evan had first mentioned meeting Caroline – and it seemed so casual, now, looking back on that, the way he just 'mentioned' the fact that he might want to write something about that, meeting her the effect it had had on him and might I help. It had seemed so casual and yet there had been nothing casual about it. We'd had a gin or two and then Evan had said, 'Please help me with it, Nin. This is writing I won't be able to do on my own,' and I'd said, 'Alright, I'll try' – remember? All this now felt like a long time ago and here we were with this pile of pages accumulated between us, and whether or not anyone would want to read them . . . That no longer seemed relevant.

I looked back fondly on the days when we were meeting at the kind of pub with muddy gumboots at the door. I looked back. Country thoughts: braces of Labradors and terriers tethered to posts, retrievers allowed indoors after a good day's work out on the hill, clustered at the fire in lodges or beneath tables in country inns . . . These ideas had been nourished by the rural sort of hostelry Evan and I had been frequenting, back in the winter when it was cold, and it had been comforting, somehow, calming, to be so nourished. The idea that the pair of us might be deep in the countryside straight off the back of a shoot or point-to-point and with little thought of the sophistications of a matte chrome bar, for example, or the kinds of gin I could now see people were interested in, in the more fashionable parts of town . . . Well, it was a lovely idea. Those Barbours hanging on hooks, the proper sort I mean, before they became silly and fashionable . . . I myself did own one of the old Barbours, inherited from an aunt, and I had worn it on occasional country weekends when Marjorie used to invite me down 'to make up numbers' for some party or other, this before the advertising had both of us, to carry on the country and hunting analogy, in its maw, and Marjorie had had plans of marrying and having 'a whole squad of children' as she put it, and moving to Wales or the West Country. She'd always been an excellent cook and could happily have fed an army, let alone a 'squad' of her own – only she'd never met the person she would have the 'squad' with, that mythical handsome farmer she had in mind, and so instead had focused all her domestic abilities and skills on creating an extremely attractive one-bedroom flat in Chelsea. I thought fondly now of how I wore the Barbour, not only with her, in those far-off house party days, but very occasionally, too, in the early winter weeks with Evan when our writing together was just beginning and this was a 'project', we called it, that we shared. How many of us ever have life turn out in the way we expect, was where my thinking took me when I thought about that particular piece of outerwear, or me, or Marjorie, in careful detail. Experience throws up surprises at every turn.

Evan had seemed so relaxed then, back in the winter, by comparison with how he was, I could see, now. There was more colour in his cheeks back then, as though the country atmosphere of those pubs suited him. When we were children we would spend a lot of time outdoors, in hardy clothing and gumboots, so perhaps the whole atmosphere in The Walker's Friend and those other places felt comforting to us because they were somehow familiar. Now our destinations were very different. That chrome bar – matte – of The Gin Whistle. That Grapes of Wrath followed swiftly by A Tulip's Edge, neither of which carried straightforward gin or tonic but it all had to be special-shaped bottles with labels that had haikus on them or extracts from short stories. We were in another world. And the 'project', whether or not anyone was 'going to be interested', had taken us both into its depths. Evan was now talking 'novel'. Back in the lovely Cork and Bottle, he had said that his reaction to meeting Caroline would have meaning in 'a written-down account', was how he put it, in which he would have a role through his position as lodger in her home; his unspoken feelings and attitude towards her would have voice, he said. 'A presence on the page.' Now, though, more and more he was describing what was happening as being, first 'a good story', and then 'well, a novel, really, Nin'. Fixing me with a particular kind of look. 'Is what this is shaping up as, don't you agree?'

He'd raised the issue after I'd been talking to him about form, reminding him of the amount we'd written together since starting back in January, when he'd moved in to Richmond, of its shape and narrative momentum, or lack of it. I'd reminded him of how I'd raised the question early on, of the writing's 'relevance' to the general reader, and Evan had countered that it didn't matter that nothing had been said, by him, of his feelings for Caroline, that it didn't change the fact that as far as he was concerned we still had a great story here.

'Most of the strong feelings we have go unspoken,' I agreed one evening in the kind of place where I should have been wearing a little black dress. I remember we were sitting quite close together on two very spindly little chairs. It was like we were trying to keep our balance. That was A Tulip's Edge. Ever since Evan had fallen upon The Gin Whistle, with the delivery of that particular set of notes that had . . . bothered me, somewhat, we'd taken to meeting in a more Chelsea-minded part of town. It had been a move, smartish, that made me aware of the way we both dressed, Evan and I, that was articulated in the decor of not only the Whistle but also Grapes of Wrath, that temporary holding place with its illuminated bar that seemed to make of the gin-bottles light bulbs lined up along the shelf, and now this tulip-inclined establishment with its 'artisan' gins and demanding furniture.

'Most of the important thoughts we have about our lives . . . We don't say them out loud,' I said, the fine and precarious structure of the chair wavering beneath me. 'But that's not the point, Evan,' I continued. 'The fact is that people, when they read, want to read something that has substance and ballast.' I was back on the theme of content. Less introspection, more action had been my driving thoughts ever since Evan had given me those pages about his sense of, as he described it, the 'real'. For that kind of thinking would not our story make, was how I saw it. I wanted to have him see it, too.

'Readers like resolution, conflict, drama . . .' I went on. 'And you're talking about making this into a novel, your situation in Richmond, and what you think about the situation, but I have my challenges with that. "Story" or not, Evan. Or "novel", to use your new term . . . We still need a proper plot here. That's what people want from the genre: narrative. Drama and action and maybe some research, too, you know, historical research? Don't get me wrong. I'm committed. As I've said, it won't stop me writing, wondering whether people will find this interesting or not. The project is interesting I think, and it's building up, we have the whole first section done. But "novel", Evan? If it's a novel readers will want more. They'll want more than you seeing Caroline Beresford in a Richmond doorway. Novels want more!'

I finished off my drink and stood to get another round in. Back in the dear old Cork the gin was straightforward, as I've mentioned, pub gin, pub tonic. Bombay. Gordon's. When did it get to be life got so fancy? Now here we were somewhere, and alright so there was no 'matte chrome bar' at A Tulip's Edge, but just look at the place, at the gin. There was a fake library along one wall featuring books about tulipomania and tiny lamp-lit cubicles on another, each one filled with all kinds of gin named after districts in Amsterdam where the tulip craze first took hold. There was shaved ice in a bowl and the tonic had some herb or other. 'Slivers of a "Citrus Gesture"?' the guy behind the bar had put it to me when I'd asked for lemon. What were Evan and I, in our kind of clothing, doing there?

'Most people watch TV series now anyhow, instead of reading novels,' I continued. 'And when they do, read, I mean, then believe me, Evan,' I felt flushed and hectic, 'they want fiction to have stuff from the newspapers in it, the culture that's around them. You think that culture is Richmond? Positioned where it is? Last stop on the third tube option on the District Line? Think again.' I was walking away, still talking. I felt like I had a lot to say. Those herbs in the tonic may have been stimulants. 'People want certain kinds of locations, characters,' I called back at him. 'Paedophilia and wars, sex change and reality TV . . . That's a small example, of course; still I'm talking content, again, and lots of it.'

'But I don't care,' Evan replied, when I returned to the table with fresh drinks and a small bag of tissue-wrapped nuts for us to share. Tissue-wrapped nuts, for goodness' sake!

'I just want this story written down, Nin,' he continued. 'About Caroline. About my life in relation to hers. Who knows?' he remonstrated. 'Who knows?' He was rather wound up himself. 'It may turn out that I don't even have a life, that that's what my unrequited love for Caroline has made me see. That I don't have anything else I am really busy with or living for. Apart from you, I mean. I'm like an empty shell.'

'Mmmm.' I took a large sip of my Portobello Road and its strange-tasting tonic. And then I took another one. If I smoked, and if I was allowed to in a pub, I would have been lighting up a cigarette right then. 'Apart from you', indeed. What was he thinking of? I'd be taking a fag from the pack, right now, yes, a singular, deadly, good old-fashioned fag, and sticking it in my mouth. Striking the match and inhaling. Just to be doing something, anything, fiddling with a cigarette and smoking it, rather than have those words – 'Apart from you, I mean' – rushing through my head.

Yes, Evan had made his point. He'd made it alright. He'd done what I said doesn't happen in stories, oh, he'd done that. Reminding me that words do happen, they can go to work on the page and wreak an effect. He'd proved it: 'It may turn out that I don't even have a life, that that's what my unrequited love for Caroline has made me see,' he'd said, and more, showing in a sentence just how good words can be at making things real. 'No ideas but in things'* –

* The notes on 'Narrative Construction', later, refer to modernism and its ideas of 'making it real'; see the section on William Carlos Williams and the American modernist tradition in particular.

remember, that old chestnut? Sure, you might think I would know about the effect of a good sentence well enough not to be shocked by its application now – this from the advertising programmes I create, those various campaigns, the pet food and so on. Others for insurance. Sports shoes. As well as from having a good education in English literature. You'd think I might be blasé, I mean, about how easy it is to create desire and facts and resolution out of a well-turned phrase, to give meaning and shape to life because people need life insurance and new shoes and cat food and read the poetry of William Carlos Williams.

'And yet . . .' I said, when I'd regained my composure. 'And yet . . .'

Because of course he was right, the same people who read ads and know about modernist American poetry didn't necessarily also need to know about Evan and Caroline Beresford, did they? In this I was in agreement with Evan. And it's how I'd seen things back at the beginning, as well, when we were just getting started with all this. Yet here I was now, with my oldest friend whom I've known since I was four, and the pages piling up and the country pubs left far behind us now that we had the far more swanky kind of establishment in our sights – split glass bars and all the rest of it – and despite everything I'd said in the past, my reservations about introspection, those ponderings of the 'real', now that Evan seemed to be having doubts himself about whether the story had anything more to it than being just a private account of a lodger and his landlady, I had become the one who was starting to think differently. That the writing itself, so to speak, the fusing of a modernist aesthetic and life as we were living it coming together on the page in one literary gesture was the thing we were achieving. Weren't we? I thought so. Right here in the kind of place that gave you a stick of rosemary with which to stir a fancy tonic and a gin that was labelled after one of London's best known streets. Goodness me, it seemed like it. In this work of ours I was starting to feel 'deep in'.

'Deep in' was the phrase we'd bandied about earlier, when I'd told Evan about how I was adumbrating the details he was providing me with, about coffee mugs and morning conversations and so on, to provide more context, and he'd encouraged me to do that, go 'deep in' with descriptions and background for life in Richmond. And talking of 'deep', I hadn't been able to shift Petrarch from my mind, either. Or Dante. I couldn't shift the whole tradition of courtly love and my consideration of how it played out in post-Romantic culture. In films. Books. Or on TV. Or, for that matter, in the way the same tradition is expressed in the lives of other people I've known, friends, and, through reading, writers and characters alike who don't have a great deal going on but make a great deal out of what they have. So yes, I could see that novelistic thinking, which was what Evan had been getting at, what he wanted to achieve, despite lack of anything going on, was where we were headed. Word made, if you like, flesh. In that, he'd put himself in a tradition, you might say. He'd seen, as it were, the writing on the wall. After all, there's nothing so lively or romantic going on with Beryl in 'At the Bay' either, is there, that you'd think a whole

dramatic story could occur from it? Or with Will Ladis-
law and Dorothea in *Middlemarch*, come to that.* They
are just hoping, hoping, those characters, that love might
take shape, happen . . . And that hoping is all, for them, as
well as for us, the readers. It's what the whole thing, story
and words, is about.

Back in the Cork in the winter, I'd been adamant, 'I just
don't think anyone will read your book,' I'd said then. I
said it again now – in a pub that was peculiar with decor,
overwrought with tartan trim and cornicing inlaid with sets
of miniature bagpipes and violins – irrespective of my growing certainty, being 'deep in', that there could be something
of a 'novel' here, with the pages that had accumulated, all
that context – that though it was true I was now wavering
somewhat in this judgement, the fact that nothing much
was happening by way of plot was an issue still.

'But it will be a book, nevertheless,' replied Evan. 'Plot
or not. It will be, Nin.'

So alright, 'book', so 'novel'. I would have to start trying
to be relaxed about his terminology. And after all, time had
passed, as they say in the movies, winter turned to spring.
The nights were getting lighter, warmer. I'd called Evan at
work the first Thursday in March because by then I'd finished what I might describe as a sort of 'opening draft' of
the first section and though only a week had passed since
we'd last got together it seemed like much longer. That
last time we'd met at A Tulip's Edge it had been because

---

* There are notes later on 'Alternative Narrative' that address ideas of the
novel form.

the fashionable Grapes of Wrath, which we'd found that night when the Whistle had been too crowded and, to use Evan's word, 'peopled', was also too busy. It was the nature of these smart Chelsea-minded establishments with their 'bespoke' this and 'handcrafted' that to have crowds not kept at bay but positively welcomed; we'd never get a seat at the bar. A Tulip's Edge on a Thursday evening in spring would also be, I'd predicted, far too busy for the conversation and sort of Q & A Evan would be after.

So I'd suggested an alternative over the phone that was only three doors down but promised quiet and calm.

'Shall we go to The Kilted Pig?' I'd asked him. 'They have that same sort of artisan gin with heather in it that you liked that time at the Whistle, only it comes in tiny red bottles, with tartan labels, and it's quiet. There'll be no such crowds as we had to deal with at the Tulip. I found out about it online. They have crisps, made of beetroot and turnip . . .' I continued. 'There's—'

'Sure,' Evan said, without me having to persuade him further. And, 'You've read more of my last manuscript, right?'

'We can talk about that when we meet,' I'd replied.

The time between seeing him last and now had seemed long because of that reading. For as well as completing the entire opening section of his account, I'd also read a great deal more of his fountain-pen-written notes, including more of that personal material that spoke back out of his past, referring obliquely to those disconcerting remarks about the 'real', and then a whole folder's worth of something that read as a detailed narrative centred upon his time of moving to Richmond. So yes, the time in between seemed long indeed. Evan had delivered 'quite something', I was planning to tell him, that would be my phrase, when we met. 'Those pages of yours are quite something,' I would say, because they were.

'But for Caroline . . .' is how he'd started the second folder. Bold. Declarative. 'But for Caroline' and there were many, many pages to follow and all of them 'quite something' in this manner, all loaded with this quite por-tentous tone, 'But for her . . .' I'd started though, and knew I would have to finish. It was the nature of our work together, that I would 'get it all down'. Though Evan's writing was large and crazed and there was so much of it, and I had whole folios of stapled work before me on my lap, I knew I must get through it all, take notes on the lot and do a massive amount of transcription. 'But for her . . . I wouldn't know what it was to feel scared,' I read, for example. 'For myself, I mean, to be scared around anoth-er person, to so want to be around them that anything else was going to be like sickness or death. Here I was,' I had read on, 'back in London, in this part of London near enough to where I'd lived when my family was all here but that was like a place I'd never known before, never been in, visited, even – a part of London right at the end of a tube line, for chrissake, as they would say in the States. And where am I?' and so on, writing. 'Who am I? You might say being in the States is how it feels to be in Richmond, actually.'

There were pages and pages of this sort of thing, dis-cursive and declarative both. 'Like being in Connecticut

or someplace,' he wrote. 'Yeah, it did remind me of Connecticut, when I came out here that first time. It's a similar
kind of place, you might say, sitting out on the commuter
belt of a big city, only connected to it by a sort of railway
with the kinds of little stations along the route that might
have flowerpots and, nearby, a place to park your car, all
those little stations on the line out to Caroline's with guys
in suits getting off the train half cut, like in a John Cheever
short story, coming home on a summer evening from a
works drinks party or having a half in a pub in the City
before getting the 7.22 and their wives there at the station
to meet them like it was 1963. Man,' Evan had written. 'It
had been years since I'd been living in Britain, since I'd
been back. I was like a stranger in my own home town.'

I'd had to put a question mark in the margin there.
Evan had created a persona, sure, influenced perhaps by
those men in the John Cheever short stories that he'd
referenced, based on his years of living abroad, and that
was quite American in voice and tone from having had all
that time there, growing up, and then living there. But the
problem with it was that I couldn't hear Evan anywhere in
the midst of it, as being part of the narrative. All the John
Cheever stuff, those sentences and phrases, 'half cut', the
fictional aspect of the flowerpots and so on . . . It wasn't
like him. Not like I'd been able to hear him even in that
other strange section I'd read earlier, about a past relationship that had gone wrong. This 'Man, it had been years'
etc. simply didn't tie up with the boy, the person, I knew.
I'd determined to discuss it with him, when we met at The
Kilted Pig. But the minute I saw him again, in a jersey with

holes, as though he'd found it in a rag bag somewhere, I thought I'd better pull back my opinions somewhat.

'How are you feeling?' I said instead.

For some weeks now I'd been increasingly concerned about Evan. He had always been a bit on the slight side, but now he definitely had about him the appearance of someone who had lost weight. His personality, often given over to jokes and a bit of banter, now was tending almost permanently to the serious, only ever wanting to talk about Caroline. My earlier ideas vis-à-vis possible entertainments for us both that might relieve the repetitions of the pub visits – that we might have a pasta supper, go to a cafe and eat a sandwich even – these had disappeared, worn away into nothingness like the holes in the jumper before me. Evan was wasting away.

'You know,' he said now, as if he'd been reading my mind, 'all those years I lived in the US I always felt so robust. I didn't ever think of myself as an ex-pat.' He'd already ordered in the drinks, they were sitting there on the table in front of us, two tiny tumblers with the tonic presented in a cut-glass-stoppered bottle for us to share. I'd texted him details of The Kilted Pig as he knew nothing about it, even though it was actually quite near the Whistle, three doors down, actually, it was that close. Still, the modern facade could have passed him by, I'd thought, if I'd simply directed him towards the former and left him to find it on his own. Modern, sleek things have never made much impression on Evan. Even so, despite having some prior knowledge of the place – that word 'artisan' again coming into play – here he was dressed in an ancient jumper as though he were still in the Friend. No matter the content of his last pages and what he had written about Connecticut and New York-style flowerpots and so on, I thought how he couldn't look more British if he tried.

'Whenever I met any of those other guys from the firm who were over in New York for a conference or something – I had nothing to talk to them about,' he was saying now, 'about the weather or whatever, the cricket . . . I had no questions for them, no, I had nothing to say. Only it turns out now I could have asked them all, each one of them, this question: You don't know this woman, do you, who's about the same age as us? Married to a lawyer who's with Lloyds, I think it is, or maybe Citibank? Beresford, his name is. David. He set up a big operation for one of them in Hong Kong, no? You don't know Caroline Beresford? Because I just thought . . . You might have run into her. You'd remember her. I just thought you might know her is all.'

I was puzzled. Evan was doing a thing he'd played with in some of the earlier pages I'd read, imagining he'd known Caroline for much longer than he had, that they might have been students together or whatever, to give himself more action, perhaps, in the story, more things to do and say. But one thing to write it, now here he was actually talking this way to me in real life this way, fiddling around with time, changing it. Making it seem, in this conversation with me now, that he'd known the Beresfords when he'd been living in New York, as though he'd already known Caroline then, and for a long time. It was strange.

Back on the page, taking liberties, slightly, with the truth . . . well that was strange enough. But speaking this way with me directly, someone who really had known him for all this time, before he moved to America and worked in New York, who'd known him since he was five years old so really knew him, I mean, pretending he had this different, other kind of life with other people in it . . . Yes, it was more than strange. Making all these alterations to his biography, a detail here, a fact differentiation there. And the only feature not changing in any of it? Caroline. Everything altering, shifting, moving, even the surefire stuff about him I knew so well, all of it seemed suddenly up for grabs, except for one woman, Caroline. Caroline stayed. She was there, just the same, in all the fullness, reality, of her self and name. Caroline. Throughout all the words, all the paragraphs, all the sentences, she was just . . . present. In the midst. You know those lines Petrarch writes? 'So I, alas, my lady, sometimes roam,/seeking in other faces you alone,/some semblance of the one true form . . .'? Well, that just about sums it up, what Evan was doing. That despite the time changes and the fanciful idea of a persona who was also Evan having known her in a past life of them being students together . . . Despite the smearing together the real and unreal so that Evan had become someone who could have asked these British bankers he'd met on Wall Street whether they knew someone he hadn't even met yet in real time because he had created another reality altogether in which he could have asked them and could then tell me, his oldest friend, about that . . . Nevertheless, there was Caroline. For sure it was complicated, these other things Evan was writing and saying changing the texture of our story, somewhat, and its terms. I was right to feel confused. Did he actively want me to start thinking that the facts were the fiction and vice versa? I wondered. Was this all part of his new belief in the 'novel', perhaps? That he wanted me to believe that both versions were real? Or did it not matter either way because I wasn't even in it, the story? I took a sip of the Pig's hand-muddled Lewis heather and seaweed gin. Had I simply become inconsequential as far as my reading of fact or fiction was concerned? No longer part of Evan's life, if you like? Not a person who featured? After all, he seemed to be suggesting in these various comments and writings, just because I'd taken on the job of recording Evan's love story didn't mean I necessarily would have a place in it. What on earth, really, would have given me that idea?

After that meeting conducted beneath the shadows of bagpipe-encrusted cornicing with the drinks, as it were, still reeling in my head, I went home determined to assemble what would become an additional notebook for this 'novel'. For if I was to get involved in full-on fiction now, I thought the next morning, in the clear light of day, these remarks of Evan's turning and thickening the more straightforward reportage of events, I would need way more experience of structure and form than I currently had under my belt. With no more than the short story genre in my 'toolkit' as they say now, a contribution here or there in some book, plus ad work, I was going to have to learn how to manage a certain tone and approach that was long fiction's bread and butter, but that to me, copywriter with limited literary publication on my CV, was strange fruit. And, anyhow, I still wasn't sure, was it necessary? This veering off into the fanciful? Would it actually be of interest at all?

'Self-indulgent' had been the scary phrase I'd used. We'd had quite a lot to drink, and, as usual, on an empty stomach because Evan wasn't keen to go on somewhere else and have something to eat, or come back to my place so I could make us my standard platter of oatcakes and cheese.

'I've got to get back to Richmond,' he kept saying, before ordering another round.

'If you don't give this project some air,' I had been reminding him, 'let alone deliver on content, create some kind of space around it, the account of your feelings for Caroline, the whole thing is going to be . . .' and that's when I'd used the phrase: 'self-indulgent.' I said it again, recklessly perhaps, as we stood outside the pub saying goodnight.

'I know,' said Evan, then. 'You're right,' said Evan. The sign of a pig dressed in full Highland regalia swung over our heads as he considered things. 'You are always right.' He clapped both hands on my shoulders. 'Where would I be without you, Nin?' he said, 'I wonder?' And then, instead of thinking and talking to me further about the perils of being self-indulgent in this book we were writing together, simply gathered me up in a warm, gin-ish hug, tugging me on the ear as though I were a sort of pet. 'God . . .' he said, moodily, looking out into the night. We really had had about . . . what? Six? Of those strange kelpy heatherish gins? Five each? On an empty stomach? Maybe six. 'Where would I be without you?' he said again. Then, 'See you tomorrow,' and he walked off down the street.

It was spring by now, as I say, fully spring and warm enough to be out without a jacket. The sky was dark, but dark light, if that makes sense, and clear and lovely, the traffic strangely abated, so for a minute it was as though I was caught in a timeless place, neither here nor there, country nor town, London nor New York nor Hong Kong nor anywhere . . . Just me, the trees, the scent of blossom, a warm sky darkening into night. I had a lot on my mind and yet nothing. 'Where would I be without you, Nin?' I was between. In the middle of my life, but caught between its moments so I was both here and not here, in the midst, but looking on.

'In this second of being,' I murmured drunkenly to myself, parsing Virginia Woolf and a way of reading fiction that is constructed of individual moments rather than some big 'story' or other, a row of lamps was how she put it. And in that moment of saying those words, thinking about them, I knew too, undoubtedly, that, fiction or not, truth or invention, whether or not I would actually assemble into the overall text those notes of Evan's tonight, I was fully committed to this novel of his, the story, whatever it would be, of living, of love. Yes, I went home and I went straight to bed as the night took hold around me, but I was determined, as I drifted off, that my commitment made this story, as well as Evan's, mine.

# two

For sure there were developments by now. The story was proceeding, of that there was no doubt, I had the pages to prove it, but I also had to admit that there was a sort of undoing about our activity at the same time; like knitting come undone. I'd been worried about Evan for some time, that developments themselves weren't doing him any good, that all the talk was somehow occluding him. The jerseys weren't the half of it. Since I'd seen him again, even that first time when he'd just come back from the States and though, of course, he couldn't have been anything like the same boy I'd last known all those years ago, still it had occurred to me then, right away, that there was something held back about him, something doubting and unsure. He needn't have been quite so . . . restrained. Is what I'd thought then. So resistant to possibilities, options. He had always been a quiet boy but not . . . 'restrained', no. That wouldn't have been a word I would have used to describe Evan. Yet, and I'd seen this from the start, it was as if he had become, in his time away . . . careful, wary, even. And I was worried to see that. And, as the weeks went on, I continued to worry.

This concern took two forms. One: Concern over the condition of Evan himself, whether he'd been eating properly, getting enough fresh air, seeing people and going out, etc. – to the cinema or to, I don't know, various drinks parties, perhaps, or get-togethers, meeting work friends, other friends, for lunch, an evening at the theatre . . . All the activities we might embark upon ourselves, are supposed to, and expect others to be interested in, although, when I think about it, other people who might do all that are not like Evan.

And then there was: Two: The condition of the story itself. 'Our novel', Evan kept saying. By now, I'd filled a couple of notebooks with all sorts of ideas and themes, a novel's 'ballast' as I'd thought of it earlier. There were a range of questions I'd come up with that I might ask Evan at some point in my writing, about his life, and about why he'd made the decisions he had – to stay on in the US after finishing school there, why he'd decided then not to come back to London or go on to university in the UK but, rather, become American in the way people do when they move there for any length of time. That had happened to his lovely parents after all, and his sisters. It was still something my own family could not quite let go, the fact that our beloved next-door neighbours had gone away and stayed away, that the history crossword puzzle evenings for my father and Tom, my sharing homework with the girls, my mother's painting classes with Helen and all their long, long conversations together, were all things of the past. We'd always believed, my family and I, that the Gordonstons would simply go to New York for a time, and then come home again. We'd never foreseen that, instead, their letting that decision stay open with them would make them the kind of people who ended up not so much making a decision to stay as just never returning, and when you talk to them you notice they've started doing things like saying 'I guess so' instead of 'Yes, I agree', or, 'Get me some of that, will you' instead of 'Could I trouble you to . . .' or 'Please' and so on. Whatever. All that. Manners. Expressions. Their accents changing slightly and they start softening the sounds of some consonants so that when they say a word like 'city' it comes out as 'ciddy'. Though in all those respects, I have to say, Evan sounded pretty much the same as he'd always done, his sentences unfinished, short, a bit mumbly. Deeply, deeply familiar to me so that even with all my worries about his dress and appearance and now wariness, he seemed unchanged, in the most straightforward way, at heart, the same Evan I had always known.

Still, even with these many kinds of insertions, reflections, the book was in no sort of 'condition', as I just expressed it. Despite me filling in all the gaps I could between the Gordonstons, past and present, memories of letters sent, phone calls exchanged between the two families through the early years; once, a visit by my mother when she went to stay for two weeks on her own and came back with a whole new range of quite alternative-looking outfits, and so on, such was the influence of Helen Gordonston upon her. Still, even with this kind of thing occurring, lists, etc., questions put about, facts laid down; despite my writing, the notebooks being filled, so very many pages addressed to the deliberations of, and written in, our various meetings in the pubs and associated establishments in the, now, Chelsea and South Kensington area . . . We weren't getting anywhere, were we? There were all these details filled in but there was also a lack of 'substance', a certain kind of fiction editor might call it, a quality about the whole that kind of said: So what? And you'd think I had some kind of issue with this business of Evan's residency in America – which I don't – as though it had something to do with the story – which it doesn't, not really – to the extent that you might think Evan had never come back, the way I've written so much about him being away, right here for example – which he had. Because, yes, his parents had stayed on in the truly formal way and taken citizenship and his father had a Chair at Yale and so we'd lost them, my parents and brother and I, who had always loved the Gordonstons, to that far country . . . But Evan had come home. He was with me again. And none of that should have been surprising to anyone in my family either, that the Gordonstons had stayed over there,* not at all surprising because the Gordonstons had been talking that way for a while, my mother reported, when she came back from that visit of hers, the Cape Cod holiday this was, way back, in the early years, when they'd first moved out there, and it had been confirmed even as far back as then, and as the years went on, in her many conversations with Helen Gordonston about their lives and families . . . How much the Gordonstons loved it there. My mother came home that time wearing a brightly coloured sort of artist's smock she'd bought with Helen in Provincetown

---

* For they did, remember? That's already come up: How the Gordonstons left London when the author and protagonist were still children, and stayed there. Details about how both families manage being apart, when they are such good friends, are in the notes titled 'Personal History' under 'Family'.

and announced to us all at Heathrow, when she got off the plane: 'The Gordonstons will never be coming back. I can feel it. I've seen their life out there. I just know they won't return to the UK now.' It had been clear to my mother, she always says, from a summer morning in Truro, is her memory, sitting at the breakfast table under a big wide blue Cape Cod sky when Helen had said, 'Give me some of that bacon, will you?' to someone, Tom, or one of the kids, or my mother even. 'That bacon looks good,' and my mother had thought then: They've become American, the Gordonstons. It was in that form address of Helen's. That 'Give me . . .'

'They won't be coming home,' my mother said.

For sure, writing myself in a slightly American style, the writing had always been 'on the wall', as they say, writing it down here on a page as I believe I've used the expression before, to say that, as America pulls people in, so it pulled in that lovely family of ours – and therefore it was a surprise perhaps, yes, a surprise – I hadn't expected it at all – that Evan would return the way he did. 'I've decided to come back, Nin,' exactly how he put it. And my feeling when he said that, my reaction? I can't describe it. When I thought, I really had thought, that he would be away, stay away, forever. And why, I do also wonder? Did he come back, when his parents and his sisters never did? I kept returning to that theme. As I went on with the book, the work he wanted me to do, the question kept on at me, and sometimes I tried asking him but he didn't really reply. Oh, it was 'work opportunities' this, or 'career expansion' that. But none of the reasons he gave really computing, adding up, none of those reasons anything I could use in 'our' story. Only this word, 'Why?' It kept on at me, as the pages mounted up on pub tables between us, and our meetings went on. Why did you come home, Evan, tell me, why? Like in a song, but nothing like one by Neil Diamond. After all that time away, come home again, why? When, as the years had gone on, and his parents were fully committed to staying over there, in New York, and Felicity had got a job in Manhattan after graduating and my brother had stopped calling Elisabeth, and emailing her, and Evan and I had long stopped writing . . . When all the people he had grown up with apart from me had gone their own way and kind of forgotten him really, 'moved on' is what they say in the States, I know . . . Still, here he was, my dearest, oldest friend, come back from being so far away, and . . . Why, Evan? I was wanting to say, over and over, and more, as the weeks went on, turned into months. Looking at that old rag-bag jersey of his, at his hands, the way they fiddled with the tiny tulip-shaped tonic bottles on the table in A Tulip's Edge, or with the hip and square tumblers of the same sort of neat artisan gin also served under the silver vaulted ceiling of the Whistle, looking at his dear, familiar face . . . Still, Why, Evan?, saying, but in my mind only, and not out loud to the dark but increasingly spring-affected pubbish air. Why? When you had no reason, did you? When you had no reason to come home at all?

And as I say, these factors around the story were adding to the mounting worry over the 'condition' of Evan in general. His dress, appearance. Along with the state of

'Caroline', the manuscript, as I was thinking of it as. The way it was not adding up to anything, yet clearly taking its toll. And as one picks things up and reads into them for worrying information so I, too, after the somewhat confrontational conversation in the Edge, as we went on to call it, when I had talked about the fact that most of the feelings that we have in this life go unspoken, alluding to this story of his about an unexpressed love, of a great feeling that goes unrequited, and wondering whether there would be readers for such a thing in this age of 'streaming movies' and the 'televisual' and endless series of paedo-philia and sex break-outs and celebrity drama . . . When I had been quite unreserved in my opinion on that score – after, how many gins? A lot. So my concerns about Evan had me picking up on his increasing reservation, distance, and worrying also about that. After that somewhat head-on spring night, it seemed a long time passed between the reading of those stapled notes with the diary-like addition and meeting again in The Kilted Pig, during which I read all of the other pages, completing what I thought of as the opening section of 'our novel', a long time, several days.

It was true, I added them up: those 'several days'. It was a full week. The night in the Tulip's Edge when he passed over that manilla envelope, before I'd even known there was a place three doors down that we would be visiting when we next met, had been a Thursday, and then it was a full seven days and still I hadn't heard a word. And it was strange, it was, for so much time to have passed, for me and Evan. And by then, as I've already written, in those seven days, it had become, it was, fully spring.

I'd got as far, at home, as getting down that opening section, mapping out for the book a kind of shape. I'd decided that the main part of the first half would comprise notes
that Evan himself had made about moving to the Beresfords' – what that was like, meeting Caroline and David
and the boys, and names, and friends, what the house was
like, the area, all those first impressions – though not much
of that kind of detail had made it into what I'd written up
to this point. Still, my plan had been – and I had talked
to Evan about this – that I would 'map out' that 'kind of
shape': Evan arriving in Richmond, Evan settling in, Evan
getting to know Caroline – those endless cups of coffee!
It was all there, in draft. I would have included the times
she would seem to be there in the hall just when he came
in at night from work and they would stand around for
ages having a 'catch up' as she put it, or how if she wasn't
going out and David wasn't due home at any hour soon,
she'd be making a drink for them both, and would also
put in, occasionally, Evan finding himself sitting down to
join her and the boys for a kitchen supper, a 'nursery
tea' Caroline always called it though the children were
teenagers by now and barely around themselves, much . . .
There it was, the 'shape'. All these details about Evan and
Caroline fitting together to form a backbone to the story
though it was clear to me, in the general time frame of
things, in terms of Evan's presence in Richmond, Caroline
was mostly out.

Even so, I could write, I had written already in draft,
the meetings would accrue, accumulate – in pages and in
paragraphs, in writing of detail. They would, despite my

concern about the 'novel', inexorably grow. There would be, too, I would write them in, the kinds of conversations Evan and Caroline would have at those times of their 'catch ups', ideas shared, plans made. And then, so went my thinking even further, once all this was set down as 'a given', as I said firmly to Evan one lunchtime when we'd long since reverted to our more regular meetings and were having a 'Ploughman's' – yes, even in the smart environs of Chelsea and South Kensington a pub such as The Kilted Pig with its gins named after various kinds of Highland Scottish dance, Schottische and Dashing White Sergeant and so on, may offer to customers the option of a 'Ploughman's', that familiar half pint and cheese-and-pickle sandwich arrangement so familiar to those who remember 'old London' as some might call it,* only Evan and I were having Dalreavoch Waltz and Wild Thyme tonic with crisps instead – once it was all 'in place', I continued, we would, the pair of us, have a good solid base upon which to rest the bulk of the narrative. 'Evan's fundamental narrative', I was thinking of it as, because the details, when in place, would be the base upon which could sit a further investigation, of sorts, wherein I might ask him questions of a more philosophical and psychological nature, have a set of close psychoanalytical lines of interrogation that would open up further pathways to novelistic planning and so would introduce Evan himself as a fully drawn and realised character who might carry the whole weight of the

*There are notes about 'Old London' in the section 'Personal History'; see also 'Pubs'.

proceedings if love went unrequited and we had to go down that path.

There then was the triumphant plan! A plan! As I had it so figured! Well, in fact . . . ? Only arrogance, call it. Fanciness, kind of. Thinking that just because I could write ad copy, easy as jump, for some insurance company or other, or just because I could whisk out an entire campaign for dog food without even drawing breath . . . I could do the same for this project of Evan's. Who did I think I was? That these processes of mine, thoughts and ideas for a structure, were necessarily going to make it on to the page . . . Just on the basis of my planning them? That some kind of organisation on my part was going to be able to make Evan so real that I could show more and more of him by writing him, that he would become that same man to the reader I knew so well, the man they would also come to know and love? The presumption – hah! – that I could do any of that with ease. Write *that* Evan Gordonston. That person. Him. With his messy brown hair and a look that was always surprised when he saw me – 'Oh, *hello*, Nin!' as though I was the last person he expected, but smiling even so, 'Oh *hello*' – that Evan. The one with the bad jerseys. Him. It was 'fanciness', alright. To think that I could make him be someone the reader knew as well as I knew him, that I could do that by writing. I look upon myself having that idea now . . . some kind of 'plan' . . . and can only laugh. To think that, as I so envisaged it, I would be able to create a portrait of someone so vulnerable and in need of this one particular woman, this Caroline, that I would be able to show in his need of her what it was this one particular woman contained to make him so want her, what it was about her that drew from him the feeling that no other woman could hope to embody, even women he had known – that diary entry still played upon me – or a woman he knew now, whom he knew very well and always had known, still write what it was about this other person that had so taken him, filled him with thoughts and dreams and ideas of love that no other kind of book would do . . . Because, of course, it was not as easy as that. Was it? When I sat down to write it, to get beyond the 'plan'. When I tried to get down on a page what it was about this other woman that had taken him so very far away that he'd stopped eating, was getting thinner and raggedy and wan-looking, though spring had arrived, and it was warmer, lighter . . . Of course it wasn't easy at all.

Even so, I maintained my hopes. That by writing I would nevertheless come to understand this dear friend of mine and his great love. Have the answer to certain questions about Evan – that 'Why?' of mine – and more, in a fully realised portrait and account of his relations and dealings with the beloved object who resided, playing landlady to his lodger, in Richmond. That I could come to understand the nature of unrequited feeling in the Petrarchan sense of it* embodied in this man, this close, close and oldest friend from childhood, so known to me as we were so known to each other that we could just sit, for an hour or two at

* Without going overboard, there are some details about Petrarch and Laura, creativity and desire, and the *Canzoniere* at the back of the book – all pretty interesting, but very much an option as far as the extent of any additional reading is concerned. It's more of that theme again: unrequited love.

a time without speaking sometimes but comfortable even so, to be just sitting, looking out the window, maybe, or saying small inconsequential things, in The Gin Whistle as we began, at the beginning of spring, then briefly Grapes of Wrath before finding ourselves more permanently in A Tulip's Edge, The Kilted Pig and then, latterly, in that same season, the relaxed and spacious Swan and Seed with loads of outdoor seats though we rarely used them.

Therefore I kept at my work. To write on. The familiar, the known, underpinning things. With no option, is how I felt it, but to continue. And Evan, as I write, as I thought, must come to see, to accept, to realise, be given over to, in these, our relaxed and gin-drinking and crisp- and nut-munching times together, the comforts of the cloak-and-hiddenness of love. Given over entire and somehow I must get all that down, too. Those moments of: 'Eh?', saying, sometimes, when I might ask of him: 'Do you want to go out for a walk?' or 'It's raining, shall we have another gin?' Startling him, 'What?' out of reverie when I tapped his arm and said, 'Are you hungry? We could always decide on breakfast one morning, or find that cafe on the outskirts of Richmond that we went to that one time, you remember, you were keen that I went there? We don't always have to stay holed up in a pub, Evan,' and he just shook his head sadly, No, as though he'd hardly heard me.

For this was Evan now and I had to accept it. More and more vague. Becoming, yes, quite thin. Just as able as ever to crack the odd joke and make me laugh – 'I have never believed in the concept of a three-course meal,' for example, after six bags of Guatemalan hand-salted nuts in the

Edge – as well as the odd and quiet remark that would make me sit up straight in attention – 'Achilles, as you know, a boyhood hero of mine, is still a character who holds a great deal of interest for me,' late against a low-level soundtrack of *piobaireachd* one night in The Kilted Pig, for example, or, in the same place, 'A butterfly's life is quite long enough' – and 'I agree' would always be my reply.

So these frail phrases, words, to show the life of us two, together. And like butterflies, themselves, my poor thoughts, going, flitting, drifting . . . Lighting upon this memory or that, some idea. Because I knew, deep down, that 'the cloak-and-hiddenness of love' was no mere metaphor for Evan, for me. But rather that these curious comments of his I so loved, along with our silences, our easy sitting, as the rain hit the red-beaded glass windows of the Edge, or sun shone down upon our heads in the grand and lovely rooms of The Swan and Seed, as, while the weeks passed on and we came, occasionally, to sit outside there in the warmth, sometimes, our jackets and jerseys cast down on the seats beside us . . . All this, this cloth and gin and temperature, and bags of various kinds of toasted and roasted nuts, occasionally unusually wrapped, split between us . . . All this could come to be as nothing. Next to the reality of Evan's mind, his thoughts, his imagination and imagining that meant, I felt, I feel, that he was so wrapped up in hiddenness and love I may never see him again.

'Let's go in,' he always said, those early spring days, even as the sun continued to shine and everyone else at The Swan and Seed was out enjoying the weather. 'We've been sitting here long enough. We're better inside.'

# three

There were reasons, then, extended and Petrarchan, for having so many of those 'Q & A' sessions, as Evan termed them, that I was pressed to arrange with him in order for us to be able to catch up and fill in key content areas for the book we were writing that I did, for myself, also want to arrange. For how else, I was starting to think, more and more, was I to see Evan if not to find out more about his situation with Caroline? I asked myself that particular question often. Why else would he come out into the world, it was starting to seem? If not to arrange for the love story to be developed – 'got down on the page' as Evan bluntly put it – would I see him at all? So my 'Let's meet up for a Sipsmith and Fever Tree' suggestions – to be American about it, to match his habits, I suppose, that way they all have over there, of calling drinks by their man-ufacturers' names and not by sheer alcoholic description, so 'Tanqueray', so 'Hendrick's', etc., as they say in New York – were all there to make it seem casual with Evan, as though casual, casual, casual, might have been the only way, so caught, so entranced was he by life out at the end of the District Line, we could justify a meeting. Sometimes I did wonder, if I had not had the wit to suggest it, or he had not had something urgent about Caroline he needed to relay, would he even call me, speak to me? Hence my non-chalant 'Shall we get together?' messages left on his mobile when my heart was beating, actually, sometimes so much I thought that the modest baseball-sized organ nestling within me was just going to jump clean out of my chest.

And all during these weeks, Evan was becoming paler, more grubby-looking. For those old jeans and jerseys . . . They were getting more and more worn, more threadbare and stained. Even when we'd arranged to meet straight after work and he still had a suit on, he managed to convey an old-jeans-and-jersey appearance; his hair sticking up and him rummaging amongst it as though he'd just woken up; in all, in general, a pretty poor state of affairs.

By now it was always daylight when we met. With spring upon us in all its glory, aforementioned flowers and blooms at every corner and in every park, so these were daytime meetings we were having now, as I may as well describe them. With the clocks gone forward; darkness fled. So it was, in that spring light, I could always clearly see in detail the exact state of Evan's repair, as it were, in the longer lighter evenings bright as day I could look straight at him, observe all his familiar aspects and ways. We tried not to stay out late again, as we had that night at the Pig, and often, too, we'd try and get together on his lunch break, or on a morning when he didn't have any meetings scheduled, though never again was there to be a cafe involved as we'd gone to a cafe once, on the outskirts of Richmond, all those months ago, for 'context', and all we'd done was talk about our past, when we'd been children and living next door to each other in Twickenham, a part of London that wasn't that far away, actually, from the very place where we'd been sitting.

So 'Yeah,' Evan would say, or 'OK, then,' to my various proposals to visit this pub or that. And, 'Yeah,' myself, when he told me there was something about Caroline he needed me to write down. Yeah, yeah, and again another yeah. Yeah to A Tulip's Edge or more often now to The Swan and Seed. Yeah, yeah, to The Gin Whistle, still, or 'Let's go back to the Pig.' Because, as I say, never once did we vary our destinations that much, or did he come around to mine, and though he invited me to go out to the house in Richmond on a number of occasions, for some supper this, or kitchen tea that, because Caroline would love to meet me, he said, an old friend and all that . . . And oh yeah, yeah, I kept thinking, as though I might go out there, as he said he would like me to . . . I knew deep down I never would. There were the occasional evenings through the spring when I would also say 'Yeah' to his suggestion that I meet him near where he worked, in one of those pubs in Mayfair with names like The Cask or The Vault or The Chambers and they were lively enough, with all the after-work crowd, those places, on a spring evening when the weather was warming up, everyone out on the pavement and drinking and smoking like it was the eighties. But it was only ever a 'Yeah' and no more, just a slight variation on our usual routine, and afterwards, after a gin or two, we wouldn't do anything else.

'Hi,' I would say, on those occasions. I would see him through the crowd. A lone figure, not checking his phone, but just standing, in that way he used to stand when he was a boy, waiting for the next thing to happen. So standing now, and waiting for my 'Hi', just the same, actually, as he's always been.

'Hi,' I would say and then we'd order, gin this, gin that, nothing much 'artisanal' going on in Mayfair though very pleasant it was without it, even so, and Evan would fill me in on what was going on with Caroline, how much ground they'd covered that week – in a smile exchanged, or a brushing of her arm against his arm that had been registered by both parties, or in the recognition of a particular word that had been expressed – 'love', for example, as in 'Would you like a coffee?' and 'Oh, I would love that' – all this in their brief meetings in the kitchen in Richmond, or when Evan came in the front door. Or there'd be more content he'd want to pass over to me on the conversation side of things, about the kinds of subjects he and Caroline had covered over elevenses at the weekend, say, and then there'd be some discussion between the two of us as to whether there was, as Evan put it, 'anything between' him and Caroline on the basis of one or two of those get-togethers of theirs from which he could extrapolate further meaning.

'Well,' I would often say, jamming up against him for lack of space on the pavement outside The Cask, everyone shouting around us, and leaning in to each other and laughing. 'Well . . .' I would say again, thoughtfully, as though I was going to say something else, but in fact I wasn't. And he would carry on, Evan would, describing various conversations between him and Caroline giving rise to all kinds of busy and commanding thoughts that would engage him and I would say 'Well' again, sometimes, for encouragement, all the time wondering if there might be a table inside where Evan and I might be happier, on our own and indoors and away?

I write that 'never once did he come around to mine' – apart from one time, right at the beginning of all this, soon after he'd arrived back in London from America – and that's entirely true. For the fact that something happened on one particular visit when this story hadn't even begun is of no consequence to the plot or narrative,* no reason to get into it here, maybe never in this account. After all, my part in the writing is to comply – those daughters of Milton, remember? In the same way, I was to 'comply' – with Evan's ideas and requirements as far as content is concerned, and also, for that matter, with the form of this story. There was no earthly reason to go putting in early information here that serves no part in a narrative about Evan's love for Caroline. What would be the point? This is his story, not mine; his love, his feeling for Caroline and what was going to happen with that, and, as I've recorded, his reaction when I told him something rather straightforward about the quality of his own written work that had led to a gap, a breach in our communications, those long days when I hadn't heard from him, not a text or a call. With all that going on, and more, why would I start writing now about some evening that's not even included in the first section of this book, referring to something that happened before the beginning of it even,

* In Further Material at the back of the book, we come upon 'Alternative Narratives' – another instance of another story inside this one; ideas of what can and can't be told, etc.

before he moved to Richmond, met Caroline? If I was to start writing about one particular night back there in the winter, in the depths of that dark time – well, I'd never finish this section that's in hand. I would go back there, I would want to, be there with Evan and I would never want to leave. I would stay.

With that in mind, then, I'll put that 'scene that took place' – is how I'd described it on a page in an early note-book that I'd since stopped using – aside. 'Scene', for 'scene' is how it was, as though what happened that night were some kind of play. As though it wasn't real. For sure there's no space for such scenes here, not in the sense that Henry James describes them, in his quite famous essay about theatre and novel writing, that phrase of his: 'the divine principle of the Scenario' . . . No. Though Evan has talked about this book at times as being something that's a bit like a play, well a monologue really, with the figure of a tall blonde woman at the back of the stage making gestures, coming towards the front of the stage to speak sometimes, and a man responding to her but neither of them hearing each other . . . Even so, theatrical as that set-up may be, the other particular 'scene' I was referring to hardly fits the rest of the drama anyhow which is all about Evan and Caroline with no interest whatsoever in addressing something that took place in the sitting room of my flat back before this story begins. Instead, I'll intro-duce at this juncture another more pertinent meeting that occurred when the clocks had switched forwards and the evenings became suddenly much lighter. Yes. That time. 'Spring forwards', as we say, to remind ourselves how to set the clocks, adding one whole hour and with it changing the day. So writing, quite suddenly away from the winter solstice with a low lamp burning late at night in the sitting room of my flat, the doorbell ringing as if to startle me but in fact I'd been expecting it, and springing forwards instead to a time when it seems as though a much larger light were shining on us all – and this included Caroline and Marjorie and my parents and Felix and everyone I've mentioned in this story – as though, quite suddenly, one day in spring, we were, all of us, living in a different world.

By now I'd well and truly got into the thinking of Evan's 'novel' as he was happy to hear me calling it, though for the most part there was nothing much made up about it – apart from the odd 'intrusion', as I thought of certain pages myself, when Evan wanted to apply a little magical fictional realism to his narrative and have me include these in the account, or when I found myself adding details that I hadn't personally witnessed, the details of Caroline's dress and hair, filled in somewhat from Evan's more general outline, the arrangement of the kitchen with its expansive breakfast bar that overlooked the large green garden with its borders and old oaks and maples. Some rose trellis, I believe. And so on. There was plenty of this kind of thing that I was writing about quite freely in my paragraphs and pages, adding here and there where Evan had just told me about the general circumstances of the set-up in Richmond, or where I had inferred.

He was, for sure, barely leaving his lodger's quarters these late spring days, as they were at this stage of the proceedings, except to work, or meet me early to talk about

Caroline. It had been ages, ages, since we'd been out late. Something about the night was going to trouble us, was in both our minds, I believe, since that time I'd been forthright about his chances of getting a readership for this story and we'd had too much to drink . . . Something about that night, then, had made us wary of the spring weather, the warmth, the softness of the dark. We'd tried to keep our meetings to the light.

Yet here he was, one evening towards the end of March, calling up well after nine o'clock – actually it was a brief text – to ask if we could meet at the Child o' Mine, a place quite near the Seed, where we'd only ever been in the afternoon.

Of course I said 'Yeah.' As I've already noted, Evan had been looking increasingly peaky. At our last meeting, the day before, he had been wearing an old maroon-coloured jersey that had stains on the front, nasty stains that had worked their way into the wool of the jersey and he hadn't seemed to care about it one bit. Now, though, he looked even worse. His outerwear had the appearance of something spilt recently, down his trousers, down his front. Also, the jersey was not only stained, but was fraying at the cuffs and around the neckline – I mean, pieces of textile were unravelling from Evan at these places; the jersey was coming away. When I looked closer I could see a hole, a large hole under the arm, and, in general, evidence of . . . on his shirt, on his jeans . . . significant thinning.

He was 'wearing', in other words, Evan was. Wearing thin. Wearing, too, or 'coming away' as a seam comes away from the sleeve, or a hem will fall. This whole affair with Caroline, if I could call it an 'affair', these 'chats', brief brushings, of a hand, a fingertip, an arm . . . They were taking a toll. The day before I'd seen this man who was my oldest friend in the world wearing a very nasty-looking item, but it was nothing as bad, nothing, as what he had on this evening. I doubted whether this freshly stained, unravelling thing was even wool.

And worse. For when he took that off, the outer garment, if I can even call it that – Child o' Mine was like The Swan and Seed that way, it could get warm indoors – there was an equally unpleasant T-shirt underneath. And all this with tracksuit bottoms – 'sweat pants' as they say in America – and trainers.

'God, Evan,' I said to him then. 'You never used to wear this kind of stuff.'

'You mean these old sweat pants?' he'd replied, barely looking at me, he was pouring the tonic into the large tumblers of gin, 'locally produced' apparently, so-called '*terroir*', he'd already ordered.

'Exactly,' I said. The word 'incredulously' comes to mind. 'Sweat pants,' I said. 'The kind of clothing that even goes by the name "sweat pants", Evan. You'd never be in that kind of kit in the past. What's happened to you, boy?'

'There's no lemon,' said Evan, as if I hadn't spoken. He took a sip. 'Tastes alright though.' He looked like he was in a kind of a dream. Dressed in unrecognisable clothes, as though he himself could barely be recognised. The 'sweat pants' might have been peeled off the legs of a homeless person, I could talk about them forever. They, too, had stains – though in this case the stains were mainly old. Old indeed. Much older than the crusted muck that sat on Evan's chest, that I could see he displayed to the world as though it were some kind of badge, a badge of honour worn bravely across the front of his maroon.

'Hi,' said Evan, as though I had only just sat down.

'Hi back,' I replied, about to say something else, about his shoes, about those 'pants' again, but he put his hand on my arm to stop me.

'I've something to tell you,' he said. 'Thanks for coming out so late.'

He was drawn and pale, I've written that already. Ill-looking, actually, though he'd reported in an earlier meeting that he had no symptoms; he was only drawn. It's true, he certainly seemed to have lost a great deal of weight. Slight in all areas may be a good description, through the arms and torso; his hair sticking up like always, like a little boy, as I said before, as though he'd just woken up. He looked awful.

'Good God, Evan,' I said. 'Shoot.'

I wasn't fazed, despite the appearance side of things, despite his sense of drama, the lateness of the hour. After all, Evan was always reporting that he had 'something to tell'; usually it was 'something big' and then I would write it down and it didn't seem that big a deal at all.

Still, 'Shoot,' I said again, taking a sip from my gin. '*Terroir*', eh? What was all that about? And there was no lemon, he was right. And there was also no ice. What was going on in these places with the gin? Evan didn't even seem to care. His hair looked like he'd had a fright – and, by the way, I might add, quite apart from its shape, sticking up in odd angles, Evan had always had such great hair, when he was a boy. Helen used to cut it herself, creating a style somehow, but relaxed-looking, just so that it would be out of his eyes. I guess, thinking about it, in a way, that family were preparing to be American years before the actual event of them moving there. The signs were in Evan's hair. The way he wore it longer than the other boys, the way he was always in jeans and T-shirts – even in winter. He used to shake his hair back out of his eyes when he was talking to me, when we played, and when I think about it, he looked like a young American even all those years ago and well before his family moved there. These memories came back to me now, as he sat, bolt upright, at the small table between us.

'What's up?' I said now, as though we were both still nine years old. He shook his head as though his hair was as long as it used to be, and all the old charm of Evan – despite the ghastly attire – flooded back. It ran right though me.

'So good to see you, Nin,' he said then, and I could barely bear it.

And you know, it wasn't just Evan but all the Gordonstons had great hair. Helen, she had fabulous long hair, shiny dark hair that she just used to tie back in a pony tail, with a bit of string from a jam jar it looked like, but fabulous, fabulous. And Elisabeth had great hair. Felicity did. We used to compare at school – the colours in her hair! Toffee and blonde and treacle and honey . . . All those adjectives – while my own was just brown, nothing but . . . Is how it looked to me.

'Why isn't my hair brown like Felicity's is brown?' I used to ask my mother.

'In the same way mine isn't dark like Helen's is,' my mother would reply. 'It's genes, Emily. The Gordonstons are blessed.'

All that, running through me. Memory. Evan. I felt myself shaking.

'Helen is beautiful,' my mother would always say, especially after coming back from being next door at the Gordonstons', when she'd been spending time with Helen in that amazing kitchen of hers, that was full of light and windows and flowers. Helen there, in that kitchen, in the midst of some pottery project or other, some silk-screen work and all the dyes were spilling into the sink – scarlet and orange and emerald and yellow.

'She's a beautiful, beautiful woman,' my mother would say.

And there I was with Evan now in the grip of these kinds of past thoughts. The Gordonstons. Our families together. I was back in the past while also being very much attached to the present, too, in the body and proximity of Evan sitting in front of me, the feeling of him, as I say, running through me like water. I had to take a gulp of the ice-less and lemon-less '*terroir*', just to keep me steady. Steady, Evan, I was thinking. Though 'beautiful', I could write, helping to keep myself steady, though I write it again now, 'beautiful', as my mother said of Helen Gordonston, all those years ago, this was not a word I could apply readily to Evan now. Despite his shaking back his hair, catching my eye. Oh no, Evan, I was thinking. Not this time, no. Not this April afternoon. Nor last, when it had still been March and we'd stayed out late, too late. Not now, not then. No, no, Evan. Don't let me be taken, that way, back into the past. Don't look at me, please, don't catch my eye. Not now, not then. With me being with you here, and close, so close and both the days a Wednesday – I was realising, at that moment – for I know it was a Wednesday, writing it down now in this manner and all in a rush, because I always go to a yoga class on Wednesday afternoons and Evan had asked if he could meet me then, after the class, when it was still light. So, Evan. So. Don't hum like that while you touch my arm, don't catch my eye. It was only a yoga class Wednesday I am writing about here, nothing more and nothing happened, did it. Nothing then or now.

I had another sip of that *'terroir'* gin.

'So good to see you,' he said again, and he took his hand away. He looked away from me, down at the table in front of us. He had something to tell me, he went on then, and it would have full import. This would weigh in heavily to the contents of the book we were 'writing together'; it would make a difference, it would change things, he said, in our book; it was always 'our book' now, in his discussions. 'Our novel'. Though, I could say, there was nothing 'our', to my mind, about any of this, no 'our' whatsoever in a story that was about him and Caroline, nothing 'our' in it at all but only Caroline. Only Caroline and him. This, their 'novel', hers and Evan's, his – not connected to me at all but for the writing, the 'amanuensis' side of things.

So, Evan. So.

For he didn't once look up again as he was speaking, only head bowed over that table as though searching it for clues. 'Our' this, 'our' that – and less of you and me, this word 'together', I was thinking. Less of that 'our', I may as well have told him. Though he was there right in front of me, the present and the past of him, so close . . . Still. 'Amanuensis', remember. I am here only as the one who is 'getting it down'. Amanuensis, again, the writer of a story. No 'our' in it – and remember, Evan, too, it's only a yoga Wednesday after all, is what I was telling myself, reminding myself, just to keep me steady. And just because it was late and had been late that night a week ago, too, that wasn't such a big deal, anyway, it just wasn't, nor that we were here with all our past and present very close . . . None of it a big deal, at all.

'What's up?' I said. Because for fifteen years, fifteen years, I've been taking that class; it was Rosie who first introduced me to it. After we finish the session, ashtanga, we often, all of us, the whole class, go to a pizza place around the corner and I text Rosie from there, send her a message to Gloucestershire to say how much I miss her being with us, splitting a Four Seasons and having a beer.

'What's up?' I was about to say again, to put some words into play between us, between our two selves, to get something started, a dialogue, to stop that feeling of Evan still running through me so that I could barely hold myself, could barely be there at all. 'What's up? I was about to say again but then stopped, didn't.

Because I could see – why hadn't I noticed before? – when he lifted his head and looked at me again that he'd been crying.

# four

By now Evan had been living with Caroline for nearly three months. Nearly three months of him not sleeping, not eating properly, falling in love. Nearly a quarter of a year since that first day when he'd rung the doorbell of a house in Richmond and Caroline had answered and walked down the hall in front of him, knotting up that crazy beautiful blonde hair of hers in a casual twist as she called over her shoulder, 'Coffee?' Nearly three months. Nearly three. Of Evan calling me, keeping notes. Of me making notes from what he told me, and adding to them, from his notes. My only way of getting to see him, I was acknowledging increasingly, was to work on this writing project we had fixed in place; all our meetings together, first at country-style pubs in West London where people wore gumboots and kept well-behaved black Labradors seated at their feet or lying quietly under the tables and sleeping, and then, gradually, at more sophisticated establishments that were barely – one 'Ploughman's Lunch' notwithstanding – pubs at all, only occurring because of the book we had in hand. Time was passing.

'Gosh, Evan,' I said. This was the following day after that last yoga-Wednesday of a meeting that had been late at night and we'd ended up staying out even later. After I had . . . collected my wits. 'It's spring. It really is.'

We'd decided the night before that spring might have

been the reason for the emotional pitch of things, the up-set, Evan's tears. Spring, after all. It has a lot to do with most people's behaviour, it always has, not only Evan's, not only my own. 'The climate has changed, Evan,' I said. 'The temperature. The year is moving on. And where are we in all this? This story, this "novel" of ours? I think something needs to happen, by now,' I said. For we needed to move past the recent upset, get back to the job in hand. 'There are leaves starting to come on to the trees,' I continued, 'tiny and bright green, but they are there, Evan. It's been weeks since I first saw a daffodil. The birds are on the move, I can hear them, singing and making nests. So I think, you know,' I said, I was resolute, I was strangely formal, 'that you may need to speak to Caroline in some way, express . . .' I added, 'I don't know. Something. Say something to her, I mean. Of your feelings for her. Bring some gesture into play, your thoughts out in the open. Say something . . . you know . . . You must do something to make this relationship more . . . concrete, somehow. More real.'

As I say it was only the day after the Wednesday of the night before but it had seemed terrifically long, the intervening time. The space between then and now the longest period of time, actually, between any of our meet-ings – even more than that hiatus of sorts back in the late winter into early spring, over the issue of Evan's form of description, the personal nature of his writing style – this last twenty-four hours the greatest period of minutes we'd had apart, it felt like, for sure. I'd expressed last night what I was saying now, in less cool tones, perhaps – for we had stayed up late, had only arrived at the Child at nine thirty to begin with after Evan's late text – but in actual fact the gist of what I had been saying then and more succinctly now I could have expressed from any time after about the first week of Evan meeting Caroline and falling in love. For we had an issue, pure and simple, of content. The wanting thereof. We both had to face it, I'd said, clearing all other extraneous matter away, Evan's quiet tears, my own beating heart, that this whole story had lacked actual expression, action, from the start. It was clear, of course it was clear, that Evan's feelings of love had come upon him right there at the beginning of the narrative – that lovely 'ping' – but after that: Nothing. And Evan had needed, from that initial meeting in Richmond, in my opinion, some kind of 'follow-up', was the phrase I'd used the night before, bullishly even, as some kind of a pitch.

After all, I reminded him, I had this book to write. I'd been charged, Evan had charged me, with the duties of re-cord. The word 'novel', by now, as I say, making a regular appearance in the text; there were responsibilities there. There was the simple task, too, of transcribing Evan's sayings, sentences, his meanderings about Caroline. And to turn all of this, somehow, from notes to tiny incident, into something with presence and 'press', a love story we might, any of us, want to read. So —

'Aren't you going to do anything at this stage?' I asked Evan now. We were back in the Child. What's that expression about getting straight back up on a horse you've been thrown by? That was us.

'With the leaves coming out and so on?' I was saying. 'That long-ago daffodil? Aren't you going to —'

'Just get down what has happened so far, Nin,' he interrupted. He drained his drink with a grim expression. 'I'm getting in another round.'

I say again, only a day had passed but it had seemed like much, much longer. With no communication made, from him, in all that time. And not a week without incident, was my view, that had begun with, perhaps, those tears that had been shed . . . That was behind my expressing things to him late at night in the way I had, with some degree of 'press' I mean. Because a matter of some 'press' had occurred, I may say, something had happened. Something had. An incident, maybe not large, but an incident even so – which many would rate as significant, indicating a dramatic moment in a story, a way of it moving on.

Caroline had gone up, there it was, the fact of it, to Evan's room.

So the fact stands, in a paragraph of its own. That she had presented herself to Evan, Caroline had, at his lodger's quarters, she had mounted the stair. He had told me about it in the last minutes before closing time at the Child. She had stood there, late at night, and knocked on Evan's door. So, Evan. Was my thinking. Time to 'press' on, alright. I'd said as much then, as they flicked the lights on and off and gathered up our glasses. For a risk had been taken. Albeit a slightly druggy, champagne-and-wine-fuelled kind of risk, but risk nevertheless, and a charming one, to my mind, undertaken by a woman late at night after a dinner party, when she was still wrapped up in the mood of cigarette smoke and white Burgundy and conversation, the sweetness of a complicated pudding still upon her lips. It meant the story could take off. Something between them could begin.

And there were leaves on the trees! That daffodil had long ago bloomed! Of course I wanted to 'press' Evan! It's why I used the word, why writers who are amanuenses use it. For they do need to 'press' their subjects, sometimes, for details. And this was a novel, wasn't it? Evan wanted it to be? Well then it needed those details even more. I needed them. Yet, 'Just get down what has happened so far' was all I'd received in return. And, 'I'm getting another round in.'

I had noticed his old British expressions were coming back into play. It was part of the general change. There was less of the 'Let's do drinks' or 'Is there a good bar around where you live?' and more of 'Why don't we head down to the pub?' and, as I've just written, phrases like 'Let's get another round in.' There was, too, the rather more grim British fact of those jerseys, counteracted, I suppose by the ghastly 'sweat pants' though I'd noticed this evening he was back into his ordinary old jeans.

'I'll have a single this time,' I said. I was feeling light-headed. This Child we'd found ourselves in again, for the second time in a row, also had another kind of tonic it turned out, only available 'under the counter' and it was as weird and acidy-tasting, as forceful, as the peculiar *'terroir'* nature of its matching gin. Evan had put his hand over mine, and while he'd been talking about Caroline had inadvertently been stroking the back of my hand with his thumb.

'You'll have a double and join me,' he said now, and laughed recklessly and funnily. 'God, Nin.' He suddenly seemed very much the old Evan. 'You and I have known each other for such a long time . . .'

I watched him go over to the bar and fling the empty glasses down like a cowboy. Not a trace on display of his ruined eyes from the night before. 'Just get down everything that's happened so far,' he shouted back to me from the bar, as though we were at a party and about to dance – but not to 'Sweet Caroline' by Neil Diamond, rather something altogether more funky. 'Just write it down. You're a great writer,' he shouted out again. 'You could get the whole book finished standing on your head.'

So much for the Seed, I thought. Other venues. This Child o' Mine that had been the site of such revelations was manifestly, tonight, an altogether different sort of place.

The fact is that the twenty-four hours that had passed between us being there last night and now this, and the intensities around that, had been fraught. For my part I mean, I can't speak for Evan. For Evan, I have to say, though there had been clear signs of upset after the time of it happening – his distress, head bowed over the table as though in prayer, all that which, surely, had been a result of the incident? – now it was as if Caroline going up to his room had not amounted to anything much, actually, and that the incident, an enormous one as far as his amanuensis was concerned, was not going to 'press' the protagonist into action one bit. He seemed happy – look at him just now, up at the bar and cheerily ordering more of that contraband tonic, jaunty as you like from the effect of that, and some kind of upbeat dance music – just to let things sit.

It was as though his behaviour and mien retained no memory of the upset from the night before, as though nothing, in fact, had necessarily happened at all. It was the writer in me, then, perhaps, I brooded, as I waited for him to return with the drinks, who wanted to move things along? Who felt frustrated by allowing an incident such as he'd revealed to simply hang? That I'd been so taken up by it, imaginatively, the sense of drama, in a sort of literary way, that I wanted to build on it somehow, make something of it. Was it that? For Evan told me what had happened last thing the previous night and then not another word about it as we left the pub and went our separate ways. Not another mention, not a text or a message . . . I hadn't heard a word from him until his call this evening, quite late again, suggesting we meet. And in that time between, for me, it was nothing but imagining we might just have a novel on our hands after all, of imagining all kinds of things.

There'd been real tears, remember? Though he'd never explained them. Signs of upset as he raised his head, before he came near to telling me about what had happened in his room . . . Where might it all lead? So yes, I'd texted Evan in the interim, left messages – but had heard nothing from him. It was almost as though we were having some kind of stand-off or row in the period between leaving the Child in the early hours of the morning and getting his text about tonight, which we were not. In all our long friendship Evan Gordonston and I have never fought, or suffered unpleasantness of any kind. So this kind of silence that had befallen us, full of emotion . . . Well, no wonder perhaps, I, the pair of us, had been of the mind, tonight, like last, to go out late. No wonder, I thought, we were in the mind to drink hard.

And what had actually happened anyhow? It was difficult to say. I could begin, I had, I'd already made some lengthy notes, starting when I got home the night before lest the fact of what he had told me might overwhelm me somehow, make it impossible to continue writing at all, so carrying on writing and writing the next morning and all through the day when the silence from Evan was so loud it had almost made me feel ill. I had started a whole section by way of setting the scene, imagining context. It was an important thing to do. I must write. I must 'get it down', I was thinking.

Evan's room was at the top of the house. I think I've written that somewhere already? That it was a big house, the house in Richmond? As many houses are, of course, out there at the end of the District Line, for it's an old established part of town, Richmond, with inheritance a big part of the game when it comes to real estate – so large unspoiled houses, large gardens, places to park two or three cars . . . That kind of scale. And this house of that scale particularly so – was there talk of David Beresford being given it by a grandmother, on his mother's side? I think that was the case, Rosie said – for the place had that lovely, lived-in feeling, of old sofas and bits of very good furniture and so on, a lovely wide stair. All meaning that Evan's quarters, his lodgings . . . Well, it was more than a good-sized room, he said. More like a studio flat really, as he described it, not just a bedroom. Oh no. In New York they might even call it an 'apartment'.* Why, I might write, in the American way, he had his own land-ing up there! His own bathroom – 'naturally', Evan was to say to me, two weeks after moving in, as though he'd been living in Richmond his entire life – 'with a separate shower *and* a bath.'

That's how big those houses are, as I say. Is why people go there, to Richmond, even if they've not inherited, move that far out, to the edge of West London you might say, to the end of one of the option routes on the District Line, and stay. Is why families like the Beresfords even, who you might have put down on paper for Notting Hill or Chelsea . . . Is why you find them out there in Richmond with the gardens that go on forever and, more recently, the patio areas with built-in barbecues and the swimming pools, yes, there are swimming pools in Richmond.

'I mean,' Evan said to me, right back in the beginning, when he'd first moved, 'the house is huge, Nin.' We were back in The Elm Tree then. I was making a list of 'facts and practicalities' as I called them. 'The Caroline file,' said Evan. 'No,' I replied. 'I want facts, context. Background information, Evan,' I said, for though we'd been to that cafe that time, it had been nowhere near the house, we hadn't even got close. I'd had no idea about the Beres-fords' arrangement of the domestic space, decor, none of it. We'd needed to get all those details down – which is how we got on to the sheer size of his studio flat at the top of the house.

* There are notes all about the kind of scale, the lovelinesses of Richmond, at the back of this book, and a section marked 'Evan's Living Arrangements' in 'Alternative Narratives'.

'My own landing,' Evan said to me that night at the Elm. His words came back to me in Child o' Mine as I waited for him to return with our powerful cocktails that made me want to dance. They had whirled in my head, too, in the intervening hours after he'd told me the night before about Caroline going up, and I had felt so cut off from him, as though far, far away. 'I heard a knock on the door, Nin, late, at night, and it was Caroline . . . ' he'd said, just before the Child was about to close. 'She was standing on the landing outside my room and I said, quite simply, "Come in."'

Yeah, well. Stories. Novels. That's fiction for you. And 'Closing time', eh? I might have written that down, got that much recorded at least – along with that 'Come in'. But as it turned out it wasn't as if any of this narrative was exactly moving along at any kind of pace as a result, even though one may have expected it. Even with Caroline tired and confused and clearly taking something and it had been reacting weirdly with the drinks from the dinner party, the spirits and the wine . . . Still it wasn't as if . . .

'Come in,' he'd said.

Anything had happened, had it?

Had it?

Because—

'Oh leave it,' Evan had said, as we'd parted, him about to disappear into the night, when I'd asked him what it might mean, her coming up, and what might have happened next.

'Goodnight, Nin,' is all I heard.

And then the long hours had passed. And I had felt so alone.

Well, there. It was a pub of intensities, as recently noted. Evan's 'Just write it down . . .' now in the merry atmosphere of a place of dance over which formerly had reigned an attitude of introspection and of prayer. His former 'There's no need to make a big thing of it' after Caroline had gone up, his confessed 'Come in'.

The Child was, as I say, that kind of place.

It was a pub we'd found together that used not to be there. By that I mean it was something else before it was a pub. An electrical shop, perhaps? A shoe repair business? We'd seen it together, Evan and I, back in the winter when it was still pretty cold and we'd identified it as being somewhere good to go, along with The Swan and Seed, when the weather became a little warmer, when one might feel one wanted to be on holiday, kind of – Evan from his high-powered city job and anxieties about his relationship with Caroline; me from the exigencies of life as a freelance copywriter who lives alone and has thoughts of writing a long historical novel with research, the kind that sells, but who knows that she'll never be able to. It was a very nice pub. About a forty-minute walk from my flat, and you might have thought we could go back to mine afterwards, if we'd wanted, that I could have made pasta, a rice dish, that we could just wander back home after some hours of sitting, talking . . . But as I've already noted, that was not to be part of this story which takes place, the unspooling of it, mostly in pubs – with outdoor seating and in – all over the West London area. Anyhow, there was no need for any alternative entertainment of that nature, because, as I say, the Child – like the Seed – had a holiday mood, quite removed from the urban edge of the Chelsea and South Kensington establishments, that took us away from thinking about domestic circumstances, so thoughts of pasta, rice – just no. It had large tables for two people. Perfect, then, for writing a 'practical list', which was what I had brought with me, to prompt Evan – that word 'press' again – into providing some more of the story now that we were together and the rent between us, my loneliness, his shed tears, trammelled up and mended. I could lay out the pages on a table that was perfect, altogether, for writing, and for taking notes. As it turned out there was to be no writing this night, it's true – dancing was in the air! – but still I had my notes for our next meeting. I had them with me, headed: 'Evan's Accommodations'.

'Just tell me', I asked him, when we decided to go there again on a sunny afternoon later that week, 'everything you can about the house and I'll write as you speak.'

'All of it? The whole set-up?'

'Well, as you think,' I said. 'As you need.'

'OK, then,' I remember, Evan began. I'd already written down an introductory paragraph or two, so it was a case of adding to that. I began as he spoke:

'Caroline lives in a seven-bedroom house in Richmond with a self-contained studio flat at the top of the house, and you know this, Nin, you know all this . . .'

'Go on,' I said.

'My accommodations are under the eaves,' he continued. 'Shall I carry on?' I nodded. 'That's where I now live, of course, below the roof. The rooms of the house in general are large, airy. The garden is south-facing and the garden is huge. All the gardens in Richmond are. The house at the end of Caroline's road . . . They have a swimming pool there, and one might imagine that when the nights get longer, warmer, we might sit out in the garden, Caroline and I, on a summer's evening and hear the kids from down there, splashing around. The Caxton Taylors. Caroline knows them—'

'But—' I interrupted.

'Yeah, but,' Evan agreed, and sheepishly, I added that word to my notes, 'sheepishly', because—

'Yeah, I'm getting ahead of myself,' Evan said. 'I am daydreaming . . .'

'Go on,' I prompted, pressed.

'The house is nicely decorated,' he continued then. 'There's a lot Caroline has done . . .'

'Decorated?' I said. 'Like decorated new?'

'Yeah, maybe that. Like freshly painted, you know? All the walls and woodwork. And the curtains, sofas, even the older stuff . . . It's like everything in the house is really clean.'

'Sounds fancy,' I said, and wrote down 'Showhome. Big rooms. Think *Elle Decoration* or *House and Garden*. Fresh flowers in big vases. Caroline herself dresses in shades of ivory and beige and grey and the house is like that, those tones.' I added: 'Her blonde hair. The floorboards recently done, stripped and polished. Caroline has bare feet when it's cold outside. Her skin carries the honey trace of a tan.'

'When I first went there, when we had coffee that morning,' Evan said, 'sitting up at her breakfast bar, I thought then – wow. This place is fancy.'

'Caroline is fancy,' I said.

'But that's just it, Nin,' Evan said, and writing this now, I remember, he put down his drink, as though for emphasis. 'She's not. She's like us. There's this elegance to her, this calm lovely thing . . . But then there she was, standing on the landing outside my door.'

'And you said—' I still had the pen in my hand.

'Come in.' Evan looked at me, looking deep into my eyes but my eyes for him were Caroline's eyes.

'Come in.' I finally was able to write it down, as an event, as a moment on the page. Evan saying it, thinking it, reliving it . . .

'Are you OK?' Evan said to me, but he was talking to Caroline.

After the hours that had followed the evening when he'd first told me about all this, I'd put together the most general kinds of notes, starting in those long hours I'd had before seeing Evan again in which I'd had nothing to do but write, write . . . All these pages that I'd put together, ideas . . . .How she'd gone into his room, Caroline had, and told Evan all about herself. The pills, the alcohol. I'd imagined it all. How she'd talked about her marriage, how lonely she was, how scared. She'd told Evan about all the things, frankly, I'd seen coming in this story a mile off, that maybe she'd had an affair, maybe her husband had. Yes, there was the overbearing issue with David and his interest in Classical Studies, all those classes at UCL, thoughts of study towards a PhD eclipsing all aspects of their domestic life together. There was his taking of a room in Bloomsbury in association with all that and his staying there, near

Russell Square, spending nights and nights away. But she was devoted to the children, Caroline was, of course she was, devoted, so the family unit was strong, wasn't it, yet they were growing up now, weren't they, the boys, and they didn't really need her like they used to, nobody did.

'And what am I doing, Evan? With my life?' she'd said to him, that night in his room, looking up at him – by now she was sitting on his bed, she still had a wine glass from the dinner party in her hand, and was taking sips from that, while telling him everything, as though with all the time in the world. 'I am so sorry to be like this,' saying, over and over, 'I am so sorry to come in on you like this with all my . . . crap.'

None of it, really, was so surprising. Nor Evan saying that that was alright, he understood.

'It's OK,' Evan had said, and he went over and sat next to her on the bed, where she was sitting, had seated herself, after all, after Evan had said, 'Come in,' had gone straight over to the bed to sit down on it like that. So he sat down there next to her, and, like he often did with me, took up her hand in his hand.

'I wish I could help you,' he'd said.

'Oh you do,' she'd replied, shaking his hand up and down as if trying to bolster both their spirits. 'You help me more than you know,' she'd said, squeezing his hand hard and shaking it. 'Just by being here. Just knowing you are here, in the house. Up here in the lodger's room under the eaves . . . Just knowing . . .'

And Evan told me then – after I'd written all this down – that second when she'd used the word 'lodger' he'd known that he couldn't say anything to her. About his love for her. About the story of it. About any of his feelings.

'Your dear little lodger's room,' Caroline had said.

And, 'Accommodations,' Evan had replied.

He told me at the Seed, all this days later again, that that word was the only thing he'd been able to think of, to say. As though to soften the situation, make good that shaking hand, the fact that a married woman was sitting weeping on his bed . . . To make good all of that because otherwise he would fall down on the floor at her feet just as Petrarch longed to do with Laura, as Dante dreamed of so prostrating himself before his Beatrice, and say to her then: 'Don't you know I am here and in love with you?' In a full expression of courtly love,* 'Don't you know I can't stop thinking of you? Imagining you? Every waking minute, seeing your face, hearing the things you say? Before I go to sleep, when I wake in the morning . . . I can't do anything else, think anything else . . . Because everywhere is you, everything I am, you, everywhere I go, everyone I see . . .' All of it. Of that sort of thing. Straight out of Petrarch, Dante. But not nearly as well written.

He'd been looking at me then, too, I remember, as he was talking, looking at me, but really looking at Caroline.

'I knew then', Evan had said to me, as I was carefully pouring tonic into my glass so that I myself could look

* Which we know by now is a theme running all the way through this book, Petrarch's *Canzoniere* as a metaphor and inspiration for *Caroline's Bikini*, and so on. It's Further Material.

away, be taken out of, his false gaze, 'that I couldn't say a word.'

My hand was shaking.

'But I decided I would, Nin. I did. That second I decided: I would tell Caroline of my feelings – not then, not with her so out of it and emotional, not there in my constrained "accommodations", as I had so wittily termed them, there shutting off any possibility that she might kiss me – no. But I intended nevertheless. As you yourself have "pressed" me to do: To tell her everything, everything you've written so far, that is in my book, Nin. And before the week was out.'

# five

But that week had passed and more, and nothing had happened, had it? There'd been that difficult night Evan and I had had together, when we'd gone to Child o' Mine late, but that was ages ago by now and here we were still, slap bang in the middle of 'nothing'. And, as I observed him, Evan up at the bar of the Seed ordering strong drinks come to us marked 'organic' and 'designer distilled' with accompaniments of – what was this? – Grapefruit rind? Candied tamarind? – he wasn't feeling so bad, either, about the 'nothing'. Both of us, maybe, feeling that 'nothing' might just, for the time being at least, do.

It was a pub, the Seed, as I wrote a couple of pages back, that, like other places we'd been going to over the spring, was a bit further away from where I live, and was perfect for afternoon meetings, as well as being pleasant in the evenings, before it got too late. It was spacious and quiet, so easy for Evan and me to talk, and, if we wanted to – like now and I'd brought writing materials with me as I usually did – 'get down on paper' details of anything that might come to light. The tables were large so I could easily spread out all my notes that I'd wanted to bring along with me so that Evan could see them, that they were piling up, and that things were beginning to materialise in terms of content, despite absence of plot.

'Impressive,' he said, when he saw all the files and papers.

I had filled things in somewhat, as described, and when we met, before the powerful nature of the 'organic' drinks took hold and I'd realised that Evan wasn't going to say anything to Caroline about her 'coming up' that night, to his quarters, I suggested that we make the Seed our new meeting place. It was such a relief to see Evan happy again, after those tears of a couple of weeks back, that long absence of more than twelve hours that had followed them, and it felt good to have a plan. So we decided, as though organising our project together for the first time, that he would continue to bring me notes, his pages of scribbles that he would work on in his lunch break, or late at night in his lodger's quarters while below him blonde Caroline moved around in her house in the dark.

Yes, we liked The Swan and Seed. There were tall windows and big relaxed-looking sofas arranged in the Italian style – by which I mean that they were placed in corners of the room in a certain configuration favoured by the grand old Catholic houses of the Veneto and Firenze. It makes for informality and formality, both, this in-the-round seating, and is a wildly good way to sit with someone you love who does not know much about that fact, or thinks that the love you have for him is simply that of an old friend, say, two people so familiar with each other that they could be brother and sister is how long they had known each other, practically for all of their lives.

So, we sat, Evan and I, as the month went on, in those corner sofas, the spring light from the tall windows falling down upon our heads, making us drowsy if the day was fine, and as the weeks went on and the tiny leaves on the trees outside unfurled and spread themselves thick and fresh amongst the branches, the bright flowers of the season opened and bloomed.

By now it was late, late spring, and summer would be with us soon, that season of leisure and relaxation. Of sunbathing. Swimming. Yet we were, Evan and I, hardly lounging. We had a corner sofa, it was true, but I had placed a smart, square table between us, upon which we could lay down certain pages and make notes upon them, if required. How could we be at all lounging when there was so much to do? Late May and there we were deeply enmeshed in the usual conversation – who did what, and when. How did Caroline sound, when she said a particular sentence? How might Evan respond to a certain kind of silence? And I was reporting, by way of a demonstration of potential chapter headings and so on, as Evan had requested in the first place, a 'story' after all.

It was active, then, our status in the Seed. We were working. The emotions of the Child, the tears, the thoughts of dancing, worry, then relief . . . All this was put to one side because here we had this report of his, this book of mine. His account, my words. 'Our novel'. We had this between us, and after a period of strain, those 'emotions' again, it was great to have something fixed and certain, this manuscript, and yes, indeed, 'novel' which seemed to be working well enough as description for the project these late spring days. Because more and more it was seeming to me that what had happened between Caroline and Evan, from the first moment that they met that had then been sharpened, crystallised, by Caroline coming to Evan's room that night, made this account, yes, at last, 'novelistic', as the critics might say, episodic even, if pushed, and with elements of character and plot that satisfied, if I worked on it, the requirements of the genre. That pivotal visit, along with what was occurring in the Beresford family, the increasing distance between Caroline and David as exams in the *Iliad* and *Odyssey* loomed, with a huge amount of translation involved for David and long nights spent in Bloomsbury that took him far away from Richmond and the way that played out in family life, those absences of his, played out with Caroline and the three boys . . . These things coalescing, all helping make what we we were writing together a satisfactory narrative, despite its uncertain beginnings, something – to refer back to a much earlier and somewhat contentious remark of mine – that 'people might just want to read' after all.

But it was also clear that at some point I was going to have to tackle that 'nothing' that still hovered like a lit-up neon heart at the centre of our story: the 'nothing' that happened the night Caroline went 'up'. I knew that. I was aware. As a writer I had a responsibility, was the way I thought of it, to the reader, the publisher, the critics, bookshops . . . To deliver on something coming out of that nothing, that the current state of affairs could not go on for much longer, that these pages, intriguing though they may be, were not limitless. At one point, I was clear, Evan was going to have to make a decision about where he was going with all this, what he was going to do. We'd had our time in the dark, as it were, of him saying and also not saying, expressing and also not expressing, what he felt; months passing since that midwinter day Evan had first knocked on the door and seen Caroline for the first time, winter into spring and now nearly into summer, yes. Summer with its swimming and swimsuits on its way.

'You can't stay silent about your emotions forever,' I told him, the square and useful table firmly between us. 'You have to speak. Tell Caroline. Especially now that it's been some time since she's been to your room . . .'

My voice trailed off. I looked out the window. Italians and old Catholic families know the benefit of room arrangement. The sofa was perfectly positioned for me not to have to face Evan while I spoke. I could look away while still being intimate with him, could speak freely while maintaining formality, be that amanuensis, thanks to the exact siting of the pub furniture; to feel pain and be friendly both.

'You love her and you must tell her so,' I said then, and turned back to give Evan what, in a certain kind of novel, would be described as 'a bright smile'.

Now it was Evan's turn to look away. That sounds like a line in a novel too: 'Now it was Evan's turn, etc.' As though this whole thing were premeditated, had been rigged from the start. That word of his from before – 'scene' – with all its connotations of artificiality, is what I seem to be suggesting, a sort of choreographed formality, as though our very meeting had been arranged as a sort of play, a description of something that had already happened and was now to be enacted in faithful reproduction. Altogether, I was thinking: It was as if the more I wrote about Caroline, thought about her, the situation, everything that was going on, the less I felt myself to be me. Not that I was turning into someone else, only that I had become someone who was less and less, someone not so much a person with feelings of her own as a writer who had done their research, who wasn't even an author, not even the sort who might stand behind the action and direct it – what's that expression critics use? 'Pull the strings'? Not even that. Only reporting, researching, note taking. That was who Emily Stuart was now. Only 'amanuensis' – to another's words, another's drama, another's life, Evan Gordonston's, and him thinning and disappearing, too, in a different way, becoming slighter and more and more badly dressed, wasting away before my eyes, as the shape of my papers, by contrast, took materiality and bulk and form.

And where were we, in all this? As the tall windows looked down upon us and the sofa held our forms in its comfortable embrace? Where? Is what I continued to think as the weeks went by, as I swirled my curious gins of one type or another, less *terroir* now and more hand-produced, or 'curated', as one young man behind the bar at the Seed informed me, 'Slow River' and 'Dundee Gold' and 'The Minister's Choice's, and mixed in with tonic from the small and expensively crafted bottles on sale that you could take home with you if you wanted to. And, 'I don't know what to do, Nin.' Evan saying, 'I don't know that I can do . . . anything, you see. I may love her but I can't tell her so,' and me answering 'You must' – because Evan was going to have to 'do' something, any minute, he would have to make this story go ahead and become a book. He was going to have to confess to Caroline, make a statement to her about his feelings, or embrace her, invite her in some way to understand how he felt, put his hand to her cheek, in a gesture of care and tenderness, or gather her up somehow, or lean in towards her, or take her fingers in his hand, or squeeze her hand or – I don't know – something. Something was going to have to 'take place' – finally to come together to be a book.

Or not.

I suppose there was the issue of that as well, hovering in the midst, a 'nothing' in itself, that 'or not'. But is it possible for something NOT to happen in a novel, I was asking myself in the notes I was making in my flat, late at night. And after all, it wasn't actually as though 'nothing' had happened either, even though I'd started to think, after Caroline had gone up and nothing further was forthcoming from Evan, that nothing was the reality here. Because, look. There was the state of him. Of Evan himself. That was a thing that had happened, wasn't it, as a result of love? Evan had changed. He was now officially very thin and very pale and was dressing in peculiar ways – those 'sweat pants' weren't the half of it – and he was taking days off work and dreamy, often, in his attitude now, when we met. He was less inclined to make jokes, make me laugh. He had become serious, less likely to think about, for example, let alone suggest, going dancing.

I noticed it as the days became brighter, this alteration, a sort of – ironical, given the season – fading. Even when I met him after work he would have a skewed look about him, as though his suit had become twisted on him, slightly back to front somehow, the buttons of his jacket wrongly fastened, or his cuff and trouser hems half down. I thought: That kind of turn-out wasn't 'nothing', that was for sure. To be dressed that way with the sort of job he had . . . Evan's body was telling a story of emotion having taken hold and there was no way any career in finance was going to intervene. He was in love with Caroline and that was the story, his story, the whole story. There was nothing 'nothing' about it.[*] He couldn't stop thinking about her,[†] imagining being with her, writing about her, recording various minute details.[‡] 'Today she wore her hair running down her back like a waterfall' was one sentence I'd underlined in something he'd written down, with a view to giving the whole some serious editing; 'Today she wore a dark lipstick like plums' another. So, yes, nothing wasn't nothing. Not one bit. It was all adding up to one big something. And on top of that something – and I had to keep this in mind – Caroline had already gone up, in my mind and in reality, she'd gone up, uninvited, for the reason of her own need, to his room.

'That', I said to Evan, 'is the key here.' We were back in the Seed. Since the days had been getting so much warmer it was like we couldn't stay away. We'd realised there was so much of that space inside, was part of it, and no one except us, it seemed, keen to be there as they were all outdoors. No music played, there was none of that kind of distraction. All the entertainment was taking place outside

* See 'Reprise'/'Petrarch' and 'Courtly Love', it's all in the back of the book.
† As before, 'Reprise'.
‡ 'Reprise' again, for it's all in the back of this book if you want to know more . . .

and as it became warmer shadows seemed to deepen in the corners of the Seed and we quite liked that, Evan and I, to be that far away from other people and the light.

'That she came up to your room', I said, 'is key. That she was unhappy and she told you so. That she spoke of the strains in her marriage, of her medication. And that she sat on your bed.'

Evan nodded. He looked down into his empty glass. The glasses in the Seed were tiny. He seemed barely able to suggest another round, a nut, a piece of lemon that he might eat it through. This was my friend, my oldest friend, before me, so lost and so undone, and all because of a woman he loved who had come to his room to importune him and who had been, as I'd written down before, that close to him, so very close.

'In the context of all that's been going on here,' I said, in firm tones, for I needed to be firm, my heart was breaking, 'and I am not being ironic, Evan,' I said, 'because a lot has been going on –' I gestured, 'in this pile of pages in front of us –' I indicated certain papers for his attention, a section marked 'Caroline's Confession', for example, other whole sections describing Evan's life in Richmond, David's mounting interest in classical composition, the three boys' homework schedules, lists of friends, Caroline's hairdresser appointments, a new sofa bought, the kitchen counters replaced, and so on, and so on . . . 'All this indicates a whole lot has been happening,' I said. 'But the visit to your room . . .' I faltered, 'that's something we can build on.' I went to take a sip of my drink, but my glass, too, was empty. 'It makes the novel, her coming in on you like that, into the sort of thing people might really become involved in, with action of that sort, and drama and so on. The alcohol. Pills. Caroline coming up . . .' I said. My voice was firm, but I felt I could hear it shaking . . .

Still, I went on. I had to. For the sake of what we were trying to do here, I had to do that, irrespective of how difficult it was for me to 'press' on. Still I must. 'Press'. 'Her confessing to you, confiding . . . It makes it a love story,' I said. 'A novel about the two of you being together, in your room, a story about Caroline and you and all she is to you, all she can be . . .'

Evan sat, he was quiet. His tie was hitched around his neck like a hangman's knot.

'Evan?' I said. 'Evan?' It was as though he hadn't heard me. My tremulous voice, my saying these sentences and phrases I felt I had to say . . .

'Are you listening to me at all?'

Later, after getting home that night, writing everything down – what I'd said, what Evan hadn't said – feeling the effect of the four or five Dundee gins from the Seed's vast stores, and on an empty stomach . . . I did wonder about this moment in the book. Where it was going, yes, as always. But where we were going, too. The two of us. Going. Whether we could bear it, actually. To be the Evan Gordonston and Emily Stuart who sat in a pub that had now become familiar, sitting in a way that by now we had been trained to so sit, in the Italian fashion, to be at once very close together, very very close, and also far away.

'Evan.'

Evan Gordonston.

Sitting together in the grand Catholic style, beneath tall windows.

'Are you listening to me?'

Saying.

'Evan?'

Finding ourselves together, so often, Evan and I, in that aforementioned grand style, sitting, and so close . . .

But far away from each other as well.

Speaking, or trying to, but sometimes not speaking at all because we did not have to, two old, old friends who have known each other since childhood . . .

And no need to speak then, with all that past behind us, to say any words. And then sometimes we would just catch each other's eyes and smile.

'Endings', as someone said, some novelist maybe? 'are for weaklings . . .'

So, then, The Swan and Seed. A familiar place for us to be, that spacious room with its tall windows, broad sofas, its quilted tapestries of rampant swans. So the weeks went on. A love affair discussed, dissected. Questions were asked against feather-filled cushions. Lists made. There in The Swan and Seed, just as we'd had lists made and writing achieved in Child o' Mine, A Tulip's Edge. And so on. And so on. The Gin Whistle. The Kilted Pig. Time passing. Seasons' change. There was Grapes of Wrath, and before that, too, The Elm Tree and The Walker's Friend, still time passing, always passing. The Cork and Bottle, passing still. Wound all the way back to winter's dark, time, and forwards again to the fullness of late spring, summer in the air and an intense gin from Suffolk with 'hints of pomegranate' served in tiny tin tumblers with a tonic that barely fizzed and a pea placed carefully in the bottom, no ice cubes at all. How far we'd come, Evan and I from the black Labrador beginnings of our story. So far to find ourselves now somewhere with an ending still quite far away. A place all of tall windows and grey sofas, of natural light and the sun coming down upon our heads as we sat indoors. While the rest of the world drifted outside to the pavement and the music was taken up there that would make others want to dance, not us, for there we remained, set in among the grey sofas in a grey room, no matter how sunny it was outside, we were set, Evan and I, in pale shades of grey.

# six

By now it was indeed nearly summer, but, yes, I, too, was wearing pale grey. As grey as grey, as winter's skies, and cold rain showers, as grey as Evan who may have been dressed in jeans, alright, but had on a greyish jersey as well; a 'jumper' we would have called it when we were little, wearing jumpers my mother had knitted for both of us in matching wools, both of us going exploring in the green beyond the end of our road, before the new houses were built there. By now we were both of such similar colours, Evan and I, in mood and appearance all in the hushed tones of shadows, of the grave. And this despite the long days, the light and warmth . . . It was as though we were both fading away: me into writing, becoming someone who did nothing more than report other lives, and Evan because of his simple but devastating unrequited love for Caroline Beresford, a woman who, though she lived right there with him in a large house in Richmond, may as well have been a young girl attending a Florentine church in an early fourteenth-century poem,* a glittering icon herself in some cathedral there, all gold and candle-lit and burning, while her lover loitered in some shadowy corner unseen by any saint or mother of God . . . So we

* There are some notes on Petrarch's story, how he came across Laura after a certain Easter service, naturally it's in the relevant section at the back of the book.

continued. All grey, grey, more grey. Late May gone into June and soon it would be July and the schools breaking up and everyone away on holiday then; every day it was getting warmer and warmer.

The Beresfords, Evan said, had been invited to a party.

'A party?' I said, jolted into awareness.

Indeed, a party – he'd seen the invitation, he said – with cocktails and beach towels and swimwear, a suburban sort of thing, in Richmond, with shades of LA.

'A pool party, Nin,' Evan said. 'Imagine it.'

'Well . . .' I stirred the remains of a drink in my glass.

'That's not for the likes of us, Evan,' I replied.

For he had not, of course he had not, been invited. It was an invitation extended to the Beresfords at No. 47 from the Caxton Taylors down the road at No. 23. All of Chestnut Way would be going, Evan said. Homeowners, that was to say, and their families. Not lodgers. That kind of party would be another kind of scene altogether.

'Hmmm . . .' I continued. For this kind of talk seemed irrelevant. We were only to continue sitting there, it seemed, fabricating together our 'story'. Fabricating, writing . . . Exempt from all invitations, simply sitting quietly like old, old people in the new place I'd found, a small and singular establishment named The Pincushion ('and Thistle' it also said in brackets, though we never referred to it that way), on my way back from the Seed one night. It was the kind of pub with no outdoor seating whatsoever but only a single room, though spacious enough, with little in the way of lemon rinds and nuts and tamarinds, or fancy decor and Italian sofas . . . A perfect place, you might say, for those of us who have no pool parties to go to, no place in the sun, who prefer to dress in grey.

There, in the cool interior, we continued. I had my papers. Evan had his ideas. It was a good choice, this new find of mine, for our meetings. It had the quietness, the table space we needed. It had the kind of interior that seemed never to have felt a breath of fresh air. I had first glimpsed it after a particularly intense evening with Evan at the Child, when he'd wanted to go back there, to that place of tears and confession, to go through some journal extracts with me – all based on details of Caroline's weekly schedule following the night she went 'up', that was all shopping and telephone calls and lunches with friends. She'd said, 'I'm so sorry about last night,' to Evan the next evening, when they passed each other at the front door and he was coming in from work and she was leaving to meet friends for drinks. She'd given him a hug and said, 'I'm sorry I was so ghastly last night, but you'll forgive me, won't you?' Sounding so light-hearted and merry, Evan reported, in journal notes, that it was hard to believe she'd been upset the night before, adding, 'It's these pills the doctor has me on,' with a radiant smile. 'Honestly, I think they make me completely mental! I should be locked up!' and laughing. Evan noted in fountain pen after this section of reported speech that he hadn't known what to say. Her scent was everywhere, he wrote, something orangey and bright. She was wearing a tiny dress and cardigan and high, high gold sandals, running out the door and on her way to the car, calling back over her shoulder, 'The boys have had tea but there are some oven chips left over if you fancy them! Let's catch up tomorrow before you go to work! I'll be up early and we can grab a coffee!'

In this way, then, we continued. Away from others, out of the season's time, cut off from the world. I had my work, my writing of this down, my life. Despite Christopher and Marjorie who otherwise I might have completely forgotten about phoning me on a weekly basis to please go out, get some sun, meet up with them, take on extra advertising work or whatever, I was pretty deeply involved by now in the project of Evan. 'This book of his is taking all my time,' I texted Christopher when he sent me a message: '???', and, 'I'll get back to the pet food campaign next month,' I promised Marjorie in the same way, and 'No he doesn't want to,' as I left as a message on Rosie's machine, after she'd left one on mine telling me that she thought I should tell Evan to leave Richmond. Despite all these imprecations, suggestions, commands, even, from friends. 'It's crazy you're spending so much time with Evan,' Christopher had said to me, point blank, after calling me one night to invite me on a street-cleaning rally and barbecue. 'And what about work?' he'd added, the old practical sums-and-ledgers side of him coming out once again to play. 'It's not as if you can afford to pass on the assignments Marjorie sends on to you. And when were you last at that liberal gallery of yours, too, for that matter? She tells me you're doing nothing with your time that's economically viable or sound.' As was true. I wasn't. I'd forgotten all about my catalogue research and writing and my going along to man the front desk in Hoxton. I'd forgotten when Marjorie had last emailed me a pitch. Yes,

I was aware of all the work outstanding, outstanding, in my capacity as a freelance writer, even so I was unable to do anything but go through and through Evan's many pages of notes, and writing, and my own. Sorting, sifting. Telling Christopher I'd call him back. Arranging. Texting Marjorie, 'Soon.' Trying to make, all the time, of so many quick hugs and merry laughs a great love story, grand drama, a novel that would light up the reader with excitement and sense of increase.*

One thing I had, and it was important, was a list of all the elements comprising Evan's quarters under the eaves. I needed these elements for 'context'. There we were, going through the list, on a warm night in late June, the only people in The Pincushion, a strange kind of place, when I look at it objectively – what a name for a pub! – for why were we there, in the back streets of Acton, not close to Richmond, and certainly far away from me? It was a list made up of items, contents . . . that were contained within 'My Lodger's Quarters', as Evan had headed up one of his pages. There was a flatplan neatly drawn up in a kind of grid to show the different features of the room – 'Bed Area', 'Window Recess', 'Door Entranceway', etc. – all details that had come into play the fateful night Caroline, emotional, tired, influenced heavily by both alcohol and prescription medication, had gone up to Evan's room and knocked on the door and he had said, 'Come in.'

---

* i.e. that the world might become a bigger and more interesting place thanks to a good novel. See the note, later on, 'Narrative Construction', with its reference to Katherine Anne Porter and her idea of literary 'increase', if interested. No need at all if not.

All these elements were to provide, as he put it, 'key context'.

'Key context? What do you mean?' I'd said it too, when he first brought up the phrase months and months ago, when this whole thing first began.

But Evan had just smiled, sadly and mysteriously. As though 'context' were all.

As I say, by now an invitation had arrived at the Beresfords'. It had come in a week or so ago, for a party down the road that was to be held in early July. I wasn't sure why this particular invitation was so relevant – after all, the Beresfords received a great number of party, dinner, drinks invitations – but it seemed to have taken hold of Evan's imagination even so. He had mentioned it several times, 'Imagine. A "pool party" in London, Nin! Can you imagine it?' and 'Can you even think of such a thing?'

I had to shake my head. I couldn't. We were sitting in a reproduction nineteenth-century tavern in Acton – how far away from a 'pool party' could we be? From all that glamour? Blue water? A fully developed patio area with built-in barbecue and booth seating? The very idea of it, the lit-up afternoon picture of it . . . All belonged somewhere else, far, far away from where my own imagination resided. Such a party was nowhere near where our book was set, as far as I was concerned, in a street of family houses, with traditional gardens, trees in leaf. But still Evan kept returning to it, perhaps it was all those visits to California he'd alluded to in that strange writing, the confessional notes about a failed relationship in Palo Alto, that so took him up, a reminder of a past life. Or maybe it was simply the excitement of the invitation itself, printed in bright colours on thick, expensive card, the dress code 'Swimwear' there on the bottom right-hand corner. Either way, he couldn't stop referring to the exact nature of the event – 'Pool Party' – that he'd seen advertised so gaily on the kitchen mantelpiece, next to the Beresfords' 'Daily Planner Noticeboard' that had the date for the same circled in Caroline's own hand.

When I questioned him about his interest, his answer was that the party was indeed 'relevant'. As far as he was concerned, the night when Caroline 'came up', as Evan handily described things – a sort of summary for her arriving in his room that way, that night, dishevelled but still as lovely as ever – had been 'the start of something'. The pool party, to his mind, seemed to continue that 'something', would be part of it and was therefore 'relevant', he said, he was sure. Conversations, he believed, following the arrival of the invitation, that took place at the Beresfords' were more open, honest, than they had been before, Evan was sure of this. Even David had said that the idea of a pool party was fun and that he would definitely go along with the boys, would organise some kind of watersports activity they could all be part of. Caroline had told Evan this, along with other details about her marriage – his disinterest in their domestic life on the whole, in their social life, his time increasingly being spent at the office, or in the flat he rented near UCL where he was now coming to the end of his first undergraduate degree and 'looking at getting a distinction grade' in Greek, as he'd told her, but using the time in general, to be away, in some classics library or other, some don's room or research facility, meeting place, from her.

These details, as Caroline put it to Evan, were 'the facts'.

So it was that when she 'came up' that night there had been a confrontation, of sorts, between her and David some days before, Caroline raising the issue of some of the same 'facts', conveyed by a mutual friend, the details of which she need not concern herself but thought David should be aware of by now, that his absences, time away, hours spent on those courses of his delivered on and around the Bloomsbury campus of the University of London . . . were having an effect. On their family life. Social life. On the boys. His lack of presence a growing issue in their marriage by now, whether he was away or at home, because even when at home he would only be in his study, a book on his lap and those long legs of his stretched out in front of him, all the time in the world, reading, making notes, practising the Greek alphabet in a little Moleskine notebook he kept now, always, in his pocket.

These 'facts' were of the essence, according to Evan, that 'context' of his. Not that Caroline drank three more pre-dinner cocktails than was usual when David told her he would be late for the dinner party she'd organised at their home, that she'd shopped and cooked for, planned for weeks, that something was demanding his attention at work. Nor that she had had half a bottle of wine on her own after talking with him later on the phone, when the guests had gone, and that on top of the two Ativan she had taken before their arrival, no. That she 'came up' in relation to the former facts of David's life, to put the event in that wider 'context', was of the essence here. After holding so much to herself, keeping so much in . . . According to Evan, again, that is. That she 'came up' in the light of a large, large sorrow and from that so much could be confected . . . That was the vital substance here.

For until that evening, as he reminded me in his notes, Caroline never 'came up' to see Evan. Oh, she 'came up' in general, as it were. The lodgings were always scrupulously tidy because Caroline would go up there herself and 'finish off', as she put it, once her lovely cleaner, Esme, who only came once a week, had completed going through the whole house, top to bottom, including the lodger's quarters. Caroline would put out fresh flowers and towels, then, new soaps – there were always dear little soaps in the dishes, I am imagining, in that compact but nicely designed bathroom of his underneath the eaves – soaps rather in the style of the small cakes of good soap available in nice hotels.

'Yes, Nin,' Evan confirmed. 'There are always fresh flowers after she's been in,' he said, confirming, too, Caroline's status in this whole story as a kind of Laura or Beatrice.* Or as one of the later incarnations of those same women who appeared in the so-called Cavalier Lyrics of Herrick and Carew, those objects of desire and affection for whom were strewed flowers in their wake, as it were, as 'To gather flowers, Sappha went/And homeward she did

---

* Laura and Beatrice were much younger than Caroline Beresford but she shares with them certain attributes of flowers. In 'Courtly Love', later, there are details of the motifs of flora and fauna in Petrarch's work; see also the section marked 'Evan's Living Arrangements'.

bring . . . The treasure of the Spring', Herrick has it, in 'The Apron of Flowers', also underlining things somewhat with his 'Fresh strewings allow . . . To make my lodging the sweeter' in another poem. Yes, there was a precedent exactly for establishing the role of the kind of woman who could be thought of in terms of fresh flowers in the history of romance writing and courtly love. There was backstory there, built in.

'Caroline fits that bill,' I'd said, many, many weeks earlier in The Kilted Pig, over a Gordon's silver with lime tonic and crushed ice. 'Flowers . . .' I'd said then, all that time ago. 'Yes. I get it. I do.'

So, in this way, from right back then, would Evan become increasingly used to the presence of Caroline in his 'quarters' – though he himself were not there, still he would be aware of her presence in his room, and it would add to things, I could see that, week by week, the intensity of his mood. The fact that she had been in, had 'come up', and this long before the actual night when she knocked on the door. Increasingly, altogether, in our story was a sense of Caroline and her various habits – I had already written at some length about this in an earlier appendix to the earlier part of this second section – of the extent and depth of her presence in Evan's life, quoting him verbatim, from something that had come up back in the late winter in the Edge:

'She constantly replaces flowers in my room.'

If that's not the lyrics for a Leonard Cohen song, I might have replied to Evan then, but didn't, wouldn't, 'Then I don't know what is,' I said out loud now, in the muffled confines of the 'Pin'.

'What?' said Evan.

'Oh, nothing,' I replied. 'I was thinking out loud . . .'

And what flowers, I continued to ponder. Over the months that our story had passed through they would have bloomed continually, in all manner of simile and metaphor. There would have been early spring bulbs at first, all that would have been available back in the dark midwinter when the narrative began, then blossom, just a sprig or two, daffodils – there'd been an announcement of a single daffodil so long ago! – then roses. More roses, then, from Caroline's garden, standard, dwarf and patio, climbing and scented, taking us through May and into June; and onwards to a time of the year when it was warm and the leaves by now were full and dense and a thick, bright green in all the trees, and summer cushions were to be seen on the outdoor furniture of the Beresfords' garden, tubes of suncream were dotted around the terrace as though Richmond had become the South of France, or Italy . . . Not London at all, but somewhere else far away and dreaming.

No wonder the mind turned to a 'pool party' then, under circumstances such as these. No wonder my own mind, with Evan's level of interest in the event and the season warming up, so turned. There were the three Beresford boys running around the garden with their shirts off when they got home from the last days of summer term, just before the schools broke up. Caroline herself sunbathing on the grass, a bright summer cushion beneath her head . . . Richmond at this time of year was like a glamorous faraway place indeed but right here in London – the large houses with their three cars parked out on the gravel in the driveways, and, yes, there were swimming pools, in some gardens, yes, there were and one of which, down the road at No. 23, being celebrated by a party.

'Even David is going,' Evan said; he couldn't leave the subject alone. We were hunched and overdressed in our grey woollen jerseys in the snug of the Pin, nursing the same warm gins as we'd ordered when we met there. 'He's normally busy in the weekends, with Classics revision and so on,' he continued, 'but in this case . . .' His voice trailed off. He'd already told me about how excited the whole street seemed to be over the plans for down the road. It was to be a big party with most of the neighbours coming and a great group of the Caxton Taylors' friends. They were, as Caroline had told Evan, 'super-social', the Caxton Taylors, and the party was going to be quite something. Might Evan even go himself?

'Might you?' I asked him now, but he shook his head.

'Not our kind of thing, Nin,' he said. 'We've agreed that already.'

And I had to nod along with him, like the old married couple we seemed to be imitating.

'You know perfectly well that a "pool party" is not the sort of event you and I can imagine,' he went on, 'and besides, as I've told you, it's not for lodgers.' He drained his ice-less glass. 'Fancy another?' he said, indicating our empties. 'Let's get back to the story in hand.'

Well, alright, so there were flowers in his room.

That was where the story was. I had written that down.

That there were wild flowers by his bed the night she 'came up'. Well, what else, Evan? Eh? What else?

Well, by now, of course, I can say, I easily can, that Evan was more in love with Caroline than ever, more deeply caring, attentive. I can say that. By now I was fully trained in my role, was no more than the writer, after all, and so could write up something like that – 'Evan was more in love with her than ever' – just as easy as whistle. Though he hadn't said a word to her about it afterwards, her coming up, and though she herself had only uttered those few casual sentences on her way out the door in high gold sandals, still those few words had been as nourishment, encouragement; his own silence giving him a kind of energy, fuel.

We'd decided to try somewhere new. Something about The Pincushion (and Thistle) . . . We liked it, but we wanted a change. Summer in the air, perhaps? Something.

'And all those conversations between the two of you after that night,' I said. 'There wasn't a moment when you – ?'

'Listen, Nin,' he interrupted me. The new pub was called Ripeness Is All, not that far from the Pin but more Chiswick than Acton, altogether closer to the river, which seemed like a nice kind of idea, at this time of year when the world was wanting to be out on or near the water, here we were, near water at least, in another reproduction tavern that was like something out of *The Sweeney*, with not a hint of the Shakespearean mood as suggested by its name about it, only an old seventies air and not fancy at all – they probably even served a full 'Ploughman's Lunch' if Evan and I were ever to want to eat, which it seemed we did not.

'Listen,' he said again. 'Everything about this love story defies contemporary convention. You should know that by now. You're writing it down. So you should know perfectly well that the convention we are serving is not the contemporary one, but much older, it's graver somehow. God,' he said. 'If you were a poet, we would be creating an epic here, in sonnets, rhyming or in blank verse. But in prose, Nin. Prose. It may be we're doing something no one else has done in modern life. Not that I'm aware of anyway.'*

I looked blank myself, probably, talking of verse, but it was only because I was tired. Since talking with Christopher recently I'd become aware of how behind I was getting in my knowledge of current affairs, politics. It was like the world was passing me by. Christopher had called to invite me on one of his scary, quite martially inclined marches to do with cycle lanes and the proliferation of disabled parking bays in Central London and I'd just had to say 'No,' but was aware, as I was responding, how long it had been since I'd seen any of my friends. 'Rosie will be in town,' Christopher had said. 'She would love to see you as well, you know. We all would. What is this thing you are writing after all? A telephone book? It seems to have been going on for ages and Marjorie said you won't be able to get any more work from the agency if you don't start taking up some of the campaign slack, Emily. She's been giving you lots of chances. So how are you managing, anyhow? You need to work, don't you? We all do!'

---

* For a long time I wondered about including, within 'Alternative Narratives', details of the working method of *Caroline's Bikini*, along with a possible Questionnaire regarding efficacy of its approach, sense of its literary credentials, Evan's writing, etc. I am always keen to hear back from Readers, I suppose, and the Questionnaire had that in mind.

The fact is, Christopher had hit a nerve. People with right-wing tendencies often do, I've found, when it comes down to the advice they give to their financially challenged lefty friends. It's because they themselves are working all the time and know how easy it is to lose money – in their case, significant amounts of it – as well as make it, of course, and keep on making it, by doing nothing but thinking about it all the time, money. And, it's true, things hadn't been going very well on the work front. And I did have bills that needed to be paid. So Christopher was right, in his Tory way. Maybe I would miss a payment on my mortgage if I carried on as I was, this book taking me away from the world, yet I seemed to have no choice.

For as Evan's need to meet me had increased, so had I felt that I must meet that need; so as the amount he had to say about his situation with Caroline mounted, I too felt I had a lot to say. My papers, chapter headings, sections . . . They were mounting. By now I knew the colour of the carpet on the stairs up to the second floor where Evan's room was situated, the sort of jeans Caroline wore when she went to her one and only Pilates class first thing on a Monday morning and sometimes she and Evan met by the front door.

'Gorgeous to see you as ever,' she would say to Evan then, fishing for car keys in the bag where she kept her exercise clothes. Calling out from the car, through the open window, as she reversed down the drive, 'I can't wait to see you when you get home later! Can you and I have a drink together and one of our special talks?' And the look of her, reversing down that drive, waving once, and then she'd be gone. Caroline. Leaving Evan to walk out the gate and turn down the road where she'd just driven. Having to stop and calm himself, stem the roiling waves of nausea and anxiety that had set up such a reaction in him due to Caroline's words, her proximity, her tone, her touch.

His love for her was deepening, as was my own involvement, mortgage or no mortgage. Everything was becoming more cyclical, ongoing and in a state of movement but also static, fixed. The flowers were replaced, ever fragrant. It was as if they never died. So, too, Caroline had been 'up' to Evan's room ages ago by now but it might have happened yesterday, the way Evan talked about it, the way I, too, considered the scene in my mind. Or, by contrast and just as easily, taken place many many months ago indeed, years even; so it was as though an event that had only taken place in a dream. Caroline would talk, she had no trouble talking and would talk and talk and talk to Evan – despite, because of, going up – about her family, marriage, the children . . . Privacy wasn't an issue for her. So one could say this thing had happened between her and the man who had come to lodge in her home, this intimate private exchange that had taken place in his room, but it was just like the flowers she replaced each week . . . The minute the situation had become something that had happened it was as though it could be, quite simply, overwritten by some other, fresher memory.

Altogether it could have been as if, as I wrote down, to finish the end of the second section of this book, her sitting there on Evan's bed – there on the bed of a man who was not really very known to her – was normal. The most natural thing in the world. Because it could be replaced, any gesture, covered over, fresh flowers given. As if anything she might do that could be forgotten about would be normal, unremarkable, not worthy of discussion even, or apology or explanation. Because all this, everything I am writing down, was – her gestures seemed to say – really all of it was simply the most natural, quotidian, unexceptional series of events that might unfold in a life, a narrative of experience, feeling . . . It all had novel-ish texture, and depth, in that way. A reflection of life, and so on. Is what we hoped anyhow, Evan and I. And that it might indeed even be a love story, in the end, if we kept on with it. Certainly these pages we'd written were real.

**Go!**

# one

In fact, 'natural', that word . . . Really, it is at the heart of this story. For who on this earth has not known a similar love? Natural. Ordinary. Unselfconscious. The kind of love that seems so straightforward, so easy, honest and assured; other forms of romantic attachment seem artificial and highly wrought by comparison, freighted as they are by great force of expression. By contrast, how clear, how singular and constant is unrequited love, the object for whom it burns largely unaware of the intensity of heat. So the flame goes higher, burns deeper. And yes, natural, are these concepts, these ideas. That such loves might occur in most lives, in these kinds of ways – to a lesser degree perhaps, for many, that they might not have become a lodger in the way that Evan Gordonston so lodged, that they might not wish to create a document, a written story or record of their desire in order that they may make real their condition – seems something worth considering in this age of imposed feeling generated by the industries of film and entertainment with their endless replications of the same story, always the same, coinciding with shopping and the busy activities and lusts of consumption. Unspoken love, by contrast, is as natural as the air, the weather. As apt to change lives as the other sort, though rarely acknowledged, is what happens in the end when the heart has become engaged, the capacity of the mind increased.

Its silence enlarges the scale of the world.

By now it was fully summer. That conversation Evan and I had had, when he'd told me about Caroline coming up to his room and showing to him fully, in her manner and conversation, how upset she was, presenting herself to him in a way that showed all her unhappiness . . . That had taken place in what I still thought of as another season, late spring, it belonged to a different time. Though nothing had changed, Evan still not able to speak fully to Caroline, show her some emotion of his own, despite the width of her confession, her telling him of her sense of being at a loss in the world, as though there were nowhere else she could turn but to that little attic room, that there was no one else she could go to but the man who lived beneath her eaves . . . Still, it seemed that that had happened a long time ago and the story had moved on, come fully into itself with its own definitions and terms. That Evan was the man who might give Caroline solace, on that one particular night, seemed to denote it. We had our 'novel' somehow, word by word, it was there.

For how things were to take a turn. How they were to change.

Evan was tired. I had been able to see it collecting around him for some time, an air of gradual fatigue. It was there in his clothing, as seen, his posture, his appearance sitting before me, the way he felt when he hugged me goodnight. It was almost as though, as the days were getting lighter and longer and warmer, as the doors and windows of houses were being opened into the summer air, more and more of Evan Gordonston was being held back and limited in expression, more closed into himself he seemed than ever, and reserved. That wearing of the jerseys that I had seen, even when it was far too warm for wool, and the condition of those garments – stained and threadbare and fretted with holes – indicated a general malaise, a ruination of sorts, one might say, a desperation, represented by the worn-out attitude of his dress. There was a darkness about him, a wintry silence that seemed to hang about that corner of any pub in which we might meet, The Pincushion, then, more and more, Ripeness Is All. And where once we might have sat, so happily, it seems, looking back on it, in The Kilted Pig, say, or A Tulip's Edge, talking about life and love and Caroline, the sunlit times that would be ahead, the plans that could be made and followed through with gifts and holidays and bouquets of roses . . . Now to think about these aspects of love, these romantic details that might be the very definition of Evan's feelings for Caroline, seemed part of another story, another life, altogether.

The simply named Last Stand had been the most recent place where Evan and I would meet. A pub quite near Ealing, as though Evan himself no longer had the imagination to stray far in his mind from the site of that beautiful landlady's home to which he paid his monthly dues and could think of nowhere else, not really.

And that we might choose the Stand! At this time of year! When the rest of the world was at the river or in the park, or sitting outside at one of the many bars and restaurants and cafes in West London, there we were, in a traditional hostelry with dim lighting and a downtrodden feel – an indication of the state of the protagonist and his amanuensis, both. Though there'd been times in this story when Evan and I had ventured outdoors – those early days of me meeting him off the tube, remember? And walking around the corner to my local, or the Elm that was just across Brook Green, or that night we loitered outside The Gin Whistle, amongst all the other people who were there, as though we might be part of that merry crowd, and take, along with them, our drinks to an outside table . . . They were gone now. We would not sit outside. The whole attitude of that . . . merriment . . . that had reigned then, in contrast to the present mood, back there in the winter and early spring, rattling the ice in our gin and tonics as we discussed this idea or that, where Caroline had gone last night, what the boys said about their mother's serving, yet again, even though they were teenagers, of fish fingers for tea. Or talking about David's shirts, perhaps, and how Caroline always bought them for him from traditional gentlemen's outfitters in Jermyn Street, David's witty comments about the quality of the checks or stripes . . . Now we were no longer people of that ilk. There was no more discussion of that sort to be had. There was rarely a person inside the Stand, in June, late June with the sun high in the zenith, yet there we were, nevertheless, two people, two old, old friends.

So we sat, hunched over empty glasses, the lemon rind sucked dry and no ice to melt. There we were, wrung out as those rinds, is how it felt, with nothing left to say about it, this story, all feelings emptied into Caroline as though she contained them all. Everything that we might feel or think or respond to, every thought, every emotion . . . Down, down into Caroline had gone all our selves, all our dreams and hopes and will, imagination and words and sense of metaphor and simile, illustration, sound sense . . . Down, down and down and only Caroline was left, this figure with her blonde hair pulled back into a twist, adopting beach wear and thin summer dresses and sandals now that July was nearly here, her long tanned legs striding through Evan's life as though she'd never used them to ascend the stairs and come, that night, to his room, late, as though her bare feet finished in toenail polish the colour of poppies were unknown to the carpet that was fitted fully through the lodger's studio beneath the eaves.

So Caroline. Caroline. And what was left of Evan but this shell of a man now, grey husk, with no one to be with but me? What was left of me?

Things had been going badly at work. Evan's preoccupation with 'the situation at the end of the Green Line', as he came to refer to it, had meant his standards had dropped off, his levels of expertise blunted, his acumen blurred. It seemed he had botched a major deal and then, when the client had complained, laughed in his face and sent around a general email, copied in to his CEO, headed 'No Biggie' with a smiley face as a full stop. I did wonder whether Evan was going a little bit 'doolally', his mother Helen would call it, a term that may have been lost along with a whole number of personal anachronisms and expressions of that family once they had moved to America. It happened, after all, love causing derangement of the senses, erratic behaviours, unpredictability, there was massive precedent for it.* Evan had never been that great at looking after himself – I remembered that from when we were children, how he could go hours at a time without thinking about whether he was cold or hot, hungry or thirsty, soaking wet with rain or sunburned – and though years had passed between our childhood games and this livid present tense, still, I could see remnants of that careless boy I had loved to play with more than any other. It seemed, it is completely true, as if he just didn't want to bother with thinking about himself. As in those far-off days he could be hungry and not even consider going home for a sandwich, much less ask me for so much as a crisp from my packet – though I would have given him the entire contents of that bag and more, and asked my mother to make him a lovely lunch, to boot, with biscuits and fruit to follow – so now he waned and would not petition. In my flat I had a cupboard full of pasta, rice, enriching grains; I went shopping at the supermarket once or twice a month; there was nothing I couldn't have cooked for him, grilled or boiled or stewed . . . Yet as before when he had been a boy who could be so involved in a game, some adventure or other, as though it was only ever just the two of us alive together and as though the outside world did not exist, so now he seemed to have no mind for anything else but Richmond, to be entirely within the confines of that drama, appetite gone, and was fading away before me, getting thinner and thinner, more and more pale.

*By now, of course, we are well aware of this. But readers having missed earlier references might want to look later at the section marked 'Courtly Love'.

Indeed, that quality of his, of being disconnected from the world, was out and showing – a quality of forced looking deep inside his own invented world is how I might put it. Just as when he was a boy there was a concentration, focus on one thing, so it was as if any of the smaller, practical aspects of life didn't exist, to the extent that now it was as though he barely noticed me as well. He said, 'Hi,' when he came into the pub, sure, or when I arrived and he was sitting there in the dark corner, still his eyes focused on me in that kind, endearing way when he smiled, but there was no energy around his greeting, no enthusiasm, no jump or bump or go. It had been a long time since he'd shouted out, like a cowboy, from the bar of Child o' Mine: 'Just write it down, Nin! That's all you've got to do!' The seasons had turned, life moving inexorably onwards. It had been fully six months since he'd first laid eyes on Caroline Beresford and, apart from that night when she'd come up to his room and sat on the bed, nothing had happened. Nothing had happened at all.

For there'd been no further developments to our novel, nothing doing by way of narrative arc, since Caroline had sat on the bed in his room under the eaves, with Evan coming to sit next to her, and when she had, as it turns out she did, put her hand up to the side of Evan's face before leaning towards him and Evan, so shocked still with desire and surprise, could not, I think, for a second, respond and by the time he went to react it was too late, the moment had passed, and Caroline was saying, 'Oh I am so terribly sorry, Evan. It's these crazy pills the doctor gave me. They make me do crazy things . . .'

Yes, despite all that, even, a gesture of such magnitude one might think it would have appeared earlier in the story . . . That it would have been written down much earlier than at this late stage of proceedings . . . Still, nothing. No gift of further touch or look in any of this that a writer could use and adumbrate, no surprise remark or small expression of affection that would make Evan have, that simple word, 'hope'. As in, the phrase he kept using constantly now, that old cliche, well worn and done in: 'I've not a hope in hell with Caroline.' It was as though he'd never ever believed he and Caroline could be . . . might be . . . close.

So it could have been, so it seemed by his behaviour, I was starting to think, the writer was thinking, as though that fateful night had never happened. Had it? I found myself asking. Had anything happened there, really, in which case: What about this novel, eh? I wondered. I did.

'She hasn't referred to it,' Evan had reported, shortly after the incident. That was back in the days when I would 'press' him for more information, 'press' him, too, to act, to 'bring the story on' as I put it. But as those same days went on it turned out Caroline was never to say anything significant about that night. She had reverted fully to her ebullient self, full of jokes and laughter and endless telephone calls and plans to go out, and whenever she was to talk to Evan it was only to say something funny or to ask him, 'Will you be a darling and put the kettle on?' Really, it was as though the events that had taken place on that dramatic night, when it was late, after Caroline had been entertaining and doing this on her own because where was

David Beresford in all this? That man so caught up with his classical education and Greek translation classes at the University of London, when he was supposed to be home with her? Only in Bloomsbury. Indeed, how the contents of a particular sort of novel or TV reality series might reflect so well this situation of a certain sort of marriage, the relationship between Caroline and David Beresford, the husband all too often absent at the table which his wife had laid so nicely and furnished to the great pleasure of all her guests with the produce and effects of the Tante Marie cookery classes completed when she was a young woman. For only absent, more and more, was David from the family home. That's a straightforward story to tell, that one, after all. How that man was gone, gone, gone while Caroline was serving, drinking. Doing all that on her own, and not for the first time, by no means; this last instance of David's absence that had caused her to go 'up' only one in a long line of his calls from the office, his 'I won't be able to make it tonight after all,' or 'I'll be back much later. Don't wait for me,' as I can only imagine, as Evan himself attempted to imagine, in some notes he made and passed subsequently to me . . . And all the time Caroline herself having to manage everything, greeting the guests, entertaining them, talking with them, seeing them to the door . . .

And David had never come home, those Latin and Greek conjugations of his burning in her mind as much as the knowledge of his empty, open absence. The embarrassment of that, socially, the shame. That 'Introduction to Classical Greek' might have him ignore his wife and family, stay away in a private flat taken solely for the purposes of study and concentration, for his workbooks and assessment papers, where he had a desk all set up for his various kinds of homework and translation, Latin into English, and English into Greek . . . Were it not for the fact that Evan's and my text must be entwined for the very nature of our shared endeavour to succeed, so to be focused on Caroline and Evan alone, I mean, I would say all this kind of additional material was the stuff of novels indeed.

'I've given all this a great deal of thought, you see,' Evan said to me, 'in the various ways David has made himself absent from Caroline, but at the end of the day, it's not that relevant, Nin.'

For at the end of the day, there was Caroline, who was, as he reminded me, the only story that really needed to be told, the object of all his feelings, alone. Last thing at night and the boys have been in their rooms for hours, the final guest farewelled and out the door, and, really, I can imagine all this, so easily, see it in my own mind's eye, not only through Evan's, her going into the kitchen to finish off the half bottle of French Chardonnay that was left, starting to stack plates and glasses . . . All this preceding, a drama in its own way, the great drama that was her going up the stairs having thrown back the best part of a bottle of that good white Burgundy, glass still in hand, to tap upon Evan's door.

'She didn't refer to it,' Evan would come to say, over and over, in the darkening days of mood that followed the event, long after, despite the onset of summer, summer's light. 'Not as such,' he would say. 'Not as a thing she had done, or felt. It was as though it had never happened . . .'

And his voice trailed away then and the shadows seemed to deepen around him even as the days were light and warm and filled with promise and I looked at him with equal deepening of concern and attention.

'Never,' he said, his eyes cast down, and as dark, it seemed to me, as the shadows that coursed around his feet and cast a dark spread upon his gaunt cheekbones, sent ribbons of dark down the length of his body, his pensioner-style corduroy-clad legs and second-hand lambswool-bound arms . . . All dark, dark. Oh Evan. What were you doing dressed for winter walks when it was June? As though we were still in January and now it was nearly July?

For it was. By now. Full summer outdoors, and hot. June gone into July – the month of holidays and heat and suntan lotion and beach towels. The days would be long and dreamy and in Richmond there was the matter of that invitation that had arrived at No. 47 Chestnut Way:

## POOL PARTY

It had been dispatched, as we know, some weeks before, delivered confidently by hand in a large thick white envelope, pink tissue-lined, with a tiny beach ball printed on the back flap. The Caxton Taylors had made a statement.

'They have money,' Evan reported, when he'd first told me about it, back when the invitation had arrived. 'The whole thing, the invite, and so on . . . It's been printed especially for the party, Nin,' he said, and went on to describe how the beach ball motif played out on the card

inside the envelope, which was printed in pink and yellow
and green. All letterpress printing, too, he added. 'Caroline says they're loaded.' So the message had been hand-
delivered to the Beresfords in the manner of neighbours,
with all the details they might need. Below the words 'Pool
Party' figured in smaller font: a barbecue and cocktails,
special picnic food for the children. 'Dress: Swimwear', it
said, on the bottom right-hand corner. Evan made a point
of telling me. 'Time: 2 pm 'til Late.'

How could Evan and I know, I thought, when he'd first
told me about the invitation landing on the Beresfords'
mat at No. 47, sitting as we had been back then in The
Swan and Seed, that such tidings of blue chlorinated water
and sunshine could so flood a story that until now had
seemed set in its ways, somehow, well 'set', a tale of desire
and feeling and unrequited love that operated within its
own boundaries and constraints? A story of enclosed pubs
and sequestered meetings? Who would have guessed, the
story's narrator, amanuensis, could surely not have, that a
card sitting on a mantelpiece beside the Beresfords' 'Daily
Planner' might come to play such a large part in the proceedings of a prose work she was attempting; that a simple
invitation might come to direct so much of a text's future
actions and outcome that it may force the whole notion
of 'novel' from one's consciousness, only to make of its
writing something else, instead?

That it could do that? Change everything?

For these days all poor Evan could say to me was, over
and over, 'It was as if the events of that night had never
happened.' As though Caroline coming up to his room

and his failure to act were the only things that would ever take place in this story. As though the meaning of an invitation, its strange otherness and bright fluorescent printed call to a swimming pool in a garden in Richmond, would remain unknown and hidden; as though swimwear itself, the fact of it, imagined now soaked by the same chlorinated water as was advertised on a beach-ball-printed card and left puddled on the floor in the kitchen, in this story, would have no part to play at all.

# two

It was starting to seem, too, in general, as though to match this fresh sense of stasis, that the writing was changing.

'Novel? Hah!' I managed one night in the gloom of the Stand. 'Let's return to the idea of . . . Report. Or essay, maybe, Evan,' I said. 'Or a hybrid piece, part essay, part . . . Intervention. Reflection. I don't know how to describe it. But with the pool party, all that . . . We're moving into new territory, it seems . . .'

For certainly it was the case that our single piece of dramatic plot, our hope of a 'novel', so to speak, that scene of Caroline's going 'up', and all its implications and backstory and projections . . . Well, 'it may as well have never happened,' as Evan put it. It seemed by now that the activity that had occurred in the narrow confines of his lodger's quarters had been a dream Evan had had one night and from which he had woken, confused, still wrapped up by the dream, maybe, and with it the memory of an attempted kiss, the touch preceding it, all that there in his mind, but in full knowledge, too, that none of the things that had taken place had really happened. In the same way as we might kiss people in dreams, or try to, and when we see them in the flesh can look them full in the eye and know that we have never kissed them, so it was between Evan and Caroline. They look back at us, those with whom we have been intimate in our minds, and there is nothing in their look that would suggest they know anything about it. 'I am a friend only,' their look says. 'A dear, close friend you have known for a long, long time, but I could never be in love with you.'

And with Evan now, going back to the narrative in hand, it was as though the drama of Caroline's attempted kiss was no more than a figment. A dream of a kiss. A story he had conjured from his unconsciousness but nothing substantial there that he could use to build hopes on, make plans. It had simply been this rogue, wayward thing, a gesture, a moment, with the growing silences of Evan, when we met, in the gloomy rooms of the Stand, suggesting that he was pushing to the very furthest recesses of his mind the touch of Caroline that had come upon him that night, late, after her sad and unsuccessful dinner party.

'Did she even talk about her illness again?' I asked him – for that would have been a subject, one might have thought, that would bring our protagonist squarely back into a conversation about Caroline, that he could have then speculated: Was she indeed depressed? Clinically so that she needed the medication she was taking? Had she been for a long time, despite the sunny, merry exterior, someone after all who lived in the dark? That might lead to a further idea for a plot, I was thinking, were it the case. That Evan might then be someone who could help her, being outside the family as he was, not trapped by its dynamics? That he might advise her, save her, even? Help her navigate the path between the love of her three sons, the alternative intellectual life of her husband and her own happiness? He might try, Evan, to assist her in the delicate balancing act of creating and managing the 'fun scene' that was her domestic, family and social life . . . But no, Evan just sat, nursing his drink and looking down, down into the bottom of his empty glass. It was my round.

'Are you completely sure she doesn't want to talk about it?' I tried again, certain, despite his silence, that a woman who had once opened up to him in the manner of a general confession would want to do so again, but Evan just slowly shook his head: Either 'no' or 'I haven't the faintest clue', only indicating by his gesture that he had absented himself somehow, if not from Caroline, from me.

And as for me . . . Well, I was already fully aware that this essay of ours, report, genre-blending prose, whatever . . . was veering wildly off track with every paragraph. Earlier ideas of a novel – forget it. Essays might be becoming more and more popular – we might have a hope there – but this wasn't really one of those, I knew that at heart. So what chance for a general readership now? Indeed, the only thing drawing Evan and me together was the knowledge of absence in the centre of our narrative; that, at least, like a plot-shaped space, was present in this tale. For this reason, there in the Stand, a pub chosen by both of us for no sensible justification we could figure, though it made me seem such a tough, haranguing desperado of a friend, I tried one more time to fill in that odd-shaped vacuity: 'Have you thought about asking Caroline if everything is OK?' I suggested. 'If there is anything you can do to help? After all, it is quite a big deal for a woman to—'

'Stop it,' Evan said then. 'Can't you see, Nin? It's upsetting for me to imagine? To think, I mean, that there might have been more I could have done to help? That I might believe I could do something now?' His head was still down, stirring around with his fingers the three cubes of ice that were in the bottom of his glass. He was like someone meditating, working with the ice, in a far-off contemplation of a world of his own and not someone sitting in a pub with an old friend. So he sat, introspecting. So I sat, waiting. Time seemed to pass, aeons, in the silence that ensued. Then he said, from out of the depths of that other, mysterious thinking of his, 'Sometimes I wonder, Nin, if I haven't just, you know, made the whole thing up. Start to finish. From Caroline opening the door to me that sunny morning in January to last night when I helped her put the dishes away after the boys' tea and we worked together in such companionable silence it was as if I had known her for as long as I've known you . . .'

I reached out then, to Evan, I put my hand on his hand, tapped with my forefinger his two fingers that were still in the glass, cold from stirring the ice, as though to say, come on now, it's not as bad as all that. Then, quite carefully, in a similar comradely spirit, I put my index finger below his middle finger, and my middle finger on top of his. We were still in the midst of that other, ancient kind of time. Nothing moved around us, in these seconds, or breathed. It seemed that I kept our fingers so entwined for a lifetime, an exaggeration, I know, but long enough, long enough, that we both sat there that way, the two of us, looking upon our connected, finger-knit, cold and warm woven, so to speak, hands.

'Listen,' I said then, and I barely recognised my own

voice, it was so low and quiet. 'I don't think you are imagining things,' I said. 'About you and Caroline. What you
felt for her, I'm sorry, feel . . . is real. Those things she said
to you,' I continued, 'when she came up to your room . . .
That gives you something, Evan, that "companionable silence" you mentioned just now. She did not make up those
things she said. Her confession. Her speaking out. Those
words made way for a space that you could inhabit in her
life, inhabit still. She needed you then like she needs you
now. You, Evan' – at that point I tapped his middle finger
with my middle finger, my middle finger that was warm,
that had not been stirring desperately around in some glass
of ice still bearing the traces of an undefined but nevertheless class–A gin. 'It was you she came to,' I reminded him.
'You she could confide in.' I looked up, away from our
fingers and the dear little woven shape they had made because by now Evan had brought up his third finger to lay
upon my fourth and we had something of a small square
design there, between the two of us. Still, I looked away
from all that. 'It's you,' I said. 'All you. Being able to do
that, be someone Caroline felt she could rely on, that she
could think of you in that way, that you might be someone
she could go to when feeling desperate . . . It's all because
of you.' I was looking away, towards the open door of the
deserted Stand. 'You are that person, Evan,' I said, I felt
desperate and sad and lost but the truth of my words was
there, had been spoken in the hushed and darkened air.
After all, I had everything written down. And, 'You and
Caroline,' I finished with. 'You're real, alright.'

I smiled then. Something had been achieved and I knew

it. Though I felt myself to be sadder than I had ever been in my life, though Evan's hand by now was warm . . . Still I smiled at my old writerly words, smiled at my dear old friend, to encourage him, to cheer him, to keep him going on. If I were a different kind of writer I might even say that 'I smiled brightly' or 'gave him a bright smile' by way of showing how different was my expression from the feelings behind it: 'She smiled brightly, despite the fact that her heart was breaking,' etc. I could write that, I suppose. Or, 'She put on a brave face though she felt tears weren't far away,' etc. It's a cliche, yes, but no doubt would do the job. Still . . . It would be a strange way of describing what was happening right now in a very ordinary pub at the edge of Chiswick. A strange way to sum up something that there didn't seem to be any words for, actually, as though I'd found myself to be someone who'd never used words to express anything before.

Evan let out a huge sigh of relief.

'I love you, Nin,' he said.

OK.

Well stop right there.

. . .

'I love you, Nin,' he said.

Because that can't be right.

. . .

And putting that sentence of his in a paragraph of its own as I have done and the ellipses and so on, making it into something of a big deal . . .

I'm going to stop right there.

Just stop.

Because making something of a conclusion, at this point, doing that now, at this stage of the project, as though that sentence was an achievement gained . . . Would be . . . Madness. It would make no sense in any of this story at all. After all, the second after Evan said: 'I love you, Nin,' he then said, 'I knew you would comfort me. I knew you would say the right thing.'

So, there.

I have done the right thing, you see? Stopped in the 'nick of time' as people say, about just this kind of situation exactly. Stopped absolutely at the right time, just when I should have.

Nick of time.

I'll say so.

'That's fine,' I responded promptly, noting to myself that 'promptly', that particular smart and businesslike word. Then, 'Absolutely.' Followed by, 'You can tell me everything,' and adding, 'It's what this book is all about.'

'Hmmm . . .' Evan waggled his finger, still knit up with mine, in a companionable way. He gave me a long and detailed, some would say 'searching' look. 'It's true,' he said then. 'That everything I say to you, everything that happens here, that we talk about . . . You make it seem concrete, Nin. You do. You make it that all this has happened.'

'Is happening,' I corrected him.

'Is happening,' he said. 'I stand corrected. You're right. It is, it's now. This story, it's present tense. So this relationship between me and Caroline—'

'Is – you see? – happening,' I finished for him. 'We're talking about it now.'

'Yes,' said Evan, and he unlaced his fingers from mine then, and picked up his drink, that empty glass. 'Yes,' he said again, this time as though to himself.

I need to state here that all this . . . context . . . with which Evan was so preoccupied, this content, factual detail, thinking . . . It had been building up over that particular sort of party, a 'pool party' as it was referred to, in a new world sort of way, that was being organised at No. 23 on the first Saturday of July. An event that had begun with the invitation arriving from the Caxton Taylors, that had sat up on the mantelpiece in the airy and sunny kitchen of the Beresford home at No. 47, and events developing from there. Now that phrase 'Pool Party', on the invitation, was finally to be put to use, the dress code observed, water to be entered. There were those attractive printed pink words on a white background with a beach ball trim, the little blue splashes around 'Pool' and 'Party' and another beach ball in one corner striped fuchsia, lime green and yellow.

'Pool party indeed,' I'd said to Evan, when he had first told me about it, and it was clear it was an idea that had taken hold of his imagination. 'We don't have "pool parties" in London, do we? Yet here one is. In black and white. Or rather, in shades of fluorescent pink and blue. I can hardly believe it.'

We had decided to meet somewhere else, for some reason, in the days that followed. I don't know why. Something to do with those interlacing fingers, perhaps? Certain words spoken? Or simply the sheer imminence, and indeed immanence, of the party itself, mere days away now, that might indicate a shift? Something, too, about the inevitability of the summer, the approach of holidays? About a feeling that the story itself, that we were involved with, was set to move on, to conclude, as surely as, all over London, families would shortly leave town to go away? Whatever the reason, or reasons, we'd come to sit ourselves down somewhere new on the bright, hot afternoons that led up to the party on the Saturday. A place no closer to Richmond or mine or any of the other pubs that we'd been frequenting during the course of this story that it might have been selected for convenience or continuity, or, most recently, to break from that continuity, a place we had chosen for no reason except that it was there and had no feeling at all of the season about it. The Empty Barrel it was called, a dark, windowless corridor of a pub, it seemed to me, right off the Talgarth Road.

'I guess people do have swimming pools in Richmond,' I said, when Evan and I sat down together. 'I knew someone whose father had a swimming pool at his house in Wimbledon and when you think of it, Richmond and Wimbledon . . . They are similar, kind of. That large garden of the Beresfords . . .'

'Could easily accommodate a pool,' said Evan. 'I've often thought that. From the moment it was obvious that summer was on its way, I've wondered more than once whether Caroline would like a pool at the bottom of their garden.'

It's one thing to imagine a pool, though, dream about one . . . Here were neighbours now, just a few doors down from the Beresfords, actually possessed of the same. A kidney-shaped, blue-tiled construction sunk into their garden, filled to the brim and sparkling with clear chlorinated water and all ready to host a party around its cool matt slate patio area. A pool party, with swimming and a barbecue and cocktails, that was set to start at two in the afternoon and run to 'whenever', Pamela Caxton Taylor had told Caroline when she'd called her up to say they'd love to come and was there anything she could bring?

'Just yourself and your bikini,' Pamela had replied. 'Absolutely no one – and I mean no one – is allowed to come unless they are suitably attired. It's right there on the invitation, Caroline—' she'd said.

Dress: Swimwear.

And so, in the American way of expressing things, it sure was.

Evan had told me about that invitation in such detail it was as though I could see it myself: the big, expensive, brightly printed card stuck up there on the mantelpiece beside the Daily Planner, 'Swimwear' in bright pink script, below the address and time. The entire thing on thick white stock edged with the same fluorescent pink and with 'a bright pink tissue-lined envelope to match', Evan had reported, girlishly, adding, as he'd mentioned before: 'I mean, Caroline has always said the Caxton Taylors are absolutely loaded.'

I am now trying to fix times and narrative order as clearly as I can. There, first of all, are the fingers entwined in the darkish Stand on a Monday afternoon in early July, then, some days later, there we are, under the Hammersmith Flyover off the Talgarth Road, in a deserted, dank corridor of a place, several discussions later, with a party in mind. The two pubs weren't connected, but I was starting to think Evan had chosen the particularly desperate character of the latter with a purpose: A new pub for a new chapter, perhaps? A development, kind of? A conclusion, of sorts? Or an ending? Either way I am highlighting the time of year here, the part of the season where everything can be seen, and for what it is: good or bad, lovely or terrible, attractive or grim. Just as despite the hot and summery month of July, here we were, nevertheless, in the darkest pub I have ever known, in deep, deep shadow, Evan looking as low as I have ever seen him in an old grubby pullover and loser jeans.

So much for Monday. At the Stand. Then there was the Tuesday and the Wednesday and the Thursday to follow, and Friday, all meetings set in the dank Empty Barrel . . . A whole week of dark, dark days that led right up to the night before the party, sitting there, set fast, unspeaking in the gloom.

Then. The Saturday of the party arrived. It came and went.

A Saturday, a Saturday night, passed by. 'From morn/ To noon . . . from noon to dewy eve', as John Milton's faithful amanuenses inscribed in that great poem of his so many of us love that is about something else entirely. And the 'dewy eve' in turn went on to become full night, for night fell, it deepened, it turned light again . . . And then finally, finally a phone call came through to me the following morning.

'I have much to tell you,' Evan said then. 'I think we might be getting ready to finish our book.'

# three

At this point I feel I need to recap. I've written – of course
I have, I have written so much! To the extent that I feel
like Evan, with that exclamation mark of his! – but somehow there seem to be missing pieces in what I've put together, information not given, parts not listed or left out.
Any project of this sort does need . . . 'ballast' is a word
I've used before. Though it's a bit robust, maybe. So . . .
Underpinning, then. A kind of cross-stitching under the
pattern of the whole. Think of Petrarch in the details of
those poems of his, the amount of fine, fine embroidery
that went into the figured, satiny whole of his poetry sequence that came to be known as the *Canzoniere*, the production of which, in each and every section, was sewn and
fastened and stitched to make up the length of figured silk
that was that finished work; and Dante, too, no shortage
of trammelling in *The Divine Comedy*, in line after line
of carefully worked tapestry and nothing but an under-
threading there, in brightly coloured wools. No Beatrice
without her rooms and streets and tables also woven in, no
Laura, no love at all without the knotting and threading
and work of words.

So for this reason, I can see now, more in the way of a
backstory might be in order. To 'recap' the situation, as I
say, of the circumstances of a lodger of some six months
who had returned to London two weeks prior to relocation

to make contact with an old friend from childhood who subsequently knew someone who knew of a house in West London that was a bit of a 'fun scene', as she put it, way back then, the owners of which had always been keen to rent out in part, the top-floor studio, to interested parties.

There was, by now we have it clear, the opening 'vision' of the project, as Evan defined it in his notes, his first sighting of the woman who was to become the object of this book, the point to which all narrative strains: Caroline in that wrap skirt, her blonde hair twisted into a sort of pony tail, and the way he felt 'something begin', also found in his notes, from the moment he first saw her and how that feeling, that 'something' – that 'ping' of his, remember? – grew.

And yes, there were details, present from the start, that may have gone unaccounted in these pages – details of conversations had, looks exchanged, confessions made, that together comprise a good deal of what became a flowering, a blossoming, as the seasons turned from winter to spring to summer's languorous days . . . The spread, the budding and the flowering, fruiting, of a long and heartfelt, all-consuming love. The kind of deep emotion expressed in prose that's the stuff of books and poems, both past and present, poetic and factual, entertaining and literary – in this case is reflected in a sort of 'essay', I was now calling it, 'intervention', also, or a set of thoughts and ideas laid down by an amanuensis on her page.* For, how, in the

* In terms of footnotes, by now all is reprise, reprise . . . Themes of love and literary background, 'Courtly Love' and 'Narrative Construction' . . . There's no end to it, really, the history of unrequited love in literature . . .

weeks that followed the beginning of this book, we see its protagonist, in the tradition of those established texts, seeking to describe his feelings and dreams, circumstances, to a friend who would 'get it all down', as well as writing a journal himself that at first he'd planned to publish as his own work but soon passed over to his amanuensis as contributing towards the 'project' we would develop together, as we called it first, then later 'novel', or 'story', now agreeing that the thing had a different shape again.

'Why don't you just take all these pages,' Evan had said, way back in the winter, when this whole idea was just beginning, passing me over a bundle of notes. 'And do with them what you can, Nin,' he'd said. And remember, too? How back there towards the start of all this I actually enclosed some sections of his writing to show intent, somehow, give a flavour of my friend's own writing and unique take on things? So my plan was to adopt a range of approaches in order to give variety to the whole, that no one might get bored.

Yes, then, with that in mind there are certainly more details that I could be adding. And I might add them. Evan's writing, verbatim. His unsent letters. His records of clothing and personal effects that were moved over in crates and packing boxes from the States. His music and books. Clothing. Cufflinks. I could put this kind of thing in, in the manner of the old masters, filling the canvas up with the rich accompaniments of domestic and civic life, by way of a shopping list or two, the transcripts of some of the messages he left on my mobile, emails, texts. As Petrarch had it: 'see how art decks with scarlet, pearls and gold/the chosen habit never seen elsewhere,/giving the feet and eyes their motion rare/through this dim cloister which the hills enfold'.

But there are other kinds of detail, too, that I feel I have been a little thin in providing. As though painting on a kind of dilution to the backdrop, as it were, of that 'context' Evan was so keen on, as though the colours on the set at the back of the stage have not been applied thickly enough and under the bright lights of the theatre show the world that is being represented as looking only wan and false. For yes, we have the house in Richmond, that much is established, those pigments set which look real enough. That wide front hall at No. 47 Chestnut Way, with the eighteenth-century chiffonier inherited from David Beresford's grandmother,* a massively valuable piece of furniture because David had always been old Annabel Beresford's favourite – perhaps it was from her that he first learned the pleasures of the Greek alphabet, the seductions of classical literature? – but treated by all the Beresfords as though it was some build-it-yourself affair from Ikea, covered as it was in water and drinks stains – several – cigarette burns – two – and an overflowing bowl filled with keys and receipts and papers. Yes, there is that table, firmly in place. A point of reference indeed for the many people exiting from a house, from a 'fun scene', in a haze of cigarette smoke and liquor and champagne, late at night after a party or a dinner when goodnights were

---

* The Beresford grandmother has been mentioned before, and 'Personal History' at the back of the book has further detail that might be of interest.

protracted and unwanted, gangs of friends holed up at the front door as though they might never leave . . .

So there's one detail right there, of that hall, that front door, that table. But what about other 'context', like Evan's room? That actual lodging place of his to which Caroline 'came up'? Has the paint not been a little thin there that I might thicken it up a bit with fresh colour? Add varnish to the whole that we might know exactly the nature of the room wherein Caroline eventually threw her arms around Evan and told him that she needed him, had to talk to him, and that he, only he, would understand?

It's a scene as though from a play, after all, and so needs to be conveyed with no sense of artifice or formality but as though all of it were real. All that is work to be done. As was begun, in earnest in certain country-style and more urbanely decorated pubs in the West London area, those hostelries with their various interiors and decorative flour-ishes from roaring fire to a long chrome bar, continued in spacious interiors with large windows to dark and spavined rooms that never saw the light of day . . . All of it, written down, to be written down still. Those big relaxed-looking sofas that had been arranged in the Italian style – remember them? – a configuration in which people can sit comfort-ably and be intimate with each other and talk, but in a for-mal way. That word 'configuration' just about sums it up.

Not that Evan and I were in any kind of configuration. We were always only ever working. Or 'Not Working', as Christopher had been saying, for months now, as though he'd committed some terrible Conservative Party mani-festo from the eighties to memory and was now doomed to deliver it up in flat monologues left on my voicemail and answer machine. 'There's nothing about what you're doing that constitutes proper, constructive work,' he intoned, on both my mobile and landline, and I could hear him rattling something in the background. A bucket full of change for some collection or other? A morris-dancing pole with all those little shaking cymbals for one of his summer fundraisers? 'You need to get out a bit, Emily. Do something proper,' he'd rat-a-tat down the line. 'Useful, gainful employment . . . It gives all of us a sense of purpose, of accomplishment, even.' Still 'work' it was to me, I could have told him, what Evan and I were doing: we were working hard. There at the largest table we could find, in whatever pub we were in, going through our various papers and ideas – the coming to Evan's room of Caroline: her gestures made there, speech given. Caroline's attempted kiss of Evan that had been – well, there is no other way to say it – rebuffed by Evan because, as he put it, 'I could not kiss her in my room in that way when she was feeling as she did . . . It would have been unfair.'

'Working, eh?' That was Christopher. And, somewhat brutally, with a rattle, 'Huh!'

'I know you're tied up but please do give me a call when you can,' said Marjorie, in more gentle tones, in a message of hers I'd kept from back when the days were just starting to get really warm. 'I'm concerned about you. And Rosie is . . . Please. Let us take you out for a picnic in the country so you can get some sun . . .'

But I was working! I was engaged and involved! There was that: 'I could not kiss her in my room in that way when she was feeling as she did . . . It would have been un-fair' of Evan's. Written down, inked heavily, in fact, on the page. What was that, to think about transcribing, effecting fully on the page, if not hard labour? It was work alright.

I'd had to have a quick intake of breath at that point, when Evan spoke the words he'd just spoken. I remember that, as a reaction.

'Unfair?' I managed.

'Taking advantage, you know,' he'd continued. 'It was late, she'd been drinking. She told me herself she was on medication and that it reacted with alcohol, with the wine . . . And she'd been entertaining, remember? The on-going "fun scene" . . . ?'

'Of course,' I muttered. 'I was the one who told you that. When Rosie told me. The house there has always been a "fun scene". I already knew that, Evan. I knew it myself.'

For some reason I couldn't put my finger on I had be-come very grumpy. Those late spring into summer days. It's a detail I realise has been absent from this narrative so far: Grumpy. Why? Because I'd been under the impres-sion that the whole scene in Evan's bedroom had rested on verbal communication only? Caroline's use of the phrase 'lodger's room' appearing at a key moment in the text, a remark that had made Evan feel stoppered in the past, unable to express his feelings for Caroline, and prevent-ed him, too, on the one dramatic occasion we had in the book from acting – that, and not anything else? Certainly, I'd had to admit, finding out later that my friend had not done anything at all or reacted to Caroline when she came to his room, not as a result of some use of word but for some old-fashioned notion of manners that didn't deny his physical desire, put a change about things, I reckon. Made me a bit cross. But was I also annoyed because this latest insertion only proved once again how we barely had a story here? How Evan seemed intent on undoing every chance of action or plot, responding to a gesture not with a gesture of his own, but only with words? Only more words? Indeed, was it my sense of myself as a narrator, a writer, after all, with a job to do to create a completed manuscript that might have the chance of being published, which so rebelled against Evan's inaction at this late junction? As though his articulacy were somehow his failure, as it were, to bring about some kind of event, as Aristotle would have it in his important treatise on drama, the elements drama needs to survive? So that then I was simply hopping mad from an artist's point of view? Or was it something else altogether? A feeling that I would never get to Evan, not really, in the way we'd been close once, now that Caroline had become something more than the woman he was in love with but stood, so it seemed, for all women everywhere, all chances, all hopes . . .

I was hounded, still, too, by the memory of that scrap of paper that had become mixed in with the rest, that I'd read back in the spring and that he surely never intended for me to see: 'You can't be real with me Evan, can you? . . .' Someone he'd thought he loved from years and years ago only showing Evan's withholding of emotion even then . . .

So yes, was it that? At the end of the day? A tiny thing, a scrap, that meant so much more? To do with Evan revealing the impossibility of ever seeing life for what it is so that of course he would opt to hold on to some unfulfilled ideal always, rather than be part of life as it's being lived? Along with the knowledge that came with it that we are not able, any of us, not just him, we are all unequipped, to make the most of opportunities and chances for happiness and love as they rise up before us. That so fixated are we upon ourselves, our little point of view, our wretched opinions and ideas, in this case 'of how things should be done', 'taking advantage', and all the rest of it, that we let fixation kill all our animal feeling and our passion and our lust?

I didn't know. I didn't have the beginning of an answer but for sure all these thoughts and more had been swirling around in my head in Child o' Mine and the Seed, long ago it seemed now, when I was getting more 'pigment' than usual from Evan than perhaps I would have liked. Not an easy thing for me to be receiving, Evan, I remember acknowledging, back then. His: 'It wouldn't have been fair.' His: 'I could not kiss her in my room.' Not easy.

For: 'It's just not how things should be done,' he'd said next. 'When I come to Caroline, with my thoughts, my feelings for her, I want it to be clear, calm . . . A "registered" place, Nin, is what I mean somehow. That she would remember and hold on to whatever I might say, so that whatever goes on between us . . . Is serious, has consequence, resultant action . . .'

'Like a scene in bloody *Middlemarch*,' I remember I muttered – and there. That word 'muttered'. I was grumpy alright.

'Well, I haven't read *Middlemarch*,' said Evan. 'Only *Daniel Deronda* . . .'

'Same thing,' I said shortly. 'Shortly.' By now fully aware of how these unpleasant adverbs of mine were kicking in, spoiling Evan's hopeful tone. 'Shortly'. 'Muttered'. Something was going on, it was obvious. The story was building, sentence by sentence, paragraph by paragraph. Ballast alright. But I hadn't wanted to write any of it in back then, only daring to include it now.

How I drained my glass! The gin had always been inferior in the Child. Their so-called '*terroir*'. The tonic was. Yet still we'd chosen to return there and to The Swan and Seed all through the spring.

And all Marjorie had wanted was to pick me up in her car, even then, and drive me out to Rosie's for the day. We could have looked at the paintings she was making, abstractions of spring blossom and lilac, as well as commissions of people's dogs, and then take sandwiches and a thermos and spread a rug out beneath some trees.

'I'm fed up with this place,' I said now, looking around me at the dark confines of The Empty Barrel. 'Can't we find somewhere else to go?'

For how the early summer light was fading from the windows; we'd been there for hours. And how I was thinking then: What was this thing I was writing anyway? To what end was I making notes in an establishment that spoke only of dearth and absence? 'Novel' I may have been calling our project together at some point, still hoped to. Perhaps one day. But, as my bitter reference to *Middlemarch* had highlighted, I knew deep down this might manage the status of essay or intervention but that there was no more chance of a novel happening here than a £50 million blockbusting Christmas feature running through its paces as though in a multiplex cinema on my pages.

Nothing was happening at all.

And I couldn't figure out any of it, my own responses, thoughts. Thinking back to the Seed, the Child. Only that I was mad alright, short-tempered and cross and with trouble in mind.

I was fed up.

More and more it was seeming to me that what happened between Evan and Caroline, if anything indeed could be said to have 'happened', could never be a drama in any kind of traditional sense of the word. I may as well have never read Aristotle. Those 'stage figures' of his – at least action occurred around them, to them. At least they 'moved on', to use the popular turn of phrase suggesting trajectory in relationships, closure. Whereas here I was stuck in the on-going feelings of Evan for Caroline that never turned into anything like drama, and yet, too, it seemed it was the very lack of any activity on the stage that kept those feelings so . . . full. So present in Evan's life that there was room for nothing more, absolutely nothing more.

Of course some elements were playing out, still – various scenes occurring in the Beresford family as a result of the increasing strains and distance between Caroline and David, the way that affected the three boys, who, after all, were growing up . . . Caroline's medication, and so on. There were David's forthcoming end-of-year exams in 'Introduction to Classical Studies', the fact that the boys and Caroline had never once been able to visit the one-bedroom flat he'd taken off Russell Square, they didn't even know the address – but all of these things, these domestic details did not come close to the central issue of Evan's and my 'story'. And as for that 'story', well . . . Evan was – surely, surely, and soon – going to have to resolve it: hamartia, hubris, catharsis, all that. Those ideas of Aristotle, that he came up with first. Otherwise how else could we ever gain relief, another classical idea, that rhetoric might force a response from us to a story that would eventually give us calm, and satisfaction, create 'relief', if the story of Caroline was left forever hanging in mid-air?

So, yes. Evan was going to have to act. To DO something. Not just sit there in his room while she fell back on his bed in an evening dress that was – as Evan had described it, 'quite cut away' – and . . . wait, silently for a 'registered time' before he could tell her how he felt and move to hold her in an embrace.

And mad?

Yes, fuming.

Hopping.

That was where this 'novelist' was at.

She ordered another round of drinks for herself and her companion.

Her friend.

Her dearest and oldest friend.

'Oh, Evan,' I said then, only able to write it down now, while in my mind Caroline had come to his room and confessed how unhappy she was and how much she had come to rely upon Evan, the knowledge of his steady presence in the home, his effect in the house, ongoing, as he lodged at the top of the topmost stair.

'Oh . . .' I started again, but didn't finish, because there was Caroline instead, I could see her, there in the room with him, telling him all that she was telling him, his own response of quiet and of calm and . . . yes, I could see, as though I had been there myself, how she had that word about her, Caroline had, of 'strength'. And so all these remarks of hers had been made – albeit in a state of inebriation and in a kind of medicated high that was also quite depressed, albeit, yes, albeit – and yet . . . And yet. With all her . . . presence. In the room. Her strength . . . Evan had just sat there. On the bed. Waiting. Doing nothing. Nothing. Then standing up. Just standing up in the room but not doing anything even then. Just standing. Like a tree. Or a telegraph pole. Is how I see him. Unmoving in his jersey. Standing there while Caroline, in a tiny silk slip of a dress, fell back upon his bed and said, 'I love you, Evan.'

'I'm fed up with it here,' I finally said, as I'd said, too, in the Child. And in the Edge, and before it in the Elm and the Seed and the Stand and all these places in this book. 'For goodness' sake,' I said, 'can't we find somewhere new?'

# four

'She actually tried to kiss you and you just stood there. You took her hands instead and shook them.'

This was a few days after that acknowledgement of my grumpy mood. But it may as well have been months ago. As it turned out, it made no difference to Evan and me, whatever he said, or I said. By now the story was nearly done, and we'd never left the Barrel actually, as I'd thought we might. The Barrel had become like home. Evan was right. There was nothing welcoming about the place whatsoever but we had come to love it even so. Its dark corridor-like interior, vaguely vibrating with traffic off the Talgarth Road, suited our deepening, unhappy mood and the gin was triple strength, barely legal.

'I wanted to calm her down,' Evan was telling me. 'That time . . . Nin, I told you. It was not the right—'

'She tried to kiss you and you turned away,' I repeated.

'I say again, it was not the right time.' Evan had a desperate and boyish expression on his face that I recognised from when he'd been five years old, something highly wrought and feverish going on in his mind but that was also the result of the rogue element of the gin.

'I know you were cross, Nin,' he said, 'a bit. About the . . . You know . . . But the time . . . for calm . . . That time . . .' He was not making a great deal of sense.

As I say, the gin was strong enough. The bottle didn't

even have a label. I was thinking, as we sat there, me looking at him, a bit hectic and flushed his dear old familiar face, about all the time we used to spend together when we were children, all the time over at his house, he at my house. The way our two mothers would say to both of us, 'You may as well move in,' depending on who was at whose. Helen Gordonston had always seemed like the quintessential artist figure to me, in her smock, with her potter's wheel set up at the end of the kitchen in a little conservatory the Gordonstons had built on after Evan had started school, my mother had told me, 'with room for a kiln as well and those lovely silk-screen processes of hers'. And then, as far as my own family was concerned, Evan always saying that my mother was like a mother in an Enid Blyton book, terrific at baking and careless, both. Oh yes, I was feeling a bit incoherent, too, but still . . . We could always get on and do exactly what we wanted, I remember, without Evan's mother noticing or telling us to come inside and have lunch. That, it seemed to us then, it still does, is an ideal circumstance of care. I took another sip of the strange potent cocktail served up in the Barrel and said, randomly, to Evan, 'Hmmm.'

I was also thinking about how he was going to have to do something here, in the third section of the book – and do it smartish. Put his hand to Caroline's cheek – as she had put hers to his – gestured back to her cheek, somehow? For hadn't she, at some point, done that, put her hand to his face that way? Or he should gather her to him, or simply lean in towards her, as I've written before – and as I was thinking all these things, or trying to, and looking at him, thinking, too, about the years we'd known each other, I was also thinking how he might do any of these things and how it would seem, to be the woman who received such gesture, such abundance of gesture. Of love and care. Of care and love.

I was thinking a great deal, scrambled, uncertain thoughts, as he sat there, familiar. But thinking, nevertheless.

Months had passed since our story had begun. This essay of ours, these pages of words. A long time, the changes of season charted in sections or chapters, I hadn't decided yet how they would be arranged, yet now here we were stuck, is how it felt, like a machine gets stuck, mid-action, and can't sort itself, can't click into gear to start up its whirring and turning again but only spins, over and over, brokenly and pathetically in the same place.

Me and Evan.

Doesn't sound too grammatical.

Evan and me.

And I myself was not exactly doing much either. I had to 'register' that myself in the dark shadows as the traffic passed by. Oh, I received. Even at this late stage, I continued to. Evan's ideas, dreams . . . But that was all I did. He may have been gloomy and thin, sad, pale and wan, but he was still passing over to me papers he'd compiled, journal entries he'd written, diaries, lists he'd made. He had started a thorough reading of the *Canzoniere** and

* There's that really lovely little edition available to the general reader, *Canzoniere: Selected Poems*, translated by Professor Anthony Mortimer (Penguin Classics, 2002), and by now enough information has been given throughout this entire 'story' with regards to the Further Material that appears

*The Divine Comedy*, and was involved in tracking down major scholarly work on Petrarch and Dante – he was, despite his melancholy and desperate mien, ordering books online and these were stacking up in a neat pile in his rooftop lodging beside the bed. He was able to tell me, too, in his more optimistic moments, about the fruits of all this research, the early Renaissance thinking behind the sheer energy of emotion – the art, the music, the sculpture and literature – all generated by the great engine of unrequited love that had hummed and sung its way through the culture of western Europe from the medieval period on. And he was writing about that, too, in his lonely lodger's quarters, about that engine. What it might mean. Where it might take a person and whether it might change them.

In many ways then, you could say, Evan was more fully active in this project of ours than I was ever going to be. Because he had gone 'right inside it', as he put it, into the writing, our content. He was busy enough. While I, all I could do was worry endlessly at the fabric of the thing we'd sewn together, this great cloth of words, picking at the hem, troubling and worrying at a stitch here, there. Might these pages ever 'find a readership'? That sort of thing. As I used to think a little about back in the days of trying out the odd short story or whatever, amongst all my copywriting work and the catalogue entries I put together for the gallery . . . Though all that activity now seemed like a long time ago and in another life.

---

in the back of this book, including a selection of Petrarch's sonnets to which some readers will refer and others can happily ignore. There's no need to add anything further there. It's done, that part of things nearly over too.

Yet I still had hopes it would all work out in the end. Marjorie had just started calling me again about a new campaign for cat litter that promised to pay fabulously well and asked, super-casually, as though she hadn't been talking to Christopher, if I might be interested.

'You can't be still working on that idea for Evan Gordonston?' she said, when I called back and told her I was interested if I could have until the end of July before I had to start. 'That's crazy, Emily. You can't afford to go without proper work for so long. What about your mortgage? Christopher did tell me he thinks you're being irresponsible on this. That he's been telling you that for some time. Promise you'll bring matters to a close with this thing between you and Evan.'

'It's not a "thing" between me and Evan,' I said. 'It's a book.'

'It's a "thing", Emily,' said Marjorie. 'And well you know it.'

'It's nearly finished,' I said. 'I hope. Just give me these few days in July.'

For really I did have a feeling that we were approaching the finishing line. In fact, I could see those words appearing on a page: 'Finishing Lines'. I was clear enough about it that I knew now was not the time to pick up extra income by way of Marjorie Clarke's advertising work overflow. Time enough for cat litter and the pet food and provisions giants, I thought. The ending was, it had to be, in sight. Otherwise there'd be nothing of Evan and me left.

That's what it felt like, for the two of us, despite, or perhaps because of, all this 'work', all his thinking and reading, and my 'laying down' of the sentences . . . It felt like we ourselves were fading away. Into words, only words, words . . . They were consuming us. There we were, still, returning, day after day for that last week in July before the pool party, coming back each time to a dark pub set under a busy flyover, to a little table, unmarked gin . . . While the rest of London sat outside in cafes and restaurant and bars . . . In the sun . . . We were inside. That thickened set-painting so necessary to a good stage play and dramatic performance? That was our world. The Empty Barrel, it was empty alright. Evan and I the only customers, and both as shadowy and cast off as the place itself.

But yes, we were there, even so, using that little table at the Barrel, to get finished with everything and reach a conclusion, the end. I was still going through more of those details I mentioned earlier. Evan had supplied me with a list comprising all the items, exactly, furnishings, accessories, of his 'lodger's quarters', all better to provide 'context', as he maintained, for that key 'scene', and I was to use the list in any way I saw fit. One might have thought I would, too – certainly I'd intended to – were it not for another event altogether that, as it transpired, was to move the story on in a way neither of us would have ever anticipated, that Evan had nevertheless intuited, I suppose, when he'd first become aware of, and excited by, the arrival of a certain invitation at No. 47.

For now, though, the contents of his latest list continued to involve us.

The accommodation itself, for Evan, up there under the eaves in Richmond, was modest. I write that never having been there, not near, not really, that time long ago at the cafe on the outskirts was nowhere close, neither to the road, nor the house – let alone the studio flat that was situated at the end of the topmost stair. But Evan had given me enough of that 'ballast', detail, description, that I could write in that much at least: 'Modest.' 'Under the eaves'. 'Topmost stair'. As though using these descriptions as a way of establishing circumstance, situation, might be a metaphor if you like, Evan's room and its position in the home, for his relations as a whole to the Beresfords and their social set. He was never, never going to be going to that pool party. Not that he'd wanted to, hoped to, wished to. He had chosen this outsider status for himself as surely as he had chosen his attire, that broken woolly jumper and the terrible 'sweat pants' and the ancient jeans and pensioner corduroy trews. He was no more inclined to don swim trunks and walk down the road with Caroline and David and the boys to No. 23 than dive straight into the lozenge- – or did I say 'kidney-' – shaped pool of the garden there, greet the Caxton Taylors on a certain Saturday afternoon and settle right in. No. He was a lodger, Evan. In Richmond, temporarily. To 'find his feet'. A lodger. That was all he was.

Yet I had to remind myself as I wrote these words, really, remind myself, with the story so far along by now, too, that Evan had had no need, never had, to be a lodger. Since coming back to London, after the years away, he had taken up a most senior position in his firm, and it was as though I kept forgetting about all this, that he had this side to his nature, elegantly slipping back into a position in corporate and legal life in the City as though he had always lived in London. For Evan, as long as I have known him, has always been like that. A man, and before that a boy, who, even when we were over at each other's house every day, was always capable and organised and with a quiet animal's ability to fit in, and alter quickly, adapt immediately, it would seem, to the new situation he found himself in. So he lost a shoe at mine? He just borrowed my brother's gumboots. So he didn't have any change for sweets because he'd forgotten to ask for his pocket money? Well, he could use mine and we could choose together because he didn't like gobstoppers. So in the same way, now, in London, he'd come straight back into a smart high-powered position with his firm and could have lived in pretty much any flat anywhere he'd chosen, still here he was, a lodger, and I could so easily forget that it might be otherwise. As though one might say to him now, 'Why not move in with me and here are the gumboots, the pound coins for as many sweets as we need,' and he might reply, 'I'd love that,' and arrive the same night with a small bag of clothes, and that would be all it would take. Instead of a preoccupation with an invitation, a host family's social plans for a Saturday in July, there'd be a knock on the door, a greeting. I'd say, 'Hello there. What took you so long?' and he would just come inside.

# five

So yes, Evan, during all this time, could have been somewhere else. He could have had his company put him up in
rooms or in a hotel, even, while he was getting settled back
in London, and he could have moved into a really central
flat in an easily accessible part of town. He would have had
people at his firm sort all that out for him. He wouldn't
have had to lift a finger, just say, 'Yes, I like it there,' and
they would have organised the movers, decorators. It's the
kind of thing high-powered firms sort out for their top-
end employees who are relocating. And Evan, though I
found it hard to believe it, was one of these. The sort who
might point to some piece of furniture and a corner of a
grand room and say to the removal guys, 'Put that there,
will you?' indicating a space over by the French windows
that looked over a garden square. I said that to Evan at
some point, 'I can see you somewhere really lovely,' I said.
'Somewhere that's close to work and I could walk to meet
you.' And then going on to describe the kind of place to
him, a flat of his own, not lodgings. 'You don't have to be
in Richmond, you know,' I said.

That was back around early spring sometime, when
Evan was feeling that things were never going to 'take off'
with Caroline, a phrase he was using a lot at that time,
static as the situation was, this weeks before Caroline
coming up to his room and falling down on the bed. I was

reminding him then that it would be possible to make a fresh start – somewhere like Notting Hill or Chelsea or Primrose Hill . . . Somewhere he could swing around the place and act a bit special if he wanted to. But no, he was to stay put as a lodger, he said, and hope that some kind of 'take off' might occur, as in a way it did, I suppose, in the sense that Caroline had been able to come 'up' as easily as she had done by the simple fact of him being a mere staircase away. At least, as Evan had figured, all through this period, and after it, he was still figuring it, he could see Caroline every day by maintaining his position within the Beresford home. He could help out with the boys some- times, 'be present' is how he put it. The Beresfords could rely on him on a sort of informal teenagers-overseeing ba- sis if ever Caroline was called away to an evening event at the last minute, as she often was so called, and with David not being there, but in the flat in Bloomsbury. 'It's easy for me to be present here' is what Evan would say to me, when I questioned this kind of arrangement and asked if it was the best use of his professional status and time. Though also, I had to remind myself, I was in no position to give Evan advice in terms of his career about what he should and shouldn't do. With my small pieces of copywriting now hanging in the balance, and poor financial manage- ment skills, I am the last person who should give anyone advice about anything, petition for anything, and besides, we've never been like that with each other, Evan and I. Even when the Gordonstons left, all those years ago, for America, I never said then, 'Oh, no, please don't go. Tell your parents, please, do tell them, to stay.' I never would.

Therefore, 'I can see you somewhere like Chelsea,' maybe, I might have said that, but nothing more. Certainly never anything like that 'Why not move in with me?' as at the end of the last section. Though no doubt him being somewhere more accessible, easy to get to, get from . . . His offices, and so on . . . Social destinations . . . Might have changed the texture of our meetings – especially as time went on and we'd found ourselves inching into the outskirts of Chiswick and Acton, as this account has indicated, most recently ending up in that Empty Barrel off the Talgarth Road. Yes, it might have changed things. Being somewhere central to begin with, that did not require him coming in from Richmond and us orienting things from there, that every night he would have to get back at some kind of decent time . . . Yes. It might have altered matters somewhat.

The area I live in myself is pleasant, and always calming to return to. Coming home, often late, from a long walk back after, sometimes, fraught discussions because things weren't moving along on the story front, or there'd been rows downstairs in Richmond, Evan had heard them from under the eaves, with the Beresfords in the grip of some unhappiness that was never quite named, David Beresford staying up all night with a Greek grammar, or not answering his mobile in the flat off Russell Square, a flat that was only supposed to be a temporary arrangement while he went through his intensive first-year immersion course – 'immersion alright,' muttered Evan grimly, there's nothing 'temporary' about anything involving 'immersion' – or something else was amiss, the boys were behaving badly at school, or there'd been an incident with the in-laws, everyone supposed to have been at a lunch with one set of parents or the other, but there'd been some mistake about the dates, Caroline had muddled them because she was feeling muddled, and there was embarrassment, too many apologies . . . Well, there were times I valued the relatively central location of my flat. A first-floor one-bedroom in a quiet street . . . I could breathe, after the exertions of the situation in Richmond, take in the deepening summer air.

For there was no doubt about it, whatever way you looked at it, the discussions between Evan and me, involving always my note taking and sometimes the handing over of Evan's own writings about proceedings . . . All of those chats and interviews, may I call them, could have been made so much more pleasant if Evan could have just popped in to mine, where it was peaceful, for a bowl of soup on the way home, or swung by on a Saturday morning and we could have had a walk in the park that's at the end of my road. Maybe the contents of our discussions would not have had quite so much of the end-of-the-District-Line about them if we had been wandering somewhere in my neighbourhood and stopping off for a tea in the sun, admiring some pretty young black Labrador who was being walked, quite nicely, on a red lead beneath the plane trees in full leaf. Just . . . Having a conversation, only talking, then. Not interviewing. Not asking. Or answering. Or filing for later some fresh bit of news or detail about Caroline's dress or social life, or discussing the quality of the notes Evan had been working on . . . We could have simply been in light and easy banter, ourselves making the subject for a change, and what we wanted, or might need.

'So I moved in one bright sunny day in January,' Evan had written, at the beginning of one such volume of papers that were handed over to me in the spirit of the usual meeting, somewhere between the two of us, increasingly oriented towards the western outskirts of the more central area, with not a light-hearted conversation about me or him in sight.

'It was early in the new year, before the schools went back and the family had gone off for a few days to their place in France.'

'I may as well give you all of this,' Evan had said, turning over the pages, as I say, still giving me all this material right up to the end. 'Make of this stuff what you will,' and he handed me about twenty sheets of A4, all in a bunch, tied up with little pieces of legal string. I sorted them out into some kind of order which I'll reproduce here, to an extent, space permitting:

'So I moved in—' he wrote.

And: Really? I thought. I said 'Are we to go through all this kind of thing again?'

'May as well, Nin,' he replied, and I read again: 'So I moved in' as he'd written down. I read and I read.

His handwriting, as I've said before, was extremely poor, but a sense of panache hung around the words written down, this because he'd used old-fashioned fountain pen with blue-black ink, on very expensive letter paper. This was engaging enough, I suppose, this imagining of Evan sitting down to write, create a stack of manuscript in the style of a nineteenth-century poet – that blue-black ink! – that I could go through and use . . . But none of it was the easy, mindless talking I dreamed of. None of it was just the two of us beneath those plane trees in leaf. It was all more story, all this, all that, more of the 'ballast' again, and all to do with Caroline, nothing to do with us, him and me, the fact that we'd known each other for such a long time and could be happy just sitting, watching that dog with a red lead I wrote about way back in the beginning of this narrative, back around the time of us going to the Elm, I think it was, in reference to those Labradors that sat under the pub tables, perhaps . . . No, it was just story, this, these fresh pages I was being given. All for the story as it always was.

'So I moved in . . . ' I started again. And tried to focus. Where was I? Only here:

'One bright sunny day in early January, just before the family returned from their house in France,' I read. 'Caroline had told me I was welcome to join them down there, it was a bit of an open-door policy, she said, and I could come and go as I pleased, but I had items I needed to move in, various tasks needing my attention.' Yes, I remembered all that from before. 'My boxes were being shipped over from the US later that month and would be in storage and I needed some time to go through some of them and decide what I'd be using for these next few months while I was in transit, as it were, before deciding properly where I was going to live. Long-term, I mean.'

I'd written there, in red pencil: 'in transit' next to the words 'in transit' for ironic emphasis. Because of course by now there was nothing 'in transit' in Richmond about Evan. That 'long-term'. That 'going to live'. These phrases applied to a certain suburb on the outskirts of West London only as far as I – or any reader, for that matter – was concerned; he may as well have intended to stay there from the beginning for his entire life. 'What!!!' I'd written again, towards the bottom of the page – to remind myself that I needed to quiz him on this, circling that word 'properly'. Then there was, I'd also seen, the way he wrote the word 'Caroline', too. 'Properly', you might say. For the way he'd written that word was nothing like the rest of his handwriting; it was neat and clear and even. The characters were perfectly, in that particular instance, formed. Caroline. It was obvious to me that just writing that word was a sort of meditation for Evan, upon her, I mean. Caroline. Caroline. Caroline. I could see at once, upon meeting the word of her, as it were, how he slowed down and made of her name a formal and 'properly' finished little piece of art.

In all, the pages gave a great deal of insight into Evan's orderly mind. That fancy paper was from Fortnum's. I used to have some myself, though they don't do it any more. I knew well too the fountain pen that he also used. With it he'd made a big list of the clothes that he'd decided to leave in storage, though none of the ghastly jerseys, I'd observed, had been included, or the ancient period jeans that gave him such a quirky, peculiar appearance; the clothing being kept was all dinner suits and sports jackets, smart shirts, loafers, 'American stuff' as he put it. Then there was an entry for books and CDs, DVDs and paintings, too, and some smaller pieces of furniture. He'd gathered a fair amount of 'baggage', as they say, in those years in the States. Still, I read on:

'So yes,' I read. 'I had things I needed to do. And seeing Caroline, meeting her for the first time, and then again to discuss the moving-in arrangements . . . In many ways it had been too much for me. I felt I needed some time alone in the house to settle in, orient myself, without the massive sense of Caroline Beresford's presence around me. I needed to normalise myself in Richmond' – 'normalise' was underlined and the reason I'd written the word 'what???' at the bottom of the page. 'I needed to spend time in the house alone and become used to myself in it.'

I stopped. That was nice. That was nicely written.

'Before Caroline came home,' he went on. 'Before she was to be in the house with me. Yes, I needed time on my own.'

I turned over. There was another half a page or so, barely legible, then this:

'I wondered, as I spent time in my attic quarters in early January, what change would be seen on her face, that beautiful face, when I looked again upon it. For she would have changed, would she not? Even a few days or so would do it. In France. With her family all around her. French food and wine. A few days can make a difference. I myself had become only too aware in the mere week since meeting Caroline of how change is vast, the way it works upon us, though time, as such, may not have passed in any great increment, though circumstances may bear—'

'No,' I said then aloud. The tone, the writing style . . . It was all wrong. Little wonder, I thought, a bit crossly, Evan had passed on the job to me in the beginning, of writing all his story down! No wonder he'd wanted me on board, to shift everything into the third person and get a bit of objective correlative, a bit of distance, going, here. This Edwardian-style outpouring on Fortnum's paper . . . It would have to be staunched. Honed as I'd been on pet food and insurance and cutting-edge gallery catalogue work, there was nothing I couldn't help him with on that front, would have been his thinking, the reason behind his appeal right at the start when he'd made a case from my involvement and I'd said, 'Alright, then, I'll try.'

Because without . . . narrative shaping . . . . Without that . . . Then what? My red pen question marks and underlinings said it all.

'Her messy blonde hair', he'd written, for example. 'How it takes up my vision' – and I'd managed to turn that into: 'As she walked away from him, after that first moment of meeting, he noticed the way her blonde hair was piled up quickly into a careless sort of ponytail that was actually, breathtakingly glamorous.' Those few lines were only a draft, but still, an improvement nevertheless, they had to be, upon the original.

Or:

'I hear her yelling at the children, three boys, and she has her hands full when friends come over and they're all partying together, with the television on some games channel, the CD player turned way up loud, but her voice is always music to my ears' – 'cliche!' I'd scrawled, and I turned it into: 'Evan found himself more and more appreciating the texture of the Beresfords' domestic life. Three boys between twelve and fifteen and with friends over all the time, Caroline dishing out juice and biscuits and making them chips and hamburgers if they stayed over for tea, she was busy for sure. Evan would sit there sometimes at the breakfast bar while she chatted to him about this and that; normally she was on her way out the door, waiting for the babysitter to arrive so she could go upstairs and change.'

'Three boys,' she would say to Evan then, as they sipped white wine together, late in the afternoon or early evening, or in the weekends over a pot of tea. 'Can you believe I have borne and whelped three boys and now have them to deal with for the rest of their lives? Can you? How many brothers and sisters do you have, Evan? You seem like someone who's come from a large family?'

And Evan would answer 'yes' or 'three' or 'maybe' . . . Not really able to respond properly or in full, or answer anything making any kind of sense because all he could do, all the time, was be thinking, it seemed: Caroline, Caroline, Caroline.

# six

'I would hear her calling for her boys, up the stairs, along the hallway, calling from the kitchen, in the garden . . . Her hands held up towards me, fingers splayed, showing, glittering in the light of day, that large engagement ring of hers, beside it, the gold wedding band: "I mean, what can I DO, Evan? I have these three growing monsters! I am mother – can you believe it – to three teenage, three adolescent BOYS!"'

Evan had signed his name under all this, and put the date. The pages, journal, papers, his Fortnum's letters, as I think of them . . . As well as the bundle of stationery that were notebooks, spiral-bound pads, and all filled with Evan's awful handwriting and these metaphors and similes of his. There were some really fancy turns of phrase that were hard to cope with at times – that 'music to my ears' and so on. Certainly, I don't know where the influence for this kind of writing had come from but it had been beneficial, throughout the long months of working together, that I had been able to nip it in the bud.

And at home I was still editing in that way, writing, I persisted. While Evan and I had continued to meet, and our conversation expanded, expanded, I mean, while staying curiously in one place, as time went on, this project developing, in its own way, even so I continued to write it down.

'Those green eyes of hers' and so on.

'Her face softer, more girlish, in repose.'

I could change it for something like: 'She has this thing she would do for emphasis, raising her eyebrows as she asked Evan a question like "Shall we have a fish finger with the boys, you and I, and to hell with it?" or "If you're not going out tonight, do you want to have a glass of wine with me?" and putting her hands on his shoulders. "Tell me that's exactly what you want to do," saying. "Hang out in the kitchen with an old housewife eating a leftover nursery tea." And Evan wouldn't be able to speak for long minutes with the loveliness of it all.'

For this was my role. To make. To shape. Evan and Caroline sitting together at the breakfast bar in the kitchen at Richmond, and yes, her looking at him with those beautiful blue-green eyes of hers and telling him every single thing about her life, is how it seemed to him. And yes, too, putting in Evan there, listening and saying, 'I suppose' and 'I see . . .' So my role was to write all that down for him to look at. I'd show him periodically where I was at and he would read through to get a sense of the thing, where we were headed, read back to himself his own reactions and feelings. And all of the pages gaining momentum, if you like, bit by bit, one after another, reaching what could have been a turning point when Caroline ascended the stair that night, late, when her dinner party was over and David still not home.

'You must think I'm such a sad case,' she'd said to him that night she came up, when she'd told him all about the latest type of medication, and her sleeping badly, and all the other details she'd wanted to relay, and Evan had said, 'Oh, no. I don't think that at all . . .' but hadn't managed to take her in his arms, hold her, but had just stood there in the centre of his room, shocked into immobility is how it had felt, he'd told me later when he'd only then come to realise what effort Caroline must have put in, what energy, to be so present and alive-seeming and vibrant, how many pills it took to buoy up the lovely will and cleverness and sense of life credited to her as maintaining a 'fun scene'.

'God, Evan, if I could only tell you the half of it,' Caroline had said, 'being married . . . Two people who are so different . . . The loneliness of it . . .'

Scattered phrases such as this, confessions . . .

'Sometimes I truly don't know how I can go on.'

Writing down about that night that became the accumulation of so many moments, impressions, that now he could see . . .

Those separate scenes all building up, accruing . . .

At the breakfast bar once, when he'd come in on her very early in the morning, before dawn, she'd just turned down the corners of her mouth and gone, 'Blah.'

That I could add in now.

Or putting in that at supper, sometimes, he'd see the boys with their eyes on the television as they ate, and Caroline just looking into space.

And how . . .

Often, Evan heard her crying on the phone.

Heard, too, the front door opening, closing, at strange times in the night.

In his room, when she came 'up' she'd wanted to talk

about all these individual moments, tell him about her life, what it was like, the person she thought she was and also couldn't be. The tablets she'd told Evan about, that the doctor had prescribed, were having an effect 'but the effect is not happy,' she said to him, this right back in March, and before she came up, long before, too, the events that followed the issue of the invitation that sat on the Beresfords' kitchen mantelpiece in June. 'Resignation,' she'd said to Evan in March, as he met her coming out of the laundry room with her arms full of clean dry sheets but her eyes red from crying. The children were growing up and 'What next?' she asked him one morning, making toast for seven and eating the burnt ends herself. 'What next when all this –' she waved her arms around at the three boys and their friends who were lying around on the sofa and floor playing some wi-fi game and jeering at each other on the screen. 'When all this is over?' she asked. 'What?'

And all he'd wanted to do, Evan, hadn't he, on all these occasions, was to gather her up and say, 'Don't worry, I'm here. I can help you,' and change everything for her in that second. Wasn't that always foremost in his mind? When in reality he did nothing, only continued to write his pages and give them to me, phoning me up to say, 'Can we meet? I feel like there's a lot here to say.'

And Caroline, through all this – and I had this down, too, in pages, in print-outs, in xeroxes, in black and white – also showed great will. She would not let herself stay mired in her sadness. She would do everything in her power to be as lovely, as laughing and funny as ever. Her remarks, I noted, stayed between them, her and Evan, in the kitchen, in the garden, on the grass, at the doorway of the laundry room as I've just written. They didn't stray off the page, as it were, into conversations with others. She was discreet. And, as I've reported, any confessions to him alone only caused Evan to feel even more deeply in love. Why wouldn't it? Such bravery? Valour? The way she kept the atmosphere light, that 'fun scene' continuing in the constant round of entertaining and socialising that was the trademark atmosphere of Richmond. So it was only when he came in some night late from work, or stepped downstairs from his quarters unexpectedly – it was the weekend, and he'd decided to go out for a walk, say, to come and meet me and have the latest discussion, he had some pages to hand over, perhaps – that he might come upon, fully, some of the unhappiness of the Beresfords.

Though David, Evan said, was always 'completely charming', with beautiful manners and 'always good fun'. Evan wanted to make that clear to me, too. 'It's important, Nin. In the essay or story, or whatever it is that we are finishing together. David is no villain in all this. Like Caroline, he is just being himself.' For the pool party, he said, David was planning to team-lead some kind of fabulous watersports activity for the boys and all the children in the road. 'He's already spoken to the other fathers about it,' Evan said. He was that kind of a 'team player', David, despite his disinterest in a City career and his love of the contemplative life; he was also someone adept at arranging a complicated game of water polo that involved sticks and several small balls, as well as organising the aqua-net and waterproof scoresheet and all the rest of it. He was quick-witted, too, full of good stories and the kinds of jaunty remarks that you might think would put the whole family at ease ... His list of pleasant attributes went on and on. Though to Caroline herself he barely said a word. He was 'cold with her', Evan told me, this early on. It was still spring, leaves on the trees but the light only half-hearted. I was wearing a scarf back then. I remember Evan arranged it around my face as he said goodbye, making it into a sort of hat – we'd been at the pub that day for some time. He'd looked deep in my eyes and said then that David to Caroline 'was cold', 'was cold with her'.

Thereafter, Evan told me – after a chill evening when he'd drawn the soft folds of a scarf around my face, tucking the ends in neatly to form the shape of an old-fashioned bonnet – thereafter he had been able often to detect tears in Caroline's eyes. 'When no one else can see them,' he said. 'I know the tears are there. When they're present,' he'd added, though dashed away when Evan had come into the room, by dint of something David had said to her seconds before – so developed, Evan's growing awareness of how the Beresford family were, the relations between them, husband and wife, father and sons. So it was becoming more and more clear to him, the fissures that were splitting the domestic unit wide open. It was there in Evan's journals. It was in his talk.

Sometimes, he said, Caroline would talk 'funnily' of how little she knew David cared for her, and how he would demean her, mostly without meaning to, some might even think what he was doing to be part of his charm. 'Well,' he might say of Caroline, she told Evan, over drinks with friends at some smart bar, 'it would be nice if she were to do something with her life' – not looking at her but at everyone else as he spoke, as though he were about to tell a joke. 'Just look at her,' he would say. 'This pretty wife of mine. Hopeless.' And 'Don't look,' she would answer, but speaking to the rest of the party, too, and seeming to ignore him. 'Please don't.' Such were the complicated relations played out between the two of them, that Evan might tell me, that I might try and get down on the page to be as real as I could.

Did they ever really communicate with each other, I wondered, those two, when they were on their own? I asked Evan the same. About David's degree, the Greek stories he was reading aloud to the boys? Did he tell his wife about his hopes, how he so longed to leave the City, get out from under his father's shadow, his father's career? Did she tell him that perhaps they might sell the house? Travel? Do something else with their lives? Caroline would have liked that, wouldn't she? To feel there were options, choices? That desire to turn into someone different, to be free?

'Who knows?' Evan replied. 'How's anyone to know anything if it's not written down, Nin? In permanent record? How can any of us otherwise be certain about a thing?'

It seemed to me that even without proof – not being there to see for myself, only put an idea together based on the bits and pieces Evan told me – the way they mostly communicated, Caroline and David, was silence. Occasionally, as I've written, he reported voices raised, the sound of something banging . . . This from far away, deep in the Beresford bedroom amidst the carpets and the quilts and the cushions, something breaking, something sharp.

Always late at night, with the boys long asleep, but Evan might find himself wakened out of a dream by a word, a harsh, harsh word. And that door again, opening, closing. Someone arriving? Someone in a hurry? Being called? Who knows.

'The next morning,' Evan said, 'David would have already left for the office and it was as though nothing had happened. I wondered,' he said, 'was it even true?' That he'd heard anything? Because Caroline would have the TV turned on the next morning, super-engaged and smiling, as if this was a holiday they were all enjoying together, not a Monday morning or a Thursday and the clock was ticking. Still there she was, dressed in jeans and a white T-shirt, her hair down like a girl, laughing at something one of the boys had said, giving them a hug. And there she was again, on a Saturday, chopping a vegetable up at the bench while she watched the news, frying bacon and pouring juice. Or on the phone, or arranging flowers in a complicated vase, mouthing to Evan, 'Coffee?' when he came in, while the person on the line continued to talk, pointing at the cafetiere and then at Evan, raising her eyebrows in question, while going 'mmmm' on the phone and sticking another long green stalk deep into the complications of her floral arrangement.

These were her mornings, Caroline's mornings. Lovely, lovely. As she herself was.

Her jeans slouchy and faded and her long legs and the sheer length of her, the sheer tanned elegant length of Caroline, ranging about in her kitchen at the beginning of all her days . . .

And of course Evan could have lived anywhere. In one of those enormous flats in Notting Hill or Chelsea. Or he could have gone for something more modest, bachelor chambers in Mayfair, maybe, or a terraced house in Barnes. He could have moved here, even, to where I live, with a nearby park and the sort of trees that when you look up into them, make you think you could be anywhere, that life could have all kinds of possibilities, outcomes . . . That we might have lived in the countryside together, Evan and I, with these same trees around us and over our heads, and all the hills at our back. As that first pub we'd met in to begin this book might have been in the countryside and we part of it. Deep in. As though we ourselves might have come in from off a remote shoot somewhere with a pair of black Labradors at our heels and a brace of pheasant in our hands and mud on our boots . . . Arm in arm, two people who've known each other for such a long, long time . . .

But in that pub we had something else we had to do. My papers, my pens and pencils and files . . . They were all laid out.

And nothing could compete with that, so it seemed. Our task in hand, this book. Nothing.

So my—

'Coffee?' Caroline mouthed at Evan, pointing to an empty mug before her and the jug there on the counter, and then to him. 'You and me?'

'And then that smile of hers,' I transcribed from Evan's volatile and deeply unreliable folk-music style of poetry: 'that smile of hers that made my life begin.'

# Finishing Lines

The day came for the Caxton Taylors' summer get-together, as already featured in the attractive invitation that sat up on the mantelpiece in the Beresfords' bright and rangy kitchen.

The whole month before had been warm – as June often is – promising a long and lovely season ahead, of endless days and blue skies. And now here we were in July and the mood at the end of the District Line 'said summer'. That was Evan's phrase – I've taken it straight out of a journal – 'and some', he added, speaking to me directly, after he'd passed over that particular group of pages bound together in a file and was describing them to me. He had these American phrases that still came out every now and then, sentences and words that had been generated by years living in New York and Chicago and Boston, all those years of his he'd had away that I couldn't imagine, not really, not think about, nor believe in. To my mind Evan had always been near to where I was, living close by. He'd never gone away. 'Those Gordonstons,' my mother used to say, 'how I do love them.'

So there we had it, on the basis of Evan's American turn of phrase, the mood in Richmond 'said summer'. It was hot enough. People were outdoors and on the streets, voices were raised. Clothing worn was light and thin and careless. The mood did indeed, all over London, say summer.

Evan himself was still wearing thick cotton shirts, though, but the jerseys – thank goodness – were now gone. He had confessed that with the atmosphere in Chestnut Way turning towards the entertainments at No. 23 the coming weekend, he had decided he had had enough of winter clothes. It was all part of that 'change of mood' he'd detected at the Beresfords', that he'd told me about the first night we met at The Empty Barrel. How there was something hopeful in the atmosphere, in the house, with the day of the pool party approaching; so something light and summery and entertaining was in the air.

As I say, this pleasant climate wasn't limited to Richmond. In the street where I live, geraniums were blooming in pots, pink and white and red, and how pretty they were, how I noticed them even more clearly emerging from the dark gloom of The Empty Barrel. There was the sweet, green smell of cut grass, too, coming from the parks; the scent of water from sprinklers casting the suburban gardens of West London with cool, all there to greet Evan, too, when he arrived 'home' at the Beresfords' after a long, hot day at work.

Everyone, it seemed, at No. 47 was excited about the party at No. 23. Caroline was, and the three boys, who were great friends with the Caxton Taylors' children; David had mentioned the watersports more than once and was definitely planning to be there, 'Most definitely,' he'd said. That there was no travel planned for work, no more exams at UCL . . . That there was a whole summer ahead before the autumn started and a new and equally demanding course on the Peloponnesian wars, the conditional conjugations in both Latin and Greek, and *The Complete Greek Myths*, seven of which were to be fully translated, from English back into the original, before the end of the first term, but not now, not now . . . . Meant that all this time was available, for him, so that there was nothing else he had to 'do', any place he needed to 'be' – other than at home with his wife and family. Was all part of the lift in mood, the lightness of the air, in Richmond. 'Yes, indeed,' he was 'very much around', he'd told Evan when they'd bumped into each other on the stair, and Caroline, for her part, seemed relieved about that, that they could all attend the neighbours' party together, that they could all be to-gether as a family as they used to be.

'Well,' muttered Evan somewhat grimly when I ques-tioned him about this, about David Beresford and his at-titude to home life, to parties, this one in particular, 'it's a case of – "Whatever",' he said, referring, in a protective and loving way to the many means David Beresford had at his disposal, as far as Evan was concerned, to break his wife's heart. 'He might say that now,' Evan said, that he was going, but who knew for sure? All those times, Evan reminded me, when David had promised he'd be home at a certain time and then wasn't, that he'd be there with Caroline, then wasn't there, saying he would host a din-ner with her and then staying on 'to catch up on work', said Evan, again 'grimly' – the adverb rather suiting his expression as he spoke, suiting the sarcasm with which he uttered the phrase – because, he was all too aware, Caro-line had mentioned all this to him, that David would say things like that, 'Oh sure, I'll be home tonight in good time, I'll bring the champagne,' only to arrive back at the house late and loaded, and the evening just about over and the guests starting to go home. Imploring, 'Please don't leave,' by way of compensation, but of course by then it was too late, as everyone was aware of the hour. Except David, Evan said. He was blissfully unaware. For his part, seeming happier than ever, according to Evan, even more handsome and charming. 'I must say, despite knowing Caroline as I do,' Evan had said once, 'I can't not like David Beresford.' I think I know what Evan means. After all, he was just doing what he wanted, wasn't he, David? Exactly. The classes at UCL were a sort of dream come true for him. He could chuck in his job any second as far as he was concerned, and just move to the flat off Russell Square and in time, after his DPhil and when he'd published a few papers, take up an academic position, there or in any British university where there was a good Classics department. He'd never wanted to be in the City. And he'd say that, too, to Evan, to anyone, in his charming way, with his charming smile, in front of Caroline. All the time. 'I never wanted any of this . . .' indicating the gracious home, the large green garden with its oaks and planes. 'Any of it.'

In the same way then, Evan was moved to add, the man could not ever really be relied upon. Watersports plan or not. 'I'll believe it when I see it,' he said of David's plan to be part of things down the road the coming Saturday. Him letting Caroline down so much a part of things for Evan by now, their marital relationship, the way they lived their life . . . Evan was moved to give me all kinds of opinions on that front. For goodness' sake, he told me, Caroline might plan a holiday, book the whole thing, pack, and then David, at the last minute, would pull out of it. There was that kind of thing happening all the time. The numberless small let-downs. Those, as well as all the complex and dark, dark secrets that can exist between a husband and wife, even if that husband and wife, like the Beresfords, seem beautifully suited and happy, with the three boys at expensive West London day schools and on track for Cambridge, with the house elegantly furnished and appointed with pleasing lodger's quarters and a domestic situation generally that was described by many as being 'a fun scene'.

As Evan said 'grimly' into his gin and tonic on more than one occasion, 'fun scene' or not, David Beresford, as already noted, knew well, was fully articulate and practised in, the many ways 'to break his wife's heart'.

Even so, there seemed none of that intention now or rancour about the place in the days leading up to the Caxton Taylors' 'Pool Party'. None of it. Evan just wanted to be sure I included it, anyhow, the 'shadow cast through the marriage', as he put it, 'to set the record straight' in the book we were putting together. Though I wasn't much interested in that sort of backstory, Evan wanting to underline all that about David's 'manners', the ferocious order of them, their application in all things to achieve precisely what David Beresford wanted from life. Adding, Evan said, and 'get it down, Nin,' he'd told me, as usual, 'that staying married to Caroline was the most complicated and cruel thing David Beresford could have done of all'.

Still, the same David Beresford had definitely said he would be there, at No. 23, that Saturday in early July, from

2 pm onwards as the invitation stipulated, in 'swimwear' also detailed, on the bottom right-hand corner, printed but as though it had been scrawled, in bright pink script with acid green embellishment, and I, for my part believed him.

He said he would help Charlie Caxton Taylor 'man the barbecue', Evan told me, 'that old trope' – the husbands holed up together fanning the flames while the women lounged around the pool in bikinis, keeping an eye on the children splashing, and talking amongst themselves. '"Man" the barbecue,' said Evan, poking into the discarded lemon rind that was left in his glass in the Barrel on the Friday night before the big day. '"Man" it,' he said. 'Those expressions are left over from the ark, Nin. Not even our fathers would do that, say, "man the barbecue" . . .' What century was David Beresford living in, anyhow? he said.

It was strange, it was, for me to hear Evan talking so much about Caroline's husband all of a sudden. There'd been little enough of him in our story, and it was rather too late now, I felt, to bring him in. 'Poor David', as I'd referred to him as, after all. Because, I suppose, of that love of his for antiquities and so on, because of being a bit out of kilter in terms of his work ambitions and his true desires. And yet now here was that same husband being ridiculed, in the same text, for his language, expressions used. For his coolness towards his wife, the various kinds of domestic treachery carried out by David Beresford in the name of his wanting to 'do his own thing' . . . It was all very well Evan giving me this now, at this junction, but too late, by now, to bring it in.

Besides, my mind was with that pool down the road.

That large cool blue shape laid out in a back garden in Richmond, tiled around the edges in an expanse of smooth dark grey slate, with a large square patio giving on to grass. In my mind's eye I could see Caroline and her friends arranged around that bright, watery lozenge, at the bottom of the garden, sunglasses on, stretched back on one of the many bright sun loungers the Caxton Taylors had placed at the pool edge. Calling out, 'Don't splash, Robbie,' or 'Careful,' but somewhat carelessly, as if they didn't really mind if they were splashed at all. 'No dive bombs, please.' When really, they weren't even thinking about their children and what their children were doing; they were thinking about their husbands and themselves.

So yes, 'Don't splash' and 'No diving'. These phrases, sentences, images, were coming to me, floating about in my mind rather like the sort of large, brightly coloured plastic toys you see floating on the surface of swimming pools around the world, gently bumping and colliding in the bright sunshine as Evan rattled at his empty glass in the gloom and darkness of the Barrel. All working together, all these various ideas, descriptions, to build up a picture of the actual party, the day itself, that particular Saturday afternoon when the neighbours were all arriving and, one by one, picking up a cocktail from one of the many young Eastern European women on hire from a catering company Pamela Caxton Taylor had found that specialised in 'London Pool Parties' – the company was called that, Caroline had explained to Evan – all dressed in fake grass skirts as though they lived in Hawaii. 'Those cocktails were a knockout,' Evan said.

But that was later.

Now I had Evan talking, and framing judgements. Wanting to add this, add another thing. So that I had, at the last minute it seemed, all these extra pages to put in, all these extra details. And it seemed also as though it took a very long time, too, for me to get there, to that 'later' – for me to hear anything about the party at all. It seemed, at one point, that it would take a whole new section of this book.

For after seeing him at the Barrel on the Friday night, all that seemed to occur for me, for my writing, was only . . . silence. Almost as dramatic and obvious as the time back in late spring when there'd been the terrible silence after him confiding in me late at night. Now, as then, I heard nothing from Evan. Nothing. After the opinions, the ideas . . . The hours passed by as long as they had seemed to pass back in the spring, with no call from him, no text. I saw him on the Friday and then . . . Not a word. All day Saturday, then Saturday evening, and nothing. Saturday night then came and went, and still . . . Not a sentence. Not a thing to write down. About the weekend. The Beresfords. Caroline. The party. Nothing. Until finally, finally Evan had called me on Sunday morning and said he was ready to meet. The end of the story was nigh, he'd told me, over the phone, in a strange, elated voice that was also calm. 'Let's meet at The Remarkable – you'll have to look it up on your computer – and I'll tell you everything,' he'd said.

'How do you know?' I would say to him there, in that extraordinary venue, in a couple of hours' time, after he mentioned those 'knockout' cocktails again and he and I were meeting for what would be our last get-together of the sort we'd been having in a London pub. 'You weren't there . . .'

'I'll tell you everything,' he would say again.

The Remarkable was a brand new pub, in both senses of the word – because it was newly built, recently opened it seemed, as well as it being the first, of all the pubs we'd ever visited, that we hadn't seen, somehow, in advance, while being at another. How 'remarkable' could it be, The Remarkable? Well, it just was. It was along from The River Cafe, and very, very fancy. I'd had to look it up on my computer to find out where it was, just as Evan had said. Gin came in tiny shot glasses carved from ice that you had to pour yourself, in one action down the side of your regular though highly frosted tumbler, tipping in the 'tonic and lime medley', as it was called, in a deft way, then stirring the whole with a crystal swizzle stick as fine as a darning needle that had also been provided, along with a bowl in which the ice shot glass could melt. Whew. The whole thing, as well, the place itself, seemed made of glass, glass windows, a glass roof. Glass doors that were open on to a green, glass tables on the grass, glassy-looking chairs and benches . . . The whole place looked like a set out of a film and nothing, nothing like any of the sorts of pubs Evan and I had got used to.

What was going on? What was going on here?

Despite its slick appearance, and perhaps because it was right next to the river and had a fountain and it was summer and the sky was bright blue, The Remarkable was the kind of place that attracted families, families with young children. The place rang with happy shouts and cries. I couldn't work out why Evan had chosen it; he'd seen it on a website one night after getting back to Richmond after one of our nights together, he said, long ago, after he'd left me, and 'had to walk it off' – his phrase for the feeling of having talked too much about Caroline and it making him feel sick, or sickened, rather, by the fullness of his feeling, to use a rather more archaic expression that might be rather more suited to the Romantic period than to that in which Petrarch and Dante were writing. He'd had a kind of indigestion, he said. It had been one of our meetings at The Kilted Pig he had left behind him, he said, me still there within its dark interior, not ordering another drink, but not able to leave either, just sitting, with an equally dark and knowing feeling within me that these nights together were, despite the increasing loveliness of the evening outside, closing us up, somehow, drawing us in.

I thought how The Kilted Pig had been a favourite for a time, of course, and typical, too, of the kind of pub Evan and I often found ourselves in in those days: a bit on the small side, perhaps, but with comfortable chairs and good-sized tables as I've written about already, in earlier pages, of course. That kind of place had suited me, I thought, had suited us, at the time, just fine. I should have known, and I kind of did, that when at last Evan called me on the Sunday morning following the pool party, suggesting a very different kind of establishment, the sort that I would need to 'look up' on my computer, that would sit next to a restaurant like The River Cafe, as it were, on that part of the river where the world goes, as it were again, to promenade . . . A place out in the open . . . In the bright air and the sun . . . A place to go to see and be seen . . . Well I did, I did know, that something was up. Something had changed. That this story was drawing to an end.

Not that any of this is to sound sorry for myself, harking back to lost pubs, for that was surely the last thing on my mind, but only to indicate that when I received that call it was like a little bell rang, 'Finishing Lines!' A high jangled note that might seem to echo and resound off the sheer glass walls of the unlikely establishment Evan had selected for our meeting.

After I hung up, I pulled on some clothes and headed straight there. I knew exactly where it was, The Remarkable, and he'd told me to get there 'ASAP' – about an hour's walk from where I live, maybe forty-five minutes, going fast, wiggling down those back roads from the end of my street that eventually lead into the side streets of Chiswick . . . So how Evan got there before me, leaving Richmond, after all – did he take a cab instead of his usual walking or the tube? – was anybody's guess.

Chiswick is nowhere near Richmond, I'd had it in mind to say. Or the Barrel. Or anywhere. 'Why do you want to meet there?' I'd said, when we were still on the phone.

'It doesn't matter,' Evan said. 'I am leaving Richmond, Nin. I'll tell you about it. And,' he added, 'The Remarkable is by the river and has cool breezes. It's a great place. You'll love it, I promise.'

When we met, minutes later, it seemed, with my clever route and his unbelievable speed – he must have taken a cab – he repeated, I noticed, the same strange sort of sentence, about the airiness of the place and how I would appreciate it, only ominously this time, is how it sounded, with him leaning towards me. 'It's lovely here, don't you think? With the cool breezes?' he said. Then, 'How, Nin, with everything I have to tell you, I need those breezes now.'

I remember feeling strange then. How I put down my glass. And as I say it was a very fancy glass – but all of a sudden it was as if that fancy place was dull, dull, dull. Nothing fancy about the table we were sitting at, about that needle of a swizzle stick, or the melting hand-carved gin-pourer made of ice. It was suddenly as though there was nothing fancy at all about any of it, or about the whole wide world. Behind Evan, his face framed by it, was a complicated arrangement of poles and ropes and ladders – a children's climbing frame. Little children, really little children, were moving all over it, fast as spiders. The climbing frame was crawling with tiny legs and arms and dotted with brightly coloured T-shirts and little pairs of shorts. I felt sick.

'What do you mean?' I said to Evan then. I felt ill. Everything was crawling. Twinkling around me, like the beginnings of a sort of migraine, was all the glass, the shining day, the ropes and silver frames, the tiny legs and little miniature pairs of shorts.

'What do you mean?' I said again. It was as though all the meetings, all the tables, all the talks, all the gin and tonics in the world, all the nuts and crisps . . . Had piled up together into one twinkling, glassy, terrible experience, as though all we'd been doing, Evan and I, all we'd been spending all these months together doing, was not speaking, exchanging, learning, thinking, imagining . . . Not writing a book at all. But only drinking the most monstrous kind of cocktail, some unholy kind of spirit, that had come to lodge, with a piece of the glass it was poured into, right in the centre of my brain. Here I was, here we were, in this terrible, terrible place, beneath the blue sky in a glassy pyramid of a building set upon the grass, moving inexorably towards some kind of conclusion, an ending, and Evan there before me, dressed as badly as he'd ever been, although, and I could see this, too, as though for the first time, there was a new loveliness in his face, a softness, a brightness, to his features. He was shining.

Yes. There he was.

'There you are,' I managed.

He looked tanned, actually. How can that have happened? He was relaxed. His thick shirt, wintry as ever, and still stubbornly worn at this time of year, was loose and groovy-looking – I saw even through my sickish, migrainey-affected eyes how fabulous the old flannel suddenly looked on him – the sleeves rolled up like he was a cowboy from a seventies TV show and his arms brown and strong, his hands strong, his fingernails clean and fine. He still looked intense, there was that issue of him having 'something to tell me', but for now he leaned over to take my hand.

'You've been amazing, Nin,' he said.

Past tense. Past tense.

A wave of nausea came over me like they say it does in all the novels.

Cliche, too. A cliche. 'A wave of nausea.' The migrainey thing doing its migrainey thing.

I thought I was going to be sick.

'All these months,' Evan said. 'Hearing me go on and on about Caroline . . . Caroline this, Caroline that . . . my love for Caroline, how I can't live without Caroline, all the things I say to Caroline, all the things she says to me . . .'

'I've tried to get it all down—' I felt so queasy I could barely speak.

'And now,' he carried on, as though I hadn't responded, the story whirling, whirling towards conclusion – that past tense! That use of the past tense! – and my sick dead feeling passing through me in waves, like sea sickness, tossed upon a glassy, gin-soaked sea . . .

'And now,' he repeated, 'we're here, you and I, things coming to an end. And you . . . You've been with me from the start.'

I turned from the table, from Evan. I was like a person on a boat. Exactly. I was exactly like that person, as though I had turned because I was about to throw up over the side. This speech coming from him, from Evan, this strange sickening-making speech and coming from him, from him of all people, my dearest, oldest friend, the person I have known since childhood when his parents moved next door and he came over and knocked on the door the first day and said, 'Hello, my name is Evan Gordonston and we live next door. Do you want to come out and play?' and my mother had said, 'Yes, go, Emily. You'll have fun,' because she'd already said hello to Helen Gordonston and had liked her immediately. Since all of that, all of this. All our past and present and future in jeopardy for here was Evan now with his strange way of speaking. I couldn't understand. I couldn't properly see. After all the conversations that had gone on since he'd come back from America, since he'd first put up at the 'fun scene' that was Richmond, all the conversations, talking, that had gone on, all those meetings of ours, all the notes and journals and . . . chat . . . Only to end in this strange new way of communicating I didn't recognise at all . . . .This way of talking that bore no resemblance to the phone calls, the texts, the emails, the journal entries, my writing . . . This new Evan with his thick shirt sleeves all rolled up and his brown hands taking mine, talking now.

There I was, turned away. Faced overboard, so to speak. The world tipping around me. No 'How are things?' or 'Fine, thanks.' No 'Meet later?' Or 'Sure.' Or even 'Was thinking of you' and 'Same' – no. This kind of inter-action we were having now was no interaction I know, was something different altogether. Though there were all those texts that finished with an xxx – still xxx-ing each other ourselves was something we would never do, never when we were five years old would we kiss so why kiss now? What reason? Why? 'Is this even happening?' I was thinking to myself as I was turned away, head down over the side of my metaphorical boat, getting ready to be sick.

'What?' I said from that position, not looking. 'What on earth do you mean?'

'Only that—' Evan replied, in the kind of way that indi-cated a new paragraph, but then saying instead of finishing that sentence, 'Eugh!' and slamming down his glass. 'This gin and tonic tastes like kids' lemonade,' he said, and I turned back then, to face him. The relief! He poked in his glass with the swizzle stick. 'It's disgusting . . .' He made a face, and pushed his glass to one side. 'Only,' he continued, 'there is something I need to tell you about me and Caroline.'

I felt another cliche then, another 'wave', only this time, of strange disappointment, that sort of peculiar relief. This new sentence, mood . . . I'd thought he'd said the story was nearly done? Only now, maybe not after all. For now there was this. Him taking up the glass again and fiddling with it. I'd been wrong. I drew breath. I straightened myself in my chair. Got ready for the next sentence, got myself prepared.

'After the party,' Evan began, 'the pool party at the Caxton Taylors' . . . Well, because of . . .'

'What?' I said now, and the sickness was gone, we were back on that old familiar territory. I could almost have reached in my bag and taken out my pad, my pen. Everything about that pool party had been like drawing teeth, as far as getting details out of Evan was concerned. Not to call me after it, or any time before or during, as he'd said he would. All through Saturday, Saturday night. To get no information out of him whatsoever . . . Only that silence of his. The empty line at the end of a mobile phone. But now, here he was, and it looked as though I were to be getting some information after all. 'Yes?' I said, expectantly. For I was ready for him. Up until this point, after all, I'd had to imagine everything for myself, from the colour of Caroline's bikini – 'Hawaiian print, cotton, pink', to match the Hawaiian theme of the invitation and the day – to the pool – 'turquoise, lozenge-shaped, edged with charcoal-coloured slate' – to, well, everything. The Beresfords, David Beresford team-leading water polo for the neighbourhood boys, young and old, 'Boys Only' as it turned out David Beresford had ordered, causing a great deal of talk at the party, that there were no girls allowed . . . I'd put all that in, I was planning how it would go. The fact that the day was hot, the guests many and those drinks, the cocktails, circulating freely as I knew they would, from the details on the invitation Evan had told me about weeks earlier, were indeed 'knockout' . . . Everything. Everything was in my mind, ready to be turned into words and sentences and substance for this book. The fact that those cocktails circulating on the fluorescent green and yellow and fuchsia-coloured plastic trays were really strong, included three kinds of alcohol, vodka, cachaça and rum, plus a mixer, and Caroline drinking more than one or two or three of them . . . Everything. I had put it all in.

Now Evan was speaking, and there it was, the details, the colours, but he was speaking now so this part was real.

'Something had happened the night before the pool party,' he said. 'I don't know what, exactly, but there was an atmosphere in the house on the Saturday morning and David and Caroline were barely speaking.' I nodded, I did quietly, actually, reach for my pen and the usual lined paper that I'd used for all of my amanuensis work. 'It was unpleasant, alright,' said Evan, and he went on to describe a sort of mounting tension so that, by the time the family went down the road together to No. 23, though all dressed in swimwear as requested, the clothes they wore on top of those garments seemed dark, funereal even, Evan had thought, watching them leave from the window of his high lodging rooms.

The water polo game was somehow part of it, he surmised, coming up as a subject of conversation the evening before, and carrying on as a theme at the party itself that quickly gained momentum, became a spirited source for debate amongst all the guests: Why, in this 'day and age' as people have it, would one segregate sport in that way? 'Boys Only' indeed. After all this wasn't the Olympics! It wasn't even a schools-type match! So why shouldn't the women and girls join in if they wanted? It was all about David, was it? the conversation ran. That he was the sort of man who wanted to control things, have a performance play out exactly as he wanted. And Caroline was leading the argument about that version of her husband from the front, Evan said, giving a range of opinions and gesturing over to David, to where he was in the pool with all the boys splashing around him. Talking about him. Imitating him. Throwing in Greek verbs and so on to agitate further. Myths about this and that, the flat in Russell Square . . .

David just ignored her.

'I'm fed up with the way you behave,' said Caroline then, rising from her sun lounger and going over to stand at the side of the pool to confront her handsome husband, who was in there, in the deep end, with her sons and the other children who were male, all these men. 'Get out of the water, boys,' she said.

'They stay where they are,' David replied. 'You're drunk. Go back and lie on your thing. Go to sleep. Whatever. We've got a game to play.'

OK, so I put a bit more detail in there than had been supplied in the original but Evan had given me the main shape of the afternoon, the turn of events, an unpleasant turn, that took hold at the glamorous party down the road and killed it. Caused everything to change.

He'd told me, when he'd called me up on the phone, giving those terse instructions, to meet him at The Remarkable straight away, that something 'conclusive' had occurred. 'Nin,' he'd said, 'I need to see you now, if you can make it, at this place just by The River Cafe between Hammersmith and Chiswick . . . You can't miss it if you come along by the water. Something has happened. It happened yesterday at the Beresfords, something that happened as a result of that pool party, and I need to see you. This minute. ASAP.'

So I was writing now, this minute, too, and ASAP and fast, and faster, reaching the end of all our pages and the things he'd said. It had been nine, ten in the morning on a Sunday when he'd called and he'd said we needed to meet straight away. So . . . Early opening hours, then, I'd thought, it must be. At this new place I'd had to look up on my computer. It must be some place. So quick. Go as fast as you can, then, run, the writing to match. The streets of London had been quiet when I set out, planning to go up the back streets and cut down the side by the park to the river. We would most certainly get a table outside, I was thinking as I left, even though the weather was fine . . .

And so I'd started walking, and walking faster, enjoying the hour, the day, wondering about Evan, what was ahead, and wondering, too, not for the first time, about why I'd never got a dog. Never. I increased my pace. Why? When I love walking, always have, have I never got a dog? When, remember, when we were growing up, Evan's family always kept dogs, spaniels – Flossie, Jo and Barney, one after the other, mother, daughter, daughter's son – and I'd always loved those spaniels, my mother had taken the ageing Barney to live with her and my father after the Gordonstons moved to America . . . So thinking about all this too, while walking faster, faster, all of this, this information running through my mind as well as wondering what Evan was going to tell me when we met, coursing through my mind – like a spaniel coursing across a field you might say, though none of the Gordonstons' dogs were working dogs – and I was running, by now, myself, I was, running, as fast as I could to get to Evan, to where I was to hear this 'last part', as he'd put it, when he'd called me, running towards the 'finishing lines' of his story, along the Riverside Promenade as it's called, towards the glass construction that is The Remarkable, and everything, everything, looked at that point . . . Amazing.

As did Evan himself.

I've written that down already. That he had a shine to him. Sunny, tanned, relaxed . . . Content. And 'content' is a very nice word. A good word, a concluding sort of word, yes, alright, it is, but calm, and clear. Fixed. A nice word.

Content.

Why then was I to feel the need of a stomach pump just seconds later? Why to feel 'content' might cause me so much ill?

'Hi you!' Evan had called over to me when I'd arrived at the lawn in front of The Remarkable, had seen the sign. 'Come over and have this fancy but disgusting drink I've got for us both here and I'll tell you about what happened yesterday at the Beresfords'. What happened to me.'

And I write again: Why sick then? So unwell? That same question? When 'content' was there along with 'content', details to be given, more ballast, for an ending in store. Why sick? When that is what I was used to? Details? Ballast? Why not 'content'?

When Evan was saying, 'For it's resolved, Nin. Between me and Caroline. The thing between us . . . It's over now.'

Why wrong?

The glass shattering.

The day in shards.

Why not content, with that 'It's over now'?

But instead feeling bright, like migraine, too bright, the summons of the day – and my turning away from Evan before turning back. I felt trapped, I reached for my pen.

Only, 'Look in your heart and write,' says the poet.[*]

So Evan talked, he started to, and talked and I started, as I've said, to write it down, all of it, the weather, the guests . . . The polo playing, the mighty row, there in front of everyone, Caroline jumping in the pool to get to

[*] Philip Sidney wrote that, who's not even featured in this novel, at the beginning of his own extensive literary project; it's a small but final and lovely footnote – there will be no more.

David, shouting at him, 'I hate you!' 'I loathe you!' and nearly drowning because she'd had too much to drink, that's what everyone said, those cocktails had been very strong, and that 'poor David Beresford' would have to take her home. As he did, he must have – or did he? Caroline didn't know, had no idea, only that when she woke up, hours later it was, she was in her own bed, her bikini, still wet with swimming-pool water, in a soggy pile on the kitchen floor where she had left it.

'How do you know?' I asked Evan. It was the second 'How do you know?' I'd asked him.

'Because I saw it,' he said. 'I picked it up. I was up in my room all the time, you know, I'd been working. I'd been out for a walk but I had stuff to do, I'd figured: well the Beresfords are all out, the house will be quiet. I'll get some emailing done, I was doing that, and then at some point, late late afternoon this was, evening, dusk, Caroline called me on my mobile and said would I go up to her room, that she needed to see me, could I help her, that she didn't know what she was going to do.'

Didn't know what she was going to do.

I underlined that line. We'd been there before, hadn't we? Hadn't that been the line she'd spoken in Evan's room also, the night she went 'up'? So this was where the story had been going, was it? That still, after all this time, there was Evan. There was Caroline, and she 'didn't know what she was going to do'.

And, as I say again, there he was, there she was. And all the notes I'd already made, taken from details Evan had given me – the water polo incident and what Caroline had said, what David had said. 'Don't start laying down the law about gender to me,' saying. 'Boys and girls. Boys and girls bullshit. You don't know the first thing about it. You're drunk. You've been drunk all day . . .' and Caroline nearly drowning then and crying and then someone must have taken her home but not David after all because the next thing she knew she'd woken up in her own bed, and no one there in the house, no David, no boys, only Evan there . . . Her bikini puddled in a pile on the kitchen floor, wet footsteps still showing on the shiny tiles, leading out the kitchen to the hallway and the stairs – these details were accumulating, happening, with only pages left in this story to go, and not even pages, no, not even more than a couple of paragraphs to go . . .

'What then?' I said, I managed, I had to know. This new Evan. Resolved. Content. The story nearly over. The story done.

'What then?' I repeated.

'I ate the bikini,' Evan replied. He smiled. 'I know . . .'

He took up my hand. 'Crazy, Nin. I know. But that's what happened, it's what I did. First, yes. I went to her room like she'd asked me. I sat on the bed, we talked, she talked, I listened and I brought her a cup of tea—'

'You ate . . .' I started.

'Yes,' he smiled again. 'I cut it up, in little pieces, but yes, over the course of the evening that followed I ate it, finished the whole thing. It's resolved, Nin. The story is over. Everything that happened between Caroline and me . . .'

'Is gone,' I finished for him.

'I finished it, yes.'

'And everything else, everything that had happened before . . . ?'

'Her room, my room, her there waiting for me in her room, yes, all that, too . . .'

'Is finished.'

'Gone, yes.' Evan smiled his smile again, this new smile of his I'd never seen before, well maybe I had, but that was years ago, years and years and years ago when he and I had lived next door to each other and loved each other, spent all our time together, maybe from then, that smile, I remembered, maybe then . . .

'The last thing she said was "Stay with me, Evan,"' he said, 'before she closed her eyes. But I knew she would sleep deeply. Knew that soon, David and the boys would come home.'

'So that's when . . .'

'Yeah. I went downstairs. The bikini was there. As I've said, it was a simple thing to do. And then, when that was done, when it was, as it were, gone . . . Eaten . . . I started packing. I'm leaving Richmond, Nin. A removal company are on their way there now to get my things.'

'I see,' I may have said, but probably just nodded.

'What I love about you, Nin. About this whole project,' Evan said. 'Is that I can tell you everything. As I have told you everything from the start.'

'Even that,' I said. 'That final, final thing. That weird and strange thing that you've just said now.'

'Even that,' he replied. 'Everything.'

And a kid leapt down then and seemed to land just behind him. But it was an optical illusion, the way the swing-bars were set above his head; a tiny voice cried out, 'Yay!'

'Everything,' I finished. 'Well . . .'

My voice trailed away. I couldn't take my eyes off him.

'But even so . . .' Evan said, and he leaned over, he leaned right over. 'I couldn't have done any of this, you know, got started, gone on, created a middle, a beginning, the end of it . . . Couldn't have thought how to manage it, write it, describe it and plan it, this, the whole book, the project, the novel, essay, whatever, I couldn't have done any of it at all . . .' he said, and stood, and he pulled me up with him and we stood together, blue sky all around him, shattered glass dissolved into sun and light and water . . . 'Without,' he finished . . .

'You.'

# Some Further Material

*Caroline's Bikini*, the project undertaken by Emily Stuart and Evan Gordonston as a formal experimentation of the extended style of narrative some may call essay or reportage but that I refer to here as 'novel', is now finished. The words are done, arranged. The piece overall has a contents page and a cover and all the rest of it; my job here is simply to direct interested readers towards those particulars relating to the work that are to do with background, personal history, and so on – to paint a picture of London and a segment of society in that fine city as inhabited by those in this book who have always lived there; their activities, to an extent, revealed in addition to what is already shown, in the way that all stories continue beyond the pages of books and have no ending but send out further lines to be considered in echoes, reflections, ghostings, of the written originals.

It's like that swimming pool again, where this book started. That image of a pool that could be anywhere, in any city, country or town . . . In the same way, the splash and sounds of people enjoying themselves there, in that blue water, their voices, shouts and calls might be a kind of metaphor, a reminder that Caroline Beresford and her friends, and Emily Stuart and Evan Gordonston and their families . . . Everyone whose name has featured in this novel sits along with others we already know in our own lives, encircling each other as memories of all kinds of people we love. So our own stories are interlinking with fiction's circular lines to make one continual, endless narrative . . . A slide of clear blue water endlessly interrupted by gesture and movement, turning and shining in the light, shifting, even when the pool's watery surface is completely devoid of swimmers.

How to use these pages that follow?

As you will. There's no order, in particular; just flick straight through, or find parts you might want to read in more depth. Every section reminds you where it comes from, in Evan's story – from what conversation or scene – a reminder perhaps of earlier chapters in the novel, or hints, perhaps, in other places, of stories gone untold. The minute I started assembling these notes, I realised they could have no end. Old London? The way things used to be? Before oligarchs and giant shopping malls? The friendship that existed between the Gordonstons and the Stuarts, before the Gordonstons all moved to New York? I could write about these things forever. Then there's the section on love, its curious emanations in the beautiful poetry of Petrarch, Dante . . . Again, books have been written on that subject and though I have but scant details for you here, scholars will tell you that these stories, too, are infinite.

We want to go on and on.

For now, I'll leave my own desire to continue, not leave this story at an end, by way of this second introduction –

and a selection of stories and ideas from my own materials that run at great length in pages and pages of handwritten and printed texts. A bikini is cut, as Evan Gordonston knows, from the smallest increment of this fabric. One may assume it, Caroline's top and bottom, as Evan does, no mistake about that. But there is, Reader, so much more besides.

## Narrative Construction

Overall, one needs to consider the moment of attraction. Back on p. 29, Evan Gordonston describes this as a 'ping'; Emily Stuart on p. 25 as 'BANG', in capital letters, just like that. Either way it denotes an instant moment of romantic crisis – attraction, passion, ardour . . . All gathered together on the page when one may describe oneself as being lovestruck, as though 'hurled' off a bike, we read on p. 17. Or by Cupid's arrow, as some would have it. In *Caroline's Bikini* it is the appearance of Caroline Beresford at the front door of her Richmond home that sets Evan's heart racing, is how we see it in this story. Evan refers to this moment himself as mythic, as an aspect of faith – see pp. 29, 32, 33, when he's describing the effect of Caroline to Emily Stuart. 'It may turn out that I don't even have a life,' he says to the latter on p. 89. 'That that's what my unrequited love for Caroline has made me see.'

See also: 'Literary Context'; 'Courtly Love'.

## Literary Context

*Caroline's Bikini* has been created in a particular style and manner that Emily Stuart and Evan Gordonston arrived at together following one of their initial meetings in a West London pub. It comprises an oral account as rendered by Evan over several gin and tonics that were served with occasional bags of nuts and crisps, along with transcripts of notes and journals and various papers he also provided that were then gathered up together and fashioned into one document by Emily, in the hours when she was not talking with Evan, and later, also taking notes herself as part of those discussions.

In this way, Stuart describes herself as 'amanuensis' to Evan Gordonston – meaning, literally, that she saw herself, throughout the entire process, as standing by, at Evan's hand, to take down details of whatever he had to tell her that day or evening and deliver this up again to him in neat, orderly sentences and paragraphs.

The dictionary definition is precise and useful when we think of Emily Stuart's key role in the 'novel', as it was later termed by Gordonston, as it describes perfectly the way such a writer is both necessary to the project in hand and yet curiously invisible. *Chambers's Twentieth Century Dictionary* presents it thus:

*Amanuensis*: n. one who writes to dictation: a copying secretary.

On p. 7, when Gordonston first suggests this manner of his relationship with Stuart, in terms of the prose project underway, she, immediately, is made to think of Milton, a favourite poet of hers who, she remembers from English Literature classes at university, dictated his great epic *Paradise Lost* from bed, first thing in the morning, is how she sees it, after a long night of composing before he went to sleep. He had become blind and widowed in the latter stages of his life and was looked after by his daughters, who would take down as dictation great portions of the poem that he was ready to deliver to them, 'possibly before breakfast was even served' – she made a note of that somewhere and it has stuck. She knows there are other accounts of the poet's life in which others were called upon by the poet to help in the same way – students, friends, even the young poet Andrew Marvell. But Stuart has it in mind that the daughters were the main amanuenses in the story she's interested in. It seems he would have the stanza fully developed in his mind and would then simply recite it through at length, from memory. On other occasions, after breakfast had been served, perhaps, he would compose new lines of the poem and develop these as one of his daughters was making the copy, reading back portions of the text as they went along, much in the same way Emily Stuart would recount lines of Evan Gordonston's own writing and conversation as *Caroline's Bikini* proceeded.

The key difference between the practices of the great English poet and a somewhat diffident copywriter and occasional short story author might be this: that Stuart also had a role in the composition itself, adumbrating details given her by her friend, or, in some places, filling in gaps where Gordonston had neglected to provide key material or had had simply no idea that some detail or other might be necessary.

The other differentiation, naturally, is quality, volume and content of the work in hand. In order to write the complete poem, consisting of 10,550 lines and 79,810 words, Milton was reliant upon his memory to a far greater extent than either Gordonston or Stuart in imagining, fashioning and editing his mighty epic, the point of which was the poet's not insubstantial intention to 'justify the ways of God to man'. It is a work that has continued to influence and shape the English-speaking world unto this day and the story of the love of a middle-aged banker for a woman in West London is, of course, much less in scope in every respect. Indeed, *Caroline's Bikini* might be seen as being rather more of a record of events than a piece of literature. Certainly Emily Stuart, resisting the importunacies of Evan Gordonston, in his desire to make something larger of the story – a 'novel, even' as he has it by the second section of the book – tends towards this view. As she reminds Gordonston on several occasions, if this project, though it could seem quite 'full on' at times (p. 53), 'was ever, ever going to get finished some day, move on . . .' (p. 57) there would have to be rather more 'going on' than was in evidence in the current version of the text they were creating together.

As it is, *Caroline's Bikini* follows the current matrix in its development: 'project' (also, later, 'document') to 'book' to 'novel' to 'essay' (also referred to as 'intervention' and 'report'). NB these terms become interchangeable as the story moves on. Indeed that word 'story' features, and some readers may wish to note the heading of the final section, 'Finishing Lines', as having some relevance in this context. In general, the ontological differences in nomenclature suggest the variations of thought as the author moves from one consideration of the project to another: a 'document' is not an 'essay', etc.

Throughout the work, however, Emily Stuart maintains her role of amanuensis, as previously noted. She holds in mind certain memories of John Milton and his daughters and returns to these, periodically, as well as the great poem itself, though her readings are not detailed in the story here. She loves the lines about how he made his poem come together which they all memorised in that *Paradise Lost* class she went to in first year, from the invocation to Book IX:

> If answerable style I can obtain
> Of my celestial patroness, who deigns
> Her nightly visitation unimplored,
> And dictates to me slumb'ring, or inspires
> Easy my unpremeditated verse . . .

Somewhere, in all her old university notes, Emily has a version of the following, xeroxed by a tutor, about the account left by his 'anonymous biographer', whom scholar Helen Darbishire identified as Milton's nephew John Phillips: 'And hee waking early (as is the use of temperate men) had commonly a good stock of Verses ready against his Amanuensis came; which if it happened to bee later than ordinary, hee would complain, Saying *hee wanted to bee milkd.*'

So 'amanuensis', Emily herself wrote upon that same xerox, is 'a torch beam in the shadows that writes, and writes, creating from its beam, from words spoken, a living text on white paper'. No wonder then it is a term that occurs to her in the opening pages of *Caroline's Bikini*.

## General Context: Emily Stuart and Her Love of *Paradise Lost*

Emily Stuart was always a keen student of English Literature, first meeting the epic poem *Paradise Lost* when she was about sixteen, and immediately having a sense of excitement around Milton's great literary adventure to render in English iambic pentameter the fall of man within the great heroic tradition. In addition, and more importantly, as far as the young Emily was concerned, was the fact that Milton had identified for himself a fresh and challenging literary 'project', to use Emily's own description. She fell, from the very outset, she says, for the way the great poet had imagined his way into a story using sources that already existed – from the Book of Genesis through to the *Iliad* to the very latest in scientific thinking, and with as great a frame of reference contained within that scale as one might imagine, spectacular in imaginative and intellectual reach, as was articulated so precisely in the footnotes given in her schoolgirl edition of *Paradise Lost*, the version edited by John Carey and Alastair Fowler in 1971.

'He made a world for himself,' Stuart replied, when asked why precisely Milton interested her as a poet. 'He imagined his way into the poet he was going to be from . . . way back. Then it was simply a case of educating himself, learning about the world and being fully in that world, and the time would come for him to enter into the place of his poem. And to write from that place. I love that,' she concluded.

Readers may also want to note some interesting coincidences here: *Caroline's Bikini* is set, for a large part, around the various pubs and hostelries of West London; Emily Stuart herself lives in an area on the borders of Hammersmith. John Milton lived in Hammersmith. 'Not that that means anything at all,' Stuart is keen to emphasise. Only that it seems 'kind of nice', 'that we are neighbours, in that way'. There is, too, the other interesting feature: that Milton lived and wrote in 'Stuart' times. Emily Stuart quite likes that coincidence as well.

## Further Notes

Emily's anxiety about how the narrative is being interrupted by a remark from Evan:

At several points, in the pages that she has accumulated in the creation of a 'report' or 'novel', the author indicates, both to Evan and to herself, her unease with the way various interlocutions are interfering with the flow or any potential drama of the prose. This is both a feature of her writing in general, but also an element that seems to continue to surprise and sometimes bother her. 'How can the story go on', as she puts it, if there are these questions and doubts about the usefulness of its content to its overall sense of purpose?

Similar reflexive moments in the text:

There are countless instances in *Caroline's Bikini* where both Emily Stuart and Evan Gordonston, individually or in conversations together, identify moments in their writing of the story that might influence it. The quality of various handwritten pages, the quantity of gin that has been taken, the time of year or manner of dress . . . These matters and more preoccupy them in ways that find themselves expressed in the four sections of *Caroline's Bikini*, either directly or indirectly. In some parts of the story the printed lines themselves seem to reflect this quality of the narrative reflexivity – where Emily has to stop herself from writing any more about something that Evan has done or might say, for example, or having to set pages to one side and not refer to them, for the danger of it causing her too much emotional disquiet. It should also be noted that occasional Americanisms from Evan stall the narrative even in its late stages, see p. 243, and various remarks from both parties about the quality of syntax, language, idiom, etc., intervene and sometimes seem to derail the narrative at key points in the story. This self-awareness about the writing process as it develops is part of the intertextual quality of the story – see below, 'The Meta-narrative of *Caroline's Bikini*'.

## The Meta-narrative of *Caroline's Bikini*

The over-arching idea that lies behind both the making of the story of Evan Gordonston's love for Caroline Beresford and its expression is rested on a cycle of fourteenth-century love poems, the *Canzoniere* by Petrarch.

To this end, the reader should bear certain remarks made by Evan Gordonston about the nature of the 'project' he and Emily Stuart have undertaken with a reasonable amount of reservation: i.e. this is very much a 'story', or, as is suggested by Stuart early on, a 'report'. It is not, as Gordonston might have it, a 'myth' or narrative of that stature. Indeed, the scattered nature of the original *Canzoniere* (as they were originally known, all the poems, as scattered 'pieces') might furnish a useful metaphor for Stuart's narrative approach in *Caroline's Bikini*. She would by no means attest to having created anything more formal than that, a sort of gathering together of information that at one point in the story she hazards may even be a kind of 'essay, even'.

The poems of the *Canzoniere* are, as they inform Stuart's own approach, both scattered and fragmentary but also unbroken in the sense that together they make up a sequence of sonnets written over a period of some forty years. In this sequence they describe the course of a love affair that is unrequited, though no less present or meaningful than a consummated romance. Of course the idea that one may make art in order to express an emotion stands behind much of the western literary tradition, as does the notion of poetry itself as being one of the most meaningful expressions of love and desire. Still, the *Canzoniere*, like Dante's great project, occupies a place in our minds given over to the contemplation of the beloved as an end in itself and as such inspires many writers to create work that may also be substituted for the reality of the love affair itself.

Though prose, *Caroline's Bikini* draws on this poetic tradition as an example of what I call 'writing reality' – a form of literature that does not seek to imitate life so much as to generate it. By writing up an account of Gordonston and Beresford, the author, with scant literary experience and success as a known stylist (there's talk of a few short stories, and contributions to various volumes only, that have been published; for the most part Stuart is the author of pet food and insurance campaigns), is able to make real the circumstances of 'a great love', as she puts it. She writes it into being on the page and the work that is created is itself the physical representation of that love.

See also: 'Courtly Love'.

## Modernism and 'Making It Real'

A key element of the project in hand is the modernist impulse to create a 'machine of words', as the American poet and short story writer William Carlos Williams put it. The idea of making a piece of work that requires no information outside its own frame of reference to fully exist as 'real', that could be said to be all-encompassing, in the way it articulates and builds a world, this is fundamental to Stuart's understanding of *Caroline's Bikini*. Her wish is to create 'in paragraphs and sentences', as she puts it, a story that is not so much made up, in the imagined sense of the word, as made up of real-life words and phrases and ideas.

To this end, it is hoped, the author will be able to make something that is larger than the sum of its parts, a building together of pages and concepts that together come to have meaning and emotional charge quite outside the experience or imagination of the writer herself. The Southern American writer Katherine Anne Porter is cited, in this context, with reference to her ideal of 'increase', i.e. that the work of literature itself, the result of that construction of words, may lead to an experience that, for the reader, enlarges and adumbrates his or her world. There is, too, inherent in the Southern writer's ideal, the concept of mystery, that 'increase' may also be of a more transcendental kind.

## Personal History

This section covers a range of background relating to the Stuart and Gordonston families, referred to largely on pp. 8, 9, 11, 55, 58, 59 and 64, along with some other general details about the writer's life and achievements.

See also: 'Personal Social History'.

### Family

The Gordonston and Stuart families lived next door to each other throughout a formative period well before that described in *Caroline's Bikini*. Tom and Helen Gordonston moved, with their three children, Elisabeth, Evan and Felicity, into 17 Berkshire Lane in Twickenham six months after the Stuart family had arrived at No. 15 and from the start it was clear that the two families would become close friends and neighbours.

This was in a time that seems now to belong to another age, and a different sort of city than that which we know to be London today. Twickenham then had more of a village feel than it seems to possess nowadays; families grew up and stayed there; there was no evidence of the conspicuous consumption that now marks so many of London's residential areas; children roamed freely in the streets and parks after school, and most families had pets. The houses were large and ramshackle and comfortable, with spacious overgrown gardens featuring plum and apple trees, old oaks and sycamores. Berkshire Lane itself backed on to woods, and it was there where Evan and Emily, as children, loved to explore – making forts, hide-outs, setting adventure trails and finding ways to get lost.

From the outset the two children were friends. Margaret Stuart, her daughter remembers to this day, said to Emily, the moment the Gordonstons moved into No. 17, 'I see they have a little boy your own age. I wouldn't be at all surprised if you and he become great friends.'

The thoughts of a parent can set the tone for a friendship – that somewhat peremptory 'I wouldn't be at all surprised . . .' that would transcend years and distance. This, despite the fact that the Gordonston family left Berkshire Lane when Evan and Emily were eleven years old, and the two were not to see each other for the entire period intervening, during which Evan pursued a high-level career in international finance that took him to Tokyo and the Far East, in addition to the American cities in which he lived during this time. Emily, all through this time, though remaining in London, didn't 'pursue' any particular career at all. 'I write pet food ads' is her simple response still to the question, when put to her, 'What exactly do you do?' She is, in her own words, 'no high flyer'.

Evan, however, despite his CV, would say the same. The two friends remain as close now as ever, as though the bond that was established at the ages of four and five years is still as vivid and direct and uncomplicated as it was from that morning, with her mother's words still echoing, when Evan Gordonston came knocking on the Stuarts' front door. For the international financier is 'just Evan' as far as the Stuarts are concerned, all of them, not just Emily, but her brother Felix and mother, Margaret, and father, Alastair.

Emily herself, though she is no longer in touch with Felicity, Evan's younger sister, still counts her as a 'best friend', a phrase that in itself denotes a relationship formed in early childhood. Elisabeth, Evan's elder sister, went out for a while with Felix, a relationship that was reignited when the latter went for a visit to San Francisco whereto the former had moved permanently as a young woman; and there was talk for a long time, of a possible marriage there.

Alastair and Margaret Stuart are academics, both historians, who retired some years ago, though Alastair Stuart continues to publish on the areas of pre-Clearance Highland history and post-industrial Scotland, and Margaret edits secondary school history textbooks at GCSE and sixth form levels, and acts in an advisory capacity at various external exam boards and school reviews committees across the UK.

Felix Stuart, Emily's older brother, is also an historian, the author, amongst many other books, of *This New Land* and *Kingdom*, both of which went on to become the popular BBC series of the same names. He is currently Associate Professor of Modern History at Oxford and Visiting Monash Professor of Contemporary Historical Studies at the University of New South Wales.

Tom and Helen Gordonston still live in the United States, though following the election of Donald Trump, are now considering a return to the United Kingdom. Tom Gordonston, though long retired, continues to sit on the boards of a number of prominent financial institutions, and his wife Helen, a ceramicist and painter, shows regularly at the Dewitt Gallery in New York and Los Angeles. Their daughters Felicity and Elisabeth also live in America. Felicity keeps an apartment in New York City where she teaches dance and movement at primary school level, and Elisabeth lives with her boyfriend in Sonoma Country in California where they run a small wine and food business.

The Gordonston and Stuart families, despite the distance and years between their present circumstances and their past, continue to be in touch with each other – Helen and Margaret in phone calls and old-fashioned letters, on the composition of which they both spend a great deal of time, including photos and clippings from magazines, and lists of ideas and plans in what becomes an A4-size envelope; Tom and Alastair by email, which they use as a medium, chiefly, to exchange chess moves and acrostic crossword puzzle clues, as well as a regular letter that Alastair sends to Tom in a sort of handmade package. The children of both families are less frequently in communication with each other, though emails are sent, messages occasionally left, and 'random', as Felix puts it, cards and letters arrive from the Gordonston girls addressed to both him and Emily, and for their part, the Stuart siblings have been known occasionally to write long and complex postcards, sometimes as many as ten in a series, in return.

Evan and Emily, close friends as children, were similarly only ever occasionally in touch with each other after the Gordonstons moved to the US. There were one or two long-distance phone calls at the beginning of the separation, an email or two, but on the whole, communication between the two was scarce. However, upon Evan's return to London, the two resumed their friendship as though 'no time at all had passed', as Emily puts it in *Caroline's Bikini*. It was as though some door opened that had been closed for a while, and there was Evan. 'Hi,' he said, like he'd just that minute turned up at the door of No. 15 Berkshire Lane, the address at which Emily's parents still live. 'Do you want to come out and play?'

NB: Cultural historians and anthropologists from Margaret Mead onwards have continued to address the compelling nature of early friendships in the forging of adult ties and societies. Important works are too numerous to cite here, but Evan and Emily's story could happily feature in any contemporary study and hold its own.

'I always loved the Gordonstons,' said Emily Stuart's mother, Margaret, on more than one occasion, both within and outwith the pages of *Caroline's Bikini*. 'I'm just so thrilled, Emily, that Evan has, you know, come home.'

## Life as a Freelance Reviewer and Copywriter

Emily Stuart wondered for a long time if there was something wrong with her in not following in her family's footsteps and 'going down the history path', as she puts it. Though she excelled at the subject in school, when it came time to select a subject for university study, she opted instead for English, a discipline which had always interested her and in which she had also always done well in examinations and essays, and continued to find curious and inspiring, both – a surprising combination of reactions that she had never felt pertained in that other humanities subject that so engaged the rest of her family.

The study of English literature, however, may not necessarily fit one for life in the same way other – even non-STEM – subjects might. After graduating, Emily spent time as a waitress and coat-check girl in very fancy restaurants, worked in bars and nightclubs serving cocktails, all the time thinking about and sometimes writing short stories that were rarely published. When she was well into her thirties, following some gentle persuasion by her friends, she took up freelance work for various magazines and journals, writing reviews and critiques, sometimes interviews, and also, as time went on, learned the skills that meant she could take on the copywriting work – at first filling in for close deadlines at the last minute, completing long copy work that had already been started in-agency – that would so absorb her. After gaining further experience, she was confident in taking on entire marketing projects herself, from the original 'spec', working straight off a brief and creating the headline, subhead, selling line, and all the rest of it. Her friend Marjorie is in the advertising business and has said on more than one occasion: 'Emily would be great at this game if she would just commit to going full-time. She has what it takes – the imagination and good education – to fly. It's just that she doesn't want to. She loves being freelance and we all just have to accept that. It's the way she is.'

As a result of this choice, though, Emily's relationship with work is 'perilous and interesting', as she puts it in other terms on p. 12. There will be weeks at a time when she is doing nothing but writing long copy, ads and associated leaflets and brochures . . . The list goes on and on. And other times when there is little work around, and she considers going back to the old waitressing game – even though she is far too old for that, now, she knows. Those 'thin' times, as Marjorie puts it, are when she helps out at an art gallery over in Hoxton, manning the desk there while working on catalogue copy and indexing for forthcoming exhibitions. So there it is, her working week or month or year: 'perilous and interesting' indeed.

For there is no doubt that there is nothing boring about the texture of her day-to-day life as far as writing is concerned, and it provides more than ample scope and practice of basic skills that might allow her to embark on a longer writing project such as the one suggested by Evan Gordonston in this book. Her robust abilities as a day-to-day 'jobbing writer', as they say in the ad world, more than her list of fictional publications, which, it has to be said, is a very short one, serves her for the work in hand. When she troubles herself on p. 217 of this manuscript: 'Might these pages ever "find a readership"?' she speaks not as a capable freelance person with a top CV as far as working experience goes, but as a short story writer who would love, so very much, to publish a collection of work, or even a novel, with a distinguished house.

### Advertising Work and Copy

Emily Stuart's advertising work has been part of award-winning campaigns in the pet food and insurance worlds. She has also worked on leading brands in sports shoes, so-called 'designer' fruit juices and shakes, and personal banking, and created a 'through-the-line' presence, from billboard to fulfilment reward coupons, for a major supermarket chain. She is indeed 'capable', as indicated above.

The copy is always delivered 'clean and on time', by which advertising companies mean fully edited, finished, and to job 'spec' and deadline. She is thoroughly reliable in that way. Before the return of Evan Gordonston to London, Stuart tended to accept all offers of work that came her way, and continued to work to close deadlines in a reliable fashion. It was only later, over the writing period of *Caroline's Bikini* in fact, that she started to, first, take longer with various projects than she used to, and then later set them aside altogether.

Her general copywriting work – chiefly that for Prinn Arts in Hoxton – suffered in the same way. At one point, around the Easter period in this text, she received a call from the gallerist there, Samantha Prinn herself, asking, 'Do you even want to come in and work with us any more? It's been so long since we've seen you, and we had to give the Bill Henderson show to someone else. Let me know, will you, what you want to do?'

### Use of Current Language, Idiom, Idiolect in Contemporary Prose

Many of Emily Stuart's expressions derive from her range of copywriting work, her links, if you like, with the world of popular culture and media. Though she has never worked on any campaigns related to mobile phones or social media, she has a serviceable vocabulary of various expressions that may function in a youth-oriented market, or might do for persons around her age who are still interested in contemporary fashions and mores. 'Go hang' is one such example, as used on p. 72 of *Caroline's Bikini*; others might be 'I'm not bothered', 'move on' and 'index' as well as the more old-fashioned 'groovy', 'cool' or the compression of English in the appearance of a text or Instagram message: 'Where u at?', etc.

In the same way, when constructing this text, Stuart is aware of those moments in the 'narrative', as she continues to call it – despite Evan's suggestions and, later, demands, that it may be something else, a 'novel' and so on – that she might give shape and tone to certain sentences by letting her own, more literary, sensibility shine through. The short story writer in her then comes out to play, for example, when she suggests, in the same page referred to above, that Caroline's medication may take the simile of a 'pulse' in the paragraph – one of many, many examples.

She is also keen to let full pieces of dialogue sit complete in the text, giving life to the pages, she believes, but also letting the rhythm and sound of its interlocutions be heard by the reader. This kind of awareness of idiolect, in the crafting of a character in fiction – short story or novel – is something that Stuart, the aspiring fiction writer and literary reviewer, has 'a lot of time for', as she says. 'A character is created in the words he or she says. Not nearly enough writers pay attention to that, but I want to.'

### Reflexive Moments in *Caroline's Bikini*

There are many, many moments, throughout this text, when the reader becomes aware of the writer being aware of the overall project in hand. A fancier way of putting it would be to refer to the 'countless incidents of metatextuality' – as a dear scholar I know put it recently about another book – that we see on show as the narrative progresses.

At first, this is a subject that preoccupies Stuart as the writer of Evan Gordonston's story – there's that reference to herself from the first pages of the work as 'amanuensis' and so on – but gradually, and perhaps almost imperceptibly, the notion of self-consciousness is displayed as a growing theme of the story. Emily Stuart is a copywriter, not a novelist, so she must ask herself, over and over again: Are these pages 'good enough?', 'interesting enough?' etc. etc., to be a novel. 'I'd had opinions from the outset, truth to tell', as she puts it so declaratively and boldly early on in the first section of the proceedings. This is a theme that must and will be explored fully in the reading of *Caroline's Bikini*. See for further examples of reflexive text, pp. 12, 15, 26, 66, 104.

## Linguistic Variations in *Caroline's Bikini*

As has already been observed, there is a deal of tonal range in the text that makes up Emily Stuart and Evan Gordonston's conversation about the latter's great love for Caroline Beresford. This range is accounted for by the fact that much of the narrative is rendered in dialogue, or in notes and remarks that have the vocabulary and rhythm of both parties' speech. This much is obvious, of course. No two people will sound exactly alike on the page – no matter how close their friendship or how used they are to each other's habits of behaviour and expression. It should never be the case any more in reading than in life that one might mistake one person for another when one is in close proximity with both and listening intently to what they are saying. Such is the effect of a novel that it may bring the reader as near to the people in its pages as one might be to the range of personalities and figureheads and strangers and employers, friends, family, and whoever one comes across in life.

However, it may also be noted that there are points in this text when both voices, due to the quantity of gin taken by the protagonists, perhaps, on some occasions, or the fact of physical positioning at certain sizes of pub table, or because of the amount of reading of notes that has taken place, or number of questions asked and answers given, may seem to merge, somewhat, on the page. There are times, it is true, when Emily Stuart and Evan Gordonston may sound, almost uncannily, alike. As though they might be brother and sister, twins, even. To use an old cliche often used for family members who are very close to each other: They may well be on these occasions 'two sides of the same coin'.

Finally, it is also observed throughout the 'novel' under review that others also enter the story with their voices, so to speak. There is that 'Coffee?' of Caroline's, so bright, sometimes, it seems to ring off the page. There is that early memorable line from Rosie Howard, early on in the story, entailing the information that the house in Richmond comprises 'a fun scene'. These are just examples of a quality displayed in each of the sections of the narrative that might 'people' the text further in the way just described.

These additional personalities, in the way they are closely accounted for and reported by Stuart, contribute further towards a literary experience that the reader may feel is busy with variation and range, while continuing to return to its central preoccupations with the quality of its content, its duration, lack of plot, sense of repetition, etc., etc.

## Evan Gordonston's Vocabulary, Cadence and Syntax

When Evan Gordonston returned from living in the United States, after some three decades (actually, a bit more than that, too) away from Britain, the country to which he returned was vastly different to that which he had left – in all kinds of ways to do with an overturn of a political conservatism and the permission of rampant capitalism to predate and determine personal and social outcomes in ways that had not been able to dominate in a prior era – but these notes here focus specifically upon terms of speech, language use and syntax adopted, as well as tonal differentiation and vocabulary in everyday communication.

For that reason, certain Americanisms that Evan Gordonston had picked up while living over there, certain words and phrases that were part of his everyday speech, could also be observed in use in the wider culture. 'Do you want that to go?' a barista now asks a customer at a cafe or coffee bar. 'Hi guys' is the way most British mothers will greet a number of their daughters' and sons' friends.

Other phrases and words, though, as Emily Stuart is seen to observe frequently in *Caroline's Bikini*, seem to jump out at her, and arrive on the page fully formed from Evan Gordonston's talk, striking her with all the force of an American baseball player hitting a home run. 'The mood in Richmond just "said summer"' might be an example of this sort of variation, 'and some' . . . Not to mention various remarks and so on taken straight from Evan's personal notes and journals that display an easy familiarity with lingo from 'across the pond', as some may describe it.

Though, as the story goes on, we see Gordonston's speech start to modulate, through the influence of environment – he is back 'home' in London, after all – and due, as well, and perhaps to a larger extent, to the close contact he has with Emily Stuart over the course of the book, we can nevertheless identify an individual who has a degree of transatlantic accent, or more, tone, as well as vocabulary when he speaks.

As we read in the text itself, towards the end of the story, near the beginning of the last section on p. 243: 'He had these American phrases that still came out every now and then, sentences and words that had been generated by years living in New York and Chicago and Boston, all those years he'd had away that I couldn't imagine, not really, not think about, nor believe in.'

It's a moment in the story where we see Stuart's writing, her simple report of a fact or feature to do with her friend, seem to open up into a wider observation, one that we might be aware of when considering the 'account' of Evan Gordonston's love that is *Caroline's Bikini*: that is, that she can't 'imagine' any other Evan, 'not really', other than the one who is sitting before her, familiar to her as she is to herself, nursing a gin and tonic. Language in that sense, both hers and that of the man she describes, is all.

It takes little for her, so accustomed is she to his mood and presence, to take in, by gesture, tone and word, fresh variations of Evan Gordonston's 'turn of phrase', a 'turn' that, as the phrase itself suggests, is both surprising and capable of taking her thinking in a new direction, bending her thoughts towards the musicality and appeal of American spoken English. So we have, then, on the same page as referred to above: ' . . . on the basis of Evan's American turn of phrase, the mood in Richmond "said summer". It was hot enough. People were outdoors and on the streets, voices were raised. Clothing worn was light and careless. *The mood did indeed, all over London, say summer*' (italics, editor's own).

### Further Details of Speech, Embedded in Evan Gordonston's Past

Gordonston's levels of articulacy and expression had been influenced, of course they had, by his years, both as a teenager and young man, growing up on the Eastern Seaboard, as they call that part of America between New York and Boston, and then, as indicated above, settled into a particular pattern and diction often described as transatlantic English.

Where, as a young boy living in London, going around to Emily Stuart's house he might ask her something like 'Do you want to ask your mother if it's alright to come with me and Mum to the Victoria and Albert Museum?' he would, by the time he was a teenager living in Connecticut, greet friends with a 'Hey! Wanna go into the city with my mom and me, to see some show at the Met?'

In the same way, certain words were replaced by others. Though he would not refer to his own parent thus, he would suggest to friends that various activities might be 'run past your dad' or in a phrase like 'check it out with your mom'. Tom and Helen were 'Mum and Dad', they always would be, but the variation just noted was revealed when out with his peer group, at school or in various recreational contexts that applied when he was much older as well.

Other changes that were made in vocabulary can be suggested, in part, by the following list:

Soccer – football
Cool – great
No brainer – not worth even thinking about it
For sure – yes
Trash – rubbish
Cookie – biscuit
Eraser – rubber
So long – goodbye

In addition Evan Gordonston's lifestyle and pastimes would naturally dictate a whole new dictionary. He played 'baseball', and went out for a treat to the 'diner' or 'that take-out place that does really good fries'. He wore 'shades' in the summer when they all went to the beach at Cape Cod or the Hamptons, he 'stood in line' at the post office when sending a card or package to his friend Emily Stuart in London; at some point he nearly forgot what a queue was.

Later, once he'd started working in legal firms around Wall Street, inhabiting a much more international world and surrounded by a good number of 'Brits' as native New Yorkers called them, some of the old words and expressions returned.

This pattern of course – of returning to the past – was at its most marked in his relations with Stuart, when he physically made the return to his homeland, carried out in various pubs across West London. As noted in the text, we then see the return to 'Fancy another?' or 'Let me get another round in', the kind of expressions that, though he'd been too young to use them when he still lived in London, now returned to him as though deeply embedded in his DNA.

Finally, what may be added is the matter of Gordonston's dress. Careful readers will have noted those 'polo shirts' he referred to, when unpacking his things in Richmond; there is also the disruption in the text when Stuart notes his adoption of 'sweat pants' as he calls them, indicating a level of carelessness with his personal appearance she is not used to seeing that concerns her; as though the very term itself describes a way of being, feeling, that she is not accustomed to and that seems alien and peculiar to her. 'Tracksuit bottoms' is one thing, as she notes in an aside on p. 123, and bad enough to be wearing them outside the house, but 'sweat pants' brings his idea of trousers to a whole new level of squalor.

What's interesting though, despite the general sorts of variations indicated here, their persistence in some places, along with that slight softening or slurring of speech a British person can hear in an American voice – as noted in the narrative, 'ciddy' for 'city' say, or, we could add, a kind of 'rilly' for 'really' or a 'no WAY' for 'no way' or an occasional insertion of an unnecessary question mark: 'You're kidding me?' for 'You're kidding me!' – in general, though these patterns tend, in many people, to become fixed, Evan Gordonston, upon coming back to London and meeting up again immediately with his old childhood friend, Emily 'Nin' Stuart, seemed to lose, for the most part, those traces of American syntax and sentence order retained by most. 'He sounded', as Emily says on p. 10 of *Caroline's Bikini*, 'just the same . . . as though he'd never been gone.'

Final note: American and British idiolect and tone are interesting to consider in light of each other. The American reader is more likely to read a British voice as, unless dramatically indicated by spellings, variation in syntax, use of doggerel, idiom and so on, a generally British one, and is challenged to hear and see minute regional variations, indications of education, etc.; the same remark pertains to the British reader of American texts where subtleties outside those obvious demarcations of, say, the South, or the remote hill communities of Kentucky and Tennessee, cannot be picked up easily. Is this Wall Street banker from Connecticut or Boston? Is that young woman from Manhattan or Syracuse? Hard to tell.

## Personal Social History

Here follow details of the somewhat complicated social network – including notes on the past lives and habits of certain members of that group – that comprise a key aspect of *Caroline's Bikini*, i.e. that theme of the story devoted to explaining and adumbrating the various relationships and connections that exist between all who inhabit the world of the text.

From the beginning of the story – 'novel' or 'book' or 'report', as it is variously referred to throughout – it is clear that the various individuals in *Caroline's Bikini* are well known to each other, to different degrees, either through direct contact and a history of a past relationship, or at one or two removes from each other.

We might say that in a story where Evan Gordonston and Caroline Beresford are the 'key players', as a particular kind of critic or writer may think of them, this network emanates from the two – that they may be, if you like, suns around which the various planets of the story revolve. Without Caroline there would be no Rosie Howard, for example, no Marjorie Clarke, and so on, let alone a David Beresford or the couple's three teenage boys. Without Evan, there would be no Nin, so to speak, no 'amanuensis', no need at all to get 'all of this down'.

However, that same fact constitutes another layer of meaning and social density in the plot line: The contents of the book are further complicated by the narrative position of Emily Stuart, who, herself, in addition to writing about knowing Evan Gordonston so well and for so long within the context of this friendship group, also interacts with and responds to other characters directly herself, which in turn adds further gradation to her understanding and subsequent rendering of Gordonston himself on the page.

To further trouble this narrative position is the fact that Stuart herself has never met Caroline Beresford. She remains at a distance, as attractive and unattainable as she is to Evan Gordonston himself, through the sheer fact of never having seen her or talked with her face to face. She feels she 'knows' Caroline, she uses expressions such as that one all the way through the story, but this is only because of the detail with which Gordonston has described her, as well as from the various notes and papers with which he is at pains to furnish Stuart – to 'build a complete picture', as he puts it.

Thus, overall, there is a sense running throughout the entire project of the prose, that all who inhabit the world of *Caroline's Bikini* are familiar with each other's presence in the story – whether they meet directly in the text or not.

Rosie Howard, for example, an old friend of Stuart's, knows a great friend of the Beresfords without ever having met Caroline. Her knowledge of that 'fun scene' in Richmond comes to her through this friend's contact on p. 13: 'A friend of a friend of mine has a big and rather stunning, so I understand, house in Richmond. I don't know her – the friend, I mean, Rosie's friend – but Rosie told me she has lodgers . . .' etc. Stuart, in turn, might know something of the social milieu, it is is suggested in the text, simply by knowing Rosie so well; and though Rosie herself knows David Beresford through a friend of hers who went out with his brother, and the Beresfords senior, Jonathan and Diana, she hasn't seen David for some years, though at a party recently in Gloucestershire she did bump into Robert Beresford who talked with her about the family, his parents and his brother, as though Rosie saw them regularly and was in close touch.

The relationships are summarised below. See also pp. 24, 40.

**Emily 'Nin' Stuart** – best friend of Evan Gordonston; long-time friend of the Gordonston family; schoolfriend of Felicity Gordonston; part of a wider social group comprising family friends, some of whose parents also knew the Gordonstons through the Stuarts, including Christopher Lowden and Rosie Howard.

**Evan Gordonston** – best friend of Emily Stuart; brother of Elisabeth Gordonston, who went out with Felix Stuart; connected through mutual friends with, among others, Rosie Howard and Christopher Lowden.

**Rosie Howard** – close friend of Emily Stuart and Ros Greenford, who does not appear in this story but is a good friend of Caroline Beresford, and of Amanda Parker who went out with Robert Beresford, David's younger brother; a good friends of the Beresfords, in general, both sons and their parents, Jonathan and Diana.

**Caroline Beresford** – married to David Beresford, mother of three teenage boys, Andrew, William and Jamie; good friends with a large and vibrant London social set, including Ros Greenford and Amanda Parker.

**David Beresford** – married to Caroline Beresford, father of three teenage boys, as above; brother to Robert Beresford who went out with Amanda Parker; a good friend of

Charlie Caxton Taylor who lives down the road at No. 47; friends too with some banking associates and colleagues, though their social contact is minimal; growing friendship with Professor James Ashford Anderson in the Classics department at the University of London.

**Marjorie Clarke** – has a successful career in advertising and can often offer Emily Stuart 'spillover' work from various briefs and commissions; is an old university friend of both Stuart and Christopher Lowden; also good friend of Rosie Howard; close friends with Samantha Prinn who, along with Betsy Forman runs the Prinn Gallery over in Hoxton which also gives Emily occasional catalogue copywriting work, and used to go out with Martin Howard, Rosie's older brother.

**Christopher Lowden** – close friend of Emily Stuart and Marjorie Clarke; has professional friendships with a wide range of low-level self-styled 'activists' in the West London area, one of whom counts Robert Beresford as a close friend.

In addition there are the parents:

**Tom and Helen Gordonston** – best friends with the Stuarts, Margaret and Alastair; Helen alone is good friends with a large group of neighbours in Connecticut, and artists working in upstate New York, also her gallerist Hilary Goldstein. Tom is somewhat out of touch with old colleagues and friends from Yale; he still enjoys exchanging sophisticated crossword puzzles and historical word games with Alastair Stuart in London.

**Margaret and Alastair Stuart** – best friends with the Gordonstons. Both also have a small but dependable friendship group based around their profession.

**Jonathan and Diana Beresford** – possessed of a wide and varied social group, including old family friends the Howards and the Lowdens.

## Old London

There is a London that still exists below the surface of
what I might call 'New London' – a city that is quieter, less
oriented towards consumerism and what might be described
as 'billboard living', less prone to the signs of conspicuous
consumption that are so in evidence all around the capital
today, from Hoxton to Knightsbridge. Endless building work
being carried out on perfectly nice houses – to fit them with
basement swimming pools, loft-style kitchens, formal gardens
and the like – is one of the many examples of a new populace
eager to spend lots and lots of money and to show that they
are doing so. Once, a perfectly stylish woman would have
a good handbag that she would use for years; now those
handbags go out in the rubbish and instead tiny stylish clutches
and purses thickened with gilt dominate the pages of *Vogue*
and *Tatler*.

These are but small examples of the changes. Dogs are now
made to be walked on leads, in most of the parks, as new
International London is not as dog-friendly as the old place
used to be; lovely department stores like Harvey Nichols are
no longer lovely – where once many were able to buy a pretty
party dress there, now they would be turned away from even
looking for such an item by the racks of leather trousers with
rhinestones priced at £3,000 or more, and skin creams with the
bones and eyes and semen of small animals, along with bits of
gold, in them.

The London that exists below all this, however, and it does
exist – beautiful old drawing rooms with good furniture,
gardens with fruit trees and some weeds, along with clusters of
ravishing old-fashioned roses, tweed coats that Granny used
to wear still hanging in the wardrobe, not one scrap of Lycra
folded in a drawer – is as vibrant and interesting as ever, with
a great number of people happy to potter in their gardens and
have friends around for drinks on a Thursday evening,

Such is the city inhabited by many in *Caroline's Bikini*. Indeed, it may well be due to the unflagging work of the likes of Christopher Lowden and his 'team of mates', as he calls them, those active in the mission of cleaning up London and restoring it to 'past splendour', as he puts it, tirelessly working on every campaign he can identify, from petitioning the council against 'meretricious building extensions that threaten to "vulgarise" the postcode' to forming 'street armies' that deal with the growing litter, as he has identified it, now present in the streets due to, in his words, 'the unprecedented consumption of convenience foods'.

A postnote: Emily's parents, Margaret and Alastair Stuart, still live in the family home in Twickenham and have no plans to sell. Margaret finds the garden a bit much in the early spring, but has a friend, Fiona Laidlaw, who lives three doors down, and they 'garden share', as they call it, helping each other out to stay on top of things with pruning and weeding. Margaret is terribly fond of Fiona, but she is nothing like Helen Gordonston, who Margaret is in close contact with through email, and, now that Felix has showed her how to work it, Skype. 'I still miss Helen,' Margaret says.

## Additional Notes

The friendship between Tom Gordonston and Emily Stuart's father, Alastair, was formed from the start, the moment the Gordonstons moved into No. 17 Berkshire Way and Alastair came over and introduced himself and asked if he could help with anything – books, he said, were his speciality: he was excellent at arranging them on the shelves, in alphabetical order, subject area and so on.

The two men saw each other most weeks. Though Tom Gordonston was in finance and Alastair Stuart an academic and writer the two appeared to have a great deal in common: Tom had always had an interest in modern history, and though that wasn't Alastair's field, his reading was wide-ranging. In addition, Tom Gordonston came to be most interested in Alastair's research in Scottish history – post-Enlightenment – and had an uncle in Inverness, with whom he used to spend a great deal of time as a boy, who wrote books on the Clearances, and so on, pre-empting a fashion for depicting that time as being more complex and nuanced than the 'genocide' it used to be described as back in the seventies, as the subject of material history takes over the broad sweep of earlier approaches.

Tom Gordonston still looks back fondly to 'The Saturdays' as he and Alastair used to call them – informal get-togethers when the two would sit with a whisky chatting about some historical finding or other, the latest books they'd been reading, a sophisticated acrostic they might be 'nutting out', as Alastair put it, together. As he went out of the door, Alastair would fish for something in his pocket – Where was it? went the charade, that he may not have the item he was after at all. Ah! But there it was. Another devilish historical crossword puzzle that Tom would be charged to think about over the next week, when they'd plan to meet again and discuss the outcome of the fiendishly difficult exercise in another one of their 'Saturdays'.

Now that he is retired, Tom Gordonston, sitting in his big house in Connecticut, looks forward to the post arriving. 'Where was the thing? . . . Ah! Here it is, arriving in the "mailbox",' as they call them over there: There's Alastair's familiar manilla envelope, his writing addressing Tom by his full name, giving his own return address also in full. Tom waits until Saturday afternoon to sit alone with a whisky and go through the contents, a note from Alastair about the challenge he has posed in this 'Saturday's' puzzle, the great difficulty and fun of the thing itself, a combination of a crossword he has found and added to with his own clues and boxes, inserting some particular General or Brigadier or other who, if you don't name him in full, will turn the whole game over into nothing but a pile of words. What a pleasure this is for Tom. What a great, great treat.

Felix Stuart, as is noted on p. 8, used to go out with Elisabeth Gordonston from when they were both seventeen and the Gordonstons were still in London. The relationship only lasted for a year – the Gordonstons were to move to America just three weeks after Felix's eighteenth birthday – but in the manner of adolescent relationships, their feelings for each other were intense.

Emily Stuart is a great deal younger than her brother and so was largely unaware of the depression Felix fell into after the departure of the Gordonstons. She herself was far too taken up with missing her best friend Evan to notice how low her brother was. As a result of his broken heart, Felix Stuart turned to work, achieving in his last year at school the results that would put him straight into rooms at St John's College, on an Oxford and College bursary. He went on to study for a PhD at Edinburgh, and is now Associate Professor of Modern History at Oxford, and Monash Professor of History at the University of New South Wales, and was previously Visiting Professor at Stanford, where, some years ago, he reignited his relationship with Elisabeth Gordonston, who lives in Palo Alto and works for Google. He says little about that time, his four years in California back when Visiting Professorships were easy enough to juggle with a full-time academic post and punishing round of book publicity tours and television appearances, but he is still single. Elisabeth, he has heard through the grapevine, married, but is now divorced. Recently an envelope arrived in his pigeonhole at Merton, postmarked California. When he is home from Sydney in a couple of weeks' time he will open that letter.

### The Kinds of People One May Meet When One Lives Alone

'The other friends from all those years ago had pretty much faded away, married, had families and moved to the country, or even further . . . ' (p. 20).

As we see in *Caroline's Bikini*, society in itself can be volatile and, in addition, the life of a freelance writer perilous, arduous, and, at times, socially inhibiting. Not only Emily Stuart, but Marjorie Clarke, too, feels the isolation from her peers, living, alone as she does, in that pretty flat of hers in Chelsea.

It's a simple case of 'having to get out there', as their mutual friend Christopher Lowden is always reminding them: there are all kinds of ways one can 'lock oneself in' to some social group or other, all protest work aside. But with their heavy work schedules and close deadlines – none of which they can afford to miss, both in terms of taking on the work in the first place and making sure it is delivered on time – both women can feel the loneliness that may kick in on a Saturday morning, say, when married friends are out with their families, dropping off gangs of boys at rugby or cricket, or arranging to meet with their children's friends' families for a big rowdy lunch somewhere after shopping.

Sometimes Emily has wondered if she should get a dog. It might take her 'out of things', a bit, and she has always loved dogs, as noted in the final pages of this novel. Marjorie has a cat, but as she herself says, 'It is not quite the same.'

As a result of all the living alone, and without a dog, the kinds of people Emily Stuart is likely to meet are mostly postmen and women, and the people in the corner shops. She goes to supermarkets, but of course, nobody talks or meets anyone in a supermarket – though she always has a nice chat with whoever is at the till and dreads, 'dreads' she says, the day that it will all go self-service.

As far as work colleagues are concerned, well, they are not 'colleagues'. They are names on the end of a phone and at the bottom of an email brief. There are the very nice people who run the Prinn Gallery over in Hoxton but they are intensely fashionable and 'theorised', as Samantha Prinn and Betsy Forman themselves describe themselves, and can be intimidating.

Having said that, they have always been delighted with the quality of the catalogue copy Emily writes, and, after all Emily is a great friend of Marjorie who is an old, old friend of Betsy – so she and Samantha can't be all that theorised, can they?

## Literary Background and Context

*Caroline's Bikini* is a novel about unrequited love that seeks to establish itself in the tradition of extended imaginative pieces of text – poetry or prose – that in themselves are an attempt to create an artefact or 'thing' that may stand in for the love object. If the love may not be possessed, then, says the tradition, we have this piece of work to stand for it. The piece of work is real – we can touch it, read it, respond to it – and it has a physicality that the missing object of desire does not. The beloved may not be possessed, but her story can be, and a text created from it, that can be held and kept and returned to.

Petrarch's *Canzoniere* is a perfect example of this impulse: the poet sees the young girl Laura coming out of church on Easter morning and falls in love with her, though never to meet her nor know her. In her absence he creates a sonnet sequence that he perfects and edits and writes for the rest of his life, over a period of about forty years, alternately hoping for, cherishing, fearing and giving up on feelings of love. In this he harks back to an earlier tradition where art and art's practice may have stood in for the declaration and consummation of passion, an approach that carries with it a wealth of literature from around the world.

So Evan Gordonston, though he doesn't know this is what he is doing, is following the grand tradition of courtly love, established as a code of habits, actions and beliefs predicated on the very idea of the revered love object who stands off at a distance, in his desire to have Nin 'make it all come together' as he says to her on p. 26 and repeatedly through the various sections of *Caroline's Bikini*.

Emily Stuart herself similarly acts within the tradition by agreeing to be Evan's scribe or 'amanuensis' as she puts it to him on the first page – although that term pertains to the writing of *Paradise Lost* by John Milton, an altogether different, and anyway much later project than the one first established by troubadours of the early middle ages and then by Dante and Petrarch in their extended poems. Stuart, by recording, interviewing, and, at times, also transcribing Evan's own notes from his original journals and papers, follows the role of various scribes from the medieval and early Renaissance monasteries, some of whom might have been responsible for the versions of Dante and Petrarch we now have to peruse and wonder at in our grand libraries and research institutions.

This issue of making 'real' something that has otherwise gone unobserved or unrequited through expression in language – emotion turned into words – is at the very heart of *Caroline's Bikini* and informs it on all levels. The relationships both of Gordonston and Beresford, and of Gordonston and Stuart, are enacted, bodily brought forth into being, if you like, in these pages. As Petrarch has it:

> It was that very day on which the sun
> in pity for his maker dimmed the ray,
> when I was captured, with my guard astray,
> for your bright eyes, my lady, bound me then.
> *Canzoniere*, Part One, 3[*]

[*] With thanks to Professor Anthony Mortimer who graciously allowed me to quote from his translations, here and elsewhere, in the Penguin Classics edition of the *Canzoniere*.

Thus, the capture of love in words on a page – not action itself – is the driving force behind the entire project the friends have generated together, and Stuart is quite right, when she protests over and over again that there is nothing about the 'novel' in any of the matters and actions under discussion for there is quite simply 'not enough going on' for it to fulfil that particular remit. 'Novel' she calls it, quite deliberately always retaining those quote marks around it, but novel . . . That is another thing altogether, and readers will judge for themselves whether *Caroline's Bikini* might work for them in that particular way. On the other hand this drive to create on the page a situation that a reader might engage with, feel emotionally attached to, might care about, even . . . This sits at the base of the project like a device, if not an engine, a complicated and powerful little mechanism that might set the whole prose work in motion.

'Make it new,' said the modernist poet Ezra Pound in his outline of the poetic project; well, then, so might *Caroline's Bikini* be, to paraphrase another poet, Wallace Stevens, no representation of an event, but the event itself, as Stevens put it: 'The cry of its own creation.'

## Courtly Love

So much of *Caroline's Bikini* is structured around and reflective of the medieval and early Renaissance tradition of a particular kind of romantic sensibility based on containment, formality and and an engraved and highly wrought form of communication and literature that was generated by ideas of concealment, ardour and unrequited love.

Courtly love began as an early medieval European literary conception of love that emphasised nobility and chivalry. Literature of that period is filled with examples of knights setting out on adventures and performing various services for ladies because of their love for them, a love, however, that exists not in the humanist and romantic terms that we understand and know, but in a particular set of conventions and practices that meant the beloved stayed distant, a figure that could never be possessed or fully understood because he or she is absent from the scene. Note: I say 'he', because it is this writer's belief that, much later, the essayist Montaigne followed in the same tradition with his *Meditations*; only in that case the object of affection was a dear friend who died tragically at a young age, and was sorely missed by the writer who then wrote him into being, as it were, with his various interventions created in his famous lonely tower. More of that later, perhaps. In general, it is true, the tradition of courtly love is that of a knight for his lady and from here on I shall refer to the object of affection as a 'she' for that reason.

Courtly love and the literary artefacts that were created around it was originally a sensibility understood only by the nobility. Knights, castles, ladies in towers . . . This is the entertainment about and for kings and queens and princesses and is still the basis for much of the literature that we give little girls in particular, at birthdays and Christmases, bound between the hard covers of a book of Fairy Tales and sprinkled liberally with glitter.

Yet, though the courtly love tradition began that way, as an entertainment for a particular few, time passed and the same ideas developed and changed to attract a larger audience. In the high middle ages, a 'game of love' developed around ideas of withholding love as a set of social practices: 'loving nobly' was considered to be an enriching and improving code of manners that would add finesse and grace to the individual and society as a whole.

If the tradition of courtly love began in palaces, by the end of the eleventh century it was more widespread and part of a fuller literary expression, finally creating a firm and nourishing base from which much of what we generally know to be our canon of literature in English and Scots was grown. In essence, the experience it described, caught between erotic desire and spiritual attainment, 'a love at once illicit and morally elevating, passionate and disciplined, humiliating and exalting, human and transcendent,' according to scholar Francis Newman in his book, *The Meaning of Courtly Love*, could be said to have generated the content of so much western literature where the same ideas play out in a range of guises.

The term, generally, it has to be said, has a wide variety of definitions and uses that brings us right up to the present day – as is evidenced by the very existence of *Caroline's Bikini*, which in itself is a description of a code of practice and beliefs that may have relevance and application today: 'And then that smile of hers', we read at the end of the third section of that novel, in 'Evan's [. . .] folk-music style of poetry': 'that smile of hers that made my life begin.'

Other references in the novel, apart from repeated iterations of Dante's poetic project, that point to a similar sensibility might include the character of Beryl in Katherine Mansfield's 'At the Bay' as well as a range of modernist texts such as Ford Madox Ford's *The Good Soldier*, Fitzgerald's *The Great Gatsby*, Hemingway's *Fiesta*.

**Traditions**

*Caroline's Bikini* follows the tradition of marking the passage of unrequited love in a series of texts or documents which, taken together, form one uninterrupted testament of the lover's feelings for the beloved, and his changing circumstances and thoughts as he charts the passage of his desire in sentences and paragraphs that attempt to achieve the high status of art.

In Evan Gordonston's case, this 'art' was never much in place but for a few moments when, in his journals and writings, he attempts a form of prose that is rather more highly wrought and formal than his usual jottings; sometimes these musings too take on the colours and heightened reality and imaginations of fiction.

In his practice, his amanuensis notes his debt to Dante and Petrarch in his 'first sighting' of Caroline Beresford at the front door of her home in Richmond that then gave way to months and months of private unspoken passion, with not a word spoken by Gordonston to the object of his desire about his feelings or thoughts about the nature and generation of his desire.

In this he follows almost exactly the story of Dante, whose Beatrice was significantly younger, of course, than the glamorous middle-aged Beresford, who underwent the same physical and emotional conversion as the West London banker. Dante claimed he first met Beatrice Portinari when she was nine years old, and claimed to have fallen in love with her 'at first sight', apparently without even talking with her. He saw her in the following years often, and might exchange some greetings with her in the street, but never knew her well. We might say, then, that his was the first sustained example of so-called courtly love in an extended literary context, that until then had been an idea rather than a reality, a poem rather than the biography of a poet.

Dante's love for Beatrice (as Petrarch would show for Laura somewhat differently) would be his reason for poetry and for living, together with political interests and writing. In many of his poems, she is depicted as half goddess, watching over him constantly and providing spiritual instruction, sometimes rather firmly. When Beatrice died in 1290, Dante sought refuge in Latin literature. He went 'into himself' in much the same way Evan Gordonston retreats from the world of society, internationalism and high finance, finding solace only in the dark recesses of various West London pubs with his dearest, oldest friend Emily 'Nin' Stuart as his guide. Note: certain questioning and doubtful readers of both Dante's *Purgatorio* and *Inferno* may see strange similarities in the roles taken up by Nin and Beatrice, in this matter of guide to dark places – an issue that may trouble those who are more literal-minded in their interpretation of the roles played out in *Caroline's Bikini* – for if Gordonston is the lover and Beresford the beloved, then who is this Stuart who might guide the former, Beatrice-like, through the depths of despair?

The *Canzoniere* by Petrarch, though, is the more active underlying theme of *Caroline's Bikini*, its inspiration and 'engine' as it has been referred to earlier in these notes. It is a work of detail and imagination that effects reality: making into an object that could be held in one's hands as a text or book a love that was otherwise unobserved and unrequited, that had no currency in the world. Instead here it exists as a living reality: a piece of art, a 'machine of words' that can be possessed.

Petrarch saw his Laura, glimpsed her even, a fourteen-year-old girl coming out of church in Avignon on Easter Monday – and fell in love with her at once. His entire life thereafter was spent thinking about her, planning a future with her, imagining her and her impress upon him in all its detail . . . A work of the mind and of his art that resulted in the long and ornate sonnet sequence we have today.

Fully in love with someone he had never met, never even said hello to, and who he would never, in his long life, ever see again . . . This was Francesco Petrarch. Emily Stuart thinks of him from the moment Evan Gordonston reports that from the first moment he saw Caroline Beresford he fell deeply, irreparably in love: this on pp. 24–5 of *Caroline's Bikini* as follows: 'Caroline came right up behind him and extended her hand. "Hi, I'm Caroline," she'd said. And – BANG.' And 'Evan walked in the front door of the house in Richmond and, well, I'm writing it down now, it was there in his own writing, in some of the early notes, his "life changed".'

Petrarch recounts that on 26 April 1336, with his brother

and two servants, he climbed to the top of Mont Ventoux, a feat which he undertook for recreation rather than necessity, carrying with him a copy of St Augustine's *Confessions*. Standing on the summit of the mountain he took the volume from his pocket and as it fell open his eyes were immediately drawn to the following words:

'And men go about to wonder at the heights of the mountains, and the mighty waves of the sea, and the wide sweep of rivers, and the circuit of the ocean, and the revolution of the stars, but themselves they consider not.'

His response at that moment was to turn from the outer world of nature to the inner world of 'soul':

'I closed the book, angry with myself that I should still be admiring earthly things who might long ago have learned from even the pagan philosophers that nothing is wonderful but the soul, which, when great itself, finds nothing great outside itself. Then, in truth, I was satisfied that I had seen enough of the mountain; I turned my inward eye upon myself, and from that time not a syllable fell from my lips until we reached the bottom again.'

The next line that he wrote is significant for close readers of *Caroline's Bikini*:

'We look about us for what is to be found only within and close by . . . How many times, think you, did I turn back that day, to glance at the summit of the mountain which seemed scarcely a cubit high compared with the range of human contemplation.'

He spent the later part of his years in that mood of contemplation and introversion and that was when he started work on the *Canzoniere*, marking his great love for Laura, the subject of his devotion and imagination, in a poetic series that followed in content and attitude the provisions and standards of courtly love, while writing it 'new' through his private imagination and sense of personal art.

## Unrequited Love as a Creative Act

What we have, then, is reference to a central decision, made at a certain point in the artist's life, to fashion events and circumstances into art: to make of a glimpse of a girl in church, not only a set of poems in response to that glimpse, but from that set of poems create another, more fulsome text that might not only reflect the writer's feelings and hopes but educate him in them, and so help lead him to a future life of bliss.

Such is the creative engine fuelling a project – or 'report' or 'novel' – based around absence, that is at the heart of both the *Canzoniere* and *Caroline's Bikini*. Where love may not be realised or actualised, a text can be. Where a woman cannot be brought into the life of the writer as a lover and companion, a set of pages formed into a book may take her place. The love is abstract and unrealised; the words are real.

If any writer today looking for a subject or theme for a work and who is unable to find it may be so inspired by the vacancy that is at the heart of *Caroline's Bikini* to create his or her own response, then so, too, the project of Evan Gordonston and Emily 'Nin' Stuart will not have been in vain. Art needs a sense of lack to bring about its own effects; where there is no feeling of need to make up a shortfall, there will be no work.

## Creativity and Desire

As scholar Anthony Mortimer writes:

> The Laura that wakes the lyricism of Petrarch is rarely present to his physical eye; she is evoked from the past, projected into the future, recreated in absence, always transformed into a literary and aesthetic object . . . The real Laura . . . is less compelling than the poetic vision she enables, the sum of essentially literary memories that she evokes . . . The moving, breathing creature can only truly

be loved when she is immobilized by the memory and made available for contemplation in the fragile stasis of art.*

This modus operandi could be applied almost word for word to the way in which Evan Gordonston goes about setting Caroline Beresford into a permanent situation within her home in Richmond. In meetings with his friend Emily Stuart, and the conversations about Caroline that ensue in those meetings, and in the notes and journals he keeps about her, he, too, like the Italian poet, is setting down the beloved in a context to which he may return, over and over, and so revere and honour her continually through time. The 'real' Caroline Beresford, to use the phrase of Mortimer above, is not so much 'less compelling' as the version set down jointly by Stuart and Gordonston on paper, but she is the Caroline we have and know. To that extent, the Caroline of Stuart and Gordonston's creation, like the Laura of Petrarch, is fashioned from words, outlined in fact. Perhaps, yes, but enabled by the imagination. That much is equally true.

The construction, too, of *Caroline's Bikini* has about it something of a formal schedule that we see in much more established texts – following certain rules and practices that bring the piece of work into being.

Mortimer writes (and he could be referring to Gordonston and Stuart here): 'Petrarch often seems to write with the calendar at his elbow . . . The insistence on chronology, on time that passes without bringing change, underlines the poet's trapped condition as he oscillates between aesthetic contemplation and elegiac introspection, a prey to both spiritual paralysis and chronic emotional instability.' (p. xxii, *ibid*)

Much of Petrarch's structure rests on his much-imitated so-called antithetical style, best reflected in the most imitated

---

* In his edition of the *Canzoniere*.

sonnet of all in the *Canzoniere* – no. 132, 'If this should not be love':

> If this should not be love, what is it then?
> But if it is love, God, what can love be?
> If good, why mortal bitterness to me?
> If ill, why is it sweetness that torments?
>
> If willingly I burn, why these laments?
> If not my will, what use can weeping be?
> O living death, delightful agony,
> How can you do so much without consent?
>
> And if I do consent, wrongly I grieve.
> By such cross winds my fragile bark is blown
> I drift unsteered upon the open seas,
>
> In vision light, with error so weighed down
> That I myself know not the thing I crave,
> And burn in winter, and in summer freeze.

Though this is an ornate and highly formally 'made' representation of Laura by the poet, does it not remind us, just a little, of some of those strange artificialities in Gordonston's own writing, sections of which are referred to by his friend Emily Stuart as 'bad folk'? In other words, this desire to create an effect of the feeling of love on the page often results in text that is somewhat hectic and overwrought, a straining for emotional charge brought about by some literary device or other, either, as we see above, in the linking of opposites, or in the case of Evan's journal, the influence of certain kinds of folk songs or, more particularly, the lyrics of Bob Dylan poorly copied by Gordonston in lines like 'She's the "smile"' or in other places '"Good Morning" that makes my day begin' and so on.

## Practices

*Caroline's Bikini* is a novel that itself details many of the practices of courtly love as laid down in the biographies of Dante and Petrarch both – i.e. from first sighting of the beloved, the lover begins to turn away from the world to focus all his energies and thoughts and imagination upon the world and life of the beloved, attempting at all turns and at every available moment to set down his feelings and responses in highly finished literature – in the case of *Caroline's Bikini*, this 'literature' must be only the prose which is the particular signature of Emily Stuart, honed as she is on the writing of chiefly unpublished short stories and a good deal of advertising copy for insurance companies, sports shoes retail chains and pet food conglomerates.

Even so, the practices of an ancient tradition are copied and adhered to in her work – even reaching as far back, in iteration and tradition, to the Arabic influence of a version of courtly love that played out in the songs of troubadours, a group of wandering poets who would go from court to court, singing of a love that could have no earthly fulfilment, setting a precedent for the tradition that would be fully established in southern Europe some centuries later.

When Evan Gordonston is inclined, at times, with his friend Emily Stuart, to sing aloud the well-known Neil Diamond song 'Sweet Caroline' – focusing especially on the chorus of that song, and the crescendo leading towards it: 'Hands, touching hands', etc. – and at some point suggests to Stuart that they might 'dance along' to the music, he might be following in gesture and instinct an ancient tradition that had its roots, even a Neil Diamond classic played on jukeboxes and in massive crowd-pleasing stadia the world over, in the poetry of early medieval Persia and the Middle East. As Evan would say, that's 'quite a thought'.

## Role of the Beloved – General

As we know from, in particular, the 'Steady' and 'Go!' sections of *Caroline's Bikini*, the status of the idealised woman serves to underline and heighten the abject nature of him whose role it is to adore her from afar. Though the lady herself, whether she be a Florentine girl of noble birth or an attractive housewife from Richmond, has no knowledge of the desire she incites on the part of him who has come upon her, to gaze upon her while she remains unaware of that gaze, nevertheless her effect upon him is dramatic and physical. The lover sickens, thins and pines in the shadow of this great love; unable to express himself other than in the lines set down on his document that serves to prove to himself the love, the lover seems to 'fade away', as Emily Stuart writes, observing her friend in unattractive tracksuit bottoms and a jersey thickly encrusted with stains. His hair, always an attractive feature, and one shared by all his family and noted by the writer's mother ('It's genes, Emily. The Gordonstons are blessed', Margaret Stuart, p. 126), is now thin and unkempt-looking, an aspect of the lover's overall untidy and degenerate state, so lost is he to the condition of unrequited love.

The single history of this condition, as a psychological state, is one held at variance by different schools of thought and philosophy; there seems to be no 'one story' that may sum up the root and background to the feeling and its representation in art.

As the etiquette of courtly love became more complicated, so did its effects. The knight might wear the colours of his lady: where blue or black were sometimes the colours of faithfulness, green could be a sign of unfaithfulness, etc. This aspect of art presented in terms of dress and attire, however, is not a specific feature of *Caroline's Bikini* and in fact the opposite may be said to be the case. Caroline Beresford, noted for her exceptional dress sense and predilection for colours of taupe and caramel and white, does not see her sartorial palette reflected in the outfits of Evan Gordonston; the tracksuit bottoms or 'sweat pants' bear no resemblance whatsoever to the elegant bag of 'gym wear' Beresford sports as she goes out the door on her way to a Pilates class.

### Role of the Beloved – in *Caroline's Bikini*

As noted, the very existence of the beloved is the definition of her role in this narrative. Caroline Beresford need not 'do' anything, 'say' anything – though Emily Stuart, her textual recorder, may well wish her to 'act out' in various ways, so bringing about a 'novel' or 'some kind of story where something happens, for goodness' sake'.

It may be enough here, however, to note that her associations with fertility, fecundity and fruitfulness – her role as mother to 'three teenage boys!' as she cries out, through the course of sections 'Steady' and 'Go!'; her abilities to conjure up and cater for large-scale dinner parties, and her background in high-profile cookery classes and PR; her association with the 'scent of oranges' and her handy way with the interior decoration of her home: think '*House and Garden*', as Emily Stuart observes – announce her as the very essence of those traditional archetypes of femininity and submissiveness that we see through the canon of western literature, albeit a 'submissiveness' that might be traced to the Eve of that poem so loved by Emily 'Nin' Stuart, *Paradise Lost*, in other words, a submissiveness that wields a particular kind of domestic power that in turn welds the whole family into shape. This, despite David Beresford's dalliance in Classical Studies and PhD planning and so on.

### Use of Flora and Fauna

As an extension of the remarks above, we may note Caroline

Beresford's association, too, along with that 'scent of oranges', with various kinds of flowers and gardens. Her garden in Richmond is 'huge' and 'well planted' with 'old trees', 'flowering herbaceous borders' and so on; she 'goes up' to Evan's room periodically and replaces the flowers there with fresh blooms from the garden – Stuart goes on to recite these as a list, according to the season, narcissus in winter, roses in summer, and so on.

There is, also, the house in France, with Caroline's open invitation to Evan to join them there – this at a point in the story when she barely knows him, has only just met him – with its associations of rural bounty and Mediterranean ease. One imagines the flowers, the scents, the plantings, etc. (Caroline's skin, surely as a result of these visits to a rural idyll in the sun, carries always 'the honey trace of a tan') and the atmosphere of floral abundance persists even in the darkest days of midwinter in Richmond.

See former Notes and the following phrases on p. 166 of *Caroline's Bikini* for examples of this floral motif and its expression in the form of the beloved: '"There are always fresh flowers after she's been in," he said, confirming, too, Caroline's status in this whole story as a kind of Laura or Beatrice . . . Yes, there was a precedent exactly for establishing the role of the kind of woman who could be thought of in terms of fresh flowers in the history of romance writing and courtly love. . . . "Flowers," I'd said then. "Yes, I get it."'

Note, too, that key arranging of stems in a complicated vase on p. 239 – this after the invitation to the pool party has arrived in the Beresford family home and is featured in pride of place on the mantelpiece in the kitchen beside the daily planner. There are other instances of similar moments throughout the story.

## Richmond

It is remarked upon at dramatic moments or in changes of
scene that are effected in *Caroline's Bikini* that 'Evan could
have lived anywhere', that, as a key player of senior stature
in the world of international finance who was 'put up' by his
company, after all, upon first returning to London, at a suite in
the Connaught Hotel, he need not have lived in Richmond.

Richmond, to be sure, is not an unpleasant place to live. On
the contrary, this green and leafy part of London is a desirable
address for professional families from the world over, as well as
being one of the capital's postcodes that have not changed with
the generations: Richmond has always been, for a particular
sort of British family, well, Richmond. (See 'Old London' in
'Personal History'.)

However, as also noted at several junctures in this book, it is
'at the end of the District Line' and so can never be described
as a central location. Suburban, even, in mood – if that adjective
pertains in London, as Evan Gordonston suggests it may –
with its off-street parking, propensity towards swimming
pools laid out in its large gardens, and its wealth of beautiful,
accomplished middle-aged women who have abandoned
careers and any notion of independence in exchange for the
management of a large and gracious home with room, more
often than not, on the top floor for a lodger or two, Richmond
has never positioned itself amongst the often more transient,
conspicuously affluent parts of town. It is too well established
for that; too many houses, like the Beresfords', are inherited.
For sure, the estate agents who must have their way in so many
of the other SW postcodes of the capital may not in the same
way prevail in Richmond. TW is the postcode in Richmond,
and proudly so. A postcode, the close reader may have noted,
that would have been written on the backs of letters and cards
as a return address by the young Evan Gordonston, when

he lived as a child with his family next door to the Stuarts in Berkshire Way, Twickenham, all those years ago.

## Richmond: Key Geographical Facts

Sited within the Greater London area across an area of 2.08 square miles, Richmond hosts a population of some 21,500 people, a great number of whom commute into Waterloo Station or take, as has been noted in *Caroline's Bikini*, the District Line.

An information guide may cite the borough in the following terms: Richmond is a suburban town in southwest London with a large number of parks and open spaces, including Richmond Park, and many protected conservation areas including individual houses.

Richmond was founded following Henry VII's building of Richmond Palace in the sixteenth century, from which the town derives its name, and town and palace were particularly associated with Elizabeth I, who spent her last days there. During the eighteenth century Richmond Bridge was completed and many Georgian terraces were built – these remain well preserved and many have listed building architectural or heritage status. The opening of the railway station, a feature of the area noted by Evan Gordonston, in 1846 was a significant event in the absorption of the town into a rapidly expanding London.

## The House in Richmond

The house at No. 43 Chestnut Way is detailed throughout the pages of *Caroline's Bikini* – including a large portion of material that appears towards the end of that story, taken directly from Evan's pages of notes. 'Think . . . *House and Garden*', states Emily Stuart at some point, referring to the way the home has been furnished and decorated, but readers should observe, too, the relaxed atmosphere suggested by accessories as various as an old hall table and many other pieces of furniture inherited by David Beresford from his grandmother who favoured him, as well as, by contrast, that breakfast bar that features so prominently in the narrative and in the Beresfords' kitchen.

## Evan's Living Arrangements

'Evan's room was at the top of the house . . . It was a big house, the house in Richmond . . . As many houses are, out there at the end of the District Line . . . large gardens, places to park two or three cars . . . That kind of scale. And this house of that scale particularly so – was there talk of David Beresford being given it by his grandmother, on his mother's side? I think that was the case . . . for the house had that lovely lived-in feeling, old sofas and bits of furniture and so on, a lovely wide stair . . . All meaning that Evan's quarters, his lodgings . . . Well, it was more than a good-sized room, he said. Like a studio flat really . . . not just a bedroom.'

The line that follows the above is:

'In New York they might even call it an "apartment".'

Certainly, there are a number of instances in *Caroline's Bikini* when the narrator draws a point of comparison between arrangements – in all kinds of contexts, whether it be about the choice of language, or idea of good manners, or in the sense of clothing choice and dress – held up in Great Britain and as determined in the United States. Though she herself has no particular expertise or personal knowledge in this area of cultural differentiation, nevertheless she sees fit to pass judgement and hold a point of view about a range of ideals and circumstances, no doubt on the basis of an old and long-standing friendship with Evan Gordonston and because her brother, Felix, with whom she has always maintained a close bond, spent four years in California and has talked with her at length about the historical, intellectual and social circumstances of that country in the light of their family's attachment to the Gordonstons, and the Gordonstons' attachment to theirs.

For this reason, and others besides – possibly to do with her professional life as a copywriter and, as she puts it, 'short order cultural prose stylist' – Emily Stuart feels entitled to pass remarks such as that above: 'In New York they might even call it an "apartment".' Though she has never visited Evan in his temporary accommodations in Chestnut Way, nor, in the past, has ever had much reason to visit Richmond or explore its parks and greens and 'town' – there was a visit, once, with Evan to a cafe near Richmond, already remarked upon in *Caroline's Bikini* and, some time ago, another with friends listed in this text that involved an 'eco-rally' around a particular oak tree near White Lodge that had been listed for felling, sleeping out, overnight, around the tree, etc., creating copy for a leaflet that went on to be the basis for an art project with an East London collective, but, apart from a couple of walks and picnics, that was it – even so Stuart writes about Gordonston's domestic arrangements with a great amount of authority and verve. This extends not only to passing remarks about the social environs and circumstances of Richmond itself, but also to comments and reportage about the interior decoration of the Beresford home, the signification of certain pieces of furniture such as the 'chiffonier', and so on. As far as Stuart is concerned, without ever once visiting Evan at Chestnut Way, she *knows* Richmond.

What she knows about American apartments, by comparison, is anybody's guess. Whether they have 'landings', half stairs and so on, bathrooms with a 'bath and a separate shower' as Evan is keen to describe . . . Stuart can only imagine. In fact, despite her comments, there is nothing 'New York' about Evan's arrangements in Richmond, whatsoever. Evan is a lodger in a house, a very gracious house, at the end of the District Line. Is the final summation of his circumstances.

As far away from the word 'apartment' and its groovy autonomous connotations as we could think it to be.

## Alternative Narratives

As noted, from the very first page of *Caroline's Bikini*, the narrator, Emily Stuart, is concerned about the quality of the narrative. She worries about her own role as 'amanuensis' – 'I mean, I've never done this sort of thing before', she writes on p. 7 – and is concerned throughout the 'novel' as to the quality and quantity of what she refers to as 'plot'; on p. 92 we read: 'Back in Cork, in the winter, I'd been adamant. "I just don't think anyone will read your book", I'd said then,' referring later to the need for "ballast" in a story.

To this end, and because of her own uncertainties about her status as any kind of 'novelist' – after all, this is someone who has only ever written short stories, with 'ideas' for further fictions of that kind, and has never embarked upon a longer more sustained narrative form – Stuart allows, at certain pages in the text, the inferences made by Evan Gordonston, via his own pages of writing, that there may exist alongside the 'facts', as he persists in referring to them as, of his relationship with Caroline Beresford, of certain paragraphs and pages of invention, imaginings, fantasies, even.

That these sections of the text should be permitted within the overall 'project' is less a decision made by Stuart than a situation that simply develops or occurs within the pages of the story that are taking shape by her own agency.

Remember the story Gordonston creates about having met Caroline at Oxford? That's an example of the sort of thing being referred to here: a case of Stuart here transcribing a fantasy story about him knowing Caroline from a much earlier life and asking around after her in New York.

This sense of an alternative plot line, ideas about another

story, another moral universe or context, another tale that might be told, so to speak . . . There are suggestions of this appearing in other guises throughout the novel. There was that coffee taken at a cafe on the 'outskirts' of Twickenham and Richmond, when Gordonston and Stuart first get together again after so many years apart, the event that took place in her flat late at night, when Gordonston appeared at the door . . .* These scenes might be present as ideas running underneath *Caroline's Bikini* without obstructing or interfering with it; these other stories are not so much part of the 'novel' as such, but simply there, as suggestions. For overall, as the author is keen to remind us, the main energy of the project must be devoted to its two protagonists, as any further information spent on the narrator and her subject will disperse, for some readers, the overall intensity of the love affair that might seem to exist between Caroline Beresford and her 'paramour', the lodger, Evan Gordonston.

## Background

As noted, this 'novel' is a kind of literature uncertain of its own status. Were it not for Evan Gordonston's – some may say – vainglorious claim that what he had in mind to write was 'a big love story', and a 'novel', to boot, it is unlikely *Caroline's Bikini* would exist at all.

However, exist it does, thanks to his friend Emily Stuart's faithful rendition of conversations had, questions asked

---

* For there is the matter of an entire scene or number of scenes that exist early on in the proceedings, when it is still winter, that Stuart has decided, not so much to excise from the text – as there is no evidence that such a text has been written – as not to consider for inclusion, not even write about in the first place. Whether or not this editor will be able to exhort her to produce the pages under review, and then present them in time for publication, is not known at this time of writing. We are made aware though, as readers, on p. 119, and later, in other oblique references on pp. 120, 121, 136, that such a text or ideas for such a text might exist, that such writing may have import as an alternative narrative to the one we have in hand.

and answers given, of transcriptions made, of Evan's rough schoolboyish handwriting and long sections of unadulterated musings that seem to count, on his part, for 'poetry'. Thanks to Stuart's role, in short, as 'amanuensis', does the basic story line play out and express itself on the page.

Throughout the proceedings, however, the writer continues to worry at the edges of her process. Is what she is doing 'real' writing? Is it 'interesting' at all? Is it 'going' anywhere? She finds herself inserting sections of this sort of reflexive self-interrogating prose into the straightforward 'story' of Evan Gordonston and his life in Richmond.

There was no training in or background for this kind of approach to prose writing. Stuart is discovering, as she goes along, the responsibilities of the narrator and her subject, or what the writer and critic Gabriel Josipovici in a recently published collection of essays described in his title of the same as 'The Teller and the Tale'.

## Working Method

As noted already, Evan Gordonston from the beginning of the project had vast unchecked ideas about the nature of the writing he was embarking upon with his friend Emily 'Nin' Stuart. While she is sure to question him and query his terms at all stages of the proceedings, Gordonston himself seems intent on ploughing ahead with the most expansive expressions of his creative ambition. So 'novel' becomes interchangeable in his mind with, at some places, 'poetry', and, we read on p. 33, dangerously, 'myth'.

Part of the reason for this, of course, is his background in and familiarity with the world of finance and international banking law. What should such an individual know of the difference between literary genres, of the kind of hubris being called up from the classical depths of western thought and creative and cultural empathy and understanding when he has been schooled in nothing but the capitalist ethos of Wall Street and the Dow Jones index, for most of his adult life? No doubt, some of the early years in Twickenham pertain – even as he gave himself over entirely to the machinations of sub-prime mortgages and national debt – and bear some kind of hold in his memory, of interchanges between his household and the one next door, of his father's love for Alastair Stuart and his encyclopedic knowledge of modern history, of his mother's pottery and artistic pursuits, her early feminist discussions about the 'self' with Margaret Stuart, not to mention a challenging and always imaginatively charged friendship with his best friend next door . . . These facts are part of Evan Gordonston as well, of course. He, after all, did draw that tomato vine mural with Stuart on the walls of his parents' conservatory and delicately fill in with watercolour the exact hues of the fruit and its leaves at all stages of its maturity. It's not as if he doesn't have a sense of art and culture and meaning, Evan Gordonston, it's just that he tended toward the extreme when describing the project that was to become *Caroline's Bikini* and had to be curbed by Emily Stuart, somewhat. 'Because all I could manage, at that moment,' as she writes, referring to her shock, rather, that Gordonston might think that the story he was putting together had the stature of 'myth', 'after he'd spoken, was that "OK".'

### Further Definitions of 'Alternative Narrative'

In addition to the kinds of themes and ideas left unexplored in the text of this novel, there are a number of occasions in the story when a further fabulation could well occur, the reader senses, the narrator imputes, though this is left sitting, somewhat, referred to but never detailed. There are many examples of this, mostly referring to the wider social set that is detailed somewhat in 'Personal History', but a clear instance of the same might also be seen on p. 44, referring now to

David Beresford, and the nature and circumstances of that man: 'Poor David Beresford . . .' Stuart writes, 'as though to describe something that was straitened about him, confident and handsome as he was . . .'

These moments, and there are many of them in the text, as mentioned before, reach out towards a different kind of novel, one established in the nineteenth-century tradition of the English realist novel that was never of much interest to the Scottish writer at any stage in the development of the genre in that country; the reason for which such moments are not taken any further than but to remark on them in these notes, here. For they were never to be included as part of the story, or explanation, or background, or context, or to provide a defence of *Caroline's Bikini*.

*Caroline's Bikini*, the work of a Stuart about a Gordonston, arranged by a Gunn . . . was never to be a prose work belonging to anything other than the Scottish and modernist project, with roots in the early Renaissance tradition of Petrarchan love poetry by way of a long-standing debt to writing by Katherine Mansfield and Virginia Woolf. As Emily Stuart says, 'The contemporary realist novel, for the most part, can "go hang".'

## Pubs

The various pubs and bars that feature heavily in the story that is *Caroline's Bikini* and could make up an entire story of their own are listed throughout with a degree of accuracy and judgement.

Altogether, the establishments are situated in the West London area, beginning, in the first section of the novel, in 'Ready', with a range of hostelries that are located around the Brook Green and Hammersmith environs, and move outwards in 'Steady' to the chic backwaters of Chelsea and South Kensington, taking up a position in the further reaches

of Acton and the seedy underpass of the Talgarth Road in
'Go!', and finally coming to rest on the sunlit expanses of
what is known as the Riverside Promenade, that pedestrian
pleasureway stretching from the sailing and rowing clubhouses
of Chiswick down through the lawns and gardens set about
restaurants such as The River Cafe and, in this novel, the
remarkable The Remarkable.

Their appearance might be recorded in order as follows:

**'Ready'**
The Cork and Bottle
The Elm Tree
The Walker's Friend
The Gin Whistle

**'Steady'**
The Gin Whistle
Grapes of Wrath
A Tulip's Edge
The Kilted Pig
The Swan and Seed
Child o' Mine
The Pincushion (and Thistle)
In addition there also features a range of Mayfair
establishments, such as The Cask and The Vault

**'Go!'**
The Pincushion (and Thistle)
Ripeness Is All
Last Stand
The Empty Barrel

**'Finishing Lines'**
The Remarkable

It is worth taking note of the various kinds of decor and ambience created in the various establishments frequented by Stuart and Gordonston. On the whole, it appears that food was not served in any of these, apart from the usual bar snacks of crisps and nuts that were presented in various ways. However, the narrative does make reference, on one occasion, to a certain kind of lunch – known more in the past than it is nowadays – as 'A Ploughman's', consisting of bread and cheese and some kind of pickle, often with a salad or crisps garnish. These were most popular back in the seventies and eighties of the last century, and are less apparent as a bar menu option in contemporary food and drink outlets.

## Gin

When the materials for this story were being collated and organised, neither the writer, subject nor editor of *Caroline's Bikini* had any idea that gin had reached such designer status and import in the world of spirits' consumption and its advertisement. At the time of writing, it was regarded by the narrator as nothing more than a convenient and pleasurable spirit to order at any time of the day or night in one's local, a drink that might enable a sense of leisure, frank and companionable conversation, and the possibility, always, of 'another round'.

Now, of course, any reader will be familiar with the bottles lined up against the back wall of any bar or restaurant, all marked 'Gin' somewhere on the label, amongst rich typographic illustration, recipes for serving, historical details and notes, and epigraphs, salutations or dedications.

'To be served with: a cranberry, slice of pink grapefruit, peppercorns, chilli, chocolate square, a strip of cucumber . . .' Such are the instructions accompanying the production and description of a glass of the beverage nowadays. Nothing is as simple as 'A gin and tonic, please, with ice' as instruction in a local pub. For any number of accessories and serving suggestions now accompany the simple pouring of that standard and much-loved British spirit, along with its companion, the bottle of tonic water.

It's become 'fancy', gin. It has become something one may order, as Emily Stuart notes in the early pages of *Caroline's Bikini*, in the American fashion of ordering by brand rather than product. So 'Tanqueray and tonic', as this writer first came upon, in New York, in the mid eighties, was heard at bars and restaurants, never just 'gin and tonic' as she knew it at home. Now it's a case of a 'Slow River and Fever Tree, please' with a rosemary swizzle stick and hold the ice.

Gins ordered in *Caroline's Bikini*, in narrative order:

Gordon's
Bombay
Tanqueray
Sipsmith
The 'kind of gin you didn't ask the price of' in The Gin
    Whistle
Dark Town
Fallen Branch
Various unnamed 'artisan' and 'designer' and '*terroir*' gins
Portobello Road – served with a 'Citrus Gesture'
The Kilted Pig own brand
Dalreavoch Waltz – served with Wild Thyme tonic water
Triple-strength unbranded gin
A final 'Remarkable' ice gin and tonic

## Reprise

In the end, in spirit and sensibility, courtly love is defined as the 'pure love' described in 1184 by Andreas Capellanus in *De amore libri tres*, still regarded by scholars as the fundamental text upon which all other narratives – including this one – are fashioned:

> It is the pure love which binds together the hearts of two lovers with every feeling of delight. This kind consists in the contemplation of the mind and the affection of the heart; it goes as far as the kiss and the embrace and the modest contact with the lover, omitting the final solace, for that is not permitted for those who wish to love purely . . .

This is the aesthetic at work in the literature that is constantly referred to throughout this project, i.e. the sonnet sequence that is the *Canzoniere* that so influences and underwrites everything that appears in these pages. Without Petrarch, where would we be?

Closing remarks, given especially within the terms and narrative construction of *Caroline's Bikini* – careful readers will note the development of the so-called 'plot' of that novel in accordance with the paradigm set out below that describes a different story, from another age, reflecting another kind of sensibility – might end with some poems by Petrarch and the nine stages of courtly love indicated in order:

Attraction to the lady, usually via eyes/glance
Worship of the lady from afar
Declaration of passionate devotion
Virtuous rejection by the lady
Renewed wooing with oaths of virtue and eternal fealty
Moans of approaching death from unsatisfied desire (and other physical manifestations of lovesickness)
Heroic deeds of valour which win the lady's heart (less applicable in this novel)
Consummation of the secret love (careful readers take note

of how this may not, or indeed may, in a different sort of
way, play out in *Caroline's Bikini*)

Final scenes as described in the literature and accompanying
art work (for this, see use of notes and additional material
as a way of continuing or extending – adapting? – the
original story of *Caroline's Bikini*)

A small but lovely reference:

A sonnet by Philip Sidney, the final line of which is
remembered by Emily Stuart in the final pages of *Caroline's
Bikini.*

> Loving in truth, and fain in verse my love to show,
> That she, dear she, might take some pleasure of my pain, –
> Pleasure might cause her read, reading might make her know,
> Knowledge might pity win, and pity grace obtain, –
> I sought fit words to paint the blackest face of woe;
> Studying inventions fine her wits to entertain,
> Oft turning others' leaves, to see if thence would flow
> Some fresh and fruitful showers upon my sunburn'd brain.
> But words came halting forth, wanting invention's stay;
> Invention, Nature's child, fled step-dame Study's blows;
> And others' feet still seem'd but strangers in my way.
> Thus great with child to speak and helpless in my throes,
> Biting my truant pen, beating myself for spite,
> 'Fool,' said my Muse to me, 'look in thy heart, and write.'

And finally . . . a selection of poems from the *Canzoniere.*

The following sample of work relates to a number of themes
and ideas also played out within the construction of this book.
A close reading will render the similarities and influences
in ways that open up *Caroline's Bikini* to fresh insights and
perhaps a revisiting by the reader of the swimming pool we
meet at the beginning of this book.

## From Part One

No. 140

Love, who within my heart still lives and reigns
and in my heart keeps his chief residence,
sometimes into my brow makes armed advance,
there plants his banner, there his camp maintains.

But she who teaches us both love and pain
and wills that burning hope, desire intense,
be checked by reason, shame and reverence,
dismisses our desire with disdain.

Then fearful Love turns to the heart in flight,
leaving his enterprise, to weep and cower;
and there he hides and dare not venture forth.

What can I do, seeing my master's fright,
Except stay with him to the final hour?
To die for love: there is no lovelier death.

No. 90

Upon the breeze she spread her golden hair
that in a thousand gentle knots was turned,
and the sweet light beyond all measure burned
in eyes where now that radiance is rare;

and in her face there seemed to come an air
of pity, true or false, that I discerned:
I had love's tinder in my breast unburned,
Was it a wonder if it kindled there?

She moved not like a mortal, but as though
she bore an angel's form, her words had then
a sound that simple human voices lack;

a heavenly spirit, a living sun
was what saw; now, if it is not so,
the wound's not healed because the bough grows slack.

No. 192

Love, let us stay, our glory to behold,
things passing nature, wonderful and rare:
see how much sweetness rains upon her there,
see the pure light of heaven on earth revealed,

see how art decks with scarlet, pearls and gold
the chosen habit never seen elsewhere,
giving the feet and eyes their motion rare
through this dim cloister which the hills enfold.

Blooms of a thousand colours, grasses green,
under the ancient blackened oak now pray
her foot may press or touch them where they rise;

and the sky, radiant with a glittering sheen,
kindles around, and visibly is gay
to be made cloudless by such lovely eyes.

## From Part Two

No. 336

She comes to mind – indeed, she's always there
whom Lethe could not bring me to forget,
as in her flowering years when first we met,
illumined by the rays of her own star.

No sooner does she come, so chaste and fair,
So rapt and set apart, than I cry out:
'It must be her, and she is living yet',
and beg the gift of some sweet words from her.

Sometimes she answers, sometimes she is mute.
Like one whose reason wakes him from a dream,
I tell my mind: 'Believe not what you see:

'you know in thirteen hundred and forty-eight,
the sixth of April, at the hour of prime,
the body let that blessed soul go free.'

This final extract, from Part One, can be read as a most
relevant summary of the project of *Caroline's Bikini* and is
worth keeping in mind when considering the work as a whole:

No. 74

I am already weary of the thought
of how my thought in you unwearied lies
and how, to flee the burden of my sighs,
my heavy life has still not taken flight;

and how, in speaking of the face so bright,
ever discoursing of the hair and eyes,
there lacks not yet the tongue, the voice that cries,
calling upon your name by day and night;

and how, upon your track, I still travail
to follow you with firm untired feet,
wasting so many steps to no avail;

and whence comes ink, and whence comes all the sheets
I fill with you: if doing so I fail,
Love is to blame, there is no fault of art.

# Acknowledgements

The author would like to thank Professor Anthony Mortimer and Penguin Books for their kind permission to use excerpts from Petrarch's *Canzoniere: Selected Poems*, Penguin Classics Series, 2002.